T0021837

Novels by Jaz Primo

The Sunset Vampire Series

SUNRISE AT SUNSET

A BLOODY LONDON SUNSET

SUMMIT AT SUNSET

(Additional Titles Forthcoming)

You can find Jaz Primo online

at the following locations:

Facebook: Jaz Primo

Website: www.jazprimo.com

Blog: primovampires.blogspot.com

SUMMIT
AT SUNSET

Jaz Primo

RUTHERFORD LITERARY GROUP
www.rutherfordliterary.com

Published by:
RUTHERFORD LITERARY GROUP L.L.C.
1205 S. Air Depot, PMB #135
Midwest City, Oklahoma 73110-4807
http://www.rutherfordliterary.com

This is an original publication of Rutherford Literary Group.

ISBN: 978-0-9828613-4-9
(Trade Paperback Format)

1. FICTION_FANTASY_PARANORMAL
2. FICTION_FANTASY_URBAN LIFE
3. FICTION_OCCULT & SUPERNATURAL

Library of Congress Control Number: 2011961661

First Printing: January 2012.
10 9 8 7 6 5 4 3 2 1

Set in Century Schoolbook.
Cover art by Albert Slark.

Printed in the United States of America.

ACKNOWLEDGMENTS

This novel is dedicated to the loyal group of *Sunset Vampire* fans who have been so kind, encouraging, and supportive of me during the journeys of Caleb, Katrina, Paige, and Alton throughout their exploits. Without fans, novels are nothing more than creative repositories of undiscovered dreams and passages...

All my love and appreciation to my wonderful wife, Lori, who continues to support, promote, and encourage my passion (or rather, obsession) for writing. Sincere, heartfelt thanks to my family and friends, who continue to bolster my confidence during the weak moments on the sometimes rocky road of the creative process. As always, thank you to my dear friends Jimmy, Jessica, Teresa, Crystal, Victoria, Amie, Lisa, and Shannon for their invaluable support, encouragement, and beta-reading. A special shout-out to Victoria and Jessica for their amazing assistance with the meticulous proofreading process!

I'm mesmerized by the creative genius of my cover artist, Al Slark. He has once again surpassed himself with the novel cover for *Summit at Sunset*. Thanks for putting such a wonderful face to my novels! My continued thanks to Brandon for his masterful assistance with "spinning the webs" and creating "font-tastic" opportunities for me. Special thanks to my wonderful editor, Julia, for her keen eyes for correction and insight into proper storyline development.

Chapter 1

House Guest

On a cool mid-April night, Caleb Taylor carefully maneuvered through the thick undergrowth of the forest. Despite the oppressive darkness from all sides, it was a beautiful moonless night for a hunting excursion. Caleb paused at the edge of a break in the trees to appreciate the evening's gentle breeze.

Enough to mask my exact location, he speculated.

He had learned not to let the prey's scent be acquired too easily by the predator, or else the hunt ended rather quickly. Glancing at the illuminated face of his new watch, he calculated the span of time that had passed since he had entered the forest.

Always fighting the clock.

Despite his preoccupation with quietly navigating his way through the pitch-black terrain, he took the time to breathe in the fresh scent of the forest. He attempted to gauge his location against the preliminary reconnaissance he had conducted prior to sunset. As he stepped past a tree and under one of the overhanging branches, he pivoted his body closer to the ground and heard a small tearing sound. With a quick tug and a sharp scrape against his left arm, he felt a stab of pain as needle-like brambles raked across his skin.

"Damn," he muttered under his breath, tentatively probing his left arm where his clothing was torn.

Glad I'm wearing older clothes, he absently credited before quietly proceeding on his way.

A minute passed before he heard a small shuffling sound not far from his location. He froze, grasped the trunk of a near- by tree, and scanned the area in the direction of the noise. His heartbeat increased slightly, and he momentarily closed his eyes to concentrate on calming himself.

Peaceful forest, calm forest, peaceful forest.

As his mantra ended and he opened his eyes, he was more at ease and continued to sweep the area visually. His eyes wid- ened with sudden recognition as he stared between the tree trunks across a distance of approximately sixty feet at what appeared to be two small orbs of bright green. *A predator's eyes.*

Realizing that all pretense of stealth had been lost, he turned and fled in the opposite direction through the bushes and tree limbs in a race against time. An image of a rabbit run- ning from a fox flashed in his mind.

Barreling like a bullet through the darkened forest, he heard the sounds of his closing pursuer. The ground dropped sharply before him, and he half-tumbled down an incline, bare- ly managing to keep his balance to the bottom. He righted him- self and turned to run, but was startled by a *whooshing* sound from above. A dark image leapt over him and landed beside him with a heavy thud. He staggered backwards with surprise at the towering presence before him, crowned ominously with glowing green eyes.

"Enough!" a woman's authoritative voice commanded. "You violated our agreement."

"W-What?" Caleb stammered.

He craned his neck upwards to make eye contact with the tall, imposing woman standing before him. Her long, red hair was pulled back tightly over her head and tied into a neat po- nytail. She had a model's high cheekbones, and her shapely form was displayed by a pair of faded jeans and long-sleeved shirt. She was beautiful and, best of all, his to adore. Katrina Rawlings was his mate.

My vampire, he proudly thought, *my love*. However, he was simultaneously concerned by her current demeanor. *My un-*

happy vampire.

"Remember our arrangement, my love?" Katrina chastised. "If you're injured, our game stops."

Their game was called Find Caleb, invented by Alton, a friend of Katrina's who had been helping Caleb establish a way to channel her need for hunting into a sport that did not kill or harm anyone. Unfortunately, though not surprisingly, he endured occasional minor injuries. Still, he easily dismissed such inconveniences in lieu of his foremost goal: pleasing her.

"C'mon, it's just a scratch, Kat," he countered using the nickname he had given her soon after they met. He had been amazed that she allowed it, because she hated pet names, much less nicknames. Only their mutual friend Paige usually got away with it.

He reached back with his right hand to touch the spot on his left arm where his shirt was torn. However, this time he felt something warm and sticky to the touch, and his arm stung when his fingers touched his skin. As he retracted his hand, he strained through the darkness to stare at his blood-covered fingertips with a wide-eyed expression.

"What the..?"

"See? How did you think I found you so quickly?" she interrupted pointedly. "Your blood scent was easily carried on the breeze to me, just as freshly-cooked hamburgers on a grill would to you."

"Yeah, I see what you mean. Sorry about that," he sheepishly offered. "I guess I'm the hamburger tonight, then."

She stared down at the handsome, twenty-six-year-old man standing before her. He was precious to her. In fact, she loved him more than life itself. And his pale, blue eyes and athletic body were simply beautiful to behold. It pleased her that he had maintained a steady exercise regimen since winter, which had only enhanced her already considerable physical attraction towards him. But it was his sincere, kind nature and caring demeanor that had captured her heart.

"More like a hot dog," she quipped.

A smile touched his lips.

Her expression softened, and she reached out gently to grasp his left arm. "Turn towards me, my love," she beckoned with a sigh. "You're so accident-prone sometimes."

"I try my best," he innocently countered.

Katrina beamed with satisfaction and conceded, "I know you do."

He's actually made great progress in a short time, she thought. *But I suppose that when vampires play rough with humans, accidents will tend to happen.*

She examined the cut on his arm and saw the blood beginning to seep into his shirt. Deftly ripping open the remainder of his sleeve, she bent down to lick the blood from his arm. Its fresh scent elicited a strong desire in her, but she forced it under her control. *No, it's not a desire*, she temporized, *it's a dark hunger, a ravaging thirst. And it wants to be quenched soon.*

"Ouch," he muttered under his breath as the stinging sensation continued in his arm. "Stupid thorns."

"If it's due to some of the brambles that I saw further back in the forest, then it's the poison in the thorns that's causing your discomfort. Let me fix that for you."

She pressed her tongue against his injured skin and held it in place for a few moments. He quickly felt the build of a soothing, numbing sensation. He was forever grateful that vampire physiology was so handy for first aid. Their saliva could both numb, and summarily heal, wounds. Such an ability enabled vampires to feed on humans, or other animals, relatively painlessly, if they so desired. Wounds healed in mere minutes, leaving no trace of offending fangs.

"There, better?" Katrina asked. She certainly felt better just from tasting his blood, which she found both addictive and irresistible.

He appreciated the lingering numbness in his arm and reached back to the wounded area, feeling no cut or abrasion.

"Good as new," he gratefully replied.

"Good," she said and bent her head down to kiss his lips

warmly.

He responded in kind and reached out to interlace the fingers of his hand through hers. Not wanting to break the moment, he gently snaked his free arm around her waist and pulled her towards him. Her soft lips were intoxicating, and he wanted the kissing to last forever. Granted, while Katrina might be an alpha vampire, the most dangerous and violent variety, she was also a passionate woman. Added to that, she was so kind, caring, and attentive towards him. Even in her most ominous of moods, he knew that she loved him. Of course, that's not to say she didn't intimidate him on occasion. *Such a small price to pay for the companion of a lifetime*, he decided.

"I love you, Kat," he whispered when their lips parted from yet another kiss. "And I love our weekend getaway."

She had suggested that they spend a romantic weekend at the forest retreat that she had picked out on the Internet. They rented a cabin, and upon arriving, ensured that its windows were blocked out with dark cardboard from the sun's lethal, ultraviolet radiation.

"As I love you," she softly replied before kissing his lips, his cheek, and the soft skin of his neck. She listened to the melodic rush of blood pulsing through his arteries and the rhythmic harmony of his heartbeat causing her thirst to build.

He noted that his lover's eyes were still glowing green, like two small emerald orbs in the darkness. That meant one of three things: she was angry, aroused, or hungry. Somehow, he felt that aroused was a possibility, but hunger was most likely given his recent open wound and her tasting him. He couldn't recall the last time that she had fed, though they had brought plastic packets of blood with them to store in the cabin refrigerator.

"Want a little nibble?" he quietly offered.

Katrina kissed his neck once more. "Do you mind?"

She's so polite to me on that topic, he noted appreciatively. She had never once taken blood from him without his approval.

It was one of the things that she had promised him after declaring him her mate.

"Happy to oblige," he replied with a grin.

She gently guided him to the ground and encouraged him to lean back against a large fallen tree trunk while adjusting his posture for easy access to his neck. While she didn't have to draw blood from the neck, it was her favorite location. *Call me a traditionalist*, she reflected.

She squatted down to straddle his body between her knees then bent towards him while placing her hands on either side of his body. Her soft lips kissed his neck and formed a seal against his skin. As she pressed her tongue against him, he felt the telltale numbness begin to grow. He held very still, and moments later, he felt an increased pressure as her fangs fully penetrated him.

Small, slurping sounds emitted from her as he lay prone with his eyes closed. The darkness and sedate sounds of the forest were soothing as he floated on a sea of euphoria. He relished such peaceful moments of tranquil bonding with Katrina. However, the time slipped away before he knew it. The slurping ceased, and she withdrew her fangs from his neck. Finally, her tongue pressed against his skin, and she gathered additional saliva to the wound area until it sealed fully.

"Thank you," she whispered before affectionately kissing his lips. *He's perfect for me*, she resolved in contentment.

"Anything for you, Kat."

They leaned back against the fallen tree trunk for a time, merely appreciating each other's company and the peaceful Georgia night. Beyond the canopy of treetops, the sky's blanket of darkness provided the perfect backdrop for a spectacle of stars, at which Caleb thoughtfully gazed. When he shivered from the growing chill in the air, Katrina extended her arm across his shoulders, pulling him close against her body.

His eyes moved from scanning the stars to gazing into her beautiful green eyes. He marveled at the wonder that was the stunningly beautiful woman sitting next to him.

She's a phenomenon! She's nearly five hundred years old, and yet, her body's cells regenerate almost magically. He envied that she would appear thirty forever.

He smirked as he pondered her angelic profile while she stared into the night sky.

Yeah, and as if that weren't enough, there's always her blazing-fast speed, tremendous physical strength, hypersensitive senses of vision, smell and hearing, and immunity to illness or diseases. Never mind that she has virtually no need to sleep, and her endurance is seemingly limitless.

As if sensing his close inspection, her attention reverted to him.

"Such a penetrating stare. What are you thinking, my love?" she softly queried.

He appears mesmerized, she recognized, *and I'm not even trying to hypnotize him.*

A knot formed in the pit of her stomach at that thought. *Not that I'd ever try that again,* she resolved. It seemed like only a few years since she had managed to hypnotize Caleb as a child to encourage him to forget about her killing his abusive father before his very eyes. The effort had worked at the time and allowed him to grow up believing that his father had simply abandoned him and his mother. Then she had departed Caleb's life until meeting him again as an adult the previous fall.

Regrettably, her hypnotic legacy had caused painful and disturbing flashbacks and other emotional repercussions for him as an adult. Fortunately, on their recent spring trip to London, a vampire psychiatrist had been able to remove her hypnotic block.

Thank goodness that instead of anger or fear he was grateful for my help. She was happy that the event actually seemed to bond them even more closely.

"Just thinking about you, Kat," he gently replied. "Pondering at how remarkable you are, you and your kind."

She rolled her eyes and mildly chastised, "I would've

thought you'd have tired of such thoughts already. There are so many more interesting things to think about, rather than vampires. We should be old hat for you by now."

His eyes widened, and he reached up to caress the side of her face with his fingertips. Her eyes curiously darted to his in return.

"You'll never be 'old hat' for me," he promised. "You're amazing, and I'm still dumbfounded to be of any interest to you at all."

She frowned over his self-deprecating train of thought. Her hand darted upwards to grasp his chin firmly between her fingertips, and she moved her face to within an inch of his. Her green eyes momentarily flashed brightly before returning to their previous hue.

"Listen closely to me, oh-human-mate-of-mine. You saved my life when you were only eight years old, at a time when I was ready to give up my existence completely. You, and you alone, gave me a reason to keep living. You gave my life meaning and purpose. If anything, vampires are nothing more than predators. However, you're an angel, wholly and completely. So I don't want to hear you say such things. Got it?"

He silently nodded, and she released her grip on his chin. He continued to stare at her in mild challenge, though he remained quiet at some length before speaking again.

"You talk about yourself like you're a monster of some kind," he whispered. "But all you've ever been to me is the object of my dreams."

Her heart fluttered as the thick emotion in his voice washed over her. Then her lips found his, and she kissed him passionately. He gratefully responded and felt her hand cup the base of his head as she pressed against his lips. They traded kisses, each enjoying the warmth and passion of the other, each sharing in the love they held for one another.

Time seemed suspended as they reveled in their nighttime paradise. However, the continually dropping temperature eventually made its presence known to Caleb. While Katrina was blissfully immune to extreme temperatures, she felt her mate shiver slightly.

"Let's return to the cabin, my love," she urged as she grasped his hand in hers and half-lifted him to his feet. Her arm instinctively wound around his waist in a semi-protective manner as they walked back up the dark incline towards the direction of their cabin.

By the time the small, nondescript cabin loomed before them, it was well past two in the morning. Caleb yawned and massaged his arms with his hands to generate some warmth as they walked through the front door. As soon as Katrina closed the door, she moved in a blur to stand before him. Her deft fingers unbuttoned his bloody shirt. A moment later, she cast it into the fireplace. The embers from the waning fire relit with the fresh fuel of his ruined shirt.

"Why don't you go ahead and take a warm shower?" she suggested as she undid her ponytail, allowing her long, red hair to cascade across her shoulders. "I'll join you momentarily."

He nodded, stifled a yawn, and made his way into the cabin's sole bathroom. She smirked at him as he departed, finding his innocent sleepiness endearing, and then added some cut firewood to the fireplace. The wood soon crackled anew as she heard the shower running in the bathroom.

Fire in the hearth, and soon, fire elsewhere, she thought as she slipped from her clothes and moved towards the bathroom to join him.

* * * *

Caleb had quickly fallen into a deep sleep after the love-making that followed their shower. Even in his exhaustion, the striking, red-headed vampire knew exactly which erotic buttons to push to elicit the amorous response she had needed from her young mate. He had performed well for her, due in no small part to the increased stamina his body had acquired from a regular regimen of exercise.

While lying in bed next to him, Katrina stretched for a moment before relaxing against him. She rolled onto her side and held his body close to hers, breathing in his body's scent and listening to the strong thrumming of his heartbeat. The bedroom was so quiet that she easily heard the sound of his blood rushing through his arteries. His regular breathing was like a soothing mantra to her, and she reveled in knowing that the human male in her arms was hers...all hers.

I adore him. He's my everything.

After a time, she grew somewhat restless. Knowing that sunrise would come all too soon, she wanted to appreciate the night and the great outdoors before having to sequester herself inside during the impending day.

Stupid sunlight, she fumed. *I used to love the sun. Now it just impedes me.*

Minutes passed before she slipped from underneath the covers, being careful not to awaken Caleb. He shifted slightly, but remained asleep as she slipped into a pair of jeans, dark t-shirt, and sneakers. Then she slipped from the bedroom to the cabin's front door. Moments later, she stood outside near their rented SUV, appreciating the night air. She closed her eyes, breathed in deeply, and categorized the host of scents and sounds around her.

She quickly identified a pair of bats flying around a nearby tree. *I can smell a raccoon not far away, too.*

The breeze blew through the trees as she registered other scents. *Hmm, tree blossoms, freshly sprouted grasses, and moisture from overnight dew. The odor of burnt wood from the cabin's fireplace. Sounds of water lapping against the shore in the nearby lake. So many sounds and scents that I never noticed as a human.*

Everything was so natural and peaceful, and it filled her with happiness to be there. She wandered through the forest, but stayed relatively close to the cabin in case Caleb needed her.

Paige complains that I worry too much. Perhaps I'm just

paranoid. Then she replayed a brief series of memories, quite dramatic and potentially fatal events that she and Caleb had shared since last fall. A number of times, such dramas had occurred under seemingly innocent circumstances. *He seems to have a penchant for attracting danger.* "Paranoid nothing. I'll stay close to the cabin," she resolved out loud.

The remaining hours passed all too quickly, and she eventually felt a telltale change in the atmosphere. When the eastern sky began to lighten with the hint of an impending Saturday sunrise, she paused to consider the beauty of the new day. Of everything entailed in being human, she missed sunrises the most. She used to revel in the feeling that a sunrise heralded the promise of a new day and the opportunity for a fresh start to life. But since her turning, the morning sun brought a new meaning: her potential death from its ultraviolet radiation.

Sensing the impending rays preparing to break across the treetops, she returned to the cabin to find Caleb still soundly asleep.

Standing in the bedroom doorway, she observed her lover and mate with a tender expression. She once more contemplated how he was the embodiment of a loving life-companion for her. She slipped from her clothes and slid beneath the covers to lie next to him. Her arm draped across his chest as she laid her head on the pillow next to his. Soon, she lazily dozed and let her thoughts roam freely.

*   *   *   *

The remainder of the weekend passed quickly. During the day on Saturday, Caleb partook in some mid-morning fishing at the lake. He had been hesitant to leave Katrina cooped up alone in the cabin, but she had insisted that he needed to enjoy the beautiful sunshine for a time.

"You're still human, after all," she had insisted. "And your body needs some sunlight once in a while. Besides, I want to read this new mystery novel I brought with me."

In the end, he had reveled in the fishing experience and even caught three nice-sized bass, which he cleaned and stored in the cabin refrigerator to have for dinner that evening. He spent the remainder of the day indoors with Katrina. They played Trivial Pursuit for a time, but the score rose astronomically in her favor, so they moved to card games. She taught him how to play a couple of variations of poker. He gaped at her dexterity, as well as the ability for her to both shuffle and deal cards so quickly that he barely saw her hands move before her. The infuriating thing was that she never even broke eye contact with him while doing so. He won as many hands as he lost, and by the end he was definitely getting the hang of how to play.

"You're good at everything, you know," he dryly observed.

She smiled in response. "Thank you. But unlike you, I've had nearly five hundred years of experience to draw upon."

He rolled his eyes at her, although he had to admit that she was probably correct, yet again.

"So, what do we do now?" he asked with a glance at his watch. There were still a couple hours of daylight left before it was safe for her to attempt leaving the cabin.

Her eyebrows playfully arched, and she adopted a predatory expression. "Oh, I have a couple of ideas," she offered as she rose from where she sat at the cabin's small dining room table.

He started to rise to meet her, but she moved in a blur to wrap him in her arms. Her lips passionately pressed against his, and she hugged him to her while herding him towards the nearby couch. As they fell over the backing and onto the cushions, he chuckled as she didn't seem to miss a beat kissing him. Once again, she pushed those erotic buttons in him, and he found his excitement quickly rising.

Then time stood still.

That evening, Caleb cooked his fish over a small grill located just outside the cabin while Katrina sat in a folding nylon chair watching from a comfortable distance. Like most vampires, she detested the scent of cooked flesh of all kinds. However, she took pleasure in watching him cook, and she appreciated the happiness emanating from him in waves. The camping trip had been exactly the relaxation that both of them had seriously needed.

As if on cue, he commented, "It's such a shame we have to leave tomorrow. This has been really nice, Kat."

She lazily twirled her ponytail between the fingertips of one hand. "It has been wonderful, hasn't it? We'll have to do this more often."

He agreed and continued frying his fish.

"Hey, Kat, I've been wondering something about vampires recently. Where exactly are vampires derived from? After all, you were all humans before your transformations. I mean, it's not magic, right?"

Katrina quietly observed him at length. *It's valid question, really*, she thought, though most of her previous partners had never bothered to delve too deeply beyond the fact of their mere existence or her incredible abilities and attributes.

As the silence grew, he tentatively spied at her out of the corner of his eye before refocusing on his cooking. She easily detected the intensity of his curiosity.

"The truth might surprise you," she began. "Actually, even among some of the oldest of our kind, there seems to be some doubt as to what the original vampires, or beings, were exactly. However, it's been generally accepted that the 'originals' couldn't have been something indigenous to our planet."

He looked up after her voice trailed off to silence, and his eyes widened slightly. "You're saying the original vampires were aliens?"

She shrugged, well-acquainted with the outlandishness of the notion. "Who knows? There may not have even been more than one originally."

"So, was it...were they humanoid or animal?"

Again, she shrugged broadly and focused past him to the forest beyond. "Whatever it or they were, their conversion process changed our bodies into what you see before you," she explained. "We may not even resemble the image of the original beings. We're all strange, mutated hybrids of them for all I know. Whatever they were, one fact remains: they were excellent predators."

He silently conceded the truth in her statement while turning the fish in the skillet. *It's an amazing premise, if true. But then, maybe it's something that will never be known. Maybe all the vampires who know the truth are all long since dead and gone.*

Eventually, he wondered out loud, "So, when and where exactly is that vampire conference supposed to happen this summer?"

When they had vacationed in England during his spring break in March, Alton Rutherford mentioned that a special vampire conference was pending somewhere in Europe during the summer. Alton was an eight-hundred-year-old vampire and one of Katrina's closest friends. He was also her former mentor and had taught her sword fighting, as well as financial investment strategies.

Katrina's mood darkened somewhat at his mention of the conference. "Early to mid-June. The exact date and location will be determined sometime in the next week or so. Alton's supposed to call me when it's set."

He tried to act nonchalant. "So, are we going, then?"

Her eyes darted to her mate. "I haven't decided yet, my love." Then she sighed with what sounded to him like resignation. "But it would mean a lot to Alton if we did."

"Oh," he casually replied as he finished cooking the fish.

She leaned forward in her chair. "Has Alton called you or something?"

He looked up at her with surprise. "Called me? No, I was just curious. I just wasn't sure whether to offer to teach this summer or not, that's all. I figured I'd wait until I knew more about your plans for us."

She settled back into her chair, gazing up at the evening sky. "I see."

Silent moments passed as she pondered the prospect. "Well, if I know Alton, we'll probably end up going," she finally conceded. "You wouldn't mind, would you?"

He shook his head and offered an innocent expression, "Not at all. I've never been to Europe. So, any chance it'll be near Romania?"

"You mean Transylvania, don't you? Caleb Taylor, I should come over there and bite you in the neck."

He playfully snickered as he carried the skillet towards the cabin. She growled under her breath, but rose from her chair and followed him inside.

Caleb made his way into the kitchen, where he popped open a container of pasta salad and dished some onto his plate beside the sizzling fish. She watched as he warmed a glass of blood for her in the small microwave and poured himself a Coke. Then he took his drink and plate to the dining table and returned to remove her glass from the microwave.

"Dinner is served," he announced while placing the glass at the table setting next to his. Then he sat down to his meal.

"Thank you," she offered as she sat next to him to sip from the glass of blood.

Yum, type A. My favorite. Caleb's blood type, in fact.

He ate in relative silence as she contentedly watched him while finishing her own liquid meal. After cleaning up the dining room and kitchen, he took her by the hand, looked into her eyes, and asked, "It's our last night here at the cabin. How about showing me more of the great outdoors?"

She was only too happy to oblige.

They spent most of the evening walking around the lake, appreciating each other's company as much as the beautiful scenery. He was amazed by how alive the forest continued to be after dark. It was like living in another world, more ominous in some ways, and yet peaceful in others. But eventually, it was time to return to the cabin, and the night passed too soon.

On Sunday, Caleb fished some more, but released his catch. By evening, they loaded their SUV and made the long drive back to Atlanta. He dozed off mid-return and was still asleep by the time Katrina turned their vehicle into their estate driveway.

The estate was in the center of five acres of property, situated among similar acreage lots in an elite neighborhood addition in the small community of Mableton, just outside downtown Atlanta. The upscale Pine Valley addition sported heavily forested properties, of which Katrina's lot bordered a scenic wooded park that sprawled throughout the addition.

The house itself was a two-story structure comprising over six thousand square feet of living space. Once parked in the cavernous multi-bay garage, Katrina gently roused Caleb, and he stretched with a wide-mouthed yawn as he exited the vehicle.

"I'll unpack the SUV," she offered. "You go get ready for bed. You have to teach in the morning, after all."

There was no argument from him as he made his way through the garage and into the house. He felt exhausted, but thoroughly satisfied with their weekend getaway.

*   *   *   *

Life returned to an unremarkable pace until Wednesday, when Caleb received a cryptic text message from Katrina during one of his history lectures at Robert Fulton Community College in downtown Atlanta where he was a faculty member.

Shipment from Alton arriving this afternoon. Can you come home early?

Fortunately, his last class that day was just prior to lunch.

The delivery service truck pulled into the driveway less than half an hour after he arrived home. The wooden crate removed from the back of the panel van by the two deliverymen was quite large, in excess of six feet long. Caleb watched closely, directing the men to place the crate in the middle of one of the two empty car bays in the garage.

As the panel van departed, he stared at the crate with a perplexed expression. Then the garage door began its closing descent, and Katrina appeared beside him as a displacement of air rushed around him. The sunlight had barely cleared where she stood, and he peered up at her.

"In a hurry or something?" he asked with a smirk as he looked down at her pale bare feet sticking out from under her faded blue jeans.

Don't get your feet burned in the process.

"Just curious," she casually replied, although she intently stared at the crate before them.

"Got a crowbar?" he asked as he scanned the periphery of the garage.

Katrina lurched forward to pry the crate lid open effort-lessly with her fingertips amidst a series of loud creaks as the nails were unceremoniously ripped from the wood. Caleb gawked at her as she dropped the lid aside on the concrete floor and playfully wiggled her fingers.

"Not necessary," she quipped.

"Show-off," he mumbled while removing the packing from the top of the open crate.

As he dug out more packing materials and laid them aside, he revealed a leather-covered couch, such as one would see in a hotel or office waiting area. However, it appeared worn and had a couple of small marks on the black leather covering. He instantly recognized it from their trip to London in March. It had to be the one he had found in the London Tube tunnels outside of an old entrance to the lower levels of the tunnel system. A number of vampires who had been spying on Alton were operating from there, and Caleb had been the one to discover them.

Katrina stepped forward and tore the side of the crate apart to gain easier access to the worn piece of furniture. She laid the crate section aside and scowled.

"I bet this is --"

"The couch from the Tube tunnels," he interrupted excitedly, then picked up a small white envelope taped to the top of the couch. Written on the front was *Caleb* in a black gothic-like script.

"It's in Alton's hand," she observed.

He opened the envelope and unfolded the letter inside, also written in the same style of script.

"Wow, really nice handwriting," he commented as he began to read.

"That's just *him* showing off," she dryly observed as she studied the message from over his shoulder.

Caleb,

How are you, dear boy? I'm sending you a token memento from your recent trip to London. Truth is, I didn't have the heart to throw it in the bin after you went to such trouble finding it for me. Tell Katrina I said it should look nice in your living room.

Plans are being finalized for a large conference in Slovenia this June. I'm hoping you will show an interest in accompanying Katrina. It should prove very educational for you, and the scenery will be breathtaking. Plan on at least a two-week stay.

Should you decide to make the journey, I'm certain you'll enjoy seeing Europe, as well as spending some quality time with Katrina. By now, she's probably already reading this message over your shoulder, so I will close. Please give her my regards. Naturally, I'll be expecting a ring from her very soon. However, please call me when you have time, Caleb.

Best Wishes,
Alton

Caleb quirked his lips as he finished reading. "He's got you pegged, Kat." But she was less amused and immediately groused, "Harrumph. Reading over your shoulder, indeed. And the couch is definitely *not* going in our living room."

His right arm snaked around her waist, and he bent his face up to kiss her lightly on the neck. She lifted her head slightly to allow his lips easier access, but muttered, "What's he up to?"

Such an unusually chummy letter for him, she reflected.

While it was obvious to Caleb that his mate was displeased with Alton's message, he was quite excited about the prospect of going to Europe. Slovenia, in particular, sounded exotic to him. Also, he had already come close to deciding not to teach this summer at the college, anyway.

If nothing else, it gives me more time with Kat.

"So," he gently ventured, "We're definitely going, right?"

Her mind raced with a host of thoughts. She contemplated Alton's message, a storage location for the couch, the prospects of the upcoming conference, and the preparations that needed to be attended to leading up to their departure. Then she peered down at her mate and noted his appraising expression. Her features softened somewhat, and she quickly kissed the tip of his nose.

"I'm considering it, my love," she replied. "Alton's correct, of course. It would be an ideal opportunity for you to see more of Europe. However, I'd like more details regarding the nature of the conference first. With Alton, nothing's ever as simple as it appears."

"It would be a longer vacation for us," he said temptingly. "I mean, I had a great time in London. But the week flew by so fast."

She noted his thoughtful expression. *Great time in London,* she sardonically recalled. *When you weren't trying to avoid being killed! Still, it's just like him to be so forgiving.*

"Too true," she muttered, still deeply in thought.

Slovenia is a curious selection. I wonder whether it's the northern or southern region.

It had been years since she had traveled to that part of Europe. The country was conveniently situated near the beautiful Mediterranean. And while the southern part was very classic and touristy, the northern part was very mountainous and often remote.

I'll call Alton later.

"Any ideas where we should place the couch?" he asked.

She warily observed him and ventured, "The Salvation Army, perhaps?"

"Hey, you can't just give away my memento-couch," he retorted with a pleading look in his eyes.

Granted, the couch isn't particularly practical, but it's a hell of a conversation piece from our adventures in England.

She rolled her eyes at him and disdainfully conceded, "Fine. But it's certainly not going in our living room."

What an utterly ugly piece of furniture, she thought irritably. *Alton has the oddest sense of humor sometimes.*

"My man-cave?" he countered. The estate's small library had been hastily converted into his study when he had moved in.

"How about the garage instead? We'll need to move furniture around in your study before it will fit."

He carefully measured her disapproving tone. At least he had won a small victory in maintaining possession of it.

Today the garage; maybe someday the study.

* * * *

A few days later, Katrina was trying her hand at baking a cake. Her cooking skills had waned in the centuries since becoming a vampire, as none of her previous human mates were the type of people that fostered such domestic endeavors in her. Aside from her only human husband, Samuel, whom she had lost to influenza while she was still a human, the only person that caused her to consider cooking was Caleb. It pleased her to cook for him, and he genuinely appreciated her efforts. She had already mastered a host of breakfast-related specialties, so desserts were her latest endeavor.

She was on her third, and most successful, attempt of the day with a devil's food cake when the phone rang. Darting to the phone with her uncanny speed, she whipped the receiver up to her ear amidst a small cloud of flour.

"Hello?" she asked in a polite, yet curious voice.

"Hello, this is Tammy Mendez with Atlanta Central Realty," the soft, feminine voice prompted. "May I please speak with Caleb Taylor?"

Katrina's eyes narrowed, and she guardedly replied, "Caleb's not in at the moment. Can I take a message for him?"

There was a pause. "Actually, I'm sorry. I thought I was dialing his cell phone when you answered, but I see that I accidentally called his secondary number. I have information for Mr. Taylor that he requested regarding available town houses in the Atlanta area. I thought he might want to go over the results and perhaps tour some of the prospects."

Katrina was caught off guard by the realtor's response, and her mind raced to understand why Caleb would be looking at town houses.

He hasn't said anything to me about this recently.

"Oh," she absently commented. "Well, you can probably reach him on his cell. He's at the college until later this evening."

"Thanks very much. I'll do that," the lady politely replied. "Sorry to have bothered you."

"No trouble at all," Katrina said before hanging up the phone with a perplexed expression. Then she glanced back towards the kitchen stove where she had been baking the cake, feeling her motivation wane by the second.

Her mind raced to try and understand the nature of the phone call.

What's going on with Caleb? Have I done something wrong? Is he unhappy living with me? Why hasn't he said anything? Is this about my not letting him put that old couch in the house? Why wouldn't he have said something?

It appears the only answers lie with Caleb.

She checked her watch and determined that there were still a couple of hours left before sunset.

Trapped at home until then, she ruminated. *I guess I should go ahead and finish his cake.*

"I can always press his face into it later, I suppose," she muttered under her breath as dark emotions began to overtake her while she mulled the topic over and over.

A couple of hours later sunset had fallen, and Katrina changed into a turquoise blouse, fashion jeans, and knee-high black leather boots. She finished tying her hair into a tight ponytail and headed towards the garage.

She made her way to Robert Fulton, where the parking lot was rather empty by that time. As she walked through the parking lot, she reflected on when she had enrolled in Caleb's history class the previous fall semester, as well as the enjoyable experience she had while listening to his lectures. He had a real gift for teaching, and she loved how fulfilling it was for him.

Her features fell slightly as a wave of sadness rolled through her at the possibility that her mate might be unhappy living with her. She breathed in heavily as she pulled the door open leading into the social sciences building.

His office door was closed, and she failed to hear anyone inside. She confirmed the time, having estimated that he was likely finishing his last class that evening. She bit her lip and decided to slip up to his classroom.

Maybe I'll stand outside and listen to the last part of his lecture for old time's sake.

Then a sinking feeling shot through her stomach as she

contemplated what the evening's conversation with him might reveal.

As she approached the classroom, she noted that the door had been left cracked open a sliver, and she heard his voice carry out of the room. She wanly smiled at the sound of him in "lecture mode" and peered in to see that his back was turned to the doorway as he scribbled notations on the chalkboard. She slipped into the classroom in virtual silence and sat into an empty seat on the back row near the doorway.

"So that's why the Texans were unable to relieve the troops at the Alamo before the Mexican Army overtook the fort. Keep in mind that the facility was never intended as a tactically defensible point, so its own inadequate design contributed to the fall of the defenders as much as their relatively outnumbered forces and poor logistics," Caleb explained, completely oblivious to Katrina's entrance.

However, as he turned and scanned the room's faces, his eyes immediately fell upon her, and he smiled.

She felt a wave of confusion flow through her as she once more sensed a disconnect between his behavior and the phone call from the realtor.

He smoothly fell back into his lecture without drawing further attention, "However, on April 21, 1836, Sam Houston and the Texan Army marched against and defeated the Mexican Army at San Jacinto. While this was a tactical victory for the Texans, it hardly resolved the issue of settlement in the largely contested Mexican territory. It's not until we discuss the Polk Administration and the Mexican War during the late 1840s that any resolution occurs on that matter. But let's stop there for tonight."

Barely two seconds following the end of his statement, the students scrambled for the door. He shook his head at their hasty departure, as well as the passing glances that a number of male students gave to Katrina on their way out. As he gathered his notes together, he failed to notice that she had moved to stand beside him. When he turned to pick up his textbook he lurched slightly at her unexpected proximity, and his eyes immediately noticed the intense look in her eyes.

She looks sad, he noted.

"Is everything okay, Kat? I was surprised to see you at the back of the room," he ventured. "Although it was a nice surprise, actually. It reminded me of when you took my class last fall."

She towered before him, staring silently down into his eyes. "I was going to ask you the same thing, actually."

He gently placed his notes and textbook back onto the podium and reached out to take her hand in his as he stared up into her eyes.

"What do you mean? Kat, what's wrong?" he pressed. But then he felt a wave of nausea in the pit of his stomach and insisted, "Has something bad happened to Paige or Alton?"

She squeezed his hand while shaking her head. "No, they're fine. It's you I'm worried about."

His eyes narrowed. *Me?*

"Caleb, are you happy with us?" she asked as her emerald eyes drilled into his. "Is this about that old couch Alton shipped to you? Have I done something that you're displeased about?"

"Hardly, Kat. I've never been happier," he countered.

"Then why are you looking at properties in the Atlanta area? Are you moving out?"

His face went blank, and she immediately sensed his confusion. His expression changed to shock, and his eyes widened as if in realization of something.

Okay, that's definitely not the response I expected from him.

"Moving out?" he asked. "Why would I move out? Are you wanting me to move?"

"What?" she retorted. "No, of course not. But I got a call for you from a realtor late this afternoon..."

His pale blue eyes reflected immediate understanding, and he welcomed the feeling of relief that settled over him.

"Oh, you mean Tammy Mendez," he said. "A fellow professor recommended Tammy after buying a new home and selling his old one through her office. And her assistance isn't for me. I'm just helping scope out a place for Paige to move into, that's all."

"A place for Paige?" she blankly asked.

A split-second later, a sense of embarrassment began to form as she registered the nature of his endeavors. Paige Turner, a young vampire that Katrina counted as one of her dearest friends, had promised to relocate from Los Angeles to the Atlanta area later in the summer. Paige was also Caleb's surrogate vampire, a designated protector for him who would take care of him if anything ever happened to her.

"So, you thought I wanted to move out?" he queried with a suspicious expression. "Kat, that's crazy! I love you, and I've never been happier living at the estate."

She had only convinced him to move in with her the past December after they confronted the dangers presented to them by a rogue vampire named Chimalma. Since then, he had enjoyed the increased time with her. He also appreciated how much their relationship had strengthened.

She pulled him to her and enveloped him in a warm embrace, heedless to the sense of foolishness that she felt. She was just so relieved that the entire affair had been merely an unfortunate misunderstanding.

I'm so paranoid, she chastised.

Caleb appreciated the closeness of her body, and his arms wound around her slim waist in response. While no longer bewildered by her behavior, he felt bad that his helpful efforts for Paige had caused her to misinterpret the situation.

"Sorry, Kat. I should've mentioned it already, but my mind's been so preoccupied with so many diversions this week."

She rested her chin on his shoulder, and her eyes narrowed to slits. "Yes, you should have mentioned it, I think. But I suppose I'll forgive you," she conceded. "This time."

"Paige texted me a few days ago to ask for my help. And honestly, I didn't expect the realtor to get back with me so quickly. I explained to her that, with Paige taking that security contract job overseas, there's all summer to scope out prospects."

"Except that you might be in Slovenia with me part of the summer," she reminded him.

He patted her lightly at the small of her back and whispered, "Well, sure, there's always Slovenia. I hope that we're able to go."

He paused for a quiet moment before adding, "But since you mentioned the couch..."

"One issue at a time, my love," she gently cautioned him.

"Oh, sure," he conceded before changing the subject entirely. "So then, aside from being surprised by realtors, what else did you do today?"

"I baked a chocolate cake for you," she offered as she parted from their embrace. She hoped that it had turned out okay.

He'll probably like the frosting, at least, she anticipated.

"I really lucked out then," he said with a delighted expression. "Chocolate's my favorite."

Luck is right. You actually get to eat it instead of being smothered by it, she contemplated, though with a vastly improved mood.

Later that evening, while consuming a sizable slice of the cake, Caleb called Paige to discuss some of the available properties the realtor had recommended. The perky vampire listened to the variety of options and locations that he described and agreed to investigate at least six prospects.

"Whatcha think, kiddo?" Paige asked after he finished highlighting the interesting ones.

"Well, the market's pretty slow here," he admitted while switching the phone to his other hand. "It's probably good odds that the homes may still be on the market by summer's end."

While refilling a glass of water for him, Katrina listened with interest to the conversation, including Paige's end of the chat. It wasn't as if she were eavesdropping, really. Had her mate desired privacy he shouldn't have sat in the kitchen, or at least should have made the overt effort of sequestering himself in one of the other rooms in the house. *He's well aware of how keen vampire hearing is.*

"Thanks, Kat," Caleb absently muttered as she sat the glass down next to his plate.

"Yeah," Paige agreed. "Things are pretty slow out here, too. I guess I'd better put my townhouse up for sale pretty soon. I'll put most of my personal belongings in storage before I leave. I want my place to be in show-worthy condition while I'm away."

He savored a mouthful of cake.

"Caleb?" she asked.

"It'll be great to have you out here, you know. We miss you," he said in a muffled voice.

"Are you eating?"

"Mm, sorry," he apologized. "Kat made this great chocolate cake."

"Twerp!"

Katrina lightly ran her fingernails down the back of his neck, marveling at her mate's keen appreciation for her friend and former pupil.

I should be thankful they pair off so well, she reasoned as a somber mood overcame her and she stepped away. *If something were ever to happen to me, I'm relying on Paige to look after him.*

"I miss you too, tiger," Paige finally offered in an uncharacteristically soft voice. While she wasn't one for displaying overtly intimate feelings to others, much to her surprise, Caleb brought that quality out in her. Suddenly self-conscious of her tone, she fell into a playful display of sarcasm. "And I miss that gruff old lady of yours too," she quipped. "Tell her I said 'hey.'"

His eyes peered across the room at Katrina, who scowled.

"Hey back at ya, shorty," she wryly retorted, knowing full well that the vampire could hear her. "Spoiled brat."

Paige chuckled at that.

"You know, it would really help my efforts if I knew what part of Atlanta you want to settle down in," Caleb ventured.

There was a pause at the other end before Paige finally

replied in a quiet voice, "Oh, I dunno. Somewhere close to you guys would be fine."

Katrina's eyebrows rose slightly as she put clean dishes away from the drain board, but she said nothing.

Makes sense, I suppose, she mulled.

Caleb's eyes slowly swiveled over to Katrina before answering, "Okay then. I'll focus my attentions within, say, twenty miles?"

"Sure, that works," Paige agreed.

They said their goodbyes, and he finished eating his slice of cake.

"This is a great cake, Kat," he offered. "Thanks for baking it for me."

She happily beamed in response. "Anytime, my love."

He tentatively looked up at her from where he sat and wondered if his conversation with Paige had somehow bothered her. "You know, Kat," he began, "If it bothers you for Paige to move so close to us..."

She moved to stand behind him, draping her arms across his chest. "No, my love. I'm perfectly fine with what we decided."

Her thoughts were momentarily lost in silent recollection. It had been less than a month since her in-depth discussion with Paige regarding the young vampire's affections for Caleb. Following that, Caleb had urged the blonde vampire to relocate to the Atlanta area. *It's probably for the best.*

"Kat?" Caleb gently asked as he sensed his mate's quiet distraction.

Katrina broke from her reverie, hugged him, and gently patted him on the chest. "Sorry," she answered. "Everything's fine, Caleb. We'll find a suitable house for Paige."

He craned his neck upwards to brush his lips against hers. "Thanks, Kat," he noted with gratitude.

If only Alton weren't so established in England, maybe he could move closer as well, he mused. He had no remaining immediate relatives, so Paige and Alton constituted the closest thing he had left to family. Since his mother's passing, he had felt so alone in the world. *Family is so important*, he silently recognized. *It's wonderful to be surrounded by those that care about you.*

* * * *

The next few weeks passed uneventfully for Caleb and Katrina. Finals and the spring graduation ceremony were both over by the second week of May. Despite the fact that she hadn't yet committed to attending the Slovene conference, Caleb declined offers to teach during the summer semester. Instead, he cleaned out his office a week later and was free to pursue a host of activities at home. At the very least, he would have a free summer to spend with Katrina.

He started his time off by reorganizing the contents of their cavernous four-car garage, including sorting items to be stored in the attic. He also tended to some plants in the large flower-beds in the front yard, though Katrina assured him the lawn service that she had contracted with could handle that. He conceded to feeling a little stir-crazy with all the free time on his hands.

One morning around four am, Caleb rolled towards the left side of the bed and found that Katrina was gone. Such a revelation wasn't unusual, given that his mate could only safely leave the house after sunset. It stood to reason that sundown to sunrise would be the prime time for vampires to socialize, roam, or hunt. So he wasn't offended when he frequently woke to find Katrina missing. He knew that by morning she would likely be lying next to him to greet him upon waking. On those few occasions when she wasn't, she was usually somewhere in the house preoccupied with one of her numerous interests.

After making a quick trip to the bathroom, he still felt restless and proceeded upstairs for a glass of ice water. He paused in the main hallway halfway to the kitchen upon hearing voices coming from the back section of the house. He immediately recognized Katrina's voice, but strained to listen to the other female voice. Moments later, a telltale giggle gave away the guest's identity.

Paige! It's Paige.

It had been less than two months since he had last seen her, but it felt longer. He easily recalled his flight to California to convince her to relocate to Atlanta so she would be closer to him and Katrina. Fortunately, she had agreed, but stipulated that she had to complete a contract security job over the summer first. Despite the delay, he was excited that she would be making Atlanta her new home in just a matter of months.

He quickly pattered through the kitchen and into the entryway to the living room at the back of the house. Katrina winked at him from her place on the couch, and their guest rose from the recliner where she had been sitting.

Paige's petite body was lithe as a ballerina's. Her youthful, twenty-something features were haloed by her blonde bob, evoking the flapper dancers of the 1920s. A set of piercing, deep blue eyes targeted Caleb, while her playful smile appeared nearly devilish against a backdrop of pearly white teeth. She had the kind of mischievous grin that made him feel as if he'd just sold his soul but relished the bargain. Her form-fitting blue jeans and high-cut Ramones concert t-shirt playfully evoked exuberant sexuality.

She took in his appearance with amusement; his slightly mussed hair looked appropriate given his ensemble of cotton sweatpants and Georgia State football t-shirt. "Hey, tiger," she purred invitingly. "Come give your big sister a hug."

He crossed the short distance in seconds, and she giggled as he hoisted her off the floor, encasing her in a bear hug. She patted him on the back with one hand while playfully pinching him on a butt cheek with the other.

"Hey," he yelped as he hugged her tightly to him. "No pinching!"

"Sisters don't typically pinch their brother's butts," Katrina observed dryly, though she considered no less a playful response from her best friend.

Paige popped a quick kiss on Caleb's cheek and quietly retorted, "We're more like kissin' cousins, really."

Katrina rolled her eyes.

"Missed you, kiddo," Paige whispered in Caleb's ear.

"Missed you, too, babysitter," he whispered back, still holding her tightly. "It's great to see you!"

Oh, I'm liking this a lot, Paige appreciated. Then she abruptly pulled away from him, teasing, "All right, you can stop groping me. It's getting just plain creepy now."

He chuckled, shaking his head, while Katrina observed the pair with a good-humored expression.

"And somebody smells particularly tasty," Paige observed with a sly expression. Her bright blue eyes gleamed as his scent generated a strong urge for his blood.

"Sounds like somebody's hungry," he countered and eyed his mate. "Want anything, Kat?"

"Just you," she suggested. "But heat up a type A for each of us, I suppose."

"My favorite," Paige remarked with approval.

"Gee, I wouldn't have guessed," Katrina mocked.

"Two type As coming up, m'ladies," Caleb crisply snapped.

Minutes later, he returned from the kitchen with two glasses of warmed blood. He placed one glass on the end table next to the recliner where Paige sat and handed the remaining glass to Katrina as she reclined on the couch.

"Thank you, my love," his mate offered appreciatively.

"Thanks, kiddo," Paige remarked and made a small space on her recliner. "Have a seat, and take a load off."

But Katrina gently cleared her throat and motioned to the empty cushion next to her. Caleb shook his head slightly at his mate's rather possessive response and wearily plopped down on the couch next to her. Truth was, he was too tired to care where he sat.

However, Paige briefly stuck her tongue out at Katrina, who scowled in silent reply.

"You're up early," Katrina absently observed before taking a sip from her glass.

"Yeah, couldn't get back to sleep," he replied with a tired sigh.

"Don't you have to teach later this morning?" Paige asked.

"Thankfully, no. The semester just ended, and I'm taking the summer off," he explained.

Katrina procured a small pillow next to her, placed it on her lap, and lightly patted it with her hand. "Why not lay your head down?" she suggested.

He shrugged and lay prone with his head on the pillow as he stared at Paige. "I thought we wouldn't see you until later in the summer. What brings you to town?"

"I'm actually headed to my contract job, but thought it would be nice to visit for a few days on my way there. Hope you don't mind."

"Of course not," Katrina insisted. "We're happy to see you."

"You're always welcome here," Caleb added with a yawn, to which Paige appreciatively winked at him.

Katrina sat her glass down on the end table to her right and pulled a comforter from across the back of the couch. She smoothly unfolded it and draped it over him. "Tell us what you've been up to," she prompted as she soothed her fingertips through Caleb's hair.

As Paige recounted her packing activities at her home in California, the preparations for her contract job, and a host of other information, Caleb was lulled into a comfortable state. Somewhere during the drone of Paige's conversation, his eyelids grew heavy, and he effortlessly fell asleep.

As Katrina waited for Paige to finish speaking, she momentarily reassessed Caleb's state of consciousness before looking at the young vampire across from her with a curious expression.

"Now that Caleb's asleep, why don't you tell me why you're really here? Not that you're not welcome here, of course, but we've known each other a long time, and I recognize when something's up with you."

The edges of Paige's mouth upturned slightly with amusement at her friend's direct query. *Always looking for the angle, aren't you, Red?* The truth was that she felt slightly uneasy about her reason for being there. Her feelings weren't something she was used to laying out for everyone to see. "Remember the conversation you and I had with Caleb at my townhouse back in March?" she asked.

Katrina nodded. *How could I forget? You confessed some strong feelings for my mate that night.*

While not entirely surprised over the revelation, she had felt a little uncomfortable with it. Still, Paige had been very open and honest with her, which had reassured her somewhat.

"Caleb said I had nothing keeping me in California anymore," Paige offered, and then paused to look over at the young man across from her to assess his state of slumber. "Well, after you both left, I didn't think too much about it. Then the past couple of weeks, I've been mulling those thoughts over a little bit. Frankly, I've been feeling a little lost without you two around. So, I figured I would stop by on my way overseas. I wouldn't mind spending a little time with our boy, in fact. Maybe scope out some of the houses that he's been nice enough to check into for me?"

Katrina was reassured that her friend seemed to be laying everything out on the table in a straightforward manner. A sardonic smile crossed her lips.

"It's silly, but it almost sounds as if we're negotiating joint custody over him, doesn't it?"

"Aren't we?" Paige insisted.

"Fair enough," Katrina amicably conceded as she continued to run her fingers lightly through Caleb's hair. "Naturally, I'm sorry if I seemed a little suspicious."

"I'd be surprised if you weren't, Red." She was all too aware of her friend's tendency for suspicion, and possessiveness, when it came to Caleb.

"Caleb was correct when he said that you're always welcome here, Paige," Katrina insisted. "Your timing's pretty good, actually. Caleb's been rather stir-crazy around here as of late with all the spare time on his hands."

Paige smirked, content with her friend's more settled manner. "Oh, I think I can take care of that for you."

* * * *

Chapter 2

∿

Messengers

*W*hen Caleb awoke, he immediately recognized two things. First, the room that he was in was dark except for the dim illumination of a digital clock on the nightstand. Second, he was lying in a bed rather than on the living room couch. Still groggy and feeling somewhat dazed and disoriented, he rolled over in bed to find Katrina staring back at him with a beguiling expression.

"Good morning, sleepy-head," she wryly offered. She could tell by the expression on his face that he was confused, which amused her to no end.

"Wha..?"

"Our bed," she supplied with a soft voice. "No, it wasn't a dream. No, you didn't walk; I carried you. And finally, you're welcome."

He took a moment to comprehend everything that she said. For one, he couldn't believe she had transported him to the bedroom without waking him. Never mind the thought of her carrying a grown man to bed seemed utterly silly, if not embarrassing. He imagined that Paige would tease him to no end about it, of course. Finally, he wondered what he was supposed to be grateful for.

"I'm welcome? For what?"

"Helping you get back to sleep, of course."

"Oh. Thanks. I think."

He squinted at his watch, noting it was almost nine o'clock, and yawned. "Well, I want you to stop carrying me to bed like some oversized rag doll," he grumbled.

She affectionately kissed the tip of his nose. "What's on your agenda for today?"

He pursed his lips. "Well, if it's a nice day, I thought I might go for a jog. Otherwise, I'm pretty open to suggestions. Why?"

"No reason. Paige would like to spend some time with you, I think."

"That would be great. You okay with that?"

"Well, she is your surrogate vampire and guardian, after all. So, yes, I'm okay with it."

His eyes narrowed slightly, and he pressed, "Why do I get the feeling that you two negotiated the terms on this already?"

"Caleb, I'm sure I don't know what you mean."

"Mm-hm."

"Why don't you get dressed, and I'll see about getting breakfast ready." She slipped from beneath the sheets in a single, fluid motion.

Before he could inquire further, she had dressed and was exiting through the doorway leading to the first floor hallway. He stared after her curiously for a few moments before finally getting out of bed.

He shaved, dressed, and went upstairs to find Katrina cooking breakfast for him while Paige sat at the kitchen counter watching her with a lazy expression. She immediately perked up as he walked into the room.

Not wanting to pass her by and seem rude, he exchanged a quick kiss on the cheek with Paige before hugging Katrina from behind. He breathed in the scent of sausage links and eggs as they sizzled away in a large pan on the stovetop.

"Good morning, Cookie," he teased.

"Cookie?" Katrina paused with a spatula in her hand.

He almost winced from her tone. "Um, it's just a historic nickname for the wagon trail cooks who used to feed the cowpokes on the cattle drives."

"Let's just stick with Kat, shall we?" she suggested.

"Right. Sorry, Kat," he apologized. He rose up on his toes and kissed the back of her neck.

"Much better," she responded, neatly slipping the cooked food from the skillet onto a nearby plate.

"I don't know how you stomach cooking dead meat for him," Paige bleakly observed while shriveling her nose. "The smell's horrible."

"I'm actually getting used to it in small quantities. Still, you do that when you love your mate. Sometimes the small sacrifices are the most meaningful," Katrina said.

She glimpsed at Paige over her shoulder with a pointed expression.

Caleb discreetly peered at the two women as he filled a glass with ice water at the refrigerator.

"Yeah, makes sense," Paige off-handedly conceded.

During breakfast, Caleb and Paige discussed their plans for the day. Once sunset arrived, Paige wanted to drive by a couple of local houses that were for sale. She also mentioned taking him out to dinner at a restaurant of his choice after they ran a special errand, about which she was tight-lipped.

It all sounded like fun to him, but he couldn't help wondering what the errand might be. The last time she had taken him on a mysterious errand, he had been forced to interact with a vampire who had nearly beaten him to death. Granted, that meeting had turned out better than he had expected.

Katrina left the pair to their own devices and occupied herself with activities in her office. Caleb couldn't help wondering if that might have been part of some arrangement between the two vampires, but he couldn't say for certain. After breakfast, he talked Paige into joining him to play a medieval role-playing game on the console in the theater room. While he already had a character drawn up for use, Paige needed to create one.

Caleb queued up his iPod on the stereo system, and Bear McCreary's "Passacaglia" began to play. Paige looked up curiously as he returned to his seat.

"You have your own soundtrack music?"

"Bear McCreary is far better than the game's music. Trust me."

Paige rolled her eyes at him.

As she scrolled through the game's available avatars, she noticed a pre-saved character called Kat, which predictably was a red-haired Amazon warrior. She adopted a wry expression and selected a petite elf archer-mage for herself.

"Cute choice," he noted as he stared up at the character images on the wall-sized screen before them.

"Cute?" she retorted. "We can't all be tall Amazon warriors, kiddo, but I can still get the job done. Perky people can be deadly too, you know."

He stared sidelong at his friend. "What's that all about?"

Her pale blue eyes darted to him then returned to configuring her avatar. "I'm just sayin'."

He stared back at her in confusion, which she noticed. She focused a piercing gaze upon him.

"What is it with you and tall, imposing women, anyway?" she pressed with a hint of annoyance. "You defy most standards, my friend. I mean, most guys that I know like women their own height or shorter, and a lot less demanding."

"What's your beef with me?" he demanded, pointing to himself with his thumb. "I'm the happy one here. You're the one who sounds annoyed."

His attention reverted to the screen before him. "And yeah, it's true that most of the women I dated in the past were my height or shorter, but what the hell does that have to do with anything? It's the nature of the person rather than their physical stature."

She dryly observed, "Yeah, right. Like you don't melt before her when she towers over you. I think it's a turn-on for you. Face it, you like imposing women."

"Imposing? Kat's not –" He broke off, flustered. "I mean, yeah, she can be, I suppose. But she's kind, loving, and --"

"I get it. You like 'em tall, angry, and mysterious."

"She's not *angry*. She's, well, *protective*."

"Uh-huh," she noted in a dubious tone. "I can be protective."

He stared at her in confusion. *Where the hell did this conversation come from anyway?*

"You're protective," he finally observed in a quiet voice. "Listen, you've saved my life on no less than two occasions since I've known you. I cherish your role as a guardian in my life, Paige, as well as my best friend."

She turned to mark him with a penetrating expression. The corners of her mouth upturned slightly with satisfaction, and she moved in a blur to close the distance between them, lightly kissing him on the check before returning to her original location next to him. It startled him, but he was nevertheless pleased.

"Okay, Harry Potter, let's go kill some trolls," she relented while saving her avatar settings.

He rolled his eyes. "My guy's a holy warrior, not a magician. And I think we're fighting Orcs."

"Yeah, yeah, whatever. You're such a nerd," she teased.

"Nothing complex here. Just some ugly little dudes with clubs who need slayin'."

They thoroughly enjoyed the remainder of the day with no more uncomfortable topics.

By late afternoon, they looked through printouts of houses for her to consider visiting. A couple of hours later, the sun had dropped below the horizon, and Katrina raised the metal shutters on the windows around the house to reveal the colorful hues of the evening sky. It was one of the few near-daylight conditions that a vampire's physiology could safely endure.

"Hey," Caleb prompted Paige as he appreciated the view of the manicured front yard via the sitting room window. "It's almost sunset. I'll race you!"

She smirked. In a blur she was opening the front door before he even got up from the couch. They both walked outside onto the front lawn, and he admired Paige's pale skin in the final moments of dusk. While a vampire's skin was pale under artificial lighting, it took on a nearly ghostly appearance at dusk or pre-dawn. He stared at her thoughtfully, finding her pallor just as eerily beautiful as Katrina's.

She acknowledged his attention, cheerfully recognizing the sense of awe in his eyes.

"Careful staring at vampires, Caleb," she warned with mock-seriousness. "We're mean and always raring for a meal."

He moved to stand next to her and reached up with one hand to touch the side of her face lightly. Her skin was soft and warm to his touch, and he smiled at her.

"Don't kid yourself. Some vampires are genuinely wonderful beings," he observed as he withdrew his hand.

Her eyes widened in momentary surprise. "So are some humans," she softly amended as her gaze met his.

Then the front door opened, and he turned to see Katrina standing at the top of the porch stairs. He stared at the beautiful woman before him.

My mate, my vampire.

She moved in a blur to stand next to him, and one arm gently draped around his waist. He swallowed hard as he appreciated her beautiful eyes in the faint glow of daylight from the horizon.

I love you so very much, he thought. The woman before him had not only saved his life as an adult, but had killed his abusive father when he was merely a child. Those memories, so recently restored, flooded back through his mind in a raging torrent. He recalled the formerly short-haired brunette named Amber who had ended his years of abuse when he was merely eight years old. *Angel Amber*, he recalled.

Katrina must have read the adoring expression either on his face or in his eyes, because she pulled him to her as she bent down slightly to kiss him on the lips. He responded only once so as not to make Paige feel uncomfortable.

Still, the blonde vampire discreetly observed the exchange. *Rub it in, Red*, she thought.

"Beautiful evening," Katrina congenially observed as she

looked to the faint glow remaining on the horizon.

"Yep, and night's finally arrived," Paige agreed as both the sky and western horizon continued to darken.

Caleb stole a fleeting glimpse of both vampires and felt immediate contentment. He realized at that moment how fortunate he was to have each of them in his life and how completely happy it made him.

"Life is good," he whispered.

Both vampires turned to look at him with satisfied expressions.

"C'mon, tiger, it's time to go out on the town," Paige insisted as she hooked one arm through his.

But Katrina maintained her grip around his waist and bent to place a final warm kiss on his lips. It was a somewhat possessive gesture, but she wanted to make a point to Paige. Caleb responded to her kiss in kind, and Katrina tossed a set of car keys to Paige.

"You two have fun tonight. Take the Audi."

"Thanks, Red," Paige replied as she tugged on Caleb's arm. *Message received.*

"We'll try to stay out of trouble, Kat," Caleb gently offered. "See you later tonight?"

"Sure," Katrina responded as she reluctantly released her grip on him. "Be careful."

As Paige pulled him behind her up the porch stairs to enter the house, she quipped, "Don't worry, you overgrown Amazon. The elf archer-mage is on top of everything."

Katrina's expression turned slightly confused. "What?"

"Never mind. I'll tell you later," Caleb called back with a chuckle before being pulled into the house behind the short vampire.

*   *   *   *

Paige changed into a pair of jeans and red camisole and slipped into a black leather jacket as she bounced down the stairs. Caleb met her in the kitchen, and she took a long look at him in his jeans and fitted black t-shirt that accentuated the definition of his chest. She flashed him a look of approval.

"Grab your leather jacket," she advised as she stuffed her license, credit cards, and cash into her jacket pockets.

Minutes later, they were on the road. Caleb thoroughly enjoyed the drive around town with Paige in Katrina's Audi. The car was an impressive piece of automotive machinery and effortlessly glided down the road. She noted his enthusiasm, silently appreciating the happiness emanating from him.

They had only driven a block from the addition before he was able to convince her that he should drive, since he knew the locations of the houses that they planned to see. The spunky vampire was happy to indulge him, doubting that Katrina let him drive very often. She knew that the red-haired vampire was a control freak, which likely extended to her driving habits.

However, their house-hunting wasn't as satisfying as Caleb's appreciation for driving was. It only took Paige a few minutes at each of the four prospects to determine they just weren't for her. The first was much larger than she wanted, and the second was in a neighborhood that she didn't care for. The third house had a nice layout from what she could see through the windows, but didn't have a basement. She wanted a sublevel room, though not one as elaborate as Katrina's. The final home on their tour was too far across town, nearly outside the county.

"Expecting trouble?" he asked when she voiced her concern.

"Babysitter's always expecting trouble," she dryly observed. "Especially when it comes to you. You seem to attract it."

He shook his head at her response, amused by both her continued reference to being his babysitter and for sounding so much like Katrina at that moment. Still, he silently conceded that his life had become a lot more exciting, and dangerous, since becoming involved with vampires.

Paige studied him with a curious expression as they stood on the front lawn of the final property.

After a moment, he broke from his reverie and asked, "So, where to next?"

She expectantly held her open palm out towards him. "My special errand. And I'll drive."

Half an hour later, they pulled into the parking lot of a Harley Davidson dealership.

Caleb gaped at her with a wide-eyed expression and challenged, "You're kidding."

"Be nice," she mildly admonished. "There's still a lot you don't know about me, kiddo."

He expectantly followed her into the main showroom. A burly-looking fellow with goatee and Harley t-shirt greeted them as they entered. Paige had apparently been shopping ahead of time, because she knew exactly what she wanted to see.

The man led them to a red and chrome touring bike, though it appeared to be built more for speed than touring. Caleb had only ridden a motorcycle a couple of times and only as a passenger when catching a ride around campus with a friend while he was a college student. Caleb had a hard time imaging the petite young woman before him commanding the road on the impressive street machine.

Paige's appeared delighted as the salesperson described some customizations that had already been made.

"How about a spin?" she asked with a menacing grin.

"Uh," Caleb stammered.

The salesperson chuckled at his reaction and offered, "Little lady, take him out, but bring him back alive."

He rolled the bike as if it were a toy towards the extra-wide doors leading out to the parking lot. Caleb marveled at the guy's strength and at how easy he made it look to move the huge cycle across the floor.

Geez, does this guy bench press these cycles in the back room or something?

Paige grabbed two visor-equipped helmets and passed one to Caleb as he absently followed behind her. The guy scowled as he noted Caleb's hesitant expression, but the man's face reflected sincere surprise as Paige easily balanced the bike between her legs and remained upright.

"Somebody's a natural," he observed.

"Somebody's had a history with hogs," she clarified then turned her attention to Caleb. "Put on that helmet and hop on, kiddo," she ordered before slipping on her own helmet.

Caleb swallowed hard as he popped the helmet over his head and moved to sit behind Paige. The engine started with a growl, and she revved it slightly.

"Arms around my waist," she ordered in a loud voice.

He tentatively wrapped his arms around her petite waist, but she reached down and grabbed one of his wrists.

"Tighter!" she ordered, and he increased his hold around her.

Caleb lifted his feet to press against the passenger foot pedals as Paige kicked the bike into gear. They proceeded at a slow pace until reaching the street, at which point she gunned the bike, and they leapt out onto the road.

"Crap!" Caleb exclaimed as his arms instinctively tightened around her waist. He thought that he heard her laughing, but wasn't entirely certain.

She was quite satisfied to feel him tightly hugging her, and she relished the wild freedom of being on a motorcycle again. This was the surprise she had been waiting all day to spring on him, and it was working out just perfectly, in her opinion. She had researched the various models on her flight from California, having decided that her new life in Atlanta would include a cycle. She had been an avid rider since the 1950s, but had not owned one in many years.

Now it's time to rekindle my relationship with Harley Davidson.

Caleb finally reconciled himself to the fact that Paige wasn't going to let them fall over on the street and was surprised that she rode so well. He had definitely found a topic to talk about over dinner later that night. Suddenly, he was happy that they hadn't eaten yet because his stomach was knotted with tension. As if by instinct, his arms enveloped her waist.

That's my boy, Paige thought, loving the feeling of his strong arms encircling her. She increased speed while weaving in and out of traffic.

They test drove the cycle for about twenty minutes before Paige made her way back to the dealership. By the time they whipped into the parking lot, Caleb had become a permanent fixture on Paige's back. She lurched the cycle to a stop just outside the main doors, cut the engine, and flipped the kickstand into place with the toe of her shoe.

"Time to let go, tiger," she suggested as she lifted her helmet off. "Not that I'm complaining, mind you."

He released her with a start and slipped his helmet off just as the salesperson walked outside. They both got off the cycle, and the man looked at Caleb with a raised eyebrow.

"I see he didn't fall off or throw up in the helmet," the fellow observed.

Caleb scowled but remained silent.

"Nah, I took care of him," Paige replied with a smirk.

"Lucky guy," the man said as he eyed her with an appraising look. "Well, whaddaya think?"

"I'm game," she said. "Throw in the helmet and a set of leather saddlebags and you've got a deal."

The man seemed momentarily caught off guard by her smooth, haggle-free terms. "Done," he replied. "Come on in, and we'll knock out the paperwork."

"My new toy," Paige cooed as she followed the guy into the showroom.

"Him or the bike?" the guy asked, gesturing with his thumb towards Caleb.

She merely giggled in response as Caleb blushed in three shades of red. *Both*, she silently confirmed.

As Paige completed the sale, Caleb browsed the host of accessories on display. After a few minutes, his eyes settled on the one-piece leather riding suits, immediately recalling something he had once seen in a vampire movie. He beamed with satisfaction as he turned to stare across the showroom where Paige was standing.

"Oh, babysitter," he cooed softly.

Paige's head pivoted in a blur, and her blue eyes expertly targeted him in her sights. After a spontaneous assessment, she beheld him with a curious expression. He discreetly used the crook of his finger to beckon her to him. She said something to the salesman and wandered over.

"Wassup?" she asked.

"So, promise me you'll give me another ride on your new bike," he baited.

She frowned. "Well, *yeah*. Anytime, anyplace. I'm riding it home tonight, after all."

"Great," he said. "Tomorrow, then. Shall we say, just after lunch?"

She spared him with a deadpan expression. "Not funny, Caleb."

"Shouldn't be a problem," he optimistically ventured, pointing to the leather outfit before him. "That is, if you're wearing one of those."

Her eyes darted to the apparel display, and the edges of her mouth upturned slightly. *Smart kid.*

"Hate to tell you, Sherlock, but it's not like one of our kind hasn't already thought about that," she offered in a milder tone. "It's not without some risk and not very practical for anything but riding around. But yeah, I'll bite."

She paused with an evil grin, which merely elicited a groan from him.

"However, you have to promise *me* something," she stipulated. "If *I* give you a daytime ride, *you* have to commit to a nighttime ride."

"You're on," he agreed with a shrug.

Then he wondered what the catch was.

She seemed quite satisfied as she picked one of the black leather suits from the selection before her. She selected a set of leather gloves and briefly browsed the leather riding boots. Minutes later, she proceeded over to the counter with the additional merchandise while the salesman observed her with anticipation.

After dinner, they returned to the estate, where Katrina was surprised by Paige's purchase, but smoothly congratulated her on the acquisition. Caleb recounted a more sedate version of his test drive experience and deliberately avoided any mention of his riding agreement with Paige.

The following day, it was barely eleven o'clock when Caleb sat down to lunch in anticipation of his daytime ride. As he ate, Katrina walked into the kitchen to heat some blood in the microwave.

"Somebody's hungry early, I see."

He casually shrugged. "I've got plans at noon."

"That's nice," she remarked as she removed the glass of blood and took a quick swig. *At least he's staying active with all his spare time.* "What's on the agenda?"

"Riding with Paige," he replied around a mouthful of potato chips.

A steely expression crossed her face. "At noon?"

Paige walked through the kitchen with an armful of clothes, heading for the utility room at a speedy pace. "High noon, Red. A deal's a deal."

Katrina's green eyes narrowed to slits, and her demeanor darkened as she intently stared into Caleb's eyes. He shivered slightly at their intensity.

"What deal?" she demanded in a stern, quiet voice.

He swallowed his bite of sandwich and drank from his glass of cola. *Oh no. Not good.*

Katrina patiently waited, looming before him like a statue while staring at him flatly.

"Um," he awkwardly began, "Paige offered to give me a ride on her cycle at noon."

"Caleb Taylor!" Katrina exclaimed.

He winced slightly.

"How could you? As if you don't fully know how dangerous that is."

Paige zipped back through the kitchen wearing a mischievous grin. "Ha! I get him tonight, though."

As the blonde vampire raced upstairs, Katrina demanded, "Exactly what does that mean?"

Caleb immediately regretted the agreement with Paige. "Well, I kind of agreed to a nighttime ride in return for a day ride."

She glared at him, and he swallowed hard at the stony expression on her face.

"Kat, it's just a ride," he protested. "And, after all, she's going to wear protective gear."

Paige reappeared, twirling around like a model in her new leather outfit complete with black leather boots. A cocky expression accompanied her energetic aura as she pulled on a pair of leather riding gloves.

Katrina took a moment to stare at her friend before looking to the ceiling with exasperation.

"You're an idiot to go through with this, Paige," she said. "What if something goes horribly wrong?"

"Everything will be fine. Just a quick out and back," Paige insisted in a cavalier tone. "Keep your shirt on, Red. Tell me we haven't done far more dangerous things for far less reasons."

"We both did some stupid, careless things out of sheer ignorance when we were younger," Katrina corrected. "Now I know my limitations better and realize the consequences of failure. I won't be able to help you if something goes wrong. What if you wreck and your suit becomes torn? Your exposed skin will start burning in seconds."

Caleb didn't like the direction of the conversation, and the implications of failure generated a series of horrific flashes in his mind. *Why did I have to be so stupid?*

"Look, this was a mistake," he insisted. "We don't have to

do this, Paige. We'll wait to go riding tonight instead, okay?"

Paige let out a deep breath, shaking her head as she perched her hands atop her hips. "Honestly, Red. You wanna scare the kid by arguing about this?"

"He should be scared," Katrina growled as she cast a glare at Caleb. "I vividly recall how painfully the sun burns. Get burned badly enough, and there's no coming back from that."

Her memories replayed the past. It had only been eighteen years since she had tried committing suicide by facing the morning sun. Though she had lost her nerve at the last minute, severe damage had been done to her body. It was only the actions of an innocent, eight-year-old boy named Caleb that had saved her. The momentary recollection almost lightened her mood. Almost, but not quite.

"I know what I'm doing," Paige insisted between clenched teeth as she reached out to grasp Caleb's arm. "Hell, I did something like this a decade or more ago, anyway. And we'll both be safely back before you know it."

"Wait," Caleb protested, but Paige took his arm in her vise-like grip and pulled him towards the direction of the hallway leading to the garage.

"Oh, shut up! Honestly, the lengths you have to go to these days just to have some freakin' fun," she muttered.

"Be careful!" Katrina barked with aggravation as Caleb was dragged into the garage. *You better be careful, or I'm never going to forgive you*, she silently added.

Paige shoved her helmet over her head and thrust the spare helmet at Caleb. After putting it on, he stared into the charcoal-tinted visor on Paige's helmet, wondering if she were actually planning to go through with their plan.

"Do you see any exposed skin?" she asked in a muffled voice.

She looked almost like a black-clad astronaut in her leather outfit. He scrutinized her closely then shook his head. She flexed her arms and wrists and seemed satisfied. Then she pointed to the garage door and spun her finger in the air. He went to press the garage door button on the wall. Paige straddled the cycle and hurriedly waved him to return to her as the door rose. Sunlight permeated into the garage little by little until the garage was illuminated by the ambient glow of daylight. He hiked his right leg over the back of the bike, and she revved the engine.

She glanced back over her shoulder at him while feeling his arms slip in front of her stomach and tighten around her waist. She took a deep breath as she put up the kickstand, and they lurched out onto the driveway, marking her first journey into direct sunlight in nearly fifteen years. Despite her outward display of confidence, she wrestled with feelings of uneasiness as she realized how vulnerable the sun made her feel. Still, Paige Turner liked nothing better than a challenge.

As they rolled onto the neighborhood street, Paige steeled herself for any negative reactions. However, the charcoal-tinted visor did its job, and her face and eyes felt nothing more serious than a mild tingling sensation. The complete coverage of the remainder of her body effectively protected her. As they proceeded past the gate and out onto the neighborhood street, her confidence grew by the moment. By the time they were on the county road outside the addition, she once again felt completely in control of her situation.

However, Caleb was still concerned for his friend and silently berated himself for placing someone he cared about in potential danger for the sake of a spontaneous dare. As they smoothly coasted atop the asphalt, his imagination ran scenarios about what he should do if Paige suddenly found herself in distress from the effects of sunlight exposure. A macabre vision of feverishly trying to bury her body in dirt along the side of the road flashed in his mind. Then he realized that they hadn't even brought a shovel or any other tool for effective digging. At the very least, he thought, he could drag her into a shaded area and cover her up with something.

I'm such an idiot.

However, within ten minutes or so, he began to realize

that Paige seemed quite at ease with their circumstances, and a hopeful sense of success crept into his spirit. Before long, a feeling of guarded relief formed, which further tempered his anxiety.

Half an hour later, he was actually enjoying their daytime ride. He affectionately patted her stomach with his right hand, and she revved the engine in response.

Ever since meeting Katrina, he had bemoaned the fact that his interactions with a vampire were stunted by daylight. It was as if a moat existed between two separate worlds of day and night. Now the chasm had been bridged and realities began to coalesce with one another. However, the new dimension was tempered by the cold realization that if Paige could do this, so could other vampires. That meant his daytime kingdom was no longer pleasantly safe from direct influence by prospectively negative forces.

But then, it never really was, he rationalized with sober realization. *Blissful ignorance.*

Paige peered over her shoulder at him for a brief second, having sensed a subtle change in his body.

Everything okay back there? she wondered as she reached down with one hand to pat his arm.

Her concerns were abated by a gentle pat from his palm against her stomach.

Much better, she thought and once again focused on their enjoyable journey.

She revved the engine, which caused the cycle to lurch slightly, and Caleb's arms tightened around her waist. She appreciated the firm feeling of his body against hers.

The things I have to do for a friendly cuddle, she thought with a snicker.

By the time they returned to the estate and parked in the garage, both of them were feeling quite satisfied with themselves. When the door finally closed, Katrina appeared before them in a blur, her arms folded before her and a stern expression on her face. However, her visage was replaced with a measured sense of relief upon seeing them no worse for wear and in no distress.

My two little daredevils thankfully returned unscathed, she silently noted with a quick peck on Caleb's lips.

"See, Red? Nothing to worry about," Paige good-naturedly offered.

"It was great!" Caleb added.

"Mm-hmm," Katrina dubiously hummed as she followed them into the house.

By evening, it was time for Caleb to make good on his end of the bargain. Paige donned a pair of faded blue jeans, black t-shirt, and black leather jacket, along with her leather boots. She wandered into the front entry room where he was sprawled on the couch with his laptop surfing the Internet and quietly stood in front of him with a smirk on her face and her hands resting atop her hips.

"Evening's here, kiddo," she reminded him.

A tentative glance up at her was his only response as he closed the various programs in Windows. He still felt a little guilty about their daytime ride together, although he had enjoyed it very much in the end. Despite her virtual anonymity of being clad in leather riding gear and helmet, somehow just being outside with her during the day made him feel happy. However, he regretted the angst the act had caused Katrina. In fact, she had avoided him and Paige for most of the afternoon, remaining secluded in the lower chamber at her computer.

Paige noted his distracted body language and tried to discern the nature of his mood.

Her silent query went unanswered as he powered off his laptop, set it aside on the end table, and quietly rose from the couch. He cast an innocent, curious gander at her and asked, "Ready then?"

"Garage," she instructed in a resolved tone. "I'll tell Red we're leaving."

He shrugged and made his way towards the back of the house.

"Grab a leather jacket," she added in a raised voice. "There's an unseasonable chill outside tonight." *That, and Katrina will kill me if I let anything happen to you, including catching a cold!*

He snatched his jacket on the way out to the garage and barely had time to pick up the spare helmet before Paige appeared beside him. He started slightly with surprise, not having heard the door from the house open and close.

She giggled in response, happy to have caught him off-guard.

She activated a garage door remote from her jacket pocket and slipped on her helmet while he peered outside into the night. He noticed a peculiar fog had started to form and zipped up his leather jacket halfway.

After mounting the cycle, she motioned to him and started the engine. The motor revved to life as his leg swung over the seat.

Paige felt the satisfying, telltale warmth of his arms as they slowly wrapped around her waist.

That's my boy, she admired. *Hold on, tiger*, she added with a chuckle. *Now's my turn to have some real fun.*

She eased the bike out of the garage and quickly headed in the direction of the addition's exit. It was a wonderful night for a ride, and she was happy not to have to wear the cumbersome riding gear. She longed to feel the wind whip around her as they rode, as well as the satisfying sensation of Caleb's arms tightly wrapped around her midsection. By the time they had exited the addition onto the open road her anticipation had grown into a hunger.

They were soon racing down the asphalt county roads.

I could ride with him across the entire state tonight, she happily mulled.

As for Caleb, he eased into a state of appreciation rather quickly, and he took the time to survey the subdued landscape they passed. The foggy evening inspired ominous feelings within him, though he enjoyed spending time with Paige.

It looks kind of creepy outside tonight. Classic vampire weather.

Paige continued to increase the cycle's speed as they proceeded through the cool, foggy evening. They parted the moist air as they pressed forwards, creating a wispy swirl of fog in their wake.

There were few cars on the semi-rural county roads, and they only passed three after leaving the neighborhood. Caleb thought that the dark, oppressive conditions seemed to thwart his awareness of their velocity as they sped along. It was as if they floated on a dark sea of mist, partially illuminated by the fuzzy halo of an occasional street lamp.

Suddenly, the headlight on their cycle went out, plunging them into near darkness. Caleb's arms immediately clamped around Paige's body like a vise, and he thought that he felt her body momentarily vibrate somewhat.

Is she laughing?

The vampire took great pleasure in switching the headlight off and heartily laughed at Caleb's instantaneous, nervous reaction. Of course, her vision was well-accustomed to seeing in darkness, so she had no trouble viewing the road or surroundings around them. However, it had to be terrifying to the human melded to her back.

Now comes the payback, she resolved with satisfaction.

But even in her sense of retribution, she also felt the purely invigorating feeling of the young man's body pressed against her back. It made her feel needed and powerful. She grinned to herself despite his obvious alarm.

"Paige!" Caleb shouted after what felt like an eternity in darkness with the feeling of swift motion almost causing his stomach to feel queasy. "Stop!"

She glimpsed the view via one of her side mirrors and noticed what looked like another motorcycle shadowing them; one with its headlight likewise extinguished. Her mind raced with the possibility that another vampire was likely trailing them.

Surely that's not Katrina. She hadn't recalled seeing another bike in the estate garage, merely Katrina's and Caleb's vehicles. She instinctively increased the speed of their cycle, concentrating her attention on putting more distance between them and their mysterious follower.

Caleb's heart caught in his throat as he heard the engine revving into a higher gear and felt their velocity increase.

"Oh shit!" he barked and concentrated on keeping his stomach in check.

"Hold on, tiger!" Paige shouted, uncertain if he would be able to understand her.

She expertly maneuvered their cycle around slight curves, while concentrating both on their balance and the topology of the road. In a split second, she observed a sign on the corner of a gravel road they passed in order to mark their current location and immediately noted another small sign indicating that a scenic turnout was coming up.

Their cycle continued up a sharp incline as the turnout loomed ever closer. Her eyes darted to the side mirror, and she quickly estimated that a greater distance had formed between them and their pursuer.

Paige wheeled the cycle sharply to the left and into the shallow parking area that was bordered by metal railing. The bike skidded to a halt as she killed the engine, and Caleb practically rolled himself off the back seat while yanking the helmet off his head.

He staggered slightly off-balance, cursing. "Dammit, Paige! What the hell are you trying to do, get us both killed?!"

But she ignored him for the moment and stared off to their left towards the small entrance through which they had just passed. As she deftly removed her helmet, she heard the faint sound of another motorcycle engine gearing down and then idling in the distance. She perched her helmet on one the handlebars and focused on Caleb.

He loosely held his helmet in one hand while staring back

at her incredulously. His eyes were wide with a mix of excitement, fear, and angst.

"Well?" he demanded in a strained voice as he steadied his still-queasy stomach. "What's your friggin' problem? Is this 'scare the crap out of Caleb night,' or something?"

"Oh, stop being so dramatic," she admonished with annoyance and turned her attention back towards the turnout entrance.

"Dramatic?" he irritably countered.

"Shhh," she insisted with a quick wave of her arm.

She moved in a blur, only to reappear at the side of the county road to stare into the distance.

Just who the hell is following us? she wondered.

He fell silent as he watched her obvious distraction at something further up the road. He thought they had come from that direction, but it was quite dark, and he actually had no idea where they were.

He inspected his surroundings. He didn't think he had ever been there before, and he stared across the cliff-like view into the fog beyond the metal railing before him. The mist parted slightly in places, and he speculated that the few fuzzy orbs of light in the distance might be from some local town.

Caleb moved closer to the railing and tried to see into the darkness below. It seemed they must be some height up, though he couldn't see the bottom of the drop-off. Then he started with surprise as Paige reappeared to his right and firmly grasped his upper arm with an iron-like grip. She pulled him back away from the railing in a steady manner.

"It's a nasty drop, kiddo," she quietly warned. "Let's get you back over here away from the edge, okay? You're kind of accident-prone."

He rolled his eyes, but retreated back in the direction of the cycle. She released his arm and pulled her cell phone out with a fluid motion. He started to ask her something, but she began speaking.

"Red? We're at a turnout off the Russell-Brasstown scenic

route," she said in a quiet voice. "Pretty sure that we've got a visitor. I'm headed back with our boy. Meet me en route?"

Our boy? he wondered. *Just who came up with that little nickname?*

She snapped the phone shut and neatly slipped it back into her jacket pocket before he even saw her move. "Back on the bike, okay, kiddo?" she suggested while reaching for her helmet.

But he backed away from her. "Yeah, right. That little stunt was enough for me."

"Oh, grow up, Caleb," she tersely admonished. "I was just having some fun. Like I'd do something to endanger you."

Her chastisement caught him off guard, and he stared back at her in bewilderment. "So, that's your idea of fun?" he countered.

"We're being followed by someone. Back on the bike," she ordered. "Now, Caleb."

He hesitated, wondering what was going on. "Really?"

She loudly snapped her fingers and pointed to the cycle seat. "Do as I say."

He blinked at her suddenly demanding attitude and walked over to the bike as he slipped his helmet on. She moved in a blur, reappearing in the driver's position while straddling the cycle. The engine roared to life a second later, and she turned her head to peer at him over her left shoulder. She revved the engine once as if to punctuate her demand.

Paige hasn't acted like this before, he noted with alarm. *So serious.*

It seemed completely out of character for her, but he decided that, at the moment, the better part of valor was to comply. He hiked his leg over the back seat, and his arms slowly enveloped her waist.

But rather than a gradual start, Paige gunned the cycle, and they lurched into movement. Caleb noted that at least she had turned on the headlight. His arms tightened around her, but instead of feeling her softer body as he had earlier, it almost felt as if his arms were enveloping the trunk of a statue.

The county road seemed deserted as they accelerated through the fog. However, Paige once again noted the pursuing cycle in her mirror. The dark-clad figure appeared to be deliberately trailing them from a distance with their headlight off.

Less than twenty minutes later, Caleb saw an approaching set of headlights and fog lamps in the distance. And while he realized that they were traveling at a high rate of speed, the oncoming vehicle seemed to also be approaching them at a fast rate.

Is that who's been following us?

Only seconds passed when the vehicle appeared to slow, pull to the side of the road, and then stop with its hazard lights flashing. As they drew closer, Caleb finally recognized the Audi and saw Kat standing with her arms folded before her chest in the bright luminance of the headlights.

Paige slowed the cycle and stopped a mere foot from the front of Katrina's car. Her arm reached back around Caleb's chest and rolled him off the back of the bike with a swift motion. He had barely set his feet onto the pavement before Katrina's arm protectively wrapped around his waist and drew him before her.

"I'm going back to check out our visitor," Paige said in a raised voice that Caleb was able to understand over the purring of the motorcycle's engine.

Katrina nodded once, and Paige backed the cycle up another foot then revved the engine. The bike lurched into motion, kicking up gravel as it spun, and she raced back in the direction from which they had just come.

Caleb's mouth was agape as he pulled his helmet off and watched with awe as Paige raced away from them. She wielded the cycle as if she were some sort of stunt racer.

"Get in the car, my love," Katrina insisted as she squeezed his body slightly in her embrace to focus his attention. "Let's get you back home."

"But aren't we going to follow her?" he protested.

"Paige is an alpha and can handle herself perfectly well," she explained as she herded him towards the passenger side of the car. "She'll call if she needs help."

He stared into her eyes dubiously, but she pointedly ignored him and instead took his helmet from him and tossed it into the back seat. Then she gestured with her head towards the passenger seat and waited for him to sit down.

"Buckle up," she prompted as she closed his door, appearing in the driver's seat mere seconds later.

The velocity of her movement made his head swim.

She wheeled the car around to head in the direction opposite from where Paige had gone and propelled them back towards Mableton. Caleb worried for his friend as he studied the rear view through the side mirror, hoping that Paige would be okay.

I know Paige is capable, but we don't have any idea who our stalker is. His experiences in London had only emphasized that there were very dangerous vampires lurking in the world.

Katrina surveyed him with a hint of concern and reached out to caress her fingertips soothingly along the side of his face.

"Did you enjoy your ride for the most part?" she asked to distract him.

He cast a furtive glance at her. "Sure. I mean, it was surprising how different riding with her felt at night versus daytime." It seemed prudent to avoid telling her how alarmed he had been as they had sped through the night sans headlamp.

She sensed some evasion in his response.

"Do you remember the last time that I was speeding you away in my car following an unexpected encounter?"

He eyed her suspiciously, easily recounting when they had raced across town from the restaurant where the renegade vampire, Chimalma, had nearly trapped him last winter. It felt like an eternity since that dangerous encounter. Finally, he recalled, "Yeah, that was a bucket load of fun too."

She stifled a smirk at her mate's dry wit. *He's so adorable when he's flustered.*

"Well, unlike then, you're not in any danger this time," she explained. "It's not beyond expectation that a curious vampire might just be traveling through town. Having declared my claim to Mableton and part of Atlanta earlier this spring, there were bound to be those who would take pleasure in flaunting their unannounced defiance when traversing my territory."

Caleb acknowledged the possibility, but doubted that this was the case. Vampires didn't usually strike him as recalcitrant teenagers out to thumb their nose at authority.

Vampires usually do everything for a reason.

"Maybe," he replied in a dubious tone.

Katrina wasn't entirely convinced herself. She slipped her cell phone from her purse and called Devon Archibald, a vampire indebted to her employ as restitution for his poor judgment in nearly killing Caleb as wayward prey. She called upon him from time to time to help patrol and secure her territory.

Following her brief chat with Devon, she focused on Caleb with a confident expression. "Devon's going to patrol our area first and then around your campus. He'll let us know if something, or someone, turns up."

Caleb suddenly realized that they had already arrived at the gate entrance to their addition. *Wow, we must have been racing back here.*

Once in the estate, Katrina went to their sublevel chamber to finish some emails and call Alton while Caleb retrieved a Coke from the refrigerator and sat at the kitchen bar to reflect on the evening's events. He wondered what could have been of so much interest that another vampire would care about him and Paige so much.

After finishing his cola, he felt restless and went out to stand on the front porch to wait for Paige's return. The fog had begun to clear, revealing large patches of the night sky.

"Nice night, but you'll have to move further away from the house lights to stargaze properly," rumbled a deep baritone off to Caleb's left.

He turned in the direction of the voice and saw Devon's

hulking figure just a few feet away. The ebony-skinned vampire stood with his muscled arms folded before him. His gleaming white teeth were exposed in a wide, self-satisfied grin.

Caleb nodded at the imposing figure, having recently acquired an appreciation for the vampire who had once tried to make a meal out of him. Following their recent trip to England, Caleb and Devon had discussed the works of Shakespeare, which Caleb had brought back in a leather-bound collector's edition as a souvenir for Devon. While hardly friends, *per se*, the two had formed an increasingly comfortable rapport.

"I'm actually *Paige-gazing* at the moment," Caleb quipped. "How did you get here so fast from Marietta?"

Devon worked evenings as a security guard for a company near his home in Marietta and was a bouncer for some local clubs. A drive to Atlanta should have taken longer than the time that had passed since Katrina had phoned him.

"I was at your college's library doing some research when Katrina called," Devon said. "I was actually thinking about taking a literature class, but wanted to review some of the texts listed in the online syllabus before deciding."

Caleb immediately approved of the vampire's interest in taking a college course. Despite the stigma that large-framed, muscled men typically garnered, Devon was highly intelligent, often rivaling Caleb's own grasp of various literary subjects.

"That's great," he said. "I'll be happy to recommend some good professors, if you're interested."

"I'd appreciate that," Devon replied. "But what I'm most interested in is finding out more about who it is that I'm supposed to be looking for."

Caleb rehashed his and Paige's brief experience that evening, to which Devon intently listened as he spied a sole car traveling past their driveway gate. There was not much for Caleb to relay, actually. As Devon walked out into the large front yard in the direction of the driveway, Caleb followed.

"I hear a motorcycle," Devon offered, cocking his head to one side.

"It's probably Paige," Caleb ventured, though he couldn't hear anything yet. A few moments later, he recognized the roar of Paige's new Harley. As the entry gate opened, he moved to stand in the middle of the driveway.

Paige pulled the cycle alongside the young man and idled the motor as she slipped her helmet off. Devon folded his arms before him with a curious expression.

"Did you catch up to him?" Caleb asked, taking in the confident manner with which she perched atop her seat. He was again impressed by the petite vampire's ability to manage the cycle beneath her.

"Him?" she challenged.

Caleb shrugged. "Whomever."

"Whoever they were, they took off as soon as I headed after them," Paige absently explained. She focused her attention on him with a narrow-eyed expression. "So, did you tell Mother Hen all about your ride?" she asked.

As if on cue, Katrina appeared on the front porch as Caleb sneered.

She's wondering if I told on her or not.

"I told her it was quite different riding with you at night," he said.

Katrina appeared beside him in a blur with an expectant look on her face.

"Sorry, Red," Paige replied to her unasked question. "They took off, and I wasn't able to catch up."

"Hmm," Katrina replied as she casually draped one arm across Caleb's shoulders. "Any ideas?"

Paige shrugged. "Only one. They're riding a fast machine to outrun me, I'd venture."

"Caleb seemed to enjoy his ride tonight," Katrina said, baiting her friend with a penetrating expression.

"Yeah?" the blonde vampire hedged. "Well, that's good. It was fun, after all."

Caleb curled one arm around Katrina's waist, gently guiding her in the direction of the house. "Well, I guess that's a wrap for now, then."

Katrina relented and allowed herself to be led back towards the house. Paige watched them depart for a few moments then proceeded up the driveway towards the garage with a self-satisfied expression. She admired Caleb for his judicious silence. Later, Devon reported the results of his patrol of Mableton, but he had found nothing by the time he headed back to Marietta. Paige even went on a nighttime prowl on foot, but she also found nothing. Katrina remained at the estate, suspicious of prospective vampire interests in either her or Caleb. After their London experiences in March, she wondered if her assistance to Alton in the subway raid had placed her on the radar of any opposing vampire factions.

Her mind continued to contemplate a host of possibilities and scenarios as she lay in bed snuggled beside Caleb. She reveled in his body's proximity as his arm tightened around her body from behind. He stirred slightly, and she caressed his arm. His lips briefly pressed against her bare shoulder, and she appreciatively purred while he drifted back to sleep.

This is perfect, she thought in appreciation, reveling in the warmth of his body against hers. *This is all I need.*

*   *   *   *

The next day was uneventful for the most part. Caleb went grocery shopping to acquire items that he needed to do a barbeque that evening. Granted, he was cooking only for himself, but any occasion to fire up the grill required serious planning in his mind.

Hey, it's a guy thing, he rationalized.

The strange events of the previous evening had been all but forgotten by the time sunset arrived. Despite the waning daylight, the prominent shade on the east side of the house provided enough protection that Katrina and Paige comfortably moved out onto the back porch to watch Caleb prepare the grill. The two vampires perched on patio lounge chairs while sipping warm blood from glasses as they observed him. Eventually, following a final trip into the house to finalize preparations, Caleb returned holding a large plastic Frisbee.

"Anyone feel like tossing this around while I cook?" he baited.

Paige considered the atmosphere with a quick peep at the sky and set her glass aside on a nearby table. "Go for it," she challenged.

With a single swipe of his arm, the disc hurtled through the air and into a deeper region of the backyard. Paige moved in a blur to chase it as Katrina chuckled. The youthful vampire caught it with one hand just inches before it touched the ground, giggling with satisfaction.

"Red!" she called while tossing the Frisbee to her left across the large expansion of yard towards the trees of the adjacent property.

Katrina sped out of her chair and into the yard like a bullet as Caleb placed meat onto the grill.

Damn, that was fast! He once more marveled at the speed that vampires were capable of moving compared to humans.

"Oh Ca-leb," Katrina taunted a few seconds later.

"Bring it on," he chuckled as he closed the lid of the grill.

The rapid exchanges among the trio often left Caleb struggling to keep up. Both vampires heartily laughed or giggled as they watched him either triumph or flounder in his efforts to catch the elusive disc. On one occasion, Paige sped ahead of Caleb to catch him before he nearly slammed into the trunk of a large tree while concentrating on snatching the Frisbee from midair. Soon afterwards, he recalled his grilling responsibilities and raced to attend to his food before it burned on one side.

After turning the meat, Caleb expertly threw the Frisbee back towards Paige. The vampire caught it smoothly with one hand as it started to pass behind her back. He shook his head at her graceful motions as she deftly propelled the glow-in-the-dark plastic disc towards Katrina, who sped backwards in a blur to match the high velocity of the Frisbee as it sailed towards the northern extreme of the property line. With a ten-foot leap, she snatched it from the air then propelled it back towards Caleb.

He laughed as he ran southwards towards the wooded tree line of the opposite end of the property. While not a vampire, he was both athletic and fast for a human, and he closed the distance to the Frisbee as it began losing altitude. The disc spun downwards at an angle as he reached with outstretched fingers to grab it in mid-air. Paige giggled and playfully cheered in support of his efforts. With confidence, he slung the disc towards Paige, who was positioned to his right, halfway between his and Katrina's positions.

However, as Paige ran backwards to line up a perfect catch, something from the edge of the tree line behind Caleb caught her attention out of the corner of her eye. She immediately changed direction to run towards him with wide-eyes.

"Down, Caleb!" Katrina shouted in horror.

An arrow hissed through the air at Caleb. He still had a puzzled look on his face as Paige slammed into him. She twisted and expertly rolled her slim body beneath his so that he didn't impact the ground directly, landing upon her instead. The arrow imbedded in the turf at a slant not two feet from where they lay.

Katrina was already racing towards Caleb as another arrow arced in the air towards his location. Paige immediately rolled him beneath her and presented her petite back as a protective shield for his body. His eyes were wide as he watched the second shaft drill into the ground mere inches from the first shaft. He turned his head to stare up into Paige's bright blue eyes, fearful that she might be hit by additional arrows plummeting towards them.

"Don't worry, I'm durable," she reassured him.

Despite acknowledging the truth in her statement, he frowned.

"Crap!" he exclaimed as a third shaft impacted the ground barely a foot away from the first two.

Katrina squatted next to them, glancing down to ensure that they were uninjured and scanned the tree line for only a second before racing towards it with a deep-throated growl. "Stay here!" Paige ordered before racing after Katrina, her eyes ablaze with fury.

Everything had happened so fast that Caleb barely registered her departure, staring instead at the three wooden arrows stuck in the ground. He quickly rose to his feet to move next to a large tree trunk for partial cover and strained to hear anything beyond the sound of the wind rustling the trees and his heartbeat pounding in his ears. The sun had set completely, and darkness enveloped the backyard except for the dim illumination provided by the ornate lamps surrounding the patio area.

He absently dusted the seat of his jeans to remove stray grass and dirt as he scanned the periphery of the backyard. Then his eyes focused on a dark-skinned figure standing at the northern end of the property line near some pine trees. The figure appeared to be a dark-haired man wearing dark slacks and a turtleneck shirt. His hands were held out to his side, and he appeared to be unarmed.

"Vampire," Caleb muttered, to which the figure inclined his head in polite acknowledgement. The mere fact that the visitor could hear him from that distance was additional confirmation of his suspicion.

The figure made a brief beckoning gesture with his right hand, as if summoning Caleb towards him, and said, "Truce. I bring a message."

Caleb hesitated, and then saw the figure hold up a folded piece of paper in his left hand. He looked to his left and saw no sign of Katrina or Paige, so he shrugged and walked towards the figure.

Okay, call me crazy, but he seems peaceable enough. He said "truce," right?

*   *   *   *

Katrina and Paige raced through the woods onto the adjacent properties, searching frantically for the individual who had launched the arrows, but they found nothing.

"We should've heard or seen them by now. There's no way that a human could move that fast," Katrina angrily muttered.

"One of us then," Paige growled from thirty feet away, having easily heard her friend's comment.

"Harrumph," Katrina grunted and waved Paige to continue off to the right while she canvassed the left.

* * * *

Caleb tensely stood before the vampire, though sporting the bravest expression that he could muster on short notice. He silently berated his body's anxious heartbeat for giving away his true demeanor to the stranger. However, a corner of the vampire's mouth upturned slightly, and his irises began to glow with a yellowish hue. The stranger's eyes scrutinized Caleb in an instant.

"Greetings, Caleb Taylor," he offered. "I regret that I don't have time for pleasantries, but I'm sure you understand."

"I'm afraid you have me at a disadvantage," Caleb countered. "We've never met."

The stranger sagely agreed. "Yes, you are at a disadvantage at the moment. And yes, I also know that you're afraid."

Caleb frowned, squaring his shoulders with bravado in response. However, the figure held out his empty palm in a peaceable gesture with a facial expression that spoke of a parent stilling the actions of an animated child.

"We're aware of your meeting with Alton in London," the vampire plainly stated. "And we hope that your mate hasn't committed to a course of action, yet."

"Your contacts in London? The ones in the Tube tunnel system?" he pressed.

The vampire appeared perplexed. "Tube system? No, our

contact observed you while site-seeing in the city."

Not from the Tube system? Caleb pondered with a blank expression. *I didn't recall seeing any other vampires while site-seeing.*

Noting the young man's obvious confusion, the stranger hastily continued, "I represent parties of a moderate mindset, and we are not supportive of Alton's agenda for the summer conference. We hope that your mate will consider remaining neutral in the matter and abstain from attendance."

"Why not tell her yourself?" Caleb queried, hoping to stall the stranger until either Katrina or Paige could return.

The ebony-skinned stranger held up the note in his left hand and extended it towards Caleb. "Katrina's reputation precedes her, and she might not receive us in a manner that we would prefer. We had to take a small risk to draw her away while we instead reached out to you," he explained. "The note explains everything. Please give it to your mate."

"Ever hear of trying email or a phone call?" Caleb challenged.

The vampire shook his head. "You are most amusing, young man. But the new ways are not always mine. I still prefer the traditional methods of our kind. I leave you in peace. For now."

The stranger focused on something beyond Caleb, causing him to peer back over his shoulder. By the time he looked back, the figure had already blurred into the trees north of him.

Caleb's eyes scanned the surrounding area, finally settling on a lone figure standing less than fifty feet to his left. A woman in similar dark clothing to the stranger's and carrying a hunting bow looked at him with a sneer. By the glow of one of the estate's eaves lights, he confirmed that she had short auburn hair and pale skin. Her eyes momentarily flashed hazel, and she briefly winked at him before turning to disappear in a blur of motion.

"Damned if life doesn't keep getting stranger with these vampires," he muttered after letting out a deep breath. Then he heard what sounded like two charging bulls coming from the forest of the neighboring property to the south.

* * * *

After a few minutes, Katrina stopped, realizing that there was no sign of the intruder, no scent, and no other obvious trail to follow. Paige instantly appeared at her side.

"Nothing. No trace at all," Katrina growled.

Paige cocked her head to one side and whispered, "Wait. What if this weren't an attack? What if it were a diversion?"

Katrina's face showed momentary surprise. "Diversion from what?" Then her mind instantly formed a picture of her mate, and she turned in a fury to speed back to their property. Paige became a mirrored blur at her heels.

When they broke from the tree line, they instantly spied Caleb standing with his back turned to them at the north end of the yard.

Relief poured through Katrina as she determined that her mate appeared unharmed. She stopped just short of him, reverting to a human-like speed. She walked up behind her mate and wrapped her arms around his upper shoulders and across his chest while resting her chin on the top of his left shoulder.

Paige stopped beside him, curiously looking up at his face.

"We lost them," Katrina softly lamented. "Not sure who they were, but they're gone now."

"Yep," Caleb said. "They just left. The female vampire was the one with the bow."

Katrina's heart froze and her eyes widened as she realized how easily she could have just returned to find her lover's corpse. A sharp intake of breath from Paige marked the short vampire's response, while her eyes reflected unsettled surprise at Caleb's revelation.

Caleb felt Katrina's grip tighten around him to a nearly uncomfortable level.

"I'm sorry, my love. You could've been killed. We were foolish to leave you alone and unprotected."

"Who knew, Kat? In the end, they only wanted to pass along a message," he reassured her, though he still felt somewhat anxious. "Besides, you had no way of knowing."

"What message?" Katrina growled.

He recited what the stranger had said and tried to hold up the note in his right hand, but Katrina's continued embrace trapped his arms in too vise-like a manner for him to move.

Instead, Paige glanced down and retrieved the message from his hand. "Crushin' our boy, Red," she casually observed as she unfolded the note.

Katrina's grip loosened considerably, and she kissed him on the cheek in silent apology. He appreciated their closeness despite the serious circumstances and relaxed in her arms.

"It's in Latin," Paige offered, handing the note to Katrina. "I never quite mastered Latin."

Katrina released Caleb and quickly read the note. Despite the darkness, her vampire vision had no problem discerning the text.

Paige watched her face for a reaction to the contents, and then absently sniffed the air. "I think your stinky dead meat is burning, kiddo."

"Crap!" Caleb cursed as he raced over to the patio grill. He grabbed the metal tongs and flung the grill cover open, only to be met by a billowing cloud of smoke.

Katrina's eyes flickered to him in a moment of distraction then concentrated on the note again as she wandered in his direction. Paige darted across the yard to retrieve the arrows and the Frisbee then returned to walk beside Katrina. She observed Caleb's ministrations with mild amusement as he hastily pulled the meat off the grill and transferred it to a platter.

A few minutes later, everyone returned inside the house, and Caleb checked on French fries baking in the oven. The vampires sat on barstools at the kitchen island counter while Caleb removed additional side dishes from the refrigerator to place them on the countertop. Then he went into the small downstairs basement to retrieve some blood for Katrina and

Paige. As he heated it in the microwave for them, Katrina stared at Paige with a dark expression.

"The note indicates that a group of moderates of our kind prefer the traditional manner in which vampire matters have been handled to this point. They don't favor any form of union or organization. And since I'm well respected in the vampire community right now, they would prefer that I not allow my status to be misappropriated as a figurehead in Alton's latest venture this summer."

Caleb placed a plate, flatware, and a glass of iced water on the counter between Katrina and Paige. He retrieved the two heated glasses of blood and placed one before each of the women.

"Thanks, tiger," Paige said before returning her attention to Katrina. "So, exactly what do you intend to do?"

Caleb removed the fries from the oven and piled some on his plate. He filled the rest of his plate with half-burned, grilled brisket and slathered it with barbeque sauce. Then he sat on the remaining barstool between the two vampires.

Katrina wryly smirked at the heaping portion of food on her mate's plate then looked at Paige. "I'm not sure. But I'm not ready to declare either way for now. I think that I'll keep an open mind."

"Alton's counting on you," Paige warned.

Katrina frowned. "That may be. But then, so is Caleb. And his best interests come first."

Caleb stopped eating, and he peered at Katrina's emerald eyes with a wary expression. Her gaze appeared steely and somewhat distant, and he recalled seeing that look once before. "Oh, no, you don't," he sternly warned as his heart rate rapidly increased. "You've got that 'I'm going to lock him up safely in the house' look again, and that's sure as hell not going to happen."

Katrina arched an eyebrow at her mate and shook her head with a sigh. *He's never going to let me live that down, is he?*

She recalled when she had gained his permission to try and

save him from Chimalma and secured him in the estate under Paige's watchful eye until she and Alton could hunt down their enemy. It had nearly driven him crazy to be locked up in the house for days on end. *Still, he did give his permission to let me protect him.*

Paige snickered and stole a crispy French fry from Caleb's plate. He noticed her and curiously surveyed her as she crunched on it.

"It's okay, my love," Katrina assured him. "I promise not to overreact."

Caleb accepted that and returned to eating.

"Why don't you tell me about the woman with the bow again," Katrina prompted.

He shrugged. "Beautiful woman with short, auburn hair."

However, he became distracted as Paige snatched a longer fry, dipped it into her glass of blood, and then ate it. He groaned. "Eww, gross."

"Hush," Paige muttered and promptly procured another of his fries.

"Ahem," Katrina cleared her throat, used her hand to grasp his chin, and gently rotated his face towards her to recapture his attention.

"Sorry," he sheepishly offered as he stared into her eyes.

She adopted a forgiving expression, briefly kissed him, and encouraged, "You were saying?"

"She winked at me before she disappeared," he recalled, to which Katrina adopted a less-than-amused visage as she released his chin.

"Careful, kiddo," Paige mock-warned. "She might have her eye on you for more than just target practice."

Katrina flashed her friend a dirty look, but Paige shrugged and innocently replied, "Hey, I'm just sayin'."

"But I still wonder about the male vampire," Caleb said. "He seemed older somehow, like Alton does at times, although he could pass easily for his thirties or so. And his yellow eyes were unique."

Something that he said struck a nerve in Katrina, and her attention bored into her mate with sudden intensity. "Yellow eyes?"

"Yeah, they were ominous-looking," he replied. "Kind of eerie, actually."

Katrina pursed her lips as Paige watched with sudden interest.

"Know that one, Red?" she asked.

"I think so," Katrina replied. "He sounds just like a vampire I encountered while traveling through northern Africa back in the early 1900s. If he's who I'm recalling, then he's an ancient one. I think his name was Hakizimana."

Caleb and Paige both looked at Katrina.

"It means 'God Saves,'" Katrina explained.

"Yeah, well, I think he said his name was Ted," he said.

Katrina stared at him as if he had just turned into a frog before her eyes, while Paige exclaimed, "*Ted?* He said his name was *Ted?*"

He chuckled while holding up one hand, admitting, "Sorry, I made that up. I just wanted to see your faces. It was priceless."

Katrina rolled her eyes and shook her head. Paige snickered while mussing Caleb's hair with one hand. "Good one, tiger."

Then she stole another of Caleb's French fries.

He smiled at Paige's compliment. "He actually never told me his name. You know, in the end, neither of them seemed overtly hostile. Still, I was ready to fight for my life, if necessary."

"You didn't challenge him, did you?" Katrina asked.

Caleb shrugged. "Not really. I was just resigned to stand up to them."

Paige stopped chewing a fry, and her pale blue eyes narrowed. She shot at glance to Katrina with a look of concern.

Not a good approach, kiddo, she recognized.

"On that topic," Katrina sternly began, "the next time

something like that happens, you don't approach them. You run, either to me or Paige, as fast as you can. Understood?"

He clenched his jaw, not wanting to just turn and run every time a vampire showed up on his turf. He thought that he made a fairly level-headed decision earlier that evening, and it had turned out to be correct.

"So, I should just stand there and get eaten?" he snapped.

Katrina took a deep breath. "No, but you're not equipped to confront a vampire, particularly multiple vampires. Promise me you won't do anything careless like that again."

"Fine," he replied in a tight voice while stabbing two fries with his fork.

She had misgivings about his sincerity, but let the topic drop. *It's only going to antagonize him further by harping on the subject*, she resolved. But she worried about his taking too many chances around vampires. He was very fragile as a human, and his life could be snuffed out in a moment. That was something that she couldn't endure.

He slowly returned to eating, and the three of them silently sat through the rest of the meal. Katrina and Paige somberly observed him as they drank their glasses of blood. Even Paige's previously playful mood of stealing fries had abated. When he finished, he cleaned up and then rinsed the dishes before placing them in the dishwasher.

"I'm going to confer with Alton and see what he thinks," Katrina finally offered. She popped a kiss on Caleb's cheek then retreated down the hallway with the note in hand.

He activated the dishwasher then leaned against the counter watching Paige. "Thanks for covering me in the yard this evening."

She darted from her seat to embrace him warmly. "No problem, kiddo. Babysitter's always on duty."

Like I could do anything less for him. He's such an important part of my life now.

He fondly recalled her self-appointed nickname when he had first met her last fall.

Geez, my friends would never let me live it down over that "babysitter" business, if they ever heard about it. Still, he knew that in her own quirky way she meant well. *Paige is one of the best friends that Katrina or I could ever have.*

*   *   *   *

Chapter 3
Nights on the Town

*I*n the sublevel room, Katrina conferred with Alton on the note passed to Caleb in the backyard. However, the elder vampire had no additional information to provide her, other than that he was already aware of interests forming on either side of the issue related to the summer conference. He recommended proceeding with caution regarding further interactions with the faction, though she had already been resigned to do that even before calling him. Still, she promised to keep him apprised of the situation.

When he asked her for confirmation as to whether she and Caleb intended to attend the conference, she told him that she hadn't decided for certain. He seemed less than pleased, but wisely didn't press the issue with her.

I'll do whatever's in Caleb's best interests, she reaffirmed after hanging up the phone.

The following evening, Paige mentioned to Katrina that she wanted to take Caleb on another evening ride on her Harley. It was against her normal modus operandi, but given the previous evening's events, she considered it the better part of valor to run her plan past Katrina first.

"Sure, Paige," Katrina said. "I appreciate your cooperation with me on this issue."

Paige stared intently into her friend's eyes. "No problem. But someday soon, you and I are going to have a chat about how overprotective you still are with our boy."

"He's a human, Paige. He needs protection from our kind."

"And yet, he's not helpless," she challenged. "Consider how far he's come since you first met him last fall. Hell, he's practically a firecracker by comparison."

Katrina silently acknowledged her friend's point.

"He means so much to me. I've already lost one husband and two children. I can't bear losing him, too," she whispered.

"Then don't drive him away by smothering him."

The silence grew between them as Katrina merely stared at her.

"Listen, Red. I know you 'love him more than life itself.' I get it," Paige said, "You're just trying to protect him. You're Wonder Woman to his Steve Trevor. But every good superhero knows when to lighten up a little."

Katrina chuckled. "You have a weird way with analogies, Shorty."

"I'm just *special* that way," she quipped as she turned to depart.

"Have fun, but please be careful," Katrina said.

"Not to worry, Red. I can be a superhero when I need to be."

"And just which superhero are you, exactly?"

Paige paused with a thoughtful expression, one index finger lightly tapping on her chin. After a moment, she shook her head. "Aw, heck, I dunno, maybe Superman's cousin. Superwoman?"

"You probably mean Supergirl," Katrina dryly corrected.

"Whatever," she countered with a dismissive wave, once more on a mission. "I'll leave all the nerdy stuff to you and Caleb."

Having received the approval she needed, Paige located Caleb and was happy that he jumped at the opportunity for another cycle excursion.

"I'll even try not to scare you this time," she teased.

"Oh, yeah? Do your worst."

Paige's bright blue eyes slyly narrowed, and she murmured in a lethal tone, "Oh, you really shouldn't have said that, tiger."

Much to her satisfaction, a visible shiver coursed through

his body, both from her tone and visage.

They left the house an hour or so after he ate dinner. The nighttime ride with Paige filled Caleb with an odd sense of contentment. The weather was perfect, not overly warm, even in their leather jackets. The continuous rumbling of the engine grew soothingly rhythmic as he watched the landscape flow past them in a blur of motion.

Life is good, he contemplated as he tightened his embrace around Paige's waist.

Paige felt Caleb's grip strengthen around her. A blissful feeling passed through her, and she couldn't imagine riding without him that night. While relieved that he had agreed to take an impromptu ride with her given his last experience, she nevertheless deliberately took corners a little sharper than normal in order to elicit the occasional tightening of his hug around her.

I just love this little guy, she thought contentedly.

Then she refocused on the real reason for their jaunt.

After a time, Caleb wondered if Paige had any idea where they were actually headed, or if she were merely riding in the direction the cycle was pointed in at the time. He speculated that they were not only well outside Mableton city limits, but likely outside the county. Still, he had no complaints, and the gently rolling countryside was relaxing despite the darkness.

Little did Caleb realize that Paige had affairs well in hand. She was touring the area using a progressive, methodical pattern, purposefully hunting for a specific target. Despite the odds against success, it made her feel proactive.

Some time passed before Paige's keen vision glimpsed a motorcycle like the one that had followed them the other night. She steered them off the main road and into the parking lot of a place that had all the telltale signs of being an old biker bar.

A sea of cycles was arrayed across the half-gravel, half-asphalt lot. The wood-framed building appeared to be at least forty or more years old and in only modestly maintained condition. A wooden front porch sported a series of rough-hewn wooden beams that supported the ramshackle tin front awning.

The old-fashioned porch was occupied by a throng of rough-looking bikers who were engaged in either drinking, smoking, swapping tales, or some combination thereof. Also on the porch, to one side of the front entryway, sat the motorcycle that had caught Paige's keen vision.

That's probably not the bike we're looking for, but it bears checking into.

You're freakin' kidding me, Caleb disdainfully thought as Paige slowed their approach through the parking lot.

Memories of a previous bar visit in downtown Atlanta flooded through his mind like a bad flashback. A former California punk rock singer named Gil Yeager, whom Paige had dated for a brief time, had steered them into a rough bar setting that had ended in an impromptu parking lot fight. He painfully recalled that he and Gil had barely managed to be on the winning side.

As they came to a halt, he maintained a firm embrace of Paige's waist as she straddled the cycle. She had no sooner removed her helmet when she flashed him a devilish look over her shoulder.

"Lovin' the hug, kiddo, but now you just look like you're groping me," she teased with a flash of her bright blue eyes.

She accepted his anxiety over their arrival, but it wasn't going to deter her from checking out a possible lead while also exposing him to a prospectively instructive setting.

He absently released his arms from around her and removed his helmet. His blue eyes warily scouted the crowd hanging around the front of the dimly lit building.

"I don't like this," he darkly muttered.

Paige hung her helmet over one handlebar and cast a reassuring face at him. "Stop being such a worrywart. I've been in dozens of places like this. Most of these guys are just weekend roughnecks trying to live out *Easy Rider*."

"You mean the *magazine*?" he demanded.

Another inspection of the nearest female patrons confirmed

that none of them looked like any of the cover models he had ever seen in an issue of *Easy Rider.*

She immediately countered with a withering expression, "No, porn-king. I mean the world's most famous biker film and anti-establishment story of the twentieth century."

"Sorry. Never saw it," he replied with a shrug.

"Just never mind," she chastised with annoyance as she snatched his helmet from him and draped it over the other handlebar.

"We could go home and rent it online now, if you'd like," he suggested.

She tightly pursed her lips, rolled her eyes, and began towing him by the arm towards the building. "Some other time. Come on, Captain Adventure."

He quickly fell into step beside her, and she draped one arm around his waist as he stretched his arm across her petite shoulders. He glanced sidelong at her as they approached the wooden steps leading up to the smoky porch and noted a self-satisfied half-leer on her face that gave her an edgy appearance.

Well, at least I have a vampire with me, he thought as they crossed the threshold into the joint.

Loud rock-n-roll roared above the din of laughing, cursing, and carousing in the bar. The scents of stale beer, cigarette smoke, and worn leather permeated the room. A trio of worn pool tables in the back was surrounded by men and women as bets were called out for whoever was shooting. A lengthy series of worn stools along the length of the bar were occupied, save for two, toward which Paige steered Caleb with the pull of her arm around his waist.

A number of eyes darted to up look at the two newest patrons with a mix of mild curiosity and assessment, much like predators sizing up new prey. Caleb's eyes darted once to Paige's to note that a subtle look of amusement had replaced her earlier scowl.

She took immediate notice to their reception, but deliberately ignored the patrons. She recognized the various expressions, having seen them on numerous occasions over the past century. But unlike Caleb, she had already determined that in a roomful of dangerous characters, she was the deadliest. It was merely that nobody else realized it yet.

How I've missed this, she reflected.

Her attention quickly returned to assessing the two dozen or more people in the room. She quickly noted that none appeared to be a vampire.

An older, balding man wearing a worn brown leather vest over a stained t-shirt stood on the working side of the bar. His eyes slightly narrowed as he studied the two while passing two bottles of beer to the two bikers before him. He sidestepped to his left and casually wiped the counter in front of Paige with a relatively clean towel.

"Haven't seen you two before. Just passing through?"

Caleb started to reply, but Paige smoothly interrupted with a shrug, "Just out for a ride tonight. My old man and I got thirsty."

The bartender snickered. "I bet. Okay then. What'll you have?"

"Got any Sam Adams?" Caleb inquired.

"Nope," the bartended answered in a clipped tone.

"Two Buds," Paige interjected as her eyes met the bartender's.

One of the man's eyebrows arched slightly. "Now, *that* we got," he confirmed and turned to reach into a closed metal cooler behind him.

He neatly popped the metal caps off each bottle and swiveled around to place them on the bar with a thump.

Paige neatly produced a couple of crumpled bills and smacked them on the bar before her. "That's the first two rounds. Next one's are yours, lover," she quipped to Caleb.

The bartender scooped up the bills and made his way to the opposite end of the bar to attend to three bikers clustered together. Paige took a swig from the bottle and casually leaned over to Caleb.

"Next time, pay attention to the lit beer signs and order what you see," she pointedly recommended. "Don't go out of your way to look like an amateur."

He filed the tip away for future reference. "Just what are we doing here, anyway?"

She took another swig of her beer and stared at him. *Poor kid*, she thought, *way too sheltered in his lifetime.*

"Looks like we're just getting something to drink," she snapped in a perky voice. "And maybe teaching my boy a little bit about bars. Might come in handy someday."

"I received enough experience in bars with Gil, thanks," he recalled with a scowl.

Paige's late boyfriend had a penchant for trouble, and Caleb was thankful that Katrina's combat training had snapped into his head at just the right time, or he would probably still be recovering from injuries.

Her expression darkened as she recalled how beaten up Caleb had gotten over that event, mostly due to Gil's big mouth. The memory sent a pang of angst through her, leaving little room for regret at having killed Gil not long after that.

"Yeah, well, this time I'm here to make sure things don't go south. Just watch and take it all in, like a tourist," she recommended with a gleam in her eyes.

"All right," he replied with a shrug. He took a long draw from his beer bottle and discreetly observed the other bar patrons.

"Don't linger on anyone, or make too much direct eye contact," she mentored. "You're at the zoo looking at the animals and watching how they behave. It's a game. Just mark the ones you think look dangerous, and I'll tell you if you're right or not."

She caught the bartender's attention again and waved him over. The man frowned slightly as he leaned against the bar to stare at her.

"Yeah?" he asked.

"Nice bike out on the front porch," she casually began. "Had my eye on one like that in town. Know whose it is?"

The man warily eyed her. "Yeah, mine now. Just bought it off one of the customers a couple of nights ago. Some wannabe biker chick, I guess. Anyway, she didn't seem like she'd been in the cycle scene long for some reason. Said she was tired of it and wanted to get it off her hands. The price was so right, I didn't think twice."

Paige sneered. "Yeah, sounds like a gal I once knew. Becky Something, I think."

The bartender cleared away a couple of nearby empty beer bottles and shook his head. "Well, this one was Lucy Jones. At least that's what the title said. Cute gal...pretty red hair."

"Well, nice ride, man," Paige complimented and took a swig of her beer. "Live it up."

"Yeah, thanks," he said with a chuckle and wandered down to the opposite end of the bar.

She turned to lean back against the bar on her elbows and looked bored as her eyes darted across the crowd. *Lucy Jones. I'll bet that's an assumed name,* she fumed. *Probably was our stalker, though. I'll ask Katrina or Alton to do a search just in case.*

"The lady I saw had auburn hair," Caleb recalled.

"Yeah. It was her, I'm sure," Paige said. "I'm willing to bet she stole the bike, forged the title, and sold it for some quick cash. At least, that's what I'd do."

He stole glimpses into the mirror behind the bar across from him, using it to mark people quickly.

"Smart kid," she complimented. "Bonus points for using your head with the mirror there."

He spent the better part of the next hour nursing two beers and picking out characters he thought looked particularly dangerous. His attention fell upon a large-framed, bearded man wearing an old denim Harley Davidson jacket. He had a weathered face and a faded scar across the left side of his jaw. A medium-framed woman hung on one of his arms as he stood talking to a short biker before him. The woman wore a scowl on her face and had some streaks of gray in her long, black hair. Her hard brown eyes momentarily caught Caleb's.

"The fellow with the woman hanging off his arm," Caleb noted. "He's dangerous for sure."

Paige took two seconds to scout the individuals and turned her head to look at him over her left shoulder. "Nice pick," she complimented. "But he's not the dangerous one. The woman is."

He vision flashed to the mirror to study the woman at greater length. *What am I missing?*

"Look at her eyes," she suggested. "They're hard and cold. Bet you she's the one who gave him the scar on his jaw."

That surprised him. "You think?"

She smirked. "I know. Seen that look before, but it's been a while."

"Yeah? On who?" he asked following a swig of beer.

Paige paused and took a drink. "Katrina. She used to look a lot like that. But not for a while. At least, not since she found you, anyway."

He frowned at Paige. He wouldn't have guessed that his mate would have maintained such a cold, hard expression. And yet he was content to learn that Katrina seemed happier as of late.

Maybe I can take a little credit for some of that, he speculated.

"Hey, Blondie," called a gruff voice from across the room near the pool tables.

Paige panned the room with a bored expression until her eyes rested upon a burly, gray-bearded fellow wearing faded jeans and a dark t-shirt commemorating a biker rally from nearly twenty years prior. The fellow was missing two bicuspids, and his scraggly gray hair was tied back into a pony tail.

"Why doncha ditch that young old man of yours for a game of eight ball?" the grizzled fellow challenged.

A middle-aged woman with graying hair also pulled back

into a tight pony tail and wearing faded jeans and a leather vest cackled. She sat on a barstool against the wall and just behind the man that had beckoned to Paige.

"Don't worry, honey, he's mine." She cackled again. "The old bear's tired of us beating his ass, so he's looking for fresh blood."

Her eyes momentarily widened at the reference to blood. *Old blood tastes just as good as new blood*, she resolved.

She looked at Caleb, who shrugged in return. "Watch and learn," she whispered as she thumped her beer bottle onto the bar behind her.

The short vampire headed across the crowded room towards the pool tables. Caleb watched as Paige dissected the old guy through two games of pool amidst chastisements, hard looks, and scowls. She was a mix of edgy charm and playful banter as she kept the mood light despite the man's overt exasperation. In the end, Paige pocketed no less than sixty dollars in friendly bets from the small crowd.

"Well, I'll be gone to hell," the man groused as he handed over his portion of the wager.

She flashed a grin in her classic sprite-like manner and bent up to kiss the old man playfully on the cheek.

"Thanks for the spending money, Grandpa," she quipped. "Blondie needs more sewing supplies, after all."

A roar of laughs erupted from the crowd as she turned to depart. The old woman sitting nearby cackled a laugh and teased, "That'll teach you, ya, old bear! Now grab what's left of your pride, and let's head back to the house."

The older couple said their goodbyes and made their way past Paige. The old woman leaned towards her and congratulated, "I watched you, Blondie. Thanks for not shamin' him too bad. He's a pretty good one, after all."

She winked at the woman, who followed the man across the room to exit the bar. A new batch of people made their way to the vacant pool table and began setting up for a new game.

Paige turned to walk across the bar back towards Caleb,

but a rough-looking man in his early thirties at the table next to her reached out to clutch her arm.

"How's about a drink with your biggest fans?" he chortled as the four other men around the table chuckled.

She sneered down at him with contempt. "How about you get to leave without a broken nose?"

"Hey, mouthy bitch! I'm just bein' friendly!" he spat as he jerked on her arm again.

She reached out with her free hand, grabbed his beer, and poured it over his head in a flourish. "Beer's on you then!" she retorted while using the distraction to pull her arm free from his grip.

The other men roared with laughter, but the fellow was less than amused, and he flew up out of his chair to launch himself at Paige. Caleb saw the entire scene develop from his vantage point at the bar and leapt up from his barstool towards the fray. Two of the men at the table immediately jumped up to intercept him.

The beer-soaked biker furiously reached out for Paige, but she grinned at him evilly as she firmly latched onto his belt. The burly man leered at her until she lifted him by the belt and slammed him onto the rickety wooden table, which collapsed under his weight as his face registered shock. The two men across from him nearly fell out of their chairs to avoid being caught beneath the table.

Caleb was halfway to them when one of the two bikers approaching him swung at his head with a balled fist. He neatly dodged the swing, only to bury one shoulder into the gut of the other biker. The man staggered backwards from the force of the blow, but the first biker had already recovered and grabbed Caleb's arms from behind to pin them. While trying to jerk free from the man's grip, Caleb slammed one foot down against the biker's instep. A curse was emitted in response, but the second biker was already ramming one fist into Caleb's gut, taking his breath.

Most bar patrons watched with astonishment while Tom

Petty and the Heartbreakers' "I Won't Back Down" blasted over the wall-mounted speakers. Paige quickly noted Caleb's plight and darted to him in a blur. She grabbed the back of the neck of the biker preparing to punch Caleb again and slammed his forehead against the bar counter.

Meanwhile, Caleb managed to pull one arm free and slammed his elbow back into the nose of the fellow behind him. The biker yelped and cursed as his hands went to his face, where blood was freely flowing from his nose.

The two men formerly sitting at the collapsed table launched themselves at Caleb and Paige. One of them solidly punched at Paige and managed to land a glancing blow against her jaw. The vampire's head twisted to the side from the impact but quickly recovered. Her irises glowed bright blue and her jaw was clenched as she thrust the flat of one hand forwards into the man's chest. His body flew up off the floor and sailed fifteen feet across the room to land against one of the old pool tables.

Caleb saw the other man's fist already heading for his face and quickly dodged the blow, causing the biker's fist to slam against the edge of the bar. A cry mixed with anger and pain erupted as Caleb followed with a quick punch to the side of the man's head. But the fellow was hearty and swiftly recovered with a swing at Caleb with his uninjured hand. Fortunately, Caleb anticipated that and countered with a simultaneous punch to his throat and foot sweep, sending the man to the floor.

However, he failed to anticipate a barstool hitting him on the back. Caleb fell forward against the bar before two rough sets of hands threw him to the filthy floor. He grabbed at one man's leg in an attempt to unbalance him, but was quickly distracted by alternating volleys of boots kicking at his ribs. He involuntarily curled up, wrapping his arms around his torso to protect himself as best as possible.

The rough character who started the affair and whom Paige had initially slammed onto the table charged at her like a bull in a roar of anger. But she used his momentum against him, deftly stepping aside and grabbing him with both hands as he lurched past her. She lifted him bodily into the air and threw him across the room to her left, where he crashed into the stereo system against the wall.

All music ceased, and Paige turned to where Caleb was being kicked in the side by the two men towering over him. She swiftly punched one fellow in the kidneys, causing him to collapse backwards to the floor with a pained groan. She grabbed the other thug by the neck and propelled him to the floor like a rag doll. A swift kick to his head rendered the man unconscious.

The room fell silent as the sound of a gun being cocked was easily registered by Paige's keen hearing. The biker whom she had thrown onto the far pool table defiantly brandished a chrome revolver in his right hand. Her blazing eyes bored into the man, and his mouth went agape as his eyes pensively widened with shock.

He fired two rounds.

Paige instantly darted to her left to grab a pool cue from a stunned biker standing near her. The bullets harmlessly impacted the bar behind her as she flung the cue across the room at her assailant. The larger end caught the biker in the throat, and the pistol harmlessly dropped from his hand as he gagged. He grasped at his throat while collapsing to his knees.

The room seemed to freeze in time as complete silence prevailed. Nobody moved as Paige used a single motion with her arm to pull Caleb to his feet next to her. Small gasps of surprise and hushed whispers began to fill the room as she quickly inspected him for damage. She was hopeful that he had escaped serious injury.

"Caleb?"

"I'm okay," he dully mumbled, though he rubbed at his chest and ribs where the bikers had kicked him. He knew he would feel like hell the next morning, but he felt fortunate given the scope of the brawl that had erupted.

Paige reached into her jacket, withdrew a large roll of cash, and slapped it onto the bar before the bartender, who held a small sawed-off shotgun in his hands. Her baleful eyes burned into his, and he quickly lowered it and laid it on the bar counter.

He swallowed hard as he surveyed the wad of cash before him. She nodded once at him, and he nodded his head in silent understanding. The take before him was likely more than the bar made on even a good weekend and would more than pay for any damages.

"Come on, kiddo. Time to head home," she quietly insisted, reaching out to wrap her arm around his waist.

She gently began herding him in the direction of the exit, careful not to squeeze his side too tightly.

The room parted like the Red Sea for Moses, and a number of faces shone in complete astonishment as the two passed by. They made it to the exit, which Paige surveyed with her senses to ensure that nobody lay in wait for them just outside.

She removed her arm from around him and instructed, "Wait outside for me, tiger. Holler if you need me."

He slowly shuffled through the open door to the porch beyond. Everyone watched with confusion at Paige's treatment of the young man, as if not quite sure how to reconcile what they had seen and heard.

She ominously turned to address the room. "Are we finished here, or is there unsettled business for me to wrap up?"

After a moment of silence, a young biker across the room piped up, "Are you talking to all of us?"

"Yeah," she evenly replied with slightly pulsating irises, standing like a statue as she pored over the faces in the room.

"Son of a bitch," whispered a shocked voice out of the silence.

"Nope, we're all good here," insisted the bartender from behind the bar in a tight voice. "Nobody saw nothin'."

"Good," she replied and turned to leave.

"Hey," called the bartender.

Paige froze then pivoted her head to stare back over her shoulder at him. "Yes?"

"Uh, maybe you could drink somewhere else from now on?"

One corner of her mouth upturned slightly. "Sure, it's the least I can do."

Then she turned to walk straight out of the bar, hearing audible exhales of relief from behind her as she crossed the threshold.

What a lovely freakin' night, she ruminated.

Caleb looked up expectantly at her as she reached the base of the bar's porch steps.

"Let's mount up, kiddo," she beckoned, though he was already beside her, matching her stride for stride.

As they reached the cycle, she mischievously turned to him. "So, what do you think of Supergirl now?"

"What?"

"Er, never mind."

"Just so you know, the guy who pulled the gun back there was on my 'dangerous list' earlier," he offered while glancing back to the bar.

She looked at him with approval. "Good boy."

He chuckled, but the pain that shot through his ribs caused him to groan. She observed him with concern as she handed him his helmet.

A number of patrons gathered on the rickety front porch to watch as the two of them put on their helmets and mounted the cycle. The engine roared to life, and Caleb's arms automatically wrapped around Paige's waist.

Moments later, they were back on the main road headed back towards Mableton.

"I thought you said they were all weekend-wannabes?!" Caleb shouted.

"Most were!" she shouted before gunning the engine into high gear. She immediately appreciated the firm feeling of his arms tightening around her.

I'm really proud of Caleb, she mused.

Then another, darker thought crossed her mind. *Katrina's going to kill me*, she dreaded.

As they proceeded home, Caleb reflected on how, despite some setbacks, his latest bar excursion had come out much better than the one that he and Gil had endured. Of course, the fact wasn't lost on him that having a vampire with him certainly altered the equation. But then, he felt he had handled himself fairly well, given the number of combatants. Certainly, he was much less injured than after his previous bar brawl. *Kat's training has really made a difference*, he credited, even as the achiness in his chest and ribs increased by the moment.

Later, they pulled into the estate garage and noticed that Katrina's car was still gone. After Caleb removed his helmet, he speculatively beheld Paige as she laid her helmet aside.

"I don't understand something about what happened tonight," he said. "They saw your eyes. That essentially 'outs' you with a bunch of humans who aren't supposed to suspect your true nature."

She admired his insight, but countered, "Ah, but exactly what nature? I didn't display any fangs. For all they know I'm a demon, or fairy, or an alien. Hell, most of them are probably trying to forget that we were ever there. A lot of people would rather just pretend they didn't see what they saw. Who would believe them, anyway? And nobody wants to open themselves up for ridicule. We never even mentioned our names."

He shrugged. "Yeah, you're probably right."

"I'm just happy that I restrained myself from going ape shit on that group. Aren't you proud of me?" she asked with an evil grimace.

His eyes widened. *Restrained herself?*

She reached out to run her fingers lightly across his cheek.

"You did well tonight, kiddo. My little knight launching from the barstool to my rescue."

"Yeah, well, just doing my part," he said proudly.

She adopted a playful expression. "Of course, I had to haul

your ass out of trouble in the end, but it's still the thought that counts."

He rolled his eyes and groaned, "Gee, thanks."

"I'm just sayin'," she added with a wink.

Soon afterward, each of them cleaned up and sought other diversions. Caleb lay on the couch watching a horror movie on the main living room television while Paige was upstairs in her bedroom to chat on the phone with Alton about their evening's investigations.

Everything went along nicely until Katrina returned home later that evening. She politely asked Caleb how the evening went, but her eyes quickly darted to his bruised cheek and knuckles. Her irises flared bright green for a second, and without even consulting him, she grabbed his wrist to inspect his hand closely. To say that she wasn't pleased was an understatement of epic proportion in his opinion.

"Are you okay? What happened?" she demanded.

"Would you believe I fell off the Harley?" he tentatively asked, though her eyes stared right through him as he spoke.

"*Paige!*" she barked in a loud, commanding voice, causing him to wince slightly as she held onto his wrist.

"Aw, crap. Here we go," Paige mildly cursed as she proceeded downstairs with phone in hand. "Guess who's home? Gotta run."

Caleb quickly removed himself to another part of the house to take some aspirin as soon as Paige began recounting the evening's events in abbreviated fashion.

She noted his hasty departure with a scowl and irritably thought, *Coward.*

However, she was too proud to admit that she actually envied him.

*   *   *   *

A search on the name used on the motorcycle title revealed little of value. Lucy Jones was a fairly common name, it seemed, as there were two humans by that name in the Atlanta area alone. One of them had reported a stolen motorcycle a day before Paige and Caleb encountered the mysterious rider on their nighttime ride. And while it had to be the vampire with the auburn hair that Caleb saw in the backyard with Hakizimana, they had very little else to go on.

As the week progressed, Caleb healed, and tensions abated between Paige and Katrina. He played diplomat to the best of his abilities and expertly managed to give appreciative attention to each of them.

He even arranged a game of Trivial Pursuit for the trio. Despite being an accomplished history major, he quickly learned never to play trivia games with long-lived vampires. To say that they wiped the floor with him was an understatement, though both women had been equally amused by the thrashing that they gave him. He did, however, enjoy the numerous topical sidebar conversations that sprung out of a number of game questions, which extended their evening game well past two o'clock the next morning.

By Friday, he suggested the three of them do something together and recommended attending a production of "Promises, Promises" at the Atlanta Civic Center. Since the story was set in the mid-1960s, Caleb thought that both of the vampires might appreciate something both nostalgic and light-hearted. He was happy when both readily agreed, and plans were set, including taking him to dinner at a fine Italian restaurant downtown.

That afternoon, both vampires partook in blood for their meal and changed into trendy evening wear. Paige selected black knit slacks, a long-sleeved red satin blouse, and strappy high-heels for the occasion, while Katrina chose a classic black leather skirt and boots with a white knit top and black leather jacket. Caleb looked smart in navy Ralph Lauren slacks and a sport jacket, but he still felt rather plain compared to the women's fashionable attire.

When Katrina's Audi pulled up before the restaurant, they

turned the vehicle over to a valet, and Caleb escorted Katrina on his right arm and Paige on his left. He beamed as a number of onlookers stared at them in passing, though he conceded most of the attention was focused on the two women and not him.

I'm just happy to be part of the scene.

As was typical, the vampires selected plain Mediterranean salads, while Caleb ordered the signature Cappalinni herb chicken pasta entrée with a Caesar salad. While waiting for their meal, he absently listened to the vampires discuss some mutual acquaintances who had contacted Katrina recently to ask her opinion on topics scheduled for the agenda during the summer European conference.

He casually panned the room for anyone who might be sitting too close to their table, but then realized that the two women were conversing in soft enough tones that anyone sitting near them wouldn't likely hear.

"Hey," he interjected during a momentary lull in their conversation. "Are we actually going to the conference?"

One of Katrina's eyebrows curiously arched. "You had doubts?"

He shrugged, recognizing that she had said very little on the subject since their strange visitors a couple of days ago.

"Well, I mean, you said that you were going to consult Alton. But you never said for certain whether we're going or not."

Katrina paused as their server brought Caleb his Caesar salad and offered him shredded parmesan. After the lady departed, she confirmed, "Admittedly, I had considered not attending. But when people press me not to do something it just makes me want to do it even more."

Caleb mock-challenged, "Don't you dare kiss me. I'm warning you."

The vampire's eyes slyly narrowed, and she instantly closed the distance between the two of them to kiss him on the lips. He happily returned one of his own.

Paige groaned. "Oh, please, get a room, why don't you?"

Katrina cast a disparaging look at her friend as Paige reached out for one of the garlic bread sticks from a basket on the table. The spritely vampire crunched on one end of the bread stick, and the two women quietly observed Caleb as he dug into his salad with a vengeance.

"I'm not convinced that unionizing our kind is the way to go just yet," Paige suddenly spoke up. "Organization can be handy, but not if it creates hostile factions where there weren't any before."

Katrina scrutinized her friend for a moment and silently conceded that she had entertained similar thoughts recently. It certainly seemed as though Alton was pushing the agenda for the conference with a near fervor, which only made her wonder what angles she hadn't mulled over yet.

"It makes me wonder a little bit too," she admitted in a near whisper.

When their entrées arrived, they quietly ate and appreciated the Italian music being played by a trio of musicians in a corner of the dining room playing violins and a mandolin. The dining room had only been moderately busy when they had arrived, but now it was nearly full with patrons.

Caleb contentedly consumed his pasta and cast an appreciative look at Katrina as she watched him eat. As was typical, both women mainly picked at their salads to keep up the appearance of common diners. However, Caleb noticed that each had consumed only part of their meal and a couple of breadsticks.

After finishing his entrée, he ordered a slice of Italian cream cheesecake and three forks and excused himself from the table.

"Go ahead and try the dessert, and I'll be back in a few minutes," he offered.

Both women nodded at him, and he made his way to the restrooms on the other side of the restaurant. Upon entering the men's room, he passed an older gentleman who was exiting. While approaching a urinal, he thought that he heard the door open and glanced to his right.

The female vampire he had seen with the bow outside the estate the other evening stood with an amused expression on her face as her hazel eyes intently watched him. She was dressed in a simple black evening dress and conservative heels, and her auburn hair was elegantly pulled up with fashionable hair clips.

"Wrong room. You want the one next door," Caleb carefully pointed out as he turned to face her. He quickly realized that she stood before the only exit in the room, and he suddenly felt both alone and vulnerable.

"Do you have a cutesy response for every situation?" she flatly asked.

He managed a slight sneer.

"Only the ironic ones, it seems," he quipped. "So, you're Lucy Jones, then?" he asked, recalling the night at the biker bar.

Yeah, as if I'll forget that night anytime soon.

The vampire's countenance darkened. "That's not my name."

Oddly enough, a song by that title by The Ting-Tings went through his mind at that moment. "So, whom do I have the pleasure of speaking to then?"

She glared at him. "That's not important right now."

His eyebrows rose slightly. "Oh, believe me, you're one of the most important people that I don't know at the moment."

"You're somewhat amusing. Now focus. We want to know if your mate is planning to attend the conference or not."

Caleb swallowed, having easily recalled Katrina's earlier comments on the subject, but not certain that it was wise to voice them. While he quickly realized that the vampire would likely be able to tell if he were lying or not, he attempted simple ambiguity.

"I'm confident that she's arrived at a decision on that issue," he replied.

"And?" she demanded with narrowed eyes.

"And I think you should ask her," he suggested. "She's just outside, but you probably already know that."

He immediately wished they had been seated at one of the less desirable tables nearest the restrooms. Normally, that seemed his misfortune, except when he really needed it. "No," she insisted. "Why don't you tell me what you know instead?"

He swallowed as he wondered if he could yell out Katrina's name before the vampire snapped his neck. Somehow, he doubted it.

* * * *

Katrina minded her watch as she and Paige made short work of the tasty dessert in front them. She frowned, wondering if her mate were feeling ill. Normally she was quite skilled at reading his body language and tone of voice.

He certainly seemed fine before he left, she considered.

Paige noted her friend's subdued manner. "What's up, Red?" Her eyes darted to the cheesecake as she cut at it with her fork. It was nearly two-thirds gone. "Caleb's going to freak when he sees what's left, you know."

Katrina's eyes scrutinized the area around the room with a piercing stare. She noted a man walk into the men's room, only to depart immediately with a curious expression and a shake of his head. Alarms went off in her head, and she rose from her seat.

"Something's wrong," she darkly muttered.

Paige's eyes immediately looked to where she was staring, and she started to rise as well. However, Katrina motioned with her hand to wave her off and ordered, "Watch the exits while I go check on Caleb."

"Got it," Paige replied, but Katrina was already quickly moving past tables and patrons towards the restrooms.

* * * *

Caleb appreciated the momentary interruption caused by the fellow attempting to enter the restroom, but his relief turned back to concern as the vampire ordered the man to leave. However, she seemed agitated following that, as if she were feeling hurried or something.

"Well?" she impatiently insisted as her hazel eyes pierced his.

He quickly reasoned that the longer he could keep her talking, the better it would be for him.

"So, the other night after you and your boss left," he slowly began, "Kat and I chatted about that very topic."

"Yes? And?" the woman intently demanded. It was clear she wasn't happy.

"Well, I personally like the idea of a European trip. And Kat's pretty keen on our spending more time abroad," he continued. "But given that I wasn't sure if I was teaching this summer or not..."

The woman's eyes angrily flashed, and her lips pursed. "I know what you're doing," she insisted. "And I should kill you just for trying, but my orders --"

"Tell your boss to ask Katrina himself," he muttered. "But remember that she hates being threatened. Or someone threatening me, for that matter."

The auburn-haired vampire disappeared through the door in a flash. He only had time to take a breath before the restroom door burst open. Katrina appeared before him, and her eyes were glowing bright green.

She immediately began assessing him for signs of harm, but he insisted, "The woman vampire, she just left!"

Her eyes registered surprise, and she turned to leave, but then stopped and looked back at him. "No," she insisted. "I'm not leaving you like I did the other night."

"Well, you're gonna have to, because if you thought I had to go a few minutes ago, I *really* have to now."

She rolled her eyes at him. "Fine. Go," she challenged and

deliberately pushed each stall door open to view them, although she sensed nobody else in the room but him.

He pointed to the exit with his forefinger.

"Fine. I'll be right outside," she added and turned to leave.

A few minutes later, he exited the men's room to find two other men standing a few feet from Katrina as they warily studied her with confused expressions. He anticipated that she must have stopped them at the door in abrupt fashion.

As they walked back through the dining room, she teased in a whisper, "You really did have to go, after all."

He blushed slightly. "I had three glasses of tea, you know," he mumbled. "And what's with the eavesdropping on my —"

"Vampire hearing, remember?" she countered, at which he made a disapproving grumble.

He momentarily fumed at the occasional indignity of a vampire's all-too-acute hearing. But his thoughts quickly returned to his recent visitor. "So, you never saw the woman then?"

"I didn't see her leave the restroom, but I had told Paige to keep an eye on the exits. Unfortunately, it appears she wasn't able to catch her before she disappeared," she quietly explained as they approached their table.

Both noted that Paige was already seated and waiting on them with an expectant expression.

"She was gone as soon as I made it out the front entrance. So, we know they're following us at least some of the time," she ascertained as she watched Caleb sit down.

"So it would seem," Katrina darkly agreed.

"They're demanding to know if we're attending the conference this summer," Caleb offered as his eyes locked onto the mostly-eaten cheesecake before him.

Paige shrugged at him when he looked sidelong at her with an expression of disdain.

"Good cheesecake?" he asked with a hint of annoyance.

"Hey, Red ate some of it too, you know. And you offered, as I recall."

"Well, we're definitely going to Europe now," Katrina stated as she ignored their exchange. *I'm getting to the bottom of this issue now, no matter what,* she thought. It angered her that they were being stalked, particularly because the tactic involved cornering Caleb for information.

Another slice of cheesecake materialized before Caleb as the server appeared out of his blind spot. He winced slightly at the momentary surprise, and she apologized upon realizing that she had startled him. Despite the dessert's unexpected appearance, he adopted an approving visage and alternated glimpses at Katrina and Paige in turn.

"Eat up, kiddo," Paige suggested. "I took the liberty of anticipating your dessert-longing angst."

He appreciatively regarded her as he picked up his fork. "Thanks."

She briefly smirked at him and murmured, "Our boy likes his cheesecake, after all."

However, her delight quickly faded as she watched him. She had to leave for her contract job overseas soon and hated the idea of leaving him. Not that Katrina couldn't take care of him, of course, but Paige wanted to be nearby if she were needed. However, she acknowledged that it was for the best, given the latest developments. Anger rose in her as she contemplated how he was being sought for information by an unidentified group of vampires. A quick peep at Katrina suggested that she probably felt the same.

"Perhaps we should forgo the Civic Center this evening," Katrina suggested.

"No," Caleb insisted, his fork suspended midway to his mouth. "We run and hide, and they win."

Katrina imperiously arched one eyebrow, but he maintained a defiant expression. Paige observed the exchange with a degree of amusement.

"Very well," Katrina acquiesced. "However, you don't go anywhere without being in proximity of Paige or me," she stipulated.

He shrugged. "Fine," he conceded. "But I can't wait to see the expressions on faces in the men's room at intermission."

The corners of Katrina's mouth upturned ever so slightly, and she agreed with a penetrating stare, "Really? Neither can I."

"You really freak me out sometimes, Kat," he admitted.

She tried not to appear astonished, even as Paige struggled to avoid laughing out loud.

"But I know that you mean well. And I still love you," he thoughtfully added.

Katrina flashed him a relieved look.

He was impressed as he watched her deftly withdraw a credit card from her purse and hold it up at perfect height for their server who had approached her from behind. All the while, her vivid emerald eyes never left his as she stared at him resolutely.

Show off, he silently challenged as she adopted a gratified expression.

The remainder of the evening was uneventful compared to dinner. Fortunately, all of them enjoyed the stage production, which particularly pleased Caleb since it had been his idea. And despite Katrina's threat in the restaurant, she maintained a respectable vigil outside the restroom during intermission.

He hated to admit that he actually appreciated the additional attentiveness from both vampires, and he made an effort to make appreciative gestures to both of them throughout the evening. He wrapped his arm around Katrina's waist as they walked and initiated a kiss or two when possible without making a public spectacle.

As for Paige, he bought her a drink during intermission and traded whispered, humorous comments with her as they took in some of the more outlandish attire of some of the patrons. He felt like he was a high school student all over again with that, but she seemed to enjoy it immensely.

By the time they drove back to the estate, he had nearly

forgotten about the confrontation in the men's room. Once he and Katrina were sequestered in the estate's sublevel room, they shared passionate, intimate time together. Afterwards, he curled up behind Katrina and tenderly held her in his arms. While it was unlikely that she would sleep, she appreciated the feeling of his body spooned against hers as they lay together. He brought so much pleasure to her and genuinely made her happy. She appreciatively listened to his breathing become more even as he drifted off to sleep.

Later, her mind wandered to the events of the past few days, including the unexpected confrontation between the auburn-haired vampire and Caleb at the restaurant. The unknown faction's persistence annoyed her, even as she admired it.

However, I refuse to be caught off-guard by them again, she vowed.

*   *   *   *

During the following week, the excitement abated somewhat as there were no further attempts at contact from the mysterious vampire faction that had been stalking them. And while Caleb was happy about that, he was looking forward to a time when his activities wouldn't need to be so closely monitored. He had free run of the estate's interior, of course. But his activities outdoors were always accompanied by either Paige or Katrina.

On one occasion, he went outside during midday to walk around the estate and appreciate the sunshine. When he walked on a portion of the property where the exterior surveillance cameras had limited visibility, his cell phone rang within minutes. Naturally, it was Katrina.

"Hi, Kat," he patiently answered. "I'm on the northeast side of the house."

Then a short figure wearing motorcycle leathers and a helmet appeared to his left. He jumped slightly before realizing that it was the outfit that Paige had purchased at the downtown Harley-Davidson dealership.

"Yeah, Paige just appeared," he muttered as his heartbeat calmed once more. "Since she's here, I think I'll take a brief stroll through the park," he ventured with a self-satisfied expression.

She shook her head back and forth and placed her gloved hands atop each hip.

He neatly slipped his cell phone back in its holder and started walking towards the gate leading into the secluded park-like area adjacent to Katrina's property.

"Not happy," Paige's muffled voice emitted from inside the helmet.

"Don't worry. We'll head back if anybody's there. Heck, they might just think you're a NASA astronaut practicing for a mission," he teased with a chuckle.

Paige's charcoal visor reflected the image of his face back at him as he looked over at her. They walked along the path leading through the park area and were the only people in the area. After they finished, Caleb walked to the back porch and plopped down into one of the patio chairs.

"Time to go inside already," Paige complained in a muffled voice.

He reclined back in the chair with closed his eyes while appreciating the warmth of the day.

"Come on," he pleaded. "It's really nice out today. Not too humid, and it's not raining. So, please, just a little while longer."

She shook her head and pulled up a chair in the shade not far from him. She sat down and leaned her helmeted head against her gloved hand, propping her elbow against the arm of the chair.

This really sucks, she thought.

If it weren't for how much she cared about the young man nearby she would probably have abandoned him to his fate. Not that she expected the recent visitors to drop by during the daytime, but she didn't want to take any chances. She realized that Katrina appreciated her efforts, as well.

He happily dozed for an undetermined length of time when he felt a few droplets of water tickle his arms and face. His eyes immediately opened to stare up into a blue sky, which confused him. He glanced over to where Paige had been seated, but she was gone. Then he looked in the opposite direction to see her standing in her cycle outfit and helmet, but holding a sprayer attached to a water hose.

"Remember what you said about rain?" she asked in a loud, muffled voice.

His eyes widened, and he threatened, "Don't you dare!"

She unleashed the full force of the sprayer upon him, and he flew out of the chair like a rocket. However, she effectively doused him as he tried to avoid the spray.

"Paige! Stop it!" he yelled while running back across the porch.

The vampire roared with laughter at his plight.

"Dammit, Paige!" he cursed as she doused his back while he fumbled with the door leading into the house.

He was drenched as he stepped onto the tile just inside the door, and he felt the cold water penetrating his shirt and jeans. He continued to hear muffled laughing from Paige behind him, followed closely by giggling from in front of him. Glancing up, he saw Katrina standing not far from him.

"I guess your idea was all wet," she managed to say before giggling again.

He ground his teeth at both the bad pun and his indignity as he stomped through the house to change clothes.

"Vampires," he muttered with annoyance as he squished down the hallway.

The remainder of the week passed quickly, and before Caleb realized it, the time came for Paige to leave town. He had thoroughly enjoyed her visit and looked forward to the time when she would permanently reside in Atlanta.

The truth was that Paige felt much the same way he did.

While Caleb sat on the edge of the guest bed watching her pack, she focused upon him and warmly smiled.

"Come on, kiddo," she encouraged. "It's not like the summer will last that long. Before you know it, I'll be back, and you can help me unpack my stuff in a new house somewhere. Besides, you're going to be preoccupied with Katrina at the conference."

"Yeah, I guess. I'm just going to miss you. We've had some good times the past couple of weeks."

She looked at him in a penetrating fashion and moved in a blur to sit beside him. She wrapped her arms around him and popped a quick kiss on his cheek.

"Getting into trouble, that is. But it's been good, hasn't it?"

He turned and kissed her on the cheek in return. "Yep, good times. And don't forget bar fights."

Her bright blue eyes flashed once, and she broadly grinned. "Just wait until I see you again, tiger," she promised. "There's more where that came from."

He quirked his lips in response. "I can only imagine."

She winked at him. *Just you wait. I'm plum full of surprises.*

By evening, it was time to take Paige to the airport, so Caleb and Katrina drove her. It gave them an opportunity to give her a final hug and wish her a safe flight overseas. Then they returned to the estate, and Katrina wrapped Caleb in her arms as they stood in the middle of the living room together.

"Alone at last," she offered in a suggestive tone, to which he bent his face up to hers to kiss her passionately on the lips. She had appreciated Paige's visit, but also enjoyed time alone with her mate.

He relished the feeling of being in her embrace and wrapped his arms around her waist to pull her closer against him. While Paige was dear to him, Katrina was the woman of his dreams, the one who ignited his passion and made him feel safe and cared for. She understood him at so many levels and accepted him for who he was. He only hoped he was able to convey to her properly how much she meant to him.

"I love you so much, Kat," he whispered.

She gazed into his pale blue eyes while considering the endearing tone of his voice. It spoke volumes, and she bent down to kiss him warmly.

This man is everything to me, she resolved.

"I love you too," she replied after their lips parted.

He took her by the hand and led her though the house in the direction of their sublevel room. While he might not always be able to convey how he felt in words, he could certainly show her. The remainder of the evening was spent doing just that in tender ways that only two loving bodies could convey to each other.

* * * *

Chapter 4

⟨✣⟩

Slovenia

𝓣ime quickly passed following Paige's departure, and by early June, Katrina and Caleb were packing for their European trip. As the Slovene vampire conference tentatively indicated only a cursory agenda, there was no way to determine exactly for how long they needed to pack. Following a last-minute call to Alton, they assembled enough for at least a two-week stay. As opposed to the suitcases they had used for their spring excursion to London, Katrina acquired actual trunks for their belongings. To Caleb, it felt as though they were moving.

"Heck, I don't even own three weeks' worth of clothing!" he had joked.

However, he quickly wished that he had kept his mouth shut, as Katrina took immediate steps to take him shopping. His wardrobe nearly doubled in a matter of days, and he was certain they had been to every upscale department store and men's clothier in the major metropolitan area.

One thing was certain; he didn't want to step foot in another clothing store for at least a few years. As Katrina insisted on tailoring for proper fitting, he had been poked throughout the process and herded like a longhorn on a cattle drive. She often alternated between contemplative and gratified expressions while supervising each fitting.

I'm so glad that I manage to keep her amused, he reflected sourly.

Despite the annoying experience, he realized that perhaps

for the first time in his life his clothes fit him perfectly. In fact, he grudgingly conceded it did make him feel more confident. Fortunately, the trip wasn't anticipated to be an entirely formal affair, so he was able to pack an ample supply of casual slacks, blue jeans, and nondescript pullover shirts. Katrina suggested that he not take many clothes that blatantly advertised he was an American. It wasn't as if his speech patterns wouldn't give that away soon enough.

"Are you afraid of terrorists or something?" he had inquired.

"Not while being surrounded by vampires. Tourists from the US just tend to flaunt themselves, that's all. You may not realize this, but American vanity makes Europeans disdainful towards the nation."

He had never actually considered that before and conceded the logic of it. He also noted that Katrina didn't refer to the US as *her* nation. She had once told him that she recognized herself to be a citizen of the world with no national affiliations. However, her current passport indicated US citizenship.

She booked their flight on the prestigious Sunset Air, a company that catered to all, but specialized in safe and luxurious air travel for vampires. While the airline did use part of their fleet to operate a competitive traditional airline for human passengers, their vampire-customized fleet was something altogether different.

Each plane sported a limited number of spacious cabins that accommodated four passengers each. Aside from the four roomy, comfortable seats, there was a small bed and separate bathroom with a shower. A large flat-panel display was affixed to the wall, and all food was prepared fresh to order. Caleb had experienced the accommodations for the first time on their trip to England. Needless to say, it made flying seem like a pleasant dream.

Another convenient aspect to using Sunset Air was their pick-up and delivery shuttle service. Of course, "shuttle" meant a stretch limousine for Katrina and Caleb, while their luggage followed them in a van. Once onboard the plane, they enjoyed the comforts afforded to them in their reserved cabin, including watching films on the large screen display, sleeping, eating, and simply appreciating each other's company. Katrina also took the time to brief Caleb on some preliminary topics.

"I'll probably be in meetings most of the day," she cautioned. "But I plan to spend most of our evenings touring the surrounding area, or perhaps doing some shopping."

He wrinkled his nose slightly at the mention of shopping, but she lightly admonished, "Oh, hush. Souvenir shopping, primarily."

Satisfied that he was properly chastised, her mood lightened while she continued, "And I'm sure the days will pass quickly for you. Between visiting with the other human companions and enjoying the daylight sightseeing, the sun will set before you know it. Besides, you won't be straying too far from the conference facility without me."

"Really? Afraid I'll get lost or something?" he teased.

"You do have a remarkable track record for trouble when you're out exploring," she wryly observed. "However, Alton mentioned that human guests are being asked to remain on the property unless escorted by vampires or conference site staff. However, the property is over a hundred acres in size. They have a golf course, tennis courts, riding stables, a small lake for fishing, arboretum, and a host of other diversions."

"Oh," he absently replied as he envisioned a stretch of tall metal fence topped with barbed wire and interspersed with occasional guard towers like some immense prison.

"I'm sure it's merely a request," she reassured him. "Hungry?"

His eyes widened with interest. "I could eat."

She rolled her eyes and pressed the staff button on her seat. In a remarkably short time, a cheeseburger, fries, and cola arrived, as well as a slice of chocolate cream pie. She marveled at her mate's seemingly bottomless appetite.

Have to work off some of those calories for him when we get to Slovenia, she thought with a slight leer while watching him eat.

It was a lengthy flight, and Caleb took the opportunity to shower and get some sleep on the small bed in their cabin. Their journey involved scheduled stops in New York City, Paris, and Zurich to take on additional passengers before finally landing in Ljubljana, the capital of Slovenia. Fortunately for the vampires, the plane touched down at Ljubljana Airport precisely as the afternoon waned towards sunset.

An indoor corridor leading from the hangar to a covered parking garage simplified the process of disembarking and transferring to the vehicles waiting to transport them to the conference hotel, located just north of Jereka. An upper roadway for embarking and arrivals was supported by a series of thick concrete pillars, which sheltered the entire disembarking and departure area. A vanguard of SUVs and passenger vans was parked next to the curb.

While surveying his surroundings, Caleb took note of the dark sunscreen-coated windows on each vehicle. He counted at least a dozen vampires among the group of twenty travelers that gathered around him. In addition, there were at least six vampires among the group of individuals helping to organize everyone. A tall, dark-haired vampire wearing a tailored gray suit approached Katrina from one of the SUVs.

"Ms. Rawlings?" he inquired in a deep, formal voice.

Katrina cautiously scrutinized the fellow before her. "Are you one of Mr. Rutherford's men?"

The vampire inclined his head in a respectful manner. "Bibbens, ma'am. Mr. Rutherford insisted that you receive a private escort to the hotel," he explained while gesturing politely to the nearby black SUV. Another suit-clad figure sat patiently in the driver's seat.

Though recalling Alton's mention of arranging for a private shuttle ride from the airport, Katrina paused. Quickly withdrawing her cell phone, she sent a text message to Alton, simply stating, *"Bibbens?"*

Seconds later the reply arrived, "*Yes, plus driver.*"
She ignored Caleb's curious expression. "That's fine, Bibbens. Lead on."

As he opened the rearmost door for entry, the vampire informed them, "We'll leave immediately. The others will follow soon after."

Katrina nodded to him as he shut their door and proceeded into the front passenger seat.

Caleb noticed that the front cab area was separated from the back by a smoked pane of glass that had a small sliding window built into it, much like he had seen in a limousine. He then spied what appeared to be a small cooler built into the console before them. Opening the lid, he spied bottled water, cans of cola, and two packets of blood.

"Alton knows how to soup up a vehicle," he commented absently while removing a can of cola. He recalled a similar amenity's being added to one of Alton's limousines in England.

Katrina reached up to caress the back of his neck with her fingertips, eliciting a small shiver.

It was well past sunset when the SUV approached the region around Jereka. While the distance was merely eighty kilometers, it took longer than expected to traverse the roads due to their often meandering and circuitous route. Unfortunately for Caleb, he was unable to appreciate the scenery due to the nighttime conditions. However, Katrina's vampire vision was uninhibited by such limitations, and she acutely studied her surroundings while seated beside him in the back seat. He dejectedly leaned back into the plush leather seat.

She noted his reaction with sympathy. "I'm sorry, my love. I know you'd like to look around. There'll be so much more for you to see once we get there."

"Thanks. I'm sure you're right," he replied, and then proceeded to close his eyes for a short nap.

Wish I had vampire vision, he lamented. *Being a human sure sucks sometimes.*

He hated to admit it, but he was often jealous of his vampire mate and her peers. While trying to drift off to sleep, he began weighing all of the pros and cons in his mind. Granted, they had to avoid daylight, which he had noticed particularly annoyed them during long summer days. But there were so many more advantages to being a vampire. Physically, they were extremely durable, immune to diseases, faster, and stronger. They had amazing vision in both light and dark conditions, keen senses of touch and hearing, and a seemingly endless amount of energy.

Hell, he darkly considered, *they only sleep for a few hours every other day while I'm spending one third of every day slumbering.*

Katrina eyed her mate and noted the tension in his body language. His arms were folded in front of him, and he maintained a tight-lipped expression. She quietly released her seatbelt and slid to the center of the seat to sit next to him, supportively draping her arm across his shoulders.

"A penny for your thoughts," she whispered into his ear before lightly kissing him on the cheek.

He kept his eyes shut and sourly replied, "Being human is such a drag."

She silently congratulated herself on gauging his mood and purred in his ear, "Well, I love you as a human. I simply adore you, in fact."

He tried to restrain the beginning of a smirk. "I'm practically blind compared to you."

"You have beautiful eyes," she cooed.

"I'm a weakling," he added. "You practically have to avoid knocking me over half the time as you speed around the house."

She was beguiled over his dour wit, grateful that his eyes were still closed. "You're resilient for a human. Your body is tantalizingly fit and attractive to me."

He paused to appreciate her compliment, but then continued, "We lose quality time together because I have to waste so much time eating and sleeping."

Somewhat true, she silently conceded. *But I don't mind*

that much, really. I enjoy sharing the time with him, no matter the circumstance.

"I enjoy watching you sleep. You're so innocent and peaceful-looking. I love listening to the sound of your heartbeat and the blood rushing through your veins. And I'm starting to enjoy cooking for you, especially now that I'm getting better at it. To tell the truth, the smell of cooked foods actually bothers me less as time passes," she said.

Disagreeably grunting as his eyes remained closed, his mind raced with additional ammunition to substantiate his dark mood.

Admittedly, she's come a long way in the cooking and food-tolerance areas, he grudgingly admitted. He began to feel a little self-conscious over his continued brooding.

He appreciated the sincere tone in her responses and whispered, "I just wish we were more equal, that's all. And it's easy to feel like my life is so out of control sometimes, whereas you have everything in such an orderly state."

She snickered and whispered in his ear, "Ah, but you already know how I like to be in control, my love."

"Ha, so true," he agreed.

He contemplated ammunition to raise additional arguments, but in the end, he merely sighed with resignation.

Katrina hugged him to her, having sensed his silent surrender. She used her spare hand to turn his face towards hers and planted a passionate kiss on his lips.

"I may have control, but you're the one who commands my heart," she insisted. "Human or not, I love you. Little else matters to me than our life together."

He slowly opened his lids and gazed into her beautiful emerald eyes. He loved her so very much and was humbled by the impact that he had on her.

"I love you too," he murmured and deeply kissed her.

After a moment, their lips parted, and she pulled away from him slightly. She leaned his head against her shoulder while lightly running her fingers through his short hair then returned to appreciate the passing scenery around them. A short time later, she sensed his body go limp against her, noting that his breathing had grown more rhythmic as he was lulled to sleep.

Katrina appreciated the quiet journey to the hotel. It gave her time to think, while occasionally glancing down at her sleeping mate. The affection that she felt for him was unparalleled, rivaled only by the love she had felt for her late human husband, Samuel. It felt odd in some ways to think of Samuel so infrequently, save for when Caleb came to mind. The association between them was uncanny, and yet comforting.

For centuries, the pain she had felt at the memories of her late husband and children eventually caused her to shut those thoughts away, relegating them to the basement of her mind where the remainders of her past human life resided. Like the earthen graves in which her family members were buried, such thoughts had been swept from the forefront of her daily musings.

But now, with the addition of Caleb in her life, she once more felt compelled to seek the comforts of what had been her human existence, if only to share them with the happiness that he brought into her life.

My love, she thought as she valued the young man next to her.

Some time later, the small sliding window before them opened to reveal Bibbens' face.

"We're ten minutes from the hotel, Ms. Rawlings," he quietly whispered in deference to the slumbering human beside her.

She acknowledged him before the glass slid quietly back into place.

Katrina lightly used the back of her fingernails to caress the side of Caleb's face, causing him to breathe in deeply. Stirring, he opened his eyes, which rolled up to seek hers in sleepy fashion. He stretched in the seat, momentarily rubbing at his eyes with his fingertips.

"Are we there?" he asked before yawning again and lazily glancing at his wristwatch.

She shook her head at his adorable manner and whispered, "Not yet, my love. But we're close. I thought that you might want to see our approach. I'm told it's quite a sight whether at nighttime or in daylight."

A few minutes later, true to Katrina's earlier statement, the white glow of lighting surrounding the conference site loomed into view from the base of the pronounced mesa before them. It appeared as a glowing oasis among the dark mountainous area surrounding them. A two-lane asphalt road cut into the sharply sloping, forested landscape with street lamps attached to metal utility poles at sparse intervals. Caleb suspected that the curvy roads were twice as dangerous to navigate at night, despite the strategic placement of sturdy-looking metal crash rails before the road seemingly dropped into nothingness.

After a short time, the monotony of the tree-lined road gave way to a rising incline. A gentle, pronounced arc revealed the conference hotel in all its majesty. An elaborate frontage of vast grassy ground interspersed with full, tall trees and an occasional park lamp spread out before the majestic driveway leading up to the main facility.

A series of tasteful exterior lights elegantly accented the gathered buildings. The central hotel was only five stories tall, but extended along the width of the numerous acres of lawn set before it. A series of windows lined each level of the hotel, and the roof was covered in a giant, coppery dome. A three-story section of the facility was connected to the hotel by a smaller, one-story length of building. The smaller section was lined with large windows across the length of the first floor, and the roof was domed with glass tiles.

"Pretty impressive-looking," Caleb mumbled, thinking, *Expensive-looking, actually.*

"And that's just the portion you can see from the front,"

Katrina explained. "There's a host of things to do here. And you missed the small town of Podjelje that we passed through earlier. It has some quaint-looking shops and restaurants." *Best of all, boredom shouldn't be an issue for him if I get stuck in prolonged meetings,* she rationalized with satisfaction.

He observed the lengthy approach to the side entrance of the conference facility. *This looks promising.*

After their vehicle circumnavigated the large curve around a central gazing pool accented by an elaborate statue of a stately-looking man riding a large horse, they parked beneath a small tent-like structure assembled before the large side entrance. The sides were drawn up, leaving the area visible from all angles, but Caleb suspected that it was intended for sheltering daytime arrivals.

Their SUV stopped directly before the glass entrance, and the vampire sitting in the front passenger seat exited to open Katrina's side of the vehicle.

This might be just the relaxing change of scenery that I need, Caleb hopefully contemplated as the driver opened the back of the SUV to remove their luggage for the approaching attendants.

As they passed through the main entrance into the lobby, it was apparent from the clusters of bodies that many of the participants had only recently arrived. Navigating their way through the busy lobby, Caleb noted a variety of humans intermingled with vampires bustling through the large open area.

As it was the first time that he had seen so many vampires all in one location, he felt slightly unnerved. Admittedly, he wasn't certain that every person he visually identified as being a vampire truly was. However, upon careful scrutiny, he had noticed that many vampires maintained a bearing and attitude that set them apart from the average human populace.

For example, a number of vampires strode through the throng of people with an air of superiority, as if waiting for the sea of humanity to part for them at will. He noticed that a number of humans deliberately shied from those vampires, often pressing closer to their vampire companions. He was immediately curious as to how other human mates related to their vampires compared to him and Katrina.

Katrina momentarily studied her mate and deciphered the curious expression on his face.

"I sense a social streak surfacing in my mate. Let's focus on getting checked in first, okay?" she whispered in his ear.

Despite the fact that their luggage would be automatically delivered to their suite, they were expected to observe the standard check-in process at the main desk. The area was crowded with those who had just arrived, as well as those who had arrived earlier but hadn't yet been checked in. While there were additional hotel employees manning the main desk, the mere size of the crowd indicated that it might be a longer wait than Caleb preferred.

Katrina visually swept the room, catching the eye of Alton and a female vampire standing next to him. He motioned for her join them.

Bending down to whisper in Caleb's ear, she apologized, "Alton's beckoning. Probably wants me to meet someone. Do you mind?"

He shrugged. "Yeah, sure. Not going anywhere anytime soon, I think."

She winked at him and made her way towards where Alton stood.

It appeared to Caleb that most of the people waiting to check in were much like him, which suggested that the menial task had been foisted upon the human vampire companions. He observed the disorderly gaggle of men and women, who ranged in ages from early twenties to mid thirties, and noticed a number of people glancing at him as well. He was struck by the notion that the scene was similar to the first day of school when all the kids sized each other up.

Suddenly, his body lurched forwards and to the left as someone slammed into his right shoulder.

"Hey!" he exclaimed as his head whipped around.

A tall, dark-haired man dressed in expensive-looking trousers and sport jacket glared at him with slightly glowing blue eyes.

"Watch where you're going, human," he growled.

Caleb's jaw clenched at the vampire's gruff tone.

"I believe *you* ran into *me*, actually," he corrected.

The vampire's right hand darted out in a blur, grasping his neck in a vise-like grip that caused him to gag slightly from the impact. Caleb's hands immediately pried at the hand gripping him, but he was unable to dislodge it. The vampire's fingers uncomfortably tightened around his neck.

"Someone should teach you to respect your betters," the vampire insisted as the people around Caleb stared wide-eyed at the exchange.

A pale hand appeared out of nowhere to grasp the vampire's wrist while another tightened around the fellow's own neck. In a blur, the vampire was thrown backwards onto the floor while Caleb was knocked to his knees from the sudden motion. The vampire's body was summarily slammed against the tile floor onto his back as a short figure wearing a navy blazer and slacks hovered over the prone figure.

Paige Turner's blue irises brilliantly blazed with rage as she glared down into the offending vampire's face.

"Touch him again, and I'll *end* you!" she growled through clenched teeth.

Caleb's eyes widened at the scene taking place before him, and his mind reeled upon realizing that Paige was his unexpected rescuer. A number of nearby humans and vampires stood watching the display with a mix of curiosity and surprise.

"Let me go, or I'll –" the dark-haired vampire threatened.

The prone vampire's left hand darted to claw at Paige's right one as it squeezed his neck, but the blonde vampire menacingly seethed, "Do something, *please*. Just give me a reason."

His hand immediately dropped away.

"Apologize," she insisted in a flat, lethal-sounding voice.

Or I'll kill you right here, she darkly resolved.

The male vampire's glowing blue eyes met hers before darting to stare up at Caleb with a fierce expression.

"A misunderstanding, human," he growled.

"Do it better," Paige flatly insisted.

The vampire paused as if considering his options then whispered, "My apologies, human."

"No harm," Caleb quietly offered as he rose from his knees to stand while rubbing at his sore neck. "Apology accepted."

Paige released her grip on the vampire, who moved in a blur to extricate himself from the rather humiliating public circumstance. Caleb watched him depart, but then his attention quickly returned to Paige as she stood and gathered him in her arms in a welcoming embrace.

"You okay, kiddo?"

"Yeah, sure, I'm fine," he murmured, still a little dazed by the rapid series of events.

Satisfied that he was unharmed, she chirped in a lilting voice, "It's good to see you, tiger." Gone was the lethal-sounding tone of moments prior as the young vampire calmed herself in practiced manner, a technique that had taken years for her to master.

He gratefully returned her earnest hug.

"*This* is your secret overseas contract job?" he incredulously whispered in her ear.

"Yep," she replied in an enterprising manner. "Captain Turner, second in command of security for the conference site, at your service. Got a swanky uniform jacket and everything."

He pulled away from her slightly to note the embroidered silver captain's bars sewn into the collar of her navy blazer, as well as the security badge over the left pocket. He was momentarily gratified by the unlikely coincidence of her position in contrast to her rebellious personality. Then the ominous circumstances of a few minutes prior returned to the forefront of his thoughts, and his countenance darkened considerably.

"Thanks for the help," he genuinely offered.

She beamed and darted to kiss him gently on the cheek.

"Babysitter's always on duty, tiger," she whispered in his ear.

I'll always be there for you whenever possible, kiddo, she silently added.

A sense of gratitude mixed with happiness washed over him, and he tightly embraced her in response. She closed her eyes for a brief moment, savoring both their closeness and the relief that he was unharmed. Then she pulled away slightly with a mischievous expression.

"Okay, break it up, or I'll have to cite you for public display of affection," she teased with a smirk in typical Paige Turner fashion.

He chuckled and shook his head at her, but quickly noticed that everyone in the immediate vicinity was intently staring at them.

Paige seemed to notice as well and announced in an authoritative voice, "There will be no fighting in my lobby! And show's over, so stop gawking."

Most people either returned to their previous activities or relocated to another part of the lobby. Moments later, the clamor of voices and activity returned to its former levels. A tall, pale-skinned man wearing a uniform similar to Paige's, but with a major's rank on the collar, stopped a dozen feet from them. The fellow's features suggested to Caleb that he might also be a vampire.

"Captain Turner? A word, if you please," the man beckoned in a displeased tone.

Aw, crap, Paige thought.

"Looks like the boss is calling," she muttered to Caleb. "Catch ya later. Gotta run," she added before turning on her heels to catch up with the man.

Caleb watched her depart and tried to refocus his attentions on the lines of people waiting to be checked into the hotel.

Okay, this is no longer any fun, he thought. *And I may have lost my place in line, too.*

Realizing that most of the humans around him were curiously staring at him, he absently rubbed at his neck again while trying to ignore them.

"You two seem to know each other," a young man wearing jeans standing next to him observed with some amusement. He was approximately Caleb's age and height, but had slightly curly blonde hair and green eyes. His accent suggested that he might be from the New England area.

"Er, yeah," Caleb acknowledged as he held out his hand to shake. "Caleb Taylor," he prompted. "Pleased to meet you."

The fellow returned the handshake. "Aiden Henderson. Nice to meet you, too."

A petite-framed young woman standing in front of Aiden turned to look at Caleb with an appraising expression. She had medium-length blonde hair and brown eyes and appeared quite trendy in her pair of Capri pants and turtleneck sweater.

The young lady thoughtfully assessed Caleb. "I thought that you were with the red-headed vamp?"

"So true," he awkwardly replied. "Actually, the blonde vampire, Paige, is my surrogate."

"You have two?!" the woman demanded.

"Not exactly," he hedged. "You see, Katrina, the red-headed lady, is my mate. It's kind of complicated, really."

Boy, is it ever, he earnestly conceded.

"Actually, I suppose you could say that *they* have *me*," he wryly added.

"So, you serve them both, then?" asked a man with a French accent and a scandalized expression who was standing in another line to Caleb's right.

"Well," Caleb began, but abruptly stopped. "Wait. Just what do you mean by 'serve'?" he challenged.

The young Frenchman laughed, followed by Aiden and the blonde lady standing in front of him. Caleb chuckled despite himself, suddenly happy for the lighter mood in the room.

The Frenchman held out his hand. "I'm Reynard Dautry."

Caleb returned the shake while introducing himself.

The blonde woman offered, "Madison Baker, but everyone

calls me Maddy."

"So, Caleb," Aiden said following the brief introductions. "You were saying about *serving* two vampires?" he pressed with a raised eyebrow. Caleb winced and shook his head as everyone else grinned at his expense.

*   *   *   *

Katrina made her way through the crowd to where Alton stood next to a medium-height Native American woman with long, jet-black hair. As she approached, she realized that the woman was a vampire, though one unfamiliar to her.

Alton warmly embraced Katrina and placed a discreet kiss on her cheek, which she returned in kind. "Welcome, my dear. I'm so happy that you and Caleb decided to attend the conference. I trust your journey was uneventful?"

Parting from his embrace, her eyes quickly darted to the stranger to her left, who pleasantly observed their exchange. "It's good to see you again, naturally. And yes, it was a lengthy, but pleasant flight here. Although Caleb was disappointed that the night spoiled any appreciable view on our drive to the hotel."

"Don't worry, he'll have more than enough time to see everything in the days to come," he replied. "But I'm being rude. I'd like you to meet Talise Penbroke. She's been kind enough to accept my invitation to attend the conference."

"Katrina Rawlings," she greeted the vampire before her.

Talise brightly smiled. "The pleasure's all mine, Ms. Rawlings. Alton was just singing your praises before you appeared in the lobby, actually. Though I only know you by the reports of your most recent exploits with Chimalma, I'm nevertheless honored to meet you."

Katrina politely nodded, and her attention returned to Alton. "You look like there's something on your mind."

"Not here," Alton replied as he gently used each arm to

steer the two women across the expanse of open lobby towards the open doorway of an unoccupied conference room.

As they glided into the room, he smoothly pressed the door closed before turning to address the two women.

"Talise appreciates my view of the need for this conference. Her specialty in international law may come in handy," he explained to Katrina.

"I'm primarily a corporate attorney, but I worked with courts in the Haig on International Law for a number of years prior to that," offered Talise.

"When the conference begins, I'll be presiding as Chair, but I'll need a Co-Chair. Talise will ensure that there's a motion to nominate you," Alton explained.

Katrina's eyes widened with surprise, and she sharply looked at her former mentor.

"Co-chair? Alton, I agreed to attend just to listen and consider, not to ride shotgun over the herd," she warned.

"Understand that your presence here is important," he quickly countered. "A number of the others respect you over the Chimalma affair. Besides, I need someone who'll keep the others in line if chaos erupts."

"Oh, so now I'm supposed to be your sergeant-in-arms, as well?" she shot back. "Alton, I promised Caleb that I'd spend quality time with him while we're here. I'm not looking for a full-time job on this trip."

The diplomatic vampire held up his hands in placating fashion. "Now, now, there'll be plenty of time available for Caleb, as well. Truth is, I really need your help on this, Katrina. A number of the attendees are representing some very powerful and suspicious elder vampires in the world, who naturally prefer their anonymity in lieu of attending. Nevertheless, their proxies may be persuaded to favorably report events if things are handled properly, which could tilt things in our favor here."

"Just what do you mean by *our favor?*" Katrina inquired.

Talise's eyes played between her two fellow vampires, somewhat like observing a tennis match in play.

Alton paused to rub his fingertips contemplatively across his lips as if stalling to consider his response.

"You know," he carefully began, "a formalized agreement among our kind might help to curtail future Chimalma-like events in the world. It could also help to reinforce the importance of communication by our kind before interloping on declared territories. Take Mableton, Georgia, for example."

Katrina silently conceded her former mentor's logic. She of all people didn't want to see another vampire charging around the world wantonly trying to kill off rivals and their mates.

"I suppose if the Co-Chair is primarily a position of formality," she hesitantly ventured.

"Oh, most assuredly," Alton quickly agreed. "Just help me keep everybody in line, that's all I ask. If we can merely maintain and encourage a civil dialogue, it might just pique the interest of enough of us to –"

"All right, I'll get the specifics from you later," Katrina interrupted with a raised hand.

She of all people knew how Alton could drone on once he was energized about one of his ventures. Then her jaw clenched with another realization.

Caleb's not going to be happy about this, she ruminated. She had promised him a sort of vacation if he accompanied her.

An urgent knock sounded at the door.

"Come," Alton announced.

The door opened only partially, and the youthful face of a female vampire with hazel eyes appeared.

"Um, Ms. Rawlings, Mr. Rutherford, there's been an event in the lobby that you should know about."

"What kind of event?" Alton crisply demanded as Katrina's focus shifted to the vampire before them.

"Everything's fine. But Ms. Rawlings' mate was involved in a disagreement with another guest," she replied.

Katrina yanked the door open, causing the vampire to lose her balance as she bolted past her with Alton and Talise closely following.

*   *   *   *

Paige casually strolled through the throng of people on her way over to her supervisor. Major Kivo Pietari was nearly six feet tall and sported short-cropped red hair. His brown eyes were dull-looking as his stare pierced through her. He may have seemed an imposing figure to most, but Paige was far from being easily intimidated.

Okay, so he's pissed, she realized easily enough. *Not that it really matters when it comes to Caleb's safety.*

The major motioned for her to follow him, and they made their way into a small clerical office off of the main lobby. Seeing nobody on duty at the desk, Pietari closed the door behind them and turned to address her.

"What the hell was that all about, Captain?" Pietari demanded while staring into Paige's bright blue eyes.

"The vampire threatened a human patron," she casually explained. "We don't allow bullies to intimidate our guests, do we?"

One of his eyebrows suspiciously rose.

"A little more restraint would have been in order, I think," he emphasized. "But then, he was no ordinary customer, was he?"

She absently folded her arms before her as she stared into Pietari's eyes. "No."

"I see. You didn't mention having a mate in your interview."

"I don't, exactly," she hedged, thinking, *It's really none of his business.*

"Then why –" Pietari pressed.

"Look, I'm that young man's surrogate vampire," she brusquely explained. "It's a special arrangement with his mate. Suffice to say, I'm a guardian of sorts for him. Listen, this isn't something I'm interested in discussing further, if you don't mind."

He silently observed his subordinate for a moment before asking, "Just who *is* his mate, exactly?"

"Katrina Rawlings."

Pietari's eyes widened in a manner that suggested the name meant something to him, which Paige noted with some interest.

Curious, she wondered.

"Oh," he replied, though in a manner that seemed forced. Then his eyes darted to hers as if in sudden recognition of something. "You know, employees for this assignment were selected because they had no complicating interests here."

"If I understand correctly, Mr. Rutherford is running this operation," Paige countered. "He hired me personally, so if you have issue with my circumstances you'll need to take it up with him."

"Never mind. I'm sure that won't be necessary," he neatly equivocated. "Well, just try to keep yourself in check from now on. We don't want to create an incident in the vampire community. Things are on edge enough as it is."

His dismissive manner irritated her, and she took great satisfaction in her next statements.

"You should be thanking me, Major. You want an incident? Just let something happen to Caleb Taylor, and you'll get to see the world's second baddest-ass vampire tear into this place with a vengeance."

"Katrina Rawlings is that much of a loose cannon?" Pietari carefully asked.

She turned on one heel and reached for the door handle to exit.

"Katrina? Perhaps."

She opened the door and glanced back over her shoulder at him with a steely expression. "But then, I was referring to *me*."

Pietari remained silent with a narrow-eyed expression as he watched his second-in-command depart the office.

*   *   *   *

Caleb finally made his way through the line with his new comrades as each checked into the hotel and were issued room keys. He, Aiden, and Maddy were chatting near a small decorative tree when they were approached by a tall, handsome, athletic-looking man dressed in business casual attire. His medium-length black hair touched the back of his open-collared dress shirt, and Caleb noticed a stethoscope draped around his neck. He looked every bit like an actor who played a doctor in Hollywood television shows or soap operas.

His brown eyes gently surveyed the faces of each of them before resting on Caleb.

"I see by the pressure marks on your neck that you're the guest who had a bad run-in with a vampire a few minutes ago," he smoothly observed as he held out his hand to shake Caleb's.

Adopting an amicable expression, he introduced himself. "I'm Dr. Ethan Reynolds, the presiding physician here at the conference. Mind if I take a quick look at your neck?"

Caleb shook the man's hand, which seemed warm and hard at the same time. While employing a firm grip, the man grasped his hand with a measured pressure. It was then that Caleb determined that the good doctor was indeed a vampire.

"You're a..." he gently ventured.

"Vampire? Yes," the doctor confirmed. "If that bothers you, I can call for one of the nurses to examine you."

"Not at all," Caleb reassured him. "It's not like that. I just wasn't expecting a doctor to be a vampire, that's all."

Reynolds reassuringly smiled. "May I?" he asked with a gesture to Caleb's neck.

"Oh, of course," Caleb replied and lifted his chin slightly to allow a better view. For some strange reason, particularly since he was a vampire, the physician's manner made him feel oddly at ease.

Reynolds' touch was gentle as he traced the skin of Caleb's neck.

"Any pain, tingling, or numbness anywhere?" he asked.

"Just a little soreness," Caleb confirmed as Aiden and Maddy curiously watched.

"Mm-hm," the doctor hummed absently while probing for tender spots. "That's to be expected, and as long as it dissipates over the next few hours, you should be fine."

"Thanks, Doc."

Reynolds inclined his head in appreciation and inquired, "Someone said that the security captain took care of things rather handily. Your mate, perhaps?"

The question caught Caleb off-guard, but he smoothly replied, "Uh, no. Paige is my guardian. Katrina Rawlings is my mate."

"I see," the tall doctor responded with a puzzled expression. "Well, I only arrived a few days ago and haven't met everyone yet. I'm sure I'll run into the captain before long."

"I could introduce you to Paige, if you'd like," Caleb politely ventured.

His response seemed to please the doctor.

"Thank you. I'd like that very much," Reynolds noted with appreciation. "Well, I should make my way back to the office," he quickly offered with a nod. "Please come see me if things don't improve by this evening. My office is on the first floor next to the interior courtyard."

"I will," Caleb replied. "And thanks again."

The doctor politely nodded to each of them and turned to make his way back towards the central part of the facility.

They watched him depart, and Maddy observed, "He seemed nice enough. I'm sure he's a real hit with the ladies."

Aiden and Caleb looked at Maddy curiously, but she shrugged and added, "If you're into his type, of course."

Before either man could inquire further, a woman appearing to be in her mid-thirties with flowing auburn hair and blue eyes appeared next to Maddy. She affectionately regarded Maddy, who reached out to grasp the woman's hand tenderly in her own.

"Are we all checked in?" the woman asked in an accent that

suggested Dutch descent.

"Aiden, Caleb, this is my mate, Rianne," Maddy offered with a pleased grin. Both men introduced themselves.

Caleb observed the couple, noting that they seemed quite smitten with each other. The thought of same-sex vampire couplings had never occurred to him until that moment. But then, given the population of similar human partnerships, it made perfect sense in retrospect.

"Pleased to meet you both," Rianne courteously responded. "Maddy, shall we make our way to the suite? I'm sure you would like to freshen up before tonight's reception," she added.

Both men watched as the couple walked towards the nearby elevators while holding hands.

"Well, I better go find my girlfriend, Talise," Aiden said.

"Yeah, I need to find Kat, too," Caleb replied. "She's probably going to be real happy when she hears --"

Aiden's eyebrows arched in amusement, at which Caleb's features fell and reddened slightly.

"And she's standing right behind me, isn't she?"

Aiden merely chuckled as Katrina's arm reached over Caleb's right shoulder, her palm resting against his chest. Patting him lightly, she teased, "Please, you were doing so well there, my little troublemaker."

Her attention was immediately drawn to the reddened marks on his neck, and her mood immediately darkened.

What the hell?

Feeling Katrina's grip tighten around him, Caleb tensed.

She saw the marks.

"Kat, this is Aiden Henderson," he quickly interjected.

Talise appeared beside Aiden as he greeted Katrina. Caleb noted the woman's obvious Native American heritage in her appearance and marveled at how vampires seemed to touch all cultures and denominations.

In turn, Aiden introduced Talise to Caleb, whose attention was distracted by Katrina's closer inspection of his neck out of his peripheral vision.

"Are you okay?" Katrina insisted.

I'm so going to make sure that someone regrets this, she vowed.

"Really, everything's fine now, Kat. It was just a misunderstanding, that's all," he reassured his mate before casting a pleasant glance at Aiden and Talise. He didn't want her going on some vengeful tear so soon after their arrival. Instead, he just wanted to forget the entire event.

"The captain of security took care of things pretty fast," Aiden said.

"Paige, that is," Caleb added as his eyes met Katrina's.

Her green eyes turned flat and steely-looking, much like Paige's had been earlier, which caused him to tense slightly.

"Paige is here? And she's on the security detail?" Katrina asked with surprise.

So, that's why she was so hedgy about her contract job, she divined. *Leave it to Paige.*

"Let's speak more about this back at the room," she suggested.

They excused themselves from Aiden and Talise and made their way to their hotel suite on the fifth floor. On their brief journey, Caleb was taken aback by the sheer number of vampires they passed in the lobby and hallways. He was happy to have made the European trip with Katrina, but wondered if the episode in the lobby portended a dangerous theme for their visit.

As they unpacked their luggage to place items in closets and drawers, Katrina insisted that Caleb explain the earlier encounter in the lobby with the rude vampire. To say that she was displeased was an understatement, and he deliberately tried to soften the edges of his story for her. That was not to say it wouldn't have pleased him to see the vampire brought low by his mate. Rather, he felt as if Paige's response had been appropriate enough for his satisfaction, a point he made by recounting her intervention on his behalf in explicit detail.

When he finished, Katrina sat on the edge of their king-sized bed.

"Well, I suppose that Paige represented me well enough in my absence."

"She was impressive, really," he heartily agreed. "She's surprisingly fierce for her size."

"She's an alpha," she noted matter-of-factly with a slight shrug.

Of which I'm very proud, she thought, once again thankful for the young vampire's helpful presence in Caleb's life.

He walked over to where she sat and kissed her warmly on the lips.

"I so love you, Kat. Thanks for bringing me with you."

Her arms slipped around his waist, pulling him onto the bed beside her. Her lips targeted his almost magnetically, and she kissed him affectionately. Despite the earlier road bump in the lobby, she was happy that she had brought him with her, as well. She merely hoped that her additional duties in the conference meetings wouldn't negatively impact her time with him.

As they kissed, his hand gently massaged the back of her neck. Moments later, his hand traced down her back and slowly slipped beneath her sweater to seek her right breast.

She parted from their kiss and whispered, "I like where this is going, but we need to get ready for the reception."

He recalled an earlier comment from Maddy's consort about the reception. "It's mandatory?" he asked.

She looked upon him sympathetically. "I'm afraid it's expected. Besides, it'll give you a chance to meet more of the human companions."

He remained silent. While intrigued to meet others, some intimate time with Katrina made all other endeavors pale by comparison.

Sensing his dour mood, she kissed him on the tip of the nose and promised, "No worries. We'll pick up where we left off later."

He watched her roll off the edge of the bed and move in a blur to the bathroom to start the shower. After a few minutes, he joined her.

Later, she applied a modest amount of makeup in the bathroom as Caleb finished cinching the knot on his fashionable new silk tie that she had bought for him back in Atlanta. He scoffed out loud at the off-center dimple below the knot, hastily undoing his tie and starting over from scratch. The truth was that he felt somewhat nervous about the upcoming reception, particularly given his earlier vampire-related misunderstanding in the lobby.

Katrina heard him scoff and offered, "I know you'd rather skip this, my love. But perhaps it's even more important considering what happened earlier. Believe it or not, most of the humans in the lobby appeared rather wary from being around so many vampires at once. You'd make quite an impression if you simply treated the vampires just like any other human."

"You think?" he asked as his second attempt with his tie was more successful.

"I'm certain of it," she confirmed while surveying her eyeliner. "Most vampires enjoy intimidating humans. It's a sort of perverse pastime with a number of them, a way of indulging their overinflated egos and sense of superiority. I suggest that you treat them politely, but no differently from anyone else you would meet in public."

Caleb frowned as he stood before the mirror. "I dunno, Kat."

She smiled with self-assurance as she ran a brush through her mane of red hair, letting it cascade across her shoulders.

"Trust me. Do you remember that textbook publishing event that we attended for one of your peers a month or so ago?"

Caleb nodded. One of his fellow professors had partnered with a Georgia University professor to generate a new history textbook that had been adopted for statewide use. The celebration had been a stuffy affair, mostly filled with other professors who were keen to brag about their latest research projects and publishing opportunities. Caleb recalled that it had been a snore-fest of epic proportion, in retrospect.

"Oh yeah, I remember."

"Remember how bored you were passing through the room shaking hands and politely listening to people drone on?" she asked. "Well, just act the same way tonight. Vampires are nothing, if not repositories of past experiences and timelines. Just look at it like a historical research project, of sorts."

"I'll try that," he replied as he peered around the corner into the bathroom. What he saw made him nearly lose his breath.

Katrina looked ravishing in a full-length black silk dress that fit her curves in all the right places. A silver necklace adorned her neck, with a large emerald pendant tastefully suspended above her cleavage. Her beautiful red hair was like a mantle across her shoulders, and emerald earrings sparkled at her earlobes. A pair of black strappy high-heels complemented the ensemble. She was simply gorgeous, and he felt the pull of her amorous nature drawing on him like gravity.

"Oh, Kat," he muttered once he caught his breath. "You're stunning."

"Thank you. And may I say, you look quite the handsome gentleman yourself," she said of his selection of dark Ralph Lauren slacks and blazer.

"Nice tie," she added as she strode up to him and cast a penetrating stare into his pale blue eyes.

The increased height from her heels required him to crane his neck up to meet her gaze fully, revealing his tasty-looking neckline to her. She felt a dual desire rise in her as his body and his blood both called to her at once. Realizing that she had not partaken in blood since their flight, she ran her tongue across her teeth as her mouth watered.

Oh, how I want him right now.

His eyes widened at the predatory expression in her penetrating stare. If he didn't already trust her so implicitly, he might have been concerned for his well-being at that moment.

"Um, Kat. Are you okay?"

With a practiced sense of self-control she reined in her thirst, vowing to partake in a glass of blood at the reception.

Maybe two or three glasses, she amended.

"Fine, my love," she softly replied while deliberately placing a single, soft kiss upon his lips.

He felt entranced as he started to kiss her again, but she abruptly pulled away and led him out of the suite. Though they passed a number of vampires and humans in the hallways leading to the reception room, he failed to focus fully on them as his eyes kept drifting to the beautiful woman beside him who held his hand. A sense of intense pride flowed through him that she had selected him out of all the men in the world.

The reception room in the main portion of the hotel was just off the atrium, a two-story area with a UV-coated glass ceiling. All manner of lush plants, small trees, and flowerbeds presented a relaxing park-like atmosphere amidst the small couches, reading chairs, and various other lobby furniture and fixtures.

The wide hallway leading to the reception room was guarded by three tuxedo-wearing vampires, two men and a woman. Each held an electronic tablet and greeted guests to ensure that their names were listed before allowing their entrance to the room beyond. As Katrina and Caleb approached, each of the vampires looked up and politely acknowledged him. Caleb thought that he recognized one of the vampires from Alton's office building during his and Katrina's trip to London in March.

"Are they Alton's?" he whispered.

"Yes," she answered simply and strode over to one of the vampires.

He politely gestured with one hand for them to proceed.

The eclectic symphonic music of Philip Glass emitted from the room as they approached, casting a stately, yet subdued, mood over the atmosphere. Everyone in attendance appeared to be dressed in either formal or elegant evening attire, and for once, Caleb felt comfortable in his wardrobe selection.

He noticed that a number of eyes, vampire and human

alike, turned to acknowledge Katrina as she passed. A vampire waiter bearing a tray of crystal champagne glasses filled with blood approached Katrina, who gratefully accepted one. She savored a swallow of the red liquid as it flowed down her throat, tempering the thirst that had built in her during the past few hours.

Caleb visually swept the large room. It appeared that he and Katrina were some of the first guests to arrive. The décor was stately, adorned with fresh arrangements of flowers in crystal vases. Along one wall was a lengthy oak countertop sporting a buffet of finger foods and appetizers that appeared to be a focal point for the few humans in the room. An elegant bar was positioned near the food serving area, and a small punch fountain twinkled from the middle of the room.

Small bistro tables were arrayed on the side of the room where the buffet was located, and a number of small tables and chairs were positioned along the wall.

The opposite wall sported what could only be described as a blood bar for the vampires. Caleb noticed that the room was served solely by vampires; no human staff members were within sight. He wondered if that were because of the potentially delicate nature of the conversations that may be conducted. *But wouldn't the human companions be considered a possible security risk, as well?*

Katrina watched the intrigue play across her mate's features with some amusement. *He's simply adorable.*

She held his hand and gently led him towards a small group of vampires standing close to the blood bar. They stopped chatting as soon as Katrina approached, and each turned to greet her.

"Katrina?" asked a tall, thirty-something-looking brunette. Her red evening gown looked captivating on her shapely frame, and her brown eyes glistened as the light caught them.

Releasing Caleb's hand, Katrina embraced the woman with one arm and warmly greeted her, "Innessa, it's so good to see you again. How is my favorite Greek goddess doing?"

The woman demurred, "Oh, hush. There are no statues of me in the whole of Greece, my dear. They stopped that by the time I was turned, you know."

Then the woman's eyes settled on Caleb. "But I see you've been doing well for yourself."

Katrina stepped back and cast a smile at her mate as he blushed.

I certainly think so, she silently affirmed.

Then she turned to greet the three others in a more formal fashion with simple handshakes.

"My beloved mate, Caleb," Katrina introduced in a possessive tone.

Caleb shook each of their hands and politely greeted them in turn. He immediately liked Innessa, but that might have been because Katrina seemed close to her. Heru was a young Egyptian male with medium-length, straight black hair and a tall, lanky build. Yat-Sen was a short, muscular Chinese vampire with dyed blonde hair and vivid green eyes.

Pekka had long brown hair, gray eyes, and a medium height and build. He claimed to be from Finland, although, in retrospect, Caleb was uncertain if any of the vampires' claimed heritages were indicative of their actual countries of residence. Somehow he doubted it. Katrina once said that vampires had to be itinerant by nature, at least every so often, or people would notice their lack of aging.

He remained silent and politely listened to the vampires' conversations ranging from recent travels to how quickly places and people had changed over the years. Soon additional guests arrived in larger numbers, and he cast a longing look at the inviting appearance of the buffet table across the room. He felt Katrina gently squeeze his hand in hers, and his attention returned to her. He then noticed the other vampires observing him with interest.

"Why don't you go get something to eat, my love?" she suggested.

I'm sure he's as hungry as I was earlier, she noted with a degree of guilt. She was already sipping on her second glass of blood and felt much better for it.

"Thanks. I'd like that," he replied to the vampires before departing.

"Such a polite young human," Yat-Sen noted as Caleb walked away.

Caleb loaded a glass dinner plate with various items from the buffet and glimpsed Dr. Reynolds to his right adding some small chunks of cheese to a small plate of fruit. The youthful-looking doctor was attired in slacks, dinner jacket, and a white silk shirt, but no tie. Much like Alton, the man wore his clothes with the charm of a playboy on the prowl. Caleb also found it amusing that Reynolds was the only vampire on that side of the room at the time.

"Foraging with humans?" Caleb quipped. "That cheese will clog your arteries, you know."

Reynolds fully focused his striking brown eyes upon Caleb with a sparkle of genuine amusement, and he grinned in response.

"I happen to like fruit and cheese, even after all these years. And as for the arteries, I'm not so worried. That's one of the perks of being a vampire, I'm happy to say. However, as your doctor, I must advise you limit your intake of high-fat foods, particularly that fried pork on your plate."

Caleb peered down at his plate.

Too true, he conceded.

His attention quickly returned to the suave vampire before him.

"If I happen to see Paige tonight, I'll be sure to track you down for a brief introduction."

Reynolds appeared genuinely pleased by the suggestion. "I'd really like that, Mr. Taylor."

"Please, Caleb," he insisted.

"Caleb, then," the vampire replied. "But only if you'll call me Ethan."

"Agreed," Caleb said with a nod.

"Dr. Reynolds? There's someone I want you to meet," an ebony-skinned female vampire wearing a blue silk dress beckoned from nearby.

"Please excuse me, Caleb. Until later," Ethan offered with a nod as he popped a small chunk of cheese into his mouth and walked off towards the woman who had called to him.

When Caleb finished loading his plate and grabbing a glass of iced tea from a nearby drink table, he spied the throng of humans gathered at the small tables not far from the buffet. Aiden waved for him to join in, and he made his way to the bistro table where Aiden stood before a plateful of food. Caleb shook hands with him and introduced himself to another young man in his late twenties named Ryan from Ireland and a young dark-skinned woman named Chloe who had a West-African accent.

"Why's everyone clustered around here?" Caleb curiously asked after sampling the food on his plate. Everything tasted amazing to him. In all the excitement of their arrival, he had almost forgotten that he hadn't eaten since before their plane landed that afternoon.

"Are you kidding?" Chloe asked as if he were daft. "Smart fish don't swim in chummed waters with sharks, my friend. My Isaac told me to sit quietly unless called for."

Caleb easily detected that she seemed unsettled by the growing quantity of vampires in the room.

Ryan agreed, "Sabira told me much the same thing. She said to mingle with the humans, so here I'll stay. I'm no chancer."

Caleb appeared perplexed, and Aiden supplied, "Someone who pushes their luck."

"Oh," Caleb said while glancing over at the other humans gathered nearby. Many spoke with each other in hushed tones with wary expressions.

These people honestly look like they're afraid of getting eaten or something.

He continued to eat and engage in pleasant conversation with Aiden and the others and made a follow-up trip to the buffet and drink table. To his surprise, the humans continued to nestle in their corner while the vast majority of the room was interspersed with crowds of vampires who mingled back and forth between the groups like a giant chat-fest. Every once in a while, a vampire would glare over at the gathering of humans, mostly with a hungry, longing expression one might expect from a predator sizing up its prey.

After Caleb finished eating, he focused on Aiden in silent question. The curly-haired man responded with a brisk nod, and they both moved in unison away from the table. Aiden appraisingly looked at Caleb as he quickly surveyed their surroundings.

He spotted Alton talking to two male vampires on the far side of the room, also accompanied by an attractive brunette woman wearing a red dress, who stood next to him with her hand gently draped across his left arm.

"You *humans* have a good evening," Caleb remarked as multiple people looked up to stare at him and Aiden.

"You two are daft," Ryan chastised in his thick Irish accent.

"Good luck," Chloe called to them.

"You're kidding," one woman commented loud enough for Caleb to hear.

He strode purposefully through the room with Aiden in tow. Some vampires briefly noted the two of them as they passed, others falling silent as they sensed a human approach. Barely halfway across the room, Aiden's mate, Talise, grabbed his arm to pull him aside, leaving Caleb by himself as he purposefully completed the final distance to where Alton stood. The dark-haired vampire immediately focused his full attention on the young man.

"Ah, Caleb, my dear boy," Alton began with overt approval. "It's so good to see you. I'm happy that you agreed to accompany Katrina to Slovenia."

Caleb reached out to shake his hand. "Me too. And it's always good to see you, Alton."

The vampire shook his hand and pulled him into a frater-
nal half-hug as the woman on his arm stepped aside with a shy
smile. Caleb suspected that the two other vampires were taken
aback by Alton's unusually warm greeting, though he wasn't
certain. As he stepped back, Alton immediately gestured to the
beautiful brunette to his left.

"Caleb, I'm pleased to introduce my companion, Dorianne
Rousseau," Alton offered with a sparkle in his eye.

The woman was about Caleb's height and appeared to be
about thirty years of age. However, her most striking feature
was her violet eyes. Though such vivid eyes were normally a
telltale sign of a vampire, he was momentarily uncertain if the
woman before him were a human or not.

"*The* Dorianne Rousseau?" Caleb inquired with a hint of
awe.

She seemed caught off guard by his hint of reverence and
curiously considered him.

"I fear that you have me confused with someone else. I'm
not anyone of notoriety," she politely countered.

Caleb demurred, "Ah, but surely someone with as beautiful
a visage and name to match deserves to be greeted as such."

She laughed in a delightful manner as Alton shook his
head and muttered, "Silver-tongued scamp."

"Please, call me Dori," the woman introduced herself as she
reached out her hand to shake his.

"Caleb Taylor. My pleasure, Dori," he offered while accepting her hand and gently grasping it.

The woman stared back at him with a look of approval.

"Ah, so you're Caleb Taylor," she slyly assessed. "I see what
Alton meant regarding your charming sense of humor."

He was genuinely caught off guard by her, and he looked to
Alton.

"I might have mentioned you to her, actually," the stately
vampire hinted.

"Indeed. I've heard enough about you already, Caleb, that I

feel I know you," she complimented him. "It's nice to finally put a face to a name, though."

Caleb didn't quite know how to respond once the tables had been so expertly turned on him, so he merely nodded politely.

Alton smoothly introduced the two vampires next to them, but later Caleb honestly didn't recall their names. His attention was repeatedly distracted by Dori and how remarkable the woman seemed. If she were human, she was the most comfortable-looking human in the room.

Why hasn't Alton mentioned her before?

His focus quickly returned to Alton.

"I'm afraid I must circulate the room a bit more to try and greet everyone before the evening passes, Caleb," Alton apologized. "However, I think it important that you and I make some time in the near future. There's much for us to discuss."

"Certainly, I understand. And I'd like that very much, Alton."

"We'll talk more again soon, Caleb," Dori promised as Alton led her away towards another group.

The two remaining vampires momentarily looked at Caleb curiously. Then each made the gesture of shaking his hand again before also gravitating to other groups of vampires. Caleb surveyed the large room until his attention focused on where the majority of humans were still gathered together.

You know, they actually look like sheep huddled together in a flock for protection, he determined. Suddenly, he was glad not to be there with them.

His eyes momentarily met Aiden's across the room, and the young man winked before returning his attention to Talise and another vampire. Caleb couldn't help but feel quite pleased with himself. Amidst the politics and hidden agendas of those around him, he felt that he had discovered a kindred spirit in Aiden Henderson.

"Hey, kiddo," Paige's voice announced, startling him slightly.

He turned to greet his surrogate vampire, noting the curious expression in her bright blue eyes as she studied him, still attired in her official security outfit.

"You looked like you were in a trance for a moment," she observed. "You okay?"

"Me? Oh yeah, I'm fine," he assured her. Then he recalled his earlier promise to Ethan. "Are you off duty now?" he asked.

"Ha! Are you kidding? The major's had me running around non-stop after the lobby incident –" She stopped midsentence, afraid it would sound like she was blaming him for what had happened.

"I should've let it go and just apologized to the jerk," he lamented. He didn't like hearing that the event had caused problems for her.

She took his chin between her fingertips, much as Katrina had done on occasion, and turned his face towards hers.

"Stop," she quietly ordered. "You did nothing wrong today, and I'd do it again without hesitation. The major's just being... well, the major. Nothing more."

"Understood," he said.

She released her grip on his chin, though her serious expression remained.

"Do you have quick minute?" he asked.

Her features relaxed somewhat, and she slyly grinned. "For you? Always."

"Great, because there's someone I want you to meet," he explained as he took her hand and led her around the groups of visiting vampires.

She followed behind him with a curious expression.

Ethan Reynolds had his back turned and was passively listening to two other vampires converse when Caleb reached out to tap him on the shoulder.

Realizing that interrupting a vampire was a bad idea, Paige started to intercept Caleb's arm and snapped, "Don't do –"

Sensing someone behind him, rather than reacting aggressively as some vampires might have, the doctor turned very slowly and surveyed them with a curious expression. Ethan's features quickly brightened when he realized it was Caleb. *He's awfully well-tempered,* Paige observed.

"Ethan, I'm proud to introduce you to Ms. Paige Turner, my surrogate vampire," he formally announced.

He quickly turned to Paige and offered, "Paige, this is Dr. Ethan Reynolds.

She warmly smiled at the doctor, sizing him up and noting that his hand was already outstretched in an immediate gesture of greeting.

Well, aren't you just Doctor McDreamy-looking?

Ethan's face appeared to light up even further as he beheld Paige. "It's a real pleasure to meet you, Captain Turner. I've only been here for a few days, so we haven't been formally introduced yet."

"No, we haven't," she agreed. "Nice to meet you, Dr. Reynolds."

"Please, Ethan," he insisted.

Paige immediately liked his smile, among other physical attributes. But while the vampire seemed sincere, she was nevertheless always on her guard.

"Well, Ethan," she began, "I suppose that you can call me Paige."

"Thanks, I appreciate that," he sincerely replied. "I look forward to working with you during the conference."

"Hopefully we won't need your services too frequently," she countered.

He shrugged. "True, perhaps. But then, I'm helpful for more than accidents and injuries, you know."

"Really? Such as?" Paige suggestively pressed.

"Well, why don't we discuss that over a drink?" he asked, chivalrously extending the crook of his left arm towards her.

She caught Caleb's attention, and he encouragingly winked back at her.

"By all means, lead on, Ethan," she replied with a gleam in her eyes.

Caleb watched them wander off in the direction of the blood bar.

They could end up becoming very interesting.

His attention quickly shifted to a dark-haired vampire standing a few feet to his left who was glaring at him with slightly glowing blue eyes. He immediately recognized the vampire from the earlier lobby incident, and his body tensed slightly.

The vampire moved slowly towards Caleb, stopping less than two feet from him and displaying a thinly veiled grimace.

"Enjoying the evening, human?" the vampire curtly inquired.

"It's just wonderful, thank you," he courteously replied, not wanting to create another scene reminiscent of the lobby.

Suddenly, Katrina appeared by his side, asking, "Care to introduce me to your friend, Caleb?"

She had been casually observing her mate from a distance and immediately sensed his tension upon viewing the vampire before him. Despite never having met him, she already had an idea who he was based upon her mate's earlier description.

"We're only briefly acquainted, actually," Caleb calmly explained despite the tension he felt inside. "We met in the lobby earlier this evening."

Katrina's left arm possessively wrapped around Caleb's waist, and she stepped forwards to address the vampire before them.

"I'm Katrina Rawlings."

The tall vampire politely inclined his head, though with a smug expression, and grandly announced, "Dominic Ambrogio."

"Caleb's my mate," she firmly noted, ignoring his air of self-importance.

The vampire's eyes widened slightly with a degree of recognition as he surveyed the tall red-haired woman before him.

"He's *your* mate and not the short blonde's?" he demanded with some surprise amidst a slightly perplexed expression.

Katrina's eyes momentarily flashed bright green, and she answered in a lethally calm voice, "Correct. My mate."

He tried to appear unshaken by the revelation, but was doing a poor job of it.

"An unfortunate misunderstanding earlier this evening, of course," he assured her.

Caleb had the impression that Katrina's reputation had preceded her and noticed that the room had fallen silent save for the ambient symphonic music playing as numerous eyes observed the quiet exchange. He momentarily realized that with a room full of vampires, no conversation was truly private. Then he spied Paige standing just to his left with a stern expression as Ethan stood beside her.

"I thought that might be the case, but one never knows nowadays," Katrina levelly replied.

"Too true," the vampire agreed. "I bid you both good evening," he added before quietly making his way towards the room's exit.

Katrina took a moment to mark the vampire's faces in the room deliberately, content that her declaration had been made to all. Some looked on in silent acknowledgement, while others dismissively looked away. Already she was getting a sense of where a subtle polarization was beginning to occur among her kind.

Although none of that matters where Caleb's safety is concerned.

Paige raised a silent toast to Katrina with a wine glass of blood, while Ethan nodded supportively before turning his full attention back to Paige. Conversations quickly began to strike up again in earnest, and everyone returned to their former distractions.

Caleb's arm reached around his mate's slim waist with pride, and he looked up at her adoringly. "I so love you," he whispered.

"You better...troublemaker," she teased as she bent her head down to kiss him once on the lips. However, her cavalier

exterior was merely a façade for the love that welled inside her
for the young man in her arms at that moment.

My safe mate.

Thankfully, the remainder of the evening continued uneventfully for everyone, and Caleb remained close to Katrina
as she introduced him to more of her peers.

By the time they returned to their suite, it was well after
two o'clock in the morning, and Caleb was nearly exhausted.
Even the sugar and caffeine from the colas he liberally consumed at the reception failed to curtail his incessant yawns.
He noted that he wasn't the only human in attendance who
had problems keeping his eyes open. Many of the vampires conceded the evening only after viewing the pitiful state of their
human companions, while vampires without human charges
lingered to continue their conversations.

Katrina slipped from her dress and high-heeled shoes as
Caleb likewise removed his clothes. Despite multiple glasses of
blood at the reception to curtail her thirst, Katrina was looking forward to partaking in some of his blood. However, it was
quickly becoming apparent by his lethargic behavior that he
was simply looking forward to going to bed.

He slid beneath the covers of the bed, and she joined him
after turning off the lights. Snuggling next to his warm body,
she kissed him on the soft skin of his neck.

"Somebody smells wonderfully tasty."

He groggily acknowledged her and suddenly realized her
intentions.

Oh, but I'm so tired, he guiltily thought.

It wasn't as if she asked for much from him, and he felt
like a heel for being so tired. Taking a deep breath with a sense
of fortitude, he opened his eyes to see her green eyes slightly
glowing back at him.

"Want a nibble?" he asked with as much enthusiasm as he
could muster.

She scrutinized him in the darkness, her vision plainly seeing the tired expression on his face and reflected in his pale

blue eyes.

I should just let him go to sleep, she reasoned as she kissed him on the tip of his nose while starting to lie down.

"Never mind. Good night, my love," she offered.

But he managed to reach out and grasp her arm, stopping her from moving away from him.

"Wait. Please, take a little nightcap first," he gently insisted.

Watching him with an endearing expression, she shook her head. "You're amazing, my love," she complimented before warmly kissing him on the lips. "I'll make this fast."

He turned his head away from her, cleanly exposing his neck. He felt her lips part as they formed a seal over his skin, and he sensed her silky warm tongue press against his flesh. The numbing sensation quickly formed and before long he felt her fangs extend into his neck with only the slightest pressure. The euphoria he normally felt when she drew blood from him seemed stronger, and his thoughts quickly drifted on a soothing sea of near unconsciousness. And for the first time since he met her, he drifted off to sleep as she drew blood from him.

She sensed him slip into unconsciousness, which momentarily alarmed her until she measured his steady breathing in conjunction with the strong beat of his pulse.

My dear, thoughtful Caleb, she silently mused as she continued to draw an additional mouthful of his blood.

She loved him totally and once again was impacted by his giving nature and how he strove to meet her needs. After pressing her tongue against his skin to seal the wounds on his neck, she curled up next to him and held him close to her while listening to the steady rhythm of his heartbeat.

*   *   *   *

Chapter 5

A Walk in the Woods

*P*aige stood in the lobby watching the bustling activity as vampires filled the area either to chat or to make their way towards the large conference room where the primary meeting was scheduled to take place. It was still early morning, and very few humans were around, mostly hotel staff.

Her thoughts drifted to the previous evening's reception and the interesting and attractive Dr. Ethan Reynolds. He had surprised her with his disarming charm and good looks, which was exactly why she needed to keep her guard up.

Could be a mole trying to glean information concerning Alton's plans, she suspiciously pondered. *But then, what if he's simply a nice guy trying to get to know me at a purely social level?*

Great, she surmised with a wry expression. *I'm turning into Katrina.*

Her eyes continued to sweep the expansive lobby and fell upon a briefcase-carrying vampire of medium height and build who had stopped to talk with Major Pietari. She recognized the brown-haired Croatian vampire as Baldar Dubravko, one of the primary investors who had funded the hotel's expansion specifically for the purposes of hosting the conference. She watched as the major conversed with Dubravko in a casual manner.

Are they previously acquainted?

As Pietari invited the Croatian into the security office, a

familiar voice sounded to distract her attention.

"Good morning, Paige. Coffee?" Dr. Reynolds brightly asked as he extended the small Styrofoam cup of steaming liquid to her.

She accepted the cup with a peculiar expression, but pleasantly regarded the handsome physician. "Thanks," she replied. Observing her reaction, Reynolds inquired, "You don't like coffee, do you?"

She took a quick sip. Though it seemed a nice blend, coffee wasn't something that she regularly drank.

"Sure, I like it well enough," she replied with a shrug. "I'm just a little surprised to see a vampire who drinks it first thing in the morning instead of a steaming cup of the red stuff.

His eyebrows momentarily furrowed. "I usually don't like drinking blood in front of other people," he explained.

She wrestled with the oddity of his statement, given that he was a vampire.

You've got a lot of layers to you, don't you? she determined. "Don't like blood, do you?" she mimicked with a mischievous look.

He knowingly grinned in response, mimicking her with an exaggerated shrug. "Well, sure. I like it well enough."

She brightly smiled over his ploy, appreciating his gentle eyes.

You do get more interesting by the minute, Ethan.

* * * *

As soon as Katrina walked through the double oak doors leading into the large, conservatively-decorated conference room, she knew from the host of vampires gathered there that it was going to be an interesting conference.

She momentarily appreciated the oversized, rectangular walnut conference table that seemed to go on forever down the length of the center of the room. Its polished surface was like some sort of launching platform for a small aircraft, and she wondered how many sections it had needed to be cut into in order to install it in the room.

Over fifty chairs were assembled around the table, with the far end vacant of seating. The end closest to the main doors sported a leather chair with a placard labeled "Chairperson – Alton Rutherford" before it.

She shook her head, never doubting that Alton had prepared for nearly everything.

Including a soon-to-be-nominated co-chair.

Vampires filed into the room and sought seats around the large table. Alton purposefully walked into the room and placed a stack of handouts and folders at the head of the table.

"Good morning, Katrina," he offered and gestured with one hand to an empty seat at the end of the table immediately to his left.

"Good morning, Alton," she politely replied, selecting instead to go to the far side of the room to a seat at the extreme end.

You'll have me there soon enough, she sulked.

Much to her satisfaction, he sourly acknowledged her before readopting his former professional visage.

Talise took the seat Alton had previously pointed out to Katrina with a friendly nod in her direction. The remaining seats were quickly filled, save for the one next to Katrina. The dark-haired vampire who had harassed Caleb entered the room and instantly located an available seat. His face quickly fell upon realizing that the only remaining place was next to Katrina.

His face turned stony as he sat down and politely murmured, "Good morning, Ms. Rawlings."

"Why, good morning. Ambrogio, isn't it?" she replied with a sardonic glare before focusing on the others around the table.

Big bully, she added as an afterthought.

Two vampires wearing black business suits reached in to close the oak doors behind them, leaving the room to those gathered around the table. On cue, silence fell across the room, and everyone looked to Alton with a mix of curious or expectant expressions.

"Welcome, everyone, to what I hope will be a beneficial dialogue for each of us," he began in a practiced tone. "This is the first of its kind to my knowledge: a vampire summit of sorts. An opportunity for us to work collectively towards mutually beneficial solutions to the host of challenges facing our kind.

"But first, let's go around the table to introduce ourselves. I'm Alton Rutherford, your chairperson," he said before gesturing to Talise to continue the introductions.

A number of the names were familiar to Katrina, many from the reception the prior evening. Still, she was surprised by how many in the room were unknown to her. Even more mysteriously, a quarter of the participants were acting as proxies for other vampires, though they merely indicated that they represented "other interested vampire parties" rather than revealing specific names. For some reason, that troubled her more than the bullies like the vampire seated next to her.

Following the introductions, Alton continued, "Now, as a matter of formality, I recommend we select a co-chair to serve in the event that I'm unable to preside over activities for any reason. Do I have any nominations or volunteers?"

Everyone curiously surveyed the faces around them for a few silent moments. Then Talise spoke up in a clear voice, "I nominate Katrina Rawlings."

"I second," announced the auburn-haired Dutch vampire named Rianne. She was a long-time acquaintance of Katrina's.

"I nominate Baldar Dubravko," announced a male vampire of Asian descent.

"Second for Baldar Dubravko," said a female vampire of Middle Eastern decent.

The room quickly fell silent, and Alton directed, "Very well. I have two nominations on the floor. I'll pass out blank cards and ask each of you to write either Baldar's or Katrina's name as your preference. The cards can be placed in this manila envelope, and we'll immediately tally the results here at the table."

Minutes later, the envelope returned to Alton, who placed the cards face-up with Katrina to his right and Baldar to his left. The process was expedient, and by the end, Katrina had received two-thirds of the vote.

"As you can see, with a definitive majority, I name Katrina Rawlings as our new co-chair," Alton announced, followed by a small round of clapping from the group.

Katrina returned polite nods in response, though inside she dreaded her new promotion.

I really just wanted to be a fly on the wall through this, she lamented.

Small murmurings of conversation began, which prompted Alton to continue, "With that concluded, let's discuss some of the key objectives of our gathering. Given the recent events involving the rogue vampire, Chimalma, it's clear that we could benefit from a formalized format for settling disputes between rival vampires and their interests."

"It's called battle," one vampire mumbled. "Kill the other guy first."

A few chuckles erupted, but silence followed a stern gaze from Alton.

"A mutual acknowledgement of declared vampire territories is a start. In addition, common rights and privileges to be observed by participating vampires may help," he soberly offered. "Furthermore, continued technological advancements by the humans suggests that we would benefit from a common approach to handling potential breaches of discovery by them or their governments," Alton continued.

"A time will come when we won't be able to hide ourselves," a female vampire interrupted. "It's going to come to war eventually."

Katrina's eyes bored into Alton from across the room with a look of concern.

A war must be avoided, she silently insisted.

"Perhaps not," Alton countered, having noted her expression. "Suffice to say, a planned and unified approach to the topic would be best."

Murmurs of agreement spread throughout the room.

"As the ranks of vampires internationally grow, addressing the problem of providing a reasonable means of financial sustainment would stabilize the vampire community. We can explore an organized mentorship for new vampires with opportunities for building financial stability through service," Alton suggested. "It's a reasonable way to shape the future of our culture, while also easing the transition of conversion."

"Too many vampires already, in my view," one vampire grumbled.

A few noises of agreement followed.

"It's my hope that we can leave this summit with an agreeable framework related to these and other issues in hopes of refining details later in subsequent conferences such as this. With some hope, we may even find absent stakeholders who choose to take part in person," Alton pointedly suggested, all the while monitoring a number of participants who were serving as proxies.

"You're expecting instant solutions to these and other problems by chatting in a room over glasses of blood?" Dominic Ambrogio sarcastically inquired.

"Though well-intentioned, the agenda does seem somewhat unrealistic at first consideration," Baldar agreed in support.

Katrina closely watched the exchange. Her suspicious mind raced as she observed the subtle reinforcement taking place. A blonde female vampire across from Katrina nodded in seeming agreement with Dubravko.

Alton raised a hand in a peaceable gesture, conceding, "Admittedly, this venture isn't without its challenges. But at the risk of validating a prescient suggestion by Mr. Ambrogio, perhaps this would be a good time for a glass of blood during which time we can properly transfer Ms. Rawlings to the head of the table where the co-chair sits."

Katrina subtly rolled her eyes and kept from groaning out loud.

I'm already regretting this.

* * * *

When Caleb woke, it was well past ten o'clock in the morning. He stretched in bed with a yawn, glancing at the empty spot next to him where Katrina had been the night before. A note lay on her pillow, and he reached over to pick it up. He took a moment to focus his still-weary eyes on the text.

Caleb,

> *Thank you for last night. I'll probably be in the conference all day, so find something enjoyable to do until evening. We'll go to dinner together and do some sightseeing. Please try to stay out of trouble, my love.*

Love,
Kat

He shook his head while lying the note on the nightstand. "I'll certainly try," he murmured.

Then he rolled out of bed and shuffled into the bathroom to shave and start the day.

* * * *

Paige sat at her small desk in the security office with a bored expression, staring listlessly at the multiple computer screens before her that displayed the various video surveillance camera images from all across the conference facility. With a series of mouse clicks, the images changed to cameras watching the outdoor areas.

Some cameras were placed outside the various buildings, while others observed from perches atop light poles. It seemed that virtually every area could be spied upon by the network of digital cameras. However, she knew that was an exaggeration, having inspected each camera location herself to familiarize herself with their placement *It's not as if every camera sees in all directions at once, either.* Though significant funds had been spent to install a reasonable network of viewing possibilities, the system failed to provide complete coverage at all times. It would have seemed like overkill for such a brief conference. The major had explained to her that the system had to be realistic to maintain after the conference ended and regular vacationing humans returned to using the facility as a scenic vacation retreat.

The door gently opened, and her eyes darted to spy Caleb as he entered. She brightly grinned at him and motioned with her hand for him to enter.

"Hey, look who's finally up and around," she teased.

"You mean you didn't see me coming?" he shot back while moving to sit in a chair set before her desk. "What kind of security captain are you, anyway?"

She cast a withering expression and pointed to the screens before her.

"Hey, I'm only one set of eyes for all these miniaturized windows, all right, Mr. Sarcasm? Hell, I can't even get all the viewing screens up at one time. Gotta cycle through three sets just to look at them all."

"You could always add another monitor to the two you already have," he suggested. "I'm sure they could add another video card and install the drivers for the –"

"Yeah, yeah, thanks for the advice, Bill Gates."

"I can tell you're having fun with this."

She snorted and shook her head. The phone rang, and she glared at it while picking up the receiver.

"Security office. Captain Turner speaking," she answered in a flat voice.

He was amused by her bored tone.

"What? Yes, ma'am, I'm sure it's a crime that the kitchen

brought cold food to your room, but it's honestly not a security matter," she explained with an incredulous expression.

He had to cover his mouth to keep from laughing out loud.

"Well, you could always withhold a tip," she suggested.

She patiently listened as the animated woman's voice complained back at her. Finally, she rubbed at her eyes with the fingertips of her free hand and said, "Um, ma'am, let me transfer you to the desk manager. Please hold."

Her fingers quickly played across the telephone's keypad, and she stated, "Yeah, this is Turner. I've got an angry eater on the line for you. Something about cold food. Good luck. Here she is."

With that, she hung up the phone and cursed under her breath.

"Geez, I hate this job already," she muttered.

He couldn't help but grin back at her in response.

At the sound of the main office door, her eyes darted to the visitor. Caleb swiveled in his seat to view a young man holding a brown leather briefcase in one hand.

The Mediterranean-looking fellow uneasily looked towards the major's office and asked, "Is Major Pietari here, please?"

Paige frowned at the man's awkward behavior, but smoothly answered, "Nope. The major stepped out, but I expect him any moment. Can I help you?"

"No," he said. "I'll just come back later."

Then he abruptly turned and departed the office in what seemed a hurried fashion.

"Strange," she observed.

Her attention quickly returned to Caleb.

"Just what are you doing down here, anyway?" she asked. "Katrina brings you all the way to Europe, and you want to just sit around a hotel security office?"

"Yeah, well, I was just on my way to get something to eat. Afterwards, I guess I'll look around the place. Kat's note said I needed to occupy my time until evening."

"Fine, but if you don't like the food, just keep it to yourself, okay, kiddo?"

He chuckled and shook his head at her. Despite Kat's absence, he was happy that Paige was around. His surrogate vampire was such an important part of his life.

As if sensing his emotions, she smiled back at him for a moment. She loved his kind nature and easy disposition and was quite attached to the young man.

Under different circumstances, he might even be mine, she thought on a whim.

However, her smile quickly faded, and she silently chastised herself for letting her thoughts stray in such a direction.

Dangerous territory, she estimated before refocusing on the monitors before her.

"Okay, okay, go get something to eat, or I'll have to ticket you for loitering," she teased with a dismissive wave of her hand.

As he rose, Major Pietari walked in and scanned the office before settling his gaze upon the sandy-haired human. Caleb immediately extended his hand. The major suspiciously peered at him before gripping his hand.

"Caleb Taylor," the young man offered with a shake.

"Major Kivo Pietari," the tall vampire replied. He shifted his attention to Paige, critically observing, "No visitors while on duty, Captain."

"Um, I was just leaving," Caleb interjected. "In fact, Paige just admonished me about loitering."

The major's sharp eyes fell upon him as if studying him for a moment. Then he merely grunted in reply.

Caleb proceeded to the door. Before closing the door behind him completely, he heard Paige inform the major, "You missed an odd little visitor a few minutes ago."

Following his visit with Paige, Caleb went to the hotel's central restaurant for an early lunch. There were only a few patrons dispersed throughout the dining room, none of whom he knew, so he quietly sat and observed his surroundings while he ate. He noticed that the staff all seemed polite, though pensive, for some reason. Perhaps they weren't used to being around vampire guests.

Then the thought struck him that he was surrounded by seemingly ordinary human staff, and he wondered how the vampires had managed to maintain any sense of privacy concerning their gathering with so many potential "loose lips" around. All it would take is one discreet phone call or email to the media, and the place might be crawling with press.

Well, maybe not the mainstream press at first, he mulled. *More likely the tabloids expecting an outlandish gathering of vampire-wannabes trying to host a Goth conference.*

He shook his head and made a mental note to ask Katrina about it later.

After lunch, he decided to familiarize himself with his surroundings and walked through the main lobby past the various support offices and conference rooms. He came upon two suit-clad vampire guards standing outside the large reception room he had been in the prior evening with Katrina. He recognized both guards from the night before and politely nodded, and each acknowledged him in recognition.

On the back side of the hotel, he came upon a small cluster of boutiques and shops presented in a manner reminiscent of a shopping mall. Light filtered down from above, and he looked up to see large glass panes laid out as an elaborate skylight that ran the length of the small corridor of shops. The light seemed terribly subtle for the clear skies, upon which he noticed that the panes were treated with what must be UV-dampening material. As he proceeded on his tour, he realized that all of the windows in and around the hotel and conference center were likewise treated.

After nearly an hour of wandering, he retrieved a digital camera from his room and journeyed outdoors. The surrounding mountains were breathtaking, and the grass and trees were lush and green. Flower gardens decorated the hotel landscape, as well as a number of small fountains and park benches. He snapped photos as he walked and idly greeted a number of humans whom he recognized as other vampire companions.

Once again, he noted the starkly different demeanors of the hotel guests from the hotel staff. The sole exception seemed to be the security guards who randomly patrolled by. The guards maintained a confident air as they casually strolled about the grounds. Caleb noted a seemingly large quantity of guards on patrol as he walked throughout the acres of land constituting the hotel property.

Paige and the major must have their hands full coordinating such a large staff, he absently determined.

He sat on a park bench facing a large expanse of forest leading away from the main hotel grounds. He made a mental note to explore the forest another time and instead merely appreciated the warm sunshine as it beamed down upon him.

"This is excellent," he muttered, closing his eyes and tilting his face skywards. "Finally, some peaceful relaxation."

Minutes passed as he basked in the sunlight, leaning back against the bench while stretching his legs out before him.

"There you are," came a familiar woman's voice.

The slight French accent was unmistakable, though Caleb started with surprise and opened his eyes to pan in the direction of the brunette-haired visitor. Only as the sunlight caressed Dorianne Rousseau's pale skin was his mind finally convinced that she was human and not a vampire.

"Hi, Dorianne."

"Dori," she pleasantly corrected him. "Is this seat taken?"

He made a welcoming gesture as he sat up from his reclined position.

"Isn't it beautiful?" she quietly observed as she sat down beside him.

"It's everything Europe should be," he acknowledged with awe.

He never thought that he would ever have the opportunity, or funds, to visit the places he had been since meeting Katrina.

I'm one lucky guy.

"I confess, I take it for granted sometimes," Dori admitted.

"My home is in Paris, but my career regularly takes me across Europe. It's a nice perk of the job."

He offered a curious expression, hoping that she would say more, but she seemed oddly content to leave it at that.

"I've been to London recently, and it was both unexpected and amazing," he offered.

He thought it best to leave out the part about mysterious vampires haunting the Tube.

"I would imagine. Alton told me about your little subterranean adventure," she said with a smirk.

He frowned at how the normally secretive vampire had shared such sensitive information with her.

"So, have you and Alton known each other long?"

She warmly smiled. "We met nearly a year ago at a business meeting in The Hague, and he immediately caught my attention. My employer assigned me the responsibility of arranging a presentation for Alton and his associates, which, as a research analyst, I specialize in. Despite my practiced expertise, his eyes kept distracting me, and I practically had to fight to remain focused."

She paused to giggle while covering her mouth with her hand in a manner that Caleb found enchanting.

"Following the presentation, I felt so embarrassed that I left the building as soon as I gathered my materials. But he took the initiative to find me before I returned to Paris and literally swept me off my feet. To say that I was pleased would be an understatement. We've been seeing each other regularly since then, actually. He's, well, wonderful in so many ways."

Caleb enjoyed her recollection, but he was surprised that Alton had never mentioned Dori to him until the previous evening.

How odd, he thought. *I wonder if Kat knows.*

However, he conceded that Alton was a very private person and a hard nut to crack. He chuckled at how often Kat found it equally infuriating.

"Have I said something amusing?" she queried.

A single fleeting view of her beautiful, violet-colored eyes was all it took for him to understand how Alton might be intrigued by her.

"Sorry," he replied. "I kind of hate to admit this, but Alton's never actually mentioned you to me."

An endearing expression played across her face, and she laughed in a beguiling manner.

"Why am I not surprised?" she said. "I suppose he does keep his cards close to the vest. Likely, he was waiting to see if things worked out between us."

"I guess they must have then," he surmised. "Because here you are."

"Yes," she noted with a satisfied tone. "I'd like to think you're correct."

They considered each other in silence, though something unsaid seemed to be settled between them. It was as if a mutual comfort zone, a chemistry, had been mysteriously established.

Caleb felt strangely at ease around Dori, and he shared how he met Katrina when she had enrolled in his history class the previous fall. However, chemistry aside, he wasn't quite ready to discuss how Katrina came upon him initially when he was eight years old. That was something altogether private, though whether Alton had already shared that with Dori or not he didn't know.

She attentively listened to him until he was finished, and the conversation moved to a variety of other casual topics. They seemed like old friends catching up on the events in their lives. Caleb enjoyed getting to know her, and before he realized it, the sun was advancing towards the western horizon.

"We'd better head back," Dori observed. "Alton mentioned our having dinner with you and Katrina when the conference adjourned for the day."

Caleb recalled the note from Kat, and they rose in unison from the bench. It had been a beautiful afternoon and an enjoyable time getting to know Dori better, though he felt as if there were so much more to know about her. He thoughtfully contemplated all that he had learned and savored the waning daylight on their walk back to the hotel.

*   *   *   *

Katrina patiently waited as the remaining vampires departed the conference room. It felt like such a long day for their first meeting, and she wondered if successive days would feel the same. Part of her wished that she had declined to attend the summit at all.

Caleb and I could've toured Europe alone, she brooded.

Yet, she held a fond, sometimes annoying, dedication to her former mentor. She realized that she would have felt intense guilt for ignoring his plea for her assistance.

So, here I am.

Alton shuffled some papers and waited for a lingering attendee to depart before closing the door behind them.

"The first day's always the hardest, breaking the ice and whatnot," he absently said in his crisp English accent.

"You've got a lot more to break than ice," she supplemented as she recognized the prevailing mindsets that had formed among the group. One third was receptive to forming a formalized interest group. One third wanted no part in any of it, and those remaining were undecided.

"We have to sway the uncommitted to tip the scales," Alton ventured.

"Why does it matter? Those who want to join into a consortium are free to, and the others can do as they please," Katrina declared.

"But you're mistaken, my dear," Alton gently disagreed. "If this conference ends without a clear consensus among the participants, everyone outside, those remaining to be recruited, will see only division. Then we're left to forming little cliques around the world, like little fiefdoms all vying for vassals. No, I lived through that failed approach nearly a millennium ago, and I won't endure it again."

She considered her eight-hundred-year-old friend and the life experiences that he drew upon to form his logic. Feudal England was something less than savory on a global level, particularly for her kind. Wars would be the likely result and the end of anonymity from the human race.

"What's next then?" she pressed.

The edges of his mouth upturned slightly.

"You and I need to frame a detailed agenda before moving forward, one based upon addressing the concerns voiced today."

"Much of today's discussions were over semantics, actually," she countered.

"Indeed. But semantics conceal larger concerns, and the better prepared we are to shape the discussion around those, the more successful we'll be," he explained.

"You're almost relishing this, aren't you? This is like some big parlor game for you, isn't it?"

"Oh, please," he retorted with a flash of his hazel eyes. "Don't assume that just because I was a feudal lord I'm playing at kingdom-building. I've seen the writing on the wall for longer than you've been on this Earth, and I knew it would come to this someday. I take it, then, you'd like to see the world cast into flames while we battle amongst both humans and ourselves?"

"Of course not," she snapped. "I just didn't want to be at the center of the matter, that's all."

He lightly patted his hand on her shoulder while standing behind her chair.

His stare grew distant as he offered, "I know that, my dear. You always were the shy one, weren't you? Never wanting to be the center of attention, yet always commanding it by your mere presence. I knew that you were an alpha the moment I laid eyes upon you."

She affectionately touched his hand in silent response. In truth, he had been the kindest of mentors to her and the dearest of friends.

"Come, my dear, let's go find our mates. We promised to join them for dinner, remember?" he offered with a final pat on her shoulder.

Katrina rose from her chair with a curious expression at his revelation. "So, you've taken Dorianne as your mate?" He paused as he gathered his paperwork into a central stack and placed it in his leather satchel.

"Actually, I meant to announce it at dinner tonight."

"I'm happy for you," she sincerely offered. She cherished having Caleb in her life, and she wished the same happiness for Alton.

He winked and held the conference room door open for her to exit.

*   *   *   *

Caleb sat on a leather guest couch in the lobby while watching the stream of vampires exit the hallway leading from the wing of conference and special-purpose rooms. His eyes expectantly swept across the group as he looked for Katrina, while Dori patiently sat beside him reading a travel magazine.

His focus settled on a younger vampire with gold-fleck eyes and short brown hair who was holding a leather briefcase in one hand. Major Pietari walked over to him, and the two of them waited for an available elevator car.

"Hmm." Something about the briefcase looked familiar to him. Then it occurred to him that the briefcase looked like the one the courier had earlier in the day when he had been visiting Paige in the security office.

"What?" Dori asked as a host of vampires and humans reunited with each other in the lobby.

Her eyes followed his to the major and his fellow vampire. She took a notepad and ink pen from a nearby table and wrote, *Major Pietari and Baldar Dubravko?*

Caleb's eyes focused on the notepad.

She wrote: *Something wrong?*

He reached over to take the pad and pen from her and wrote: *Briefcase seems important. Something I saw this morning.*

Dori's attention shifted to the two vampires just as they entered the elevator, and she spied the item in question. She turned to look at Caleb with a curious expression.

He wrote: *Who is BD?*

She took the pad from him and wrote, *Croatian. Powerful. Wealthy. Big player here.*

The wheels in Caleb's mind turned, and he wondered if the man in the security office had delivered the briefcase to Dubravko, or if it had just been a coincidence.

"What are you two up to?" Katrina asked, causing both of them to start in their seat. She distinctly heard their heartbeats jump. *Something wrong?*

Upon realizing that it was Katrina, Caleb launched himself from the couch and planted a kiss upon her lips.

"Missed you today," he muttered.

More than you know, he silently added.

"Mmm," she murmured into his kiss. Upon parting lips, she whispered with satisfaction, "I see that."

A strong duality of urges rose in her as she craved his body's blood and other carnal satisfactions.

Alton exchanged a quick kiss with Dori and wrapped one arm around her waist. "Hungry?" he asked. "I don't know about you, but I could drink a horse."

Dori groaned slightly and shook her head.

"Full disclosure, I got that one from Caleb," he innocently chimed as both Katrina and Caleb looked on with surprise at Alton's playful levity.

The four of them sat in the main dining room of the hotel chatting about their day. Due to the presence of other vampires in the area, both Katrina and Alton spoke of the conference in general terms, pointedly withholding any critical mention of their concerns moving forward. Instead, most of the conversation gravitated around Dori's and Caleb's assessment of the scenic mountainous area.

When Caleb mentioned looking forward to seeing the nearby town of Podjelje with Katrina that evening, she looked back at him with hesitation, knowing full well that he was about to be disappointed.

"Actually, my love, Alton needs my help preparing tomorrow's agenda," she carefully explained.

His face fell. "But I thought –"

"I must apologize to you both. My fault entirely, actually," Alton diplomatically interjected. "But all's not lost. Dori, perhaps you and Caleb could go to town together this evening. I'd hate for you to miss it on our account."

Dori's eyes dashed to Alton, but quickly rested on Caleb. "It's true that I'd hate to miss going to town. Won't you accompany me, Caleb?"

Caleb was disappointed in the news, but he agreed, "Sure. That'd be fine, of course."

Katrina extended her hand to gently grasp one of Caleb's and supportively squeezed it. "Don't worry, we'll arrange time together."

The group fell silent for a time as Dori and Caleb ate their dinner and Alton and Katrina sipped at glasses of warm blood. Caleb's eyes fell upon the blood-filled crystal ware and a question resurfaced from earlier in the day.

"One of the things I noticed today while looking around was that most of the staff seemed on edge," he said.

"Surely being surrounded by vampires has to unnerve many of them," Alton suggested. "For some, it may challenge religious beliefs or other preconceptions of reality."

"Yeah, that occurred to me," Caleb agreed. "But what keeps people from exploiting those revelations?"

Katrina's eyes tentatively met Alton's as she started to speak, but the stately vampire interjected on her behalf, "Caleb, a reflection on the rules that you agreed to with Katrina should plainly suggest that every human employed here risks their lives to be anything other than dutifully silent."

"But it's still a significant risk for years to come even after the conference has long ended," Caleb pointed out. "How can you monitor so many people for the remainder of their lives, no less?"

"Some of the staff are volunteers who are already employed by a number of vampires in attendance here," Alton explained. "Much the same way that many of the vampire security guards are in the regular employ of a number of us. And as for the few humans not already contracted by a vampire, they're being handsomely compensated for their discretion."

"Yet threatened, as well," Caleb suggested.

"Cautioned, my love," Katrina pointedly corrected. "Not threatened."

He accepted the admonishment and politely amended, "Of course, a poor choice of words on my part."

However, in his own mind he still felt that "threatened" was more accurate. While he didn't want his mate or the other vampires he cared about to be threatened by exposure at the hands of a careless person, he also didn't like the idea of people being ruled by heavy-handed fear.

"Which is why a conference, or summit if you will, of this nature has never been attempted before," Alton said. "This could be viewed as a risky venture as much as an opportunity. The mere congregation of vampires in such a small area at one time is unprecedented, particularly when mixed with the number of humans present. Still, it was hoped that the presence of human companions might ease the tensions of the human staff members. Thus far, I've been quite happy with the results."

"It explains the large contingent of security guards, as well," Caleb said.

"The human guards are more numerous during the day simply because vampires are more vulnerable and have to be relegated to finite locations," Alton said.

"Are you aware of any perceived threats?" Dori asked with a note of concern.

Alton lightly patted her hand. "Of course not, my dear. Merely a precaution." The group fell silent again as Dori and Caleb finished eating while the vampires nursed their drinks. Following the meal, Alton signaled to their waiter, and a bottle of wine and crystal glasses appeared at their tableside. As the waiter departed, and to all but Alton's surprise, Paige suddenly appeared at the tableside wearing both her security blazer and a curious expression.

"Am I too late?" she asked.

"Right on time," Alton answered as he served a glass of wine to each of them and raised his glass in toast.

"Though you've each known me to be an intensely private person, you're among my dearest friends. It's in that spirit that I offer a toast," he quietly announced. "To Dori, for gracing me with her presence in my life, honoring me with her love, and agreeing to be my mate."

"Congratulations to both of you," Katrina offered. "May you be very happy together." Of the group, she was the least surprised, given that Alton had alluded to a companion the previous fall during their tracking of Chimalma.

"Here, here," Caleb added.

"So, you've finally taken the plunge, old man," Paige teased, eliciting a groan from Alton while Dori giggled.

"I'm equally honored, dearest, as well as indescribably happy," Dori demurred as she gazed upon Alton with adoration, at which each person sipped from their glass.

Paige pulled up a spare chair from a nearby table while Dori warmly repeated how she had met Alton. Though Caleb had already heard the story from her earlier in the day, he appreciated the charming tone that Dori used to deliver it.

Katrina held Caleb's hand in her own while listening to the recounting, and she thoughtfully beheld him as she recalled their own courtship. However, unlike their story, Alton and Dori seemed to have shared a more methodical and graceful courtship. She was very happy for her friend and hoped that they would have a long, happy relationship together, though she fleetingly wondered if Dori would be joining the ranks of vampires at some future point. Likely, her former mentor had already weighed such prospects well before declaring Dori his mate.

One thing about Alton, he's thorough, she credited.

As Dori finished her brief story, Paige imperiously arched one eyebrow and asked, "And why are we just now hearing about Dori?"

"I'm not one to kiss and tell," Alton slyly replied.

"Rather, you're just not one to tell, period," Paige remarked before sipping at her wine.

"Alton's merely a very private person while he deliberates," Dori diplomatically observed. "I respect that, actually."

"As you can see, Dori understands me all too well," Alton said with a gracious nod.

A few minutes passed in idle conversation until Paige upended her glass, sat it on the table, and announced, "Well, sorry, but I have to run. The major wants me to personally review the perimeter of the conference grounds and then check in with each of our second shift guards before our evening briefing."

"He's sure keeping you busy," Caleb observed.

"It seems the major's big on delegation," Paige mumbled.

She patted Alton and Katrina on the shoulder, congratulated Dori and gave Caleb a quick peck on the cheek before departing the dining room in a virtual blur.

"I like her," Dori said.

"Paige is a hoot," Caleb happily agreed.

"She's quite a character," Katrina dryly observed while possessively watching her mate.

Caleb innocently shrugged, sensing that the peck to his cheek had caught Katrina's attention and not in a positive way.

"Well, I regret that Katrina and I must leave you two for the time being," Alton announced. "But I hope you'll both enjoy the sites in Podjelje." He glanced at his watch and added, "I believe the shuttle is leaving in the next twenty minutes or so."

After hasty goodbyes, Katrina and Alton retreated to Alton's room to prepare the next day's agenda, while Caleb and Dori proceeded to the front of the hotel. As they boarded the small tour bus along with a group of fellow hotel guests, Aiden Henderson and his vampire companion, Talise, waved to them. Caleb and Dori took the empty seat in front of them and turned to visit. The journey to town was less than scenic for the human passengers as the bus traversed the often darkened mountain road, but the vampires occasionally commented on the splendid surroundings, including the heights of surrounding peaks.

The small town of Podjelje was a short distance from the conference site, but it seemed farther in the shroud of darkness outside. However, the town itself was well-lit by antique street lamps and the inviting luminance cast through the windows of small, street-side shops that appeared to have extended hours for the visitors. The bus pulled to the side of the town's central street, and everyone disembarked. The driver announced that two hours remained before their planned return to the hotel, leaving ample time to browse.

Caleb noticed that a couple of the vampire security guards were among the group, while the streets were patrolled by no fewer than three other local police officers. He momentarily wondered if the townspeople knew the true nature of some of the hotel guests. Surely, it must have been unusual for a busload of tourists to show up in town well past sunset.

"A penny for your thoughts, Caleb?" Dori asked while they walked behind Talise and Aiden, who held hands in front of them.

"Aw, nothing really," he evasively replied. "Just my usual musings."

She glanced sidelong at him and observed, "I was wondering what we must seem like to the town. Most of these shops must have been asked to stay open well past their typical closing times."

He sharply looked at her. "Are you a mind-reader or something?"

She shrugged. "Me? Hardly. Just considering all of the angles."

"You're Alton's dream-mate for sure," he quipped.

She giggled as they walked the quaint town street together. They perused the various shops for over an hour, which included a bookstore, two clothing boutiques, drugstore, hobby shop, antiques dealer, and local glassware vendor. Finally, they entered a candy shop where they purchased some chocolates to share.

They continued their walk, nearly reaching the opposite end of town, when Caleb pointed to a souvenir shop set off to one side of the street next to where the forest skirted the town limits. The four of them entered the moderately-sized building, noticing that the shop also served as an import service and distributor of fine silks.

Caleb picked out a small handful of novelties and was perusing the shelves near a small window when something caught his eye. The window looked out towards the nearby forest and a small brick building that appeared to be an automobile repair shop. A small exterior light attached to the building illuminated the area enough to see four men standing next to a nondescript delivery van. Three of the men he didn't recognize, though by the uniform one appeared to be a local police official. However, he clearly recognized the fourth person as Baldar Dubravko.

One of the men accompanied the police official into the van, and the vehicle proceeded further into the forest via a worn dirt road. The other man and Dubravko watched the van depart before turning and entering the small building.

I wonder what they're up to?

"Caleb, everything okay?" Dori asked as she touched his arm to get his attention.

He jumped slightly with surprise and snapped, "Be-jeezus!"

He quickly tried to collect his wits while running his hand through his hair. "Sorry. You startled me."

She looked at him with some concern and gazed out the

window with a curious expression.

"What did you see out there?" she whispered.

He frowned at her sudden change in behavior from innocently curious to suspicious and whispered, "Baldar Dubravko, a police officer, and two other men. Not really sure what they were doing."

Dori took note of her surroundings before offering, "Let's talk about it outside."

He made his way to the front of the store where he paid for his novelties, and they walked out onto the sidewalk. Aiden whistled from down the street and waved at them as he and Talise entered another shop.

Dori turned to stroll casually alongside Caleb and asked, "Now tell me."

He recounted the strange scene and waited as she quietly mulled over his revelations.

Finally, she offered, "Maybe it's nothing, just Dubravko conferring with associates."

"You don't really think that, do you?"

"Not really. Alton suspected that Dubravko might be up to something. It's doubtful that he supports the goal of the summit, despite his financial backing for renovating and upgrading the hotel's accommodations."

"What then?" he pressed, his mind racing with a host of possibilities all at once.

"I don't know," she replied.

"We could follow the van," he suggested.

She bit her lower lip and studied her watch.

"Not a bad idea, really."

Someone cleared their throat nearby, and they turned to see a local police officer standing not far from them. He wasn't the one whom Caleb had seen from the shop window, but rather one who had been patrolling the streets when they first arrived.

"You are guests from the hotel?" the officer asked with a strong Slovene accent.

"Yes, we're just shopping," Dori replied, turning on her charm.

"The shuttle, it leaves very soon," the man observed. "You should return to the loading area," he politely suggested, though with an insistent tone.

"Yes, of course," she replied. "Thank you."

The officer watched them walk back towards the bus. Barely twenty minutes later, the bus departed for the hotel, and Caleb and Dori were still ignorant regarding the nature of Dubravko's activities.

After returning to the hotel, they bid goodnight to Talise and Aiden and looked at each other with tentative expressions as they stood near a small fountain not far from the bus.

"So, how do you feel about a daytime stroll around town tomorrow?" Caleb asked.

Dori adopted a shrewd expression. "Why Caleb, I thought you'd never ask."

Caleb took a shower and wondered when Katrina would finish working with Alton. Somehow, he suspected it would be a while, so he passed the time in the suite sitting on the couch reading some materials that he had packed in his luggage for the trip.

He pulled out a recent issue of *The Chronicle of Higher Education*, which was renowned for its insight into relevant issues of the day affecting colleges and universities. The latest issue discussed the financial challenges of colleges during the recent nationwide economic downturn. One article decried the folly of releasing non-tenured faculty members from their contracts in order to save money.

It was the last thing he remembered reading before falling asleep.

Katrina entered the hotel suite and was surprised to find the lights on, as it was well after three in the morning. She quickly spied Caleb leaning back against the couch with his head cocked to one side, his mouth slightly ajar, and a newspaper absently strewn across his lap.

The scene fondly reminded her of when she used to watch him through his apartment window from the vantage point of his fire escape.

I was quite the stalker back then, she quipped while kneeling at his side.

She lightly ran her fingertips across his cheek, concerned by how uncomfortable he appeared in his sprawled position. He stirred slightly, and she kissed him on the forehead. He smiled, suddenly realizing that she was next to him, and began to stretch.

She helped him from the couch, and he half-staggered into the bedroom. She held the covers aside as he slipped beneath the sheets, and she kissed him on the lips.

"I'll just take a shower and be right back," she promised, and then shed her clothes.

Caleb intended to remain awake for her, but quickly succumbed to sleep once more.

Katrina finished her shower and shook her head at his slumbering form as she exited the bathroom. Instead, she appreciated the time lying in bed next to him for a few hours while contemplating the early events of the conference.

It appeared that she would have less time to spend with Caleb than she had originally planned, and she hoped he would understand. Then again, it wasn't as if she were particularly happy about the development herself, and she silently cursed Alton for getting her involved at such key levels.

Yet she was beginning to share Alton's concern for the implications of an unsuccessful end to the summit and felt compelled to support him.

Time passed quickly as she lay beside him, appreciating his rhythmic heartbeat and falling into a sort of meditative trance. She even dozed for an hour or so, though she was actually still days from needing any sleep.

When she finally stirred and noted the clock on the nightstand, it was time for her to rise again. She gently slipped from beneath the sheets, dressed, applied some makeup, and lightly kissed Caleb on the forehead. After placing a note on his nightstand, she quietly departed the room.

Upon waking, Caleb immediately realized that Katrina was no longer next to him, and he groaned.

Gone already? Dammit, he silently cursed, wishing that he could be a vampire and not waste valuable time sleeping.

He never even had a chance to discuss what he saw in town the night before.

Maybe Dori told Alton, he hoped.

He rubbed his eyes and reached over to read the note on his nightstand.

Dearest Caleb,

Sorry I was so late last night, my love. It will probably be another long day in the conference, so try to do some sightseeing on your own. I'll see you tonight, and I'll make it up to you somehow. (Use your imagination!)

Love,
Kat

He placed the note back on his nightstand.

This trip is going to end up as a scrapbook full of scenic pictures and notes from Kat, he sardonically determined.

He dressed, shaved, and took the time to check his email on his notebook. After checking his personal messages, he logged into his college account.

Unfortunately, the article he had read the night before about college budgets' being tightened was prescient. Robert Fulton Community College was expecting harsh budget reductions as they looked to the new fiscal year, slated to begin July 1. Among the list of reductions in travel expenses and supply purchases was a possibility of staff reductions. Apparently, more information would be forthcoming in the coming week once the legislature had allocated funds to state agencies, including funding to higher education via the State Regent's Office.

He shook his head, hoping it wouldn't come to that.

He shut down his notebook and called Dori before proceeding to the hotel restaurant for a late breakfast. She was already seated at a table in the corner when he arrived.

"Good morning," she happily greeted as he sat down.

"Ready for a little sleuthing?" he asked in a mock-conspiratorial tone.

Her eyes darted around her. "You mean, *sightseeing*, don't you?"

He tried not to look too obvious as his eyes swept the room. Other than some other human companions eating or visiting, he didn't spot anybody within hearing range and certainly no vampires.

"Um, yeah, sightseeing," he agreed with a quirky expression.

She's awfully serious about this spy stuff, he observed.

A pensive, yet polite, waitress took their orders, and they passed the time casually visiting while waiting for their food. No mention was made about their suspicions from the previous evening or about their plans for the day other than going into town to peruse the shops at length.

Dori said that the shuttle was leaving for town within the hour. They quickly finished eating and made their way outdoors to sit and wait until the shuttle was available for boarding.

It was a beautiful day, and the scenery was breathtaking. For the first time since his arrival, Caleb looked forward to enjoying the sights unimpeded by darkness. He only wished that he could share his experiences with Katrina, and he momentarily lamented her shared chairmanship responsibilities with Alton.

Upon arriving in town, there was far more activity than the prior evening. Citizens went about their business shopping or doing errands, while tourists blended into the scene before them. Caleb noted that, unlike the previous night, there were three human hotel guards, though they sported only small side arms. No local police were evident, save for an empty patrol car parked across the street from where their shuttle was parked.

Rather than go to the souvenir shop where Caleb had seen Baldar Dubravko, Dori led him to a nearby crafts shop where they browsed at length. And while he pretended to be interested, he couldn't have been more bored in his life.

However, she seemed to gauge his interest level, because she smiled to herself as she perused the crafts. In the end, she purchased a couple of knick-knacks before they finally left.

"Oh please, do try a little harder, won't you?" she sincerely pleaded. "Patience, Caleb."

The two walked down the street in the direction of the souvenir shop, but halted some distance away from the establishment as Dori abruptly sat on a park bench beneath an awning. She removed a small ceramic figurine of an angel from her bag and examined it.

Caleb joined her. "Why did we stop?"

"So that we have a few moments to survey the area. Did you happen to look for surveillance cameras last night? I know I didn't," she whispered even while studying the delicate figurine.

She absently observed the area, much like a tourist taking in the sights.

"You have practice at this, don't you?" he suspiciously asked.

He felt there was more to the young woman than met the eye, and his curiosity was piqued.

"Me? I'm just a curious tourist passing the time? Aren't you?" she meaningfully countered. "There's an older video camera in front of that jewelry store across the street, but I suspect it's just watching the shop's entrance," she said.

They sat for a few minutes, and Caleb took the time subtly to mimic her method of casually surveying the area. It helped for him to repeat the mantra "curious tourist" in his head.

"Video camera in front of the repair shop next to the souvenir place, but I think it can only view the front of the building and maybe part of the area in front of the shop," he said while gazing at the figurine in her hand.

"Very good, Caleb," she complimented. "You catch on quickly."

"Should we try an alleyway or something?" he suggested.

Her piercing violet eyes playfully pored over him as she replied, "Alton said you were a clever young man who thought quickly on his feet. Now, I can see why."

He blushed slightly as she placed the figurine in her sack and rose from the bench. He followed, and they proceeded further up the street, turning down an empty alleyway between two shops that appeared to be used as a delivery lane to the rear of the buildings.

As they made their way out of the alleyway, they noticed an older man unloading small boxes from the back of a delivery van, though he ignored them as he traversed between the van and the interior of his small shop.

Dori signaled Caleb to follow her and led the way towards the empty field of grass stretching away from the back of the buildings towards a nearby forest.

Upon reaching the tree line behind the souvenir shop, they proceeded through the trees and made their way to the dirt path that Caleb had seen the night before.

"The van went that way," he said while pointing in a direction that led deeper into the forest.

They proceeded along the dirt road at a leisurely pace so as not to draw undue attention if they were observed.

It was a beautiful day, and Caleb appreciated the fresh smell of the forest coupled with the sounds of chirping birds. They walked for about twenty minutes, and he noticed that the mountain overlooking the town loomed before them as they drew closer.

Finally, the road ended at a small clearing next to a rocky

outcropping on a sheered-off portion of the mountainside. Butted against the rock facing stood a single-story, windowless shed constructed of stone and sporting a tin roof. A single wooden-planked door was secured with a newer-looking padlock.

Caleb surveyed the area and focused on Dori with a perplexed expression. "What's a storage building doing out in the middle of nowhere?"

She shrugged. "Maybe for storing mining equipment?"

"What mine?" he countered as he walked further into the clearing.

While rocks had cascaded down the mountain to the base, there were no visible mine entrances to be seen. He scanned the area again, impacted by how the surrounding forest loomed around them like a natural wall. It gave the small clearing a claustrophobic feel.

"This is weird," he absently muttered.

Dori moved to the wooden door and tested the lock, which was secure. "We need to take a peek inside here," she insisted.

"Gee, and I left my lock picks back at the hotel," he chided.

She offered him a withering look and walked over to the nearby rocks and stones that had piled up in places. After hefting a couple of larger stones, she selected one to carry back to the wooden door where he was standing.

"Here's your lock pick," she quipped while dropping it into his hands. "Start hammering, if you please."

He nearly dropped the large stone and rolled his eyes. He used a series of rapid bashing motions, which included missing the lock on two occasions, only to hear her giggle as she covered her mouth with one hand. But after a few minutes, his ministrations were rewarded when the metal eyelet gave way around the lock, resulting in the still-closed lock's dropping to the ground. He cast the stone to the ground and gaped at the still-secured device with frustration.

"That's fine, Caleb," she reassuringly offered. "You nevertheless dislodged the lock."

"Hey, it's one of those heavy-duty ones," he pointed out

somewhat defensively. "I mean, they're supposed to be able to take a bullet and stay locked, you know."

"I'm sure," she temporized while pulling the door open.

The hinges groaned as the door swung open to reveal that the interior was lined with a solid sheet of metal, making the door quite formidable.

"That's a deceptive-looking door," he noted.

The interior of the ten-foot-square shed consisted of old wooden benches to each side, strewn with a variety of old gardening and mining tools. The entire back wall was comprised of wood and bore only a large pegboard with poorly-maintained hand tools hanging from utility hooks.

"This is strange," she said.

She quickly felt underneath the benches and visually inspected the surfaces. Taking her lead, Caleb entered to assist.

After a few minutes of fruitless searching, Dori pursed her lips with a contemplative expression. "What are we missing here?" she asked.

He looked up and noticed a string hanging from a light fixture. He pulled it, and three bulbs illuminated the room through a single, dingy glass globe.

"Doesn't it strike you as strange that an old storage building next to a mountain has functioning electricity?"

Her eyes widened and she rushed outside to look around the perimeter of the building.

"But there's no electrical poles or exposed cabling anywhere," she observed.

Caleb stood in the open doorway with narrowed-eyes. "That means it's buried underground. But then, where's the fuse box?"

She slipped past him and shifted around old crates. Meanwhile, he shuffled the items on the pegboard to see what he might have missed the first time. While clanging tools against one another he heard Dori yell, "Hey!"

He turned to see a mustached man wearing a local police uniform gripping Dori's upper arm as he yanked her outside.

His other hand held a metal baton, which swung downwards onto Dori's thigh as she tried to wrestle from his grip. She yelped as her leg collapsed, causing her to slip to the ground. "Asshole!" Caleb barked while lurching at the man. As he cleared the doorway, another baton came out of nowhere, catching him in the lower back. He grimaced as pain shot through his midsection and had no time to react as another swing caught him across the upper shoulder. He managed to grasp the baton firmly before it could be retrieved for another swing, but he felt an immediate shocking pulse of painful electricity course through him. The crackling sound filled his ears as his body failed to respond, instead falling to the ground as he gasped for breath.

"You are under arrest for trespassing," the man hovering above him announced in a thick Slovene accent.

Caleb felt the bite of metal as his wrists were cuffed behind his back, and he heard Dori protest, "You have no reason to attack us like this!"

"Shut up!" the other officer barked at her as handcuffs were applied to her wrists.

"What were you two doing here?" demanded the officer who was hauling Caleb to his feet.

"Identify yourself," Dori insisted as she eyed the lieutenant's insignia on his collar. "For a superior officer, you're acting like a common brute."

"I am asking the questions," the man replied. "What are you doing here? I won't ask again."

"You're making a bad mista –" Caleb began, but was cut short when the lieutenant slammed his fist into his temple, causing him to stagger to the ground again.

"Stop assaulting him!" Dori demanded. "We're just tourists!"

"Bah!" the officer securing Dori countered.

"Take her to the car," the lieutenant ordered. "I'll follow with him."

Caleb tried and failed to regain his footing as Dori was led away. She kept glancing back over her shoulder at him, but the officer repeatedly pushed her before him as they walked.

A moment later, Caleb was once again distracted as the lieutenant leered at him and balled up his fists. The first blows to the side of his head and midsection hurt the worst. After that, he felt only dull throbbing and retained awareness of little else.

*   *   *   *

Chapter 6

Politics and Polemics

*I*t was late afternoon as Paige strummed her fingertips against the desktop while staring at the displays before her. She clicked her mouse to switch between the various miniature surveillance windows, expanding one at a time to review the images. She momentarily lamented taking brief turns with the rest of the security staff to do the thankless task. *Still, my staff respects me for it,* she determined, believing that it was the right thing to do. *So very unlike the major, who wouldn't be caught dead taking a turn at it.*

She enlarged the image of the front lobby entrance and noticed the returning shuttle passengers filing onto the sidewalk. As she watched the faces of the arriving humans, something subtle nagged at her.

Then she perked up and used another camera view to look outside the front entrance where she had a clear view of the shuttle. She quickly scrutinized the images of the lobby interior and realized that something was missing, or rather someone.

"Where's Caleb and Dori?" she wondered out loud.

She surveyed the small office, and her eyes settled on the auburn-haired female guard who was typing information into a computer.

"Hey, Enora," she snapped. "Come over here and cover this station. I have to check into something."

The woman got up with a nod, but Paige was already halfway to the door before the guard took two steps. She rushed down the hallway and through the lobby until she reached the main doors, though she stopped where the first set of doors stood closed; they were the ones with the UV-protective coating. She paused to await two of the human security guards who were entering.

"Problems, Captain?" one guard asked.

"Didn't you count everybody before heading back from town?" Paige insisted.

"Yeah, I counted before we left," the other guard replied. "We had twenty-three."

The first guard looked at his partner with surprise. "Twenty-three? We took twenty-five with us."

The other guard looked completely embarrassed. "Oh, shit."

Paige shook her head and ordered, "You two get back to town with that shuttle right now. You're looking for Dorianne Rousseau and Caleb Taylor. You probably remember Caleb."

Both guards sharply looked up at the mention of Caleb's name.

"Well, hell," one guard cursed with immediate recognition.

"Yeah, hell, and it's coming soon if you don't bring them back now!" Paige confirmed with a flash of her bright blue eyes.

Both men almost ran into each other as they barreled back through the two sets of sliding glass doors to board the shuttle outside.

"Just great, all the guards in the world, and I get the Keystone Cops," Paige muttered under her breath while shaking her head.

She paused and added, "Gawd, what an outdated reference. I must be getting old."

She turned to cross the lobby in the direction of the security office then stopped, wondering if she should inform Katrina and Alton. Discarding the idea, she looked outside to the waning afternoon sun, wishing she had brought her leather riding outfit and cycle helmet.

"Get a grip, Paige," she mumbled. "Kiddo probably just got distracted and missed the bus."

Just after sunset, Paige made the fifth call asking for the status of the search for Caleb and Dori. She had sent two additional human guards to help inquire around town, hoping to expedite the process.

Then the radio buzzed to life.

"Captain, we just talked to a shop owner downtown. The lady said she saw Ms. Rousseau and Mr. Taylor being driven away in a local police car earlier in the day, but she didn't recall the time," the guard reported.

Paige frowned. *Police car? What the hell?*

"I'll call the local police," she said. "In the meantime, you head over there with another guard and find out what you can."

"Well, that's the problem, Captain," the guard explained. "I called the police station a few minutes ago after we talked to the shop owner. They said they don't have anyone there by those names, but when I pressed the matter, they said there were still people in custody that haven't been processed. And they insisted that they won't discuss detainees until they've been processed."

Paige cursed under her breath and snapped, "Fine, fine. Keep trying to dig up what you can from anybody else who'll talk. I'll handle things at this end."

"Yes, ma'am," the guard replied.

Shit, she thought.

Hastily, she penned out a note for Katrina and Alton and barreled down the hallway to the conference room. The two suit-clad guards at the front of the hallway held out their hands as she started to walk past them.

"Uh, Turner, they're still in session," one guard tried to inform her.

She glared at him with blazing blue eyes and declared, "Too bad. I'm on a mission from God."

The vampires reflected surprise from her response, clearly taken aback by her insistence. As if sensing something grim, they each stepped aside. She proceeded to the door, knocked twice, and entered the room before being invited.

The room fell silent as all eyes turned to her with a mix of curiosity and incredulousness at the interruption. However, upon seeing that it was Paige in a tense state, both Alton and Katrina's expressions turned stony. The blonde vampire passed the note directly to Katrina, turned on her heel, and walked out of the room, closing the door behind her.

Katrina read the note: *Caleb and Dori in trouble in town. Detained by police. Can't get information. Three more minutes, and I'll handle it.*

She glared at Alton as she passed the note to him. He took a mere second to scan the note and immediately turned to address the group.

"My apologies, but we have an urgent matter requiring immediate attention," he explained in a firm tone. "We're adjourned until tomorrow morning."

Katrina sprang from her chair before Alton was able to push himself back from the table, but he managed to catch up to her as she barreled down the hallway towards the lobby.

He caught one of the suit-clad guards by the sleeve and ordered, "Bring a vehicle to the lobby entrance immediately."

Katrina could only contemplate dire thoughts as she scouted the lobby for Paige. Spotting the young vampire, she was at her side in seconds. Paige filled her in on what she knew, and Katrina listened even while she focused on getting to Caleb and Dori as soon as possible.

Dammit, dammit, dammit! What the hell happened?

Paige sensed her friend's concern and gently touched her arm. "Whatever's happened, we'll fix it. I promise."

Katrina forced a heavy sigh. "I know. Don't worry. We'll get to the bottom of this. Stay here."

"Oh, no, I won't," Paige protested. "Our boy's in trouble."

"Yes, you will," Katrina ordered. "I need you here to coordinate resources, if necessary. If you don't hear from me in less than an hour, you bring everyone you can trust and meet us downtown."

Paige nodded her assent with hooded eyes as she folded her arms before her.

Alton beckoned to Katrina from the front of the lobby, and she moved like a blur to the exit and the vehicle waiting outside.

Katrina barely contained her growing agitation as the SUV seemed to take a leisurely pace down the dark mountain road leading to town. In fairness, the vehicle was moving at a rapid pace thanks to the keen reflexes of a vampire driver, but any delay seemed unbearable.

Alton spent most of the time on his cell phone, which from the part of the conversation that Katrina could overhear, indicated that he was consulting with legal counsel on the finer points of Slovene law.

I don't care about Slovene law, she darkly resolved while chewing the inside of her lip. *I'm getting them out of there tonight.*

The Podjelje police station was a two-story brick building with a small parking lot and a single police car parked in front. Their SUV barely came to a stop before Katrina opened the passenger door, but Alton managed to grab her by the upper arm as he held his cell phone in the other hand.

She glared back at him with a stern expression.

"Go in, but don't attack anybody, for God's sake," he urged. "I'll follow as soon as I finish this call. I'm sure they're fine, Katrina."

She tried not to slam the vehicle's door closed too hard as she exited. The vampire guard observed her from the driver's seat as she proceeded up the front sidewalk.

The building's exterior lights cast a pale glow across the front entrance of the building as she approached the dual glass doors. The door made a swooshing sound as she deliberately controlled her strength and speed. A short hallway led into a small waiting room where a lone, young-looking police officer stood before a long, high counter idly sorting paperwork before him.

The front part of the facility appeared to be devoid of other people, which she confirmed with her keen sight and hearing as she stalked to the counter and glared at the man standing there. He warily observed her.

"I understand you are detaining an American named Caleb Taylor and a French woman named Dorianne Rousseau. I want to know the charges," Katrina commanded with authority.

The young man fumbled for a clipboard next to him and deliberately studied it for a moment. He moved to a small computer to his left, and following some quick typing, he regarded Katrina with a blank expression.

"We do not have people by those names processed here. Are you sure --" he said in English, but with a strong Slovene accent.

"Yes, I'm certain," she insisted. "They were brought in earlier this afternoon. Check again."

The officer raised an eyebrow and flipped some pages on the clipboard.

"Strange. The lieutenant mentioned two people detained, but I do not see any processing information."

"And that is proper procedure?" she pointedly countered.

The young man swallowed and appeared slightly unsettled. "Actually, no. I'm sorry, but I only arrived within the hour. Please, remain calm, and I will call my superior, Lieutenant Boleslav. He is upstairs, I believe."

He reached for the phone, but Katrina leaned across the counter to stare into his eyes. "Listen to me. I will see them now, and then you can call whomever you like."

The officer shook his head as he regarded her with a sincere expression. "I do not think I can do that."

Katrina steadied herself before asking in a lethally calm voice, "I know exactly what I'm going to do in twenty seconds. Do you?"

The man started to protest, but then frowned as if wrestling with conflicted feelings. "Things are already irregular. I will let you see them and then call my supervisor."

The young man seemed earnest in his behavior, and she detected no attempt at evasiveness.

"Fine," she replied simply. She wondered what could be taking Alton so long.

The man hesitantly opened the wooden partition to Katrina's right, thereby allowing her passage behind the counter. He led her down a short hallway where he unlocked a metal doorway at the end and allowed her to enter past him. The room held only two small jail cells, partitioned from each other by a concrete wall. Dori sat on a small bed in the first cell and launched to her feet at seeing them. Katrina noticed she had a blistered lower lip and slightly swollen cheeks, but otherwise seemed unharmed.

"Dori, are you okay?" Katrina asked.

"Never mind me, help Caleb," she urged.

Her words impacted Katrina at the same moment that she smelled Caleb's blood scent in the air. Her eyes flashed bright green, but were hidden from view of the police officer with her back turned to him. She peered around the corner wall partition to see Caleb lying on his right side with his wrists still cuffed behind him. His wrists were bloody where the metal dug into his flesh. He appeared to be only semi-conscious and had obviously been beaten from the contusions on his face, one side of which was badly swollen.

Katrina turned to glower at the officer with barely contained contempt. Part of her was breaking inside over concern for Caleb's welfare, while another part of her wanted to tear the place apart. "Open the cell," she flatly ordered.

The officer spied Caleb, and his eyes bulged to twice their normal size. "Oh no, this is horrible," the young officer protested with a look of alarm as he viewed Caleb's condition.

"You're damned right it's horrible," she snapped as her anger quickly skyrocketed. "Open this cell now!"

The officer fumbled with his keys as Caleb tried to raise

his head slightly and peer at her with squinted eyes. "Kat?" he weakly asked.

"Stay still, my love," she urged in as calm a voice as she could muster. In his wounded state, she was having a hard time tearing her eyes from his prone form.

"...beat me, but...didn't tell them anything," he muttered with a strained voice.

The implications in that simple statement impacted not only Katrina, but the officer before her.

"What?" the officer asked with disbelief.

"Katrina!" Dori exclaimed.

"Stop!" ordered a gruff man's voice.

Katrina turned to see a senior-level officer wearing a lieutenant's insignia, presumably Boleslav, holding a shotgun pointed directly into Dori's cell. Another police officer stood behind the lieutenant with an assault rifle pointed past his superior in the direction of Katrina and the young officer next to her. She noted that he had an ideal firing angle on them, which only complicated her available options.

The junior officer asked something of the lieutenant in Slovene. While Katrina didn't speak the language well, she understood some basic phrases and terminology that she had studied before their trip overseas. The young man had no idea what was taking place and was confused at multiple levels.

Boleslav ordered his subordinate to step away from the cells and leave the room. The young man looked at Caleb and Katrina and shook his head.

"They need medical attention," he insisted.

At least Katrina appreciated the junior officer's sense of ethics. Her eyes darted to Caleb, who remained prone on a cot in his cell.

"Move away, or you will be shot for aiding criminals in escape," Boleslav ordered.

It momentarily appeared that a standoff of sorts was in progress. Katrina's eyes narrowed to glowing green slits as she prepared to attack at her earliest opportunity. One problem was that the officer next to her was partially blocking her path. *Where the hell is Alton?*

The young man was visibly shaking, but he moved to stand before Katrina with his hands out in a placating fashion. In Slovene, he attempted to appeal to his supervisor's sense of proprietary and ethics, but failed to realize he was way out of his league at the moment. Katrina thought that he would be lucky to survive the next few minutes given the hard look in the lieutenant's eyes.

Alton suddenly appeared in the hallway behind Boleslav's crony and pulled him to the floor with one deft motion. The man's rifle discharged, but fired into the wall to his left.

As the lieutenant's attention was momentarily distracted, Katrina raced past the young officer in a blur of motion, knocking him into the bars of Caleb's cell. She managed to reach the lieutenant, knocking the shotgun barrel upwards. A spray of pellets blasted into the plaster ceiling.

Katrina broke Boleslav's right arm with one motion while slamming the man's head into the nearby concrete wall. His head impacted the wall with a simultaneous meaty thud and cracking sound. Fully enraged, Katrina openly growled as she picked up his body and threw it with amazing velocity.

Boleslav's body sailed across the room, impacting against the opposite concrete wall with a deep boom. It dropped lifelessly to the floor in a tangled heap as both Dori and the young officer watched in horror.

Alton rushed into the room to inspect both Dori and Caleb. Meanwhile, Katrina snatched the cell keys from the young officer's shaking hand and proceeded to unlock Caleb's cell door. She entered long enough to remove his handcuffs then casually tossed the keys to Alton, who turned to release Dori from her cell.

Katrina knelt beside her mate, gently rubbing her hands across his body to assess the damage to him.

"It's okay, my love," she cooed. "I'm here now. We're taking you to safety."

She meaningfully looked to her right at the junior officer, who was still in a state of semi-shock as he stared at her.

"Yes, yes," the officer insisted. "Medical attention for him."

"Are you okay, my darling?" Alton asked Dori as he momentarily embraced her.

"Yes, I'll be fine," she gratefully replied.

Dori hastily explained that the lieutenant had beaten Caleb, while the other officer had secured her in the police car earlier that afternoon. She recounted how Caleb was beaten again during a brief interrogation in his cell, but that she had been spared anything harsher than being repeatedly slapped.

Alton's jaw clenched as he looked at the younger officer, but Dori quickly explained that she hadn't seen the young man before.

"He just came on duty," Katrina irritably snapped as she lifted Caleb's shirt to view the bruises on his back and stomach.

"Get on the phone and call your senior officers. Get them here immediately," Alton ordered the young man. "I already called your town's mayor before I came in."

"Yes, of course," the officer dutifully stammered. "This -- this is -- no excuse. I don't understand."

"We'll talk about this soon enough," Alton interrupted him. "Go make the calls."

The man nervously slipped past Alton for the main office area. The stately vampire immediately went into Caleb's cell and stood over Katrina as she examined him.

"We need a doctor," she insisted in a tight voice.

"We'll use Dr. Reynolds back at the hotel," Alton replied. "I don't trust anyone else right now."

She merely nodded in agreement, not trusting her voice to utter anything further.

* * * *

At the hotel, a blanket from the police station was used as a makeshift gurney to carry Caleb gently from the SUV. The eyes of everyone in the lobby turned to stare with surprise as Caleb's gurney was carried at one end by Katrina and the other by Alton. Dori followed behind them with one hand rubbing at her jaw.

Dr. Reynolds was already standing in the lobby wearing his white physician's lab coat with Paige at his side, and he led them to his small examining room.

"Whoever did this is going to pay," Paige angrily muttered as she stared down at Caleb with painful disbelief as he lay on the examining room table.

I'll personally rip them apart, she promised.

Caleb weakly moaned, but his eyes remained closed as he appeared to drift in a semi-conscious state.

"The primary culprit is already dead," Katrina coldly muttered between clenched teeth.

"Good," Reynolds whispered as he used medical scissors to cut the shirt from Caleb's body, being careful not to tug on the material or cause him further pain.

Katrina's and Paige's eyes met briefly with surprise at the doctor's comment.

After a moment's pause, he added, "I'm a doctor, but whoever did this obviously enjoyed the task. The world's a better place without them."

Agreed, Katrina thought.

A momentary pang of curiosity echoed in her mind at what must have transpired in the hours that Caleb and Dori had been gone, though she realized that the time for explanations would come soon enough. Her primary focus returned to the wounded man whom she loved so dearly.

"Caleb? It's Ethan. Can you hear me?" Reynolds quietly asked as he lifted each of the young man's eyelids to quickly shine a penlight into them.

Caleb moaned again, and his eyes fluttered open.

"Ethan?" he asked.

He felt confused, and pain coursed through his midsection and head. His eyes managed to focus slightly, and he looked up into the faces of the doctor, Katrina, and Paige as each peered down upon him.

"Dori? Safe?" he asked with sudden recollection of the events at the police station, only hazily remembering arguing voices and the sounds of gunshots.

"I'm here, Caleb," Dori softly replied from a nearby chair. Alton stood with his arm gently wrapped around her shoulders.

"We need to examine you for injuries, Caleb," Ethan said.

"Ladies first," Caleb offered in chivalrous fashion.

He had no idea how injured Dori might be.

"Sorry, Caleb. This is a triage situation, and you won first pick," Reynolds lightly said.

"Lucky me," he groaned as a wave of pain shot though his stomach.

"I'll need to ask everyone else to move into my office next door, please. I need to examine him," the doctor politely instructed.

Alton gently led Dori from the room. Katrina looked at Paige and motioned with her head to the door. Paige patted her friend on the shoulder as she passed.

"I'll be right outside," she said.

After she shut the door, Reynolds looked at Katrina.

"I'm going to need a little space to work, please," he said before returning his attention to his patient. "I'll try not to hurt you further, Caleb, but you'll need to communicate with me as best you can. Can you try to do that?"

"Work your magic, Doc," Caleb said with a chuckle, which only sent another wave of pain coursing though his body.

Katrina marveled at how deftly and gently the doctor's hands played across Caleb in assessment of his condition. It was readily apparent to her that the handsome physician wielded his medical skills with both experience and passion. She had never seen a vampire with such a measured or sincere sense of duty to care for complete strangers before; certainly he was an anomaly in her centuries of encounters with her kind.

She watched as he continued to examine Caleb, and she was proud of how her mate was enduring what must have seemed a painfully slow process. When the doctor produced a small digital camera from his lab coat, Katrina's eyes flashed bright green, and her hand caught his wrist.

"It's okay," he reassured her in a soft voice. "We may need this as visual evidence in the future. I'll need to do the same with Dori. My intention is to begin their healing process immediately, which means there may not be as compelling evidence by tomorrow."

Katrina hadn't anticipated that. She reluctantly assented and released her grip on his wrist.

He offered a supportive expression and turned to take the photos. She helped to turn Caleb so he could more easily photograph the young man's back. The bruises and contusions on his body were distasteful hues of red, purple, and blue.

"You're missing my good side," Caleb weakly mumbled as he gritted his teeth to endure the discomfort of his body being rotated.

"Well, at least his sense of humor's intact," Ethan observed.

Minutes later, Katrina assisted the good doctor as he cleaned the wound areas on Caleb's body while further examining him. It amazed her that no bones were broken, though Ethan suspected that Caleb had bruised ribs.

"Would you be willing to use your saliva to close the wounds on his wrists?" Ethan asked while turning to retrieve items from a storage locker.

"You have to ask?" she shot back as if insulted.

I'd do anything to help him.

"I've learned not to make presumptions about humans relative to their vampire partners," Ethan smoothly explained.

She began licking at Caleb's wrists. The normally pleasant taste of his blood was tinged with the flavor of the rubbing alcohol the doctor had used to clean the wounds. Still, she felt useful being able to help minister to his wounds.

Familiar and soothing numbing sensations proceeded

through Caleb's wrists as he realized what was happening. Despite the pain still coursing through his body, he was suddenly so grateful for the caring vampires in his life, particularly his beautiful, red-haired mate.

Reynolds produced a handful of gauze and a small syringe. Katrina anticipated the task at hand and immediately unbuttoned the cuff of her blouse sleeve to allow access to the veins in her arm. He delicately withdrew enough blood to fill the syringe and turned to his patient.

"Caleb, I'm going to inject some of Katrina's blood beneath your skin now. My plan is for the healing to begin subcutaneously and work its way outward," he patiently explained.

Caleb briefly moaned and then managed, "Okay."

"Katrina, since you're here, would you please use your saliva to numb the areas next to his wounds while I follow by injecting the blood?" the dark-haired physician asked.

"Don't you want me to heal the actual topical wounds?" she countered.

He shook his head. "Unfortunately, no. If he's examined by other human physicians or government officials as part of an investigation, there would be too many questions about his rate of healing. However, if we begin the healing from inside first, nobody's the wiser, and Caleb still benefits. We can always use your saliva to expedite the surface healing later on," he explained.

She admired the doctor's forethought.

You're good. Much more than I could have hoped for, in fact.

For the next few minutes, the doctor injected small amounts of blood below or near the various wounds after Katrina numbed the injection points.

Caleb had already learned firsthand how robust the healing powers of a vampire's blood could be. And while the process sparked renewed waves of pain, he nevertheless appreciated the assistance.

Once Reynolds completed the injections, he turned to his

medical cabinet and retrieved a fresh syringe and a small bottle. "Just a little something to help him rest," he explained while injecting Caleb's arm with the clear liquid. "You can use the wheelchair in my office to take him upstairs to your room now." He put the syringe aside.

"Thank you, Dr. Reynolds," Katrina sincerely offered as she opened the doorway to reveal Paige standing there with a worried look on her face.

"Please, call me Ethan," he encouraged. "And you're welcome. I'll come up to check on him in a couple of hours."

Reynolds and Katrina gently placed Caleb in the wheelchair that Paige retrieved, and the two women prepared to take him upstairs. Alton and Dori entered the examining room as Caleb was wheeled out, but not before the brunette woman lightly touched Caleb on the shoulder in passing.

The lobby seemed overly busy for the evening as onlookers watched Caleb being wheeled away. A number of faces reflected sincere concern, while others appeared merely curious.

"I think I like Ethan Reynolds," Katrina mumbled to Paige in the elevator as she lightly ran her fingertips through Caleb's tussled hair.

Paige softly replied, "Yeah, me too. He's something, isn't he?"

Katrina's eyes darted to her friend as if recognizing something more in her statement, but Paige's expression quickly turned stoic.

* * * *

Katrina continued to watch over Caleb at his bedside while her mate slept. She felt so helpless just sitting, watching, and waiting. While she understood the need to curtail surface healing of his wounds, she nevertheless hated seeing the harsh appearance of his swollen face. Just imagining how painful it must have felt to him made her appreciate that Ethan had given him a sedative.

Caleb's body was slightly feverish as his immune system tried to kill the vampire blood cells that were rapidly repairing the damaged tissue below the surface of his skin.

She gazed down at his still form, wondering when he might wake. Despite his need for rest, Katrina wanted to chat with him about what had happened. She was dying of curiosity to hear his perspective on what had taken place in town. Yet she was relegated to sitting in the chair staring at him while listening to the steady rhythm of his heartbeat.

At least it's strong and healthy-sounding. That's certainly a good sign.

She lost track of time as her thoughts fluctuated between her mate, the conference, and a host of other concerns. When she heard a light rapping at the suite door, she quietly admitted Paige into the room. The blonde vampire offered her one of the two thermal mugs of warm blood, which she gratefully accepted.

"How's our boy?" Paige asked as Katrina shut the suite door behind her.

She had wanted to stay with Katrina as she watched over Caleb, but her duties interrupted her plans. Not for the first time since her arrival, she wished she were just a guest and not a key support person for the conference.

"Still asleep, but his heartbeat is strong," Katrina replied. "Thanks for stopping by."

"I'd have been here sooner, but –"

"No, it's okay. I completely understand," she interrupted as they sat next to each other on the living room couch.

"I met with Alton and Dori a few minutes ago," Paige said.

"How is she?" Katrina asked, suddenly ashamed that she hadn't called or gone by to check on Dori. Alton had done so much for Caleb and taken such an interest in him.

As if sensing her friend's concern, Paige reassured her, "She's fine. Sore, but she'll be okay. And don't worry, Alton said to tell you to stay here with Caleb. They plan to come by to see him tomorrow morning."

Katrina frowned. "But the conference –"

Paige held up her hand. "Alton's already rescheduled the start time for one o'clock, after lunch. I'll take over for you here when it's time."

Katrina nodded appreciatively. Suddenly, the conference meant so little to her by comparison to Caleb's well-being. It was as if her priorities had shifted one hundred and eighty degrees in a matter of seconds.

"Dori and Alton shared some of the details with me concerning what happened," Paige ventured.

She explained everything that had taken place from the time Dori and Caleb arrived in town that morning, as well as the suspicions they were following up on that led them to the storage building in the woods.

"But none of it makes any sense," Katrina insisted once Paige had finished.

"I know," Paige said with a shrug. "We've got nothing to go on, and the only two people truly implicated are either dead or sitting in the town jail."

Katrina's eyes narrowed. "Except for Baldar Dubravko's role in everything."

"That's if Baldar Dubravko even has a role," Paige corrected her. "Right now, all we know is that Caleb apparently saw the fellow meeting with people late one night in town. There's no grand conspiracy there. And besides, until Caleb wakes up to tell us what he saw, we don't have much more to go on."

Katrina didn't like her friend's tone and sharply looked at her. "You don't think there's anything to it? Why would the lieutenant act so wantonly towards Caleb and Dori then?"

"Hey, for all we know, the lieutenant and his cohorts don't like foreigners," Paige retorted. "All I know is our boy's seemed pretty bored and also has an active imagination."

"So, they simply mouthed off and ran into the wrong locals?" Katrina pressed. "Wrong place at the wrong time, so to speak?"

"I'm just sayin'," Paige replied.

They both fell silent and sipped at their mugs of blood for a time.

"I'm sorry," Paige finally offered in a quiet voice.

"No, it's okay. You could be right," Katrina replied.

Her eyes drifted to the bedroom beyond and became a distant stare. She recalled the recent happiness that she and Caleb had shared on their camping trip before the conference became a pressing topic in their lives.

She merely wanted to enjoy spending time with him as they built their life together. The machinations of vampire politics suddenly paled by comparison to a simple day spent with Caleb. She adored his kind nature, was drawn to his fit physique, and relished the compelling way that his blood called to her. Another moment's reflection was all that was required for her to wish that they hadn't even come to Slovenia.

*   *   *   *

As if matters hadn't already become complicated with Dori and Caleb's experience with the local police, the conference itself progressively devolved into discord and chaos. After sitting at Caleb's bedside overnight and into the next morning, Katrina was compelled to reconvene with the rest of the attendees at Alton's insistence. Though polite, she greeted her former mentor in a disinterested manner as she sat to his right at the head of the table.

You'd feel differently about this if Dori had been more seriously injured, she thought.

Then a wave of guilt flowed through her as she realized the delicate balance that Alton was trying to find in spearheading the diplomatic endeavor before them.

As if in silent reply to her thoughts, Alton slipped a small folded piece of paper to her while shuffling agenda paperwork. It read, *I can only imagine what you're feeling, and I know where you'd rather be. Just know how much I appreciate your*

help. – A.
She maintained a neutral expression as she folded the note and slipped it into her folder of paperwork. The edges of her mouth upturned slightly as she focused her attention upon him.

He turned to address the group to initiate the day's topics. For a few scant seconds, a fond feeling washed over Katrina. *Alton understands me better than I give him credit for sometimes.*

As on previous days, two opposing factions of perspectives propelled the discussions, or rather, debates. The pro-unification faction wanted to discuss far grander issues than the mere concepts of cooperative agreement among their kind.

The opposition decried the loss of independence or individual control at the mere mention of collaboration or cooperation. A much smaller group of neutrals merely listened, waiting to see who would gain the upper hand.

Alton did his best to operate as mediator, but the opposition kept leading him to take sides on a matter, as if goading him to commit to a perspective. Katrina clearly saw the tactic for what it was, a ploy for them to cry foul under the auspices that the moderator's view was biased from the start.

She admired her friend for his sense of measured patience and unwavering commitment towards his duties as chairperson. She realized how useful his past experiences dealing with squabbling English nobles many centuries ago were for the task before them. In some ways, she envisioned how suitable he would be to lead the group in a more autocratic setting.

Still, she conceded that may have been in part to how well-favored she was in Alton's eyes. She did her best not to smirk at that thought while listening to another tirade from Dominic Ambrogio on the unsuitability of the conference without a larger representative group of vampires in attendance.

Once again, Alton patiently reminded the persistent fellow that the conference's mission was to formulate basic premises to advance their kind on a global scale after the summit concluded. Katrina clenched her jaw while silently wishing she could rush over to snap the complainer's neck for impeding the discussion. *Hmm, perhaps I'm a little autocratic, too,* she assessed. The moment quickly passed, and her mood darkened again. *God, how I hate this conference.*

* * * *

By mid-afternoon, Caleb managed to sit upright at the small table in their suite wearing a t-shirt and sweatpants as he took another bite of his cheeseburger. The mere act of chewing sent aches through his jaw.

Dori sat across from him wearing designer jeans and one of Alton's long-sleeved shirts while picking at a salad with her fork. Caleb's swollen and bruised face gave him the appearance of the loser from an intense boxing match, while Dori's swollen lower lip and reddened left cheek suggested she had been in a domestic dispute.

Each was keenly aware of the aches, pain, and soreness accompanying their sorry physical states. It was their mutually unpleasant conditions, coupled with wanting to avoid the stares of staff and visitors alike, which caused them to sequester themselves in the suite in the first place.

"Still curious about that storage building?" Dori asked.

Caleb stopped chewing, glared at her with a dower expression, and mumbled, "Not on your life. I'm too sore to care right now."

"Agreed," she said with a nod. "And besides, Alton told me not to go to town without him."

He continued chewing, albeit tentatively.

After swallowing, he offered, "Yeah, Kat made it quite clear, in that stern but friendly way only she can pull off, that I wasn't to leave the conference property without her or Paige."

He felt like a child who had been grounded, though he wasn't feeling particularly adventurous, either.

"Baldar Dubravko's up to something," Dori affirmed. "We just don't know what yet."

"Not that I can convince Katrina of that," he countered. "She doesn't want me anywhere near him."

He recalled his attempts to get Katrina or Paige to go look at the storage building, but each declined on the grounds that relations were strained enough with the town while the mayor's internal investigation continued.

A knock at the suite's front door interrupted them, and Caleb shuffled slowly across the room to answer it. Madison Baker and Aiden Henderson greeted him, and he made a sweeping gesture with one arm to invite them in. He winced from the pain that shot through his shoulder at the attempt.

"Maddy, Aiden," he politely offered, "this is Dorianne Rousseau, Alton's mate."

"Dori, please," the violet-eyed Frenchwoman insisted. "And I recall being introduced to each of you at the reception that first evening."

The two visitors hesitantly glanced at each other before Aiden spoke up.

"Uh, Caleb, we just came by to check in on you and see how you're doing. We thought maybe you might want us to pick up something for you in town."

"Nah, thanks. There's not much I really need," he appreciatively replied.

Maddy and Aiden focused on Dori, who merely shook her head.

"Well, we're not actually going into Podjelje right now, given all that's happened," Maddy hinted.

"Oh?" Caleb asked.

"Alton and the other vampires voted first thing this morning to ban all hotel tourist access to Podjelje, except when in the company of a vampire," Maddy said. "At least until the investigation is over."

Caleb's eyebrows rose with surprise. "I see. So, where are you two going then?"

"Yeah, well, we're actually headed into the town of Jereka," Aiden explained. "It's further away, but a nice day trip. And it's larger than Podjelje. But we're the lucky ones because we made the first roster."

"Roster?" Dori asked.

"My mate, Talise, said that Alton convinced the other vampires to accept new traveling terms for the human companions. No groups larger than twelve, and there must be a human security person with every four tourists. It's pretty competitive getting on the roster right now. It seems that everybody's anxious to see more of the country all at the same time," Aiden explained.

Caleb and Dori exchanged meaningful looks before returning their attention to Maddy and Aiden.

"Yeah, I guess I can see the allure of venturing out," Caleb conceded.

"Well, anyway, we're leaving in the next half hour or so and wanted to check to see if you wanted anything," Maddy offered.

"Oh, well, thanks," Caleb said. "I'll probably just go down to the lobby bookstore and find something to read."

"Just a friendly word of advice for you two," Aiden offered. "Most of the human companions are pretty irritated with you that you've drastically curtailed their sightseeing liberties, so I wouldn't be surprised if you get a cold reception from them for a while."

"Oh, really?" Dori irritably asked.

"Hey, not us," Maddy retorted with an upraised hand. "We figure you two must have run into something really wrong in town. You, in particular, don't seem like the kind to cause trouble."

"But then there's Caleb," Aiden interjected, "A lot of folks think that after yesterday and the earlier scene in the lobby that first day that you might just be one."

"One..?" Caleb vaguely alluded.

"Troublemaker," Maddy said.

He adopted an offended expression, and his mouth gaped

open slightly.

That's outrageous!

Dori smirked, discreetly covering her mouth with one hand, and Aiden bit the inside of his lip while smiling.

"Oh, come on," Caleb stammered. "I'm a trouble-*magnet*, at worst."

"Hey, don't shoot the messenger," Aiden replied. "And we'd better get going. We don't want to lose our seat on the shuttle."

"Take care, you two," Maddy offered as she followed Aiden to the door. "If we happen to see something interesting, we'll bring something back for you, okay?"

"Thanks, Maddy," Dori said.

"Yeah, thanks," Caleb dejectedly replied. "Have a good time."

Aiden started to say something, but only nodded and preceded Maddy through the door. She winked and mouthed the word "troublemaker" as she closed the door behind them. Caleb immediately turned to Dori with an exasperated expression.

"Hey, admit it, you've got a track record of sorts," she temporized.

"Oh, hush," he snapped while folding his arms in front of his chest.

Troublemaker, indeed!

*   *   *   *

The conference session lasted all day and into the early evening, but Caleb spent the entire time sequestered in his suite. He felt achy, sore, and in no mood to confront negativity on the part of the other vampire companions.

Paige was quite busy, but managed to check in on him periodically, even bringing him dinner from the kitchen. The spritely vampire helped improve his mood somewhat, including finding new ways to poke fun at his unsightly condition upon each visit.

"You look like one of Mike Tyson's old punching dummies,

kiddo," she commented once. On another brief visit, she teased, "Hey tiger, I see somebody took extra turns beating ya with the ugly stick."

Ethan also stopped by to visit during midday and again during early evening. Caleb appreciated the kind and sincere nature of the vampire physician, who reminded him a little of the London vampire psychologist, Dr. Roehl Guilhelm, who had helped him recover his lost childhood memories of meeting Katrina when she had killed his abusive father. His thoughts drifted to the revelation of memories that strangely felt so fresh and recent to him despite being from his childhood.

Well, it was a long time ago, but the memories are still new to me, he reflected.

When Katrina finally returned to the suite, it was nearly ten o'clock. She attentively evaluated his condition with a pained expression. It hurt her each time her thoughts contemplated the beating he had endured at the hands of the renegade local officials. While a simmering anger still persisted, she managed to keep it in check with increasing effectiveness.

Having been cooped up in the room all day, Caleb was quite interested in the conference events. He quickly sensed his mate's disdain for the affair and tried not to delve too deeply into matters. Still, he was left with the definite impression that things weren't going well.

"I really don't know how we're going to improve the tone, much less appeal to any sense of logic among the participants," she noted with resignation.

"We're?" he pressed. "I thought you really didn't want anything to do with it?"

"I didn't, at first," she replied. "But now it's starting to feel personal. Alton's trying his best, but even his diplomatic and political skills are starting to look strained."

"So? You can always say that you tried, right?" he said.

"I'm going to do more than try," she assertively remarked. "So far I've tried to stay on the sidelines, hoping that things might wrap up quickly. But instead, things are dragging along at a snail's pace with each and every objection. So now, I'm giving it my all, right alongside Alton. We're planning to strategize some more early tomorrow morning before the group reconvenes."

"They sound like a paranoid bunch," he observed.

Her eyes narrowed to slits. "I'm beginning to feel there's much more to it than just paranoia. The anti-collaboration faction, they have their own agenda, I think. It's like they're waiting for this to fail miserably, so they can proceed with something else. Somehow, I can't help feeling like Baldar Dubravko's steering the group."

"I knew it, Kat," he remarked with an intent expression. "If Dori and I can just –"

Her gaze fell hard upon him, practically pinning him to the chair where he sat.

"Stop," she ordered in a flat voice. "You're not doing anything, my love, except recovering. Why can't you just relax and enjoy the conference like the other companions?"

"But I can help," he insisted. "Dori and I think –"

"Enough," she commanded in an uncharacteristic manner. "I don't want to hear another word, Caleb. Alton and I are well-equipped to handle this, thank you. Besides, you and Dori aren't to leave the conference site without me or Alton."

"That's not fair, Kat," he retorted while rising from the couch to pace the floor. "We're not children."

"Perhaps not," she conceded.

She covered the distance between them in a second to stand before him and reached out to grasp him gently by the shoulders and stare down into his pale blue eyes.

"But recent events are unsettling, to say the least, and I don't want to see you in anymore trouble. I can't bear to see you get injured again...or worse."

He frowned, not quite certain if she meant his own behavior was unsettling, or just that of the local authorities.

"I'm not a troublemaker," he quietly stated while looking away from her.

She used one hand to turn his face back towards hers, staring into his eyes in a penetrating fashion. Her predatory visage bore into him, and she whispered, "You are a troublemaker, but I'm confident I can fix that."

He started to say something, but was silenced by her soft lips pressing against his as her palm cupped the base of his neck. Despite his sore lip, he immediately responded to her passionate kiss, forgetting his objections entirely.

Gone was the angst over their conversation, replaced only by his desire to be loved and wanted and embraced. His arms slipped around her waist as her kisses continued, and he hungrily pressed his sore lips to hers.

She relished their intimate contact, but pulled her lips from his long enough to resolutely stare back into his eyes.

"You'll remain on conference grounds for the time being."

He started to assert himself, but she quickly kissed him on the lips again.

"Promise me," she persisted as she pulled away from the kiss.

"For now," he quietly acquiesced. In his mind, he wasn't giving in so much as diplomatically conceding to a respite.

It wasn't exactly what she wanted, but it was the best she could hope for at the moment.

"Trouble with a capital 'T,'" she mildly chastised. "Come here, Mr. Trouble," she added, gently slipping her arm around his waist and guiding him towards the bedroom.

Despite his achy and sore condition, he managed to slip from his clothes, and they lovingly shared each other's bodies for the first time since their arrival in Slovenia. Their shared passion was tender, and each thoroughly enjoyed the companionship of the other. Then time stood still, at least for a few hours.

*   *   *   *

The next day, Caleb felt the cold stares of some of the other guests while making his way to the restaurant for breakfast. Fortunately, he was too sore and tired to care. Local investigators appointed by the mayor and police commissioner arrived after breakfast to interview both him and Dori. Much to their surprise, Alton attended Dori's interview, while Katrina was present for his.

To Dori's and Caleb's surprise, both Katrina and Alton encouraged them to be forthcoming with any information, save for their suspicions involving Baldar Dubravko. As for the storage building incident, both firmly held to the suggestion that the building had been broken into prior to their arrival, and they were merely curious. It was their position that they intended to notify someone, but the lieutenant and his officer showed up to engage them hostilely without provocation before they could explain, which was partly true, at least.

The only downside to the interview was the way that Katrina's intense stare penetrated into Caleb's eyes when she sensed the subtle change in his story involving the storage building's breach. However, she said nothing either during or after the interview.

In truth, he had already disclosed the entire story to Katrina beforehand, so it wasn't as if he were hiding anything from her. Still, it was unnerving to realize that he was being closely evaluated by her. Despite that, the investigators gave no indication of perceived doubt or suspicion, so he felt comfortable with his responses in the end.

Alton later informed Caleb, Dori, and Katrina that the investigators weren't getting a great deal of cooperation from the surviving officer who had attacked Dori, though Alton didn't mention where he had acquired that inside information. He suggested that the incident could erupt in unpopular media coverage, possibly generating an international buzz, which wasn't in Slovenia's best interests. He conveyed his suspicions that the case would be handled internally in the department, though Caleb was inwardly surprised that the story hadn't leaked out to at least a local news source yet.

The focus quickly fell upon the conference again, and both Katrina and Alton returned their attentions to vampire politics and subsequent debates. However, Dori and Caleb's attentions weren't so easily diverted, and the two met in Alton's suite to discuss matters further.

"Time to refocus on our objective," Dori said. "Dubravko's worth watching."

"We're stuck here for a while, you know," Caleb lamented. "All he has to do is leave the site, and we're in the dark."

He stretched his body's lean muscles, experiencing a series of aches and pains for his effort. While Katrina's blood had significantly healed his wounds, a great deal of recuperation still remained.

"Dubravko stays in the hotel for the most part, you know," she observed. "Besides, we still have to follow up on the storage building connection. There has to be something of interest in or around the area."

"And just how do we do that?" he asked.

"There's more to the process of investigation than skulking around the forest, Caleb."

"Who are you? Nancy Drew?"

It wasn't the first time he wondered about the woman's background, about which she had been cagey at best.

"Quaint reference, but no," she replied. "I have some additional venues of investigation that I'll follow up with. In the meantime, why don't you keep an eye on Dubravko's activities on-site?"

He stared at her in bland fashion. "Have you ever tried to sneak up on a vampire?"

She shook her head slightly and rolled her eyes. "Honestly, Caleb. And to think I once said you were quick-witted. Loiter in the lobby until he leaves the conference sessions, and discreetly observe him from a distance. It's not like you're not expected to be relegated to the conference property. Everyone knows you're grounded."

"Bad analogy, Dori," he said with a withering expression.

"Sorry," she quickly apologized. "Listen, just maintain a low profile and observe. There's no crime there, and it may reveal something tangible to follow up on."

"Well," he conceded, "I suppose it wouldn't hurt to camp out in the lobby for a time. Perhaps catch up on my reading?"

"Good idea," Dori agreed.

However, he was suspicious over the ease with which she had directed him. Somehow he had the impression that she had the more interesting angle to delve into, while he was relegated to nothing short of a child's errand.

"I'll let you know when I uncover anything," she offered.

"You do the same."

Caleb spent the next two days sitting in the lobby reading novels, magazines, or idly passing time on his notebook computer. When not enjoying one of the comfortable chairs or couches, he would perch on a stool at one of the bistro tables placed just outside the lobby restaurant. Fortunately, the bar staff would serve food and drinks there, even outside of the dining room's normal operating hours. And it was fairly scenic because he could appreciate the view of the grounds through the large floor-to-ceiling sections of coated glass that framed the perimeter of the lobby.

On the afternoon of the first day, Ethan, Aiden, and Maddy each briefly stopped by to visit and ask how he was feeling. However, most people gave Caleb a large berth, often completely ignoring him. That evening, Dubravko exited the conference and went directly to the security office carrying his telltale leather briefcase. Soon afterwards, Katrina and Alton appeared and accompanied him and Dori to dinner, idly watching them eat while chatting.

The next day, Caleb woke early enough to escort Katrina to the lobby, where he lingered long enough to notice Dubravko exit the elevator with Major Pietari before heading down the hallway leading to the conference room. By late afternoon, the conference let out early as Caleb dozed on the couch with a novel laid across this lap. He jolted awake in time to see Dubravko and Dominic Ambrogio enter the elevator and proceed to the upper floors.

Thinking he had gleaned nothing of value, he started to take a walk outside, but then halted upon realizing that he had missed something. For some reason, Dubravko hadn't been carrying his briefcase. He walked back into the lobby just in time to see Major Pietari carrying Dubravko's distinctive briefcase into the elevator. He watched as the car descended to lower level one, the basement area.

Why is Dubravko the only vampire carrying around a briefcase? Perhaps he hauls around a lot of cash with him wherever he goes?

"Whatcha up to, kiddo?" Paige asked seemingly out of nowhere.

Caleb lurched with surprise, and his head whipped around. "Geez, Paige!"

Her eyes immediately narrowed. "So, like I asked, whatcha doin'?"

You're up to something, my little friend.

"Oh, just hanging around," he evasively replied while glancing outside. "Not like I'm going anywhere interesting, you know."

"Hmmm. Yeah, so I've noticed. In fact, I've been observing you for the past two days, in between the major's endless errands, of course. Anyway, it seems like you've spent a good deal of your time just sitting around."

"Just healing," he replied. "Doctor's orders, after all."

"Uh-huh. Let's chat," she suggested while wrapping one of her petite arms around his waist and leading him across the lobby in the direction of a small, unused conference room on the other side of the building.

"You look good in a blazer, by the way."

"Whatever," she chimed, refusing to be distracted.

She ushered him into the small conference room and shut the door behind them.

"Okay, spill," she insisted as her bright blue eyes penetrated into his.

"Spill what?" he innocently asked, even as his heartbeat increased slightly.

"What you're doing hanging around the lobby. You're waiting for something, or watching someone."

"Aw, come on," he irritably countered. "I'm not bothering anybody."

"Stop spying on Dubravko," she flatly stated. "You're just going to piss him off, and that'll make things harder on Alton and Katrina."

He silently stared back at her.

How the hell did she know?

"Look, behind all this cute, playful exterior is a competent vampire," she chastised. "I'm actually good at what I do, kiddo."

He folded his arms before him, shaking his head slightly.

"I've never implied otherwise," he countered. "But if you're that good, then tell me what the major's doing with Dubravko's pet briefcase."

She blankly stared at him for a moment as she considered his request.

Briefcase? she wondered.

"Um, I dunno...let's think about that. Oh yeah, the major is in charge of security. So, it's likely containing valuables and needs to be secured. Hell, for all I know, the paranoid weasel probably keeps his secret 'usurp-the-conference-plan' in it or something."

The Croatian jerk's a pain in the ass, that's for sure.

"Somebody sounds kind of angsty. Maybe you need to cut down on the caffeine a little," he quipped with a playful shake of his finger.

Her eyes narrowed dangerously. "Don't push my buttons, punching bag boy."

He returned a bland, less-than-amused expression.

"Okay, so the major is securing the briefcase. Securing it where, exactly?" he asked.

She frowned at him. "Who's asking the questions here, tiger?"

He threw up his arms with exasperation and stormed across the small room towards the door.

"Well, crap! I can't even –"

She darted out with her hands to grasp him by the shoulders and steady him in one place.

"Okay, okay, just chill. I'll play, if you'll just take a deep breath."

He focused upon her with a flat, unimpressed stare.

"Probably the vault," she said. "Before the conference, they installed a really secure, bank-sized vault on the basement level. Then they walled off that section of the basement so that the primary controlled access is through the lobby elevator. But you still need a code for the car before it even stops there. There's a fire escape, but it's only a one-way exit in the stairwell. Kind of overkill in my opinion, but then, nobody asked me."

He pondered that for a moment.

"Can we get into the vault?"

"Dammit, Caleb!" she snapped with a bright flash of her blue eyes.

She took a deep breath and deliberately calmed herself before planting her hands firmly atop her hips.

"Kiddo, you're killin' me here. No, nobody but the major and the hotel manager can get in the vault. And no, I'm not asking for access, or for a tour for you."

His shoulders slumped.

I sure hope Dori's having better luck than I, he lamented. Of course, the Frenchwoman hadn't said much to him the past day or so.

"Can't you just play nicely for once?" she wearily implored. "I'm going crazy trying to keep up with things around here as it is. Hell, I haven't even had time to do more than drink a cup of warm blood now and again, much less get any rest."

"Look, please just check out what the major's doing in the

vault –" he urged before being cut off by Paige's holding up her hand for silence.

She cocked her head to one side and moved so quickly that the air whirled around him. The door to the room swished open, and she stood outside pivoting her head so fast that she seemed to view all directions at once.

She froze, cocked her head to one side again, and listened. Finally, she shrugged while reentering the room and closed the door behind her.

"Did you hear somebody?"

"See? Now you're making me paranoid," she chastised.

"I'm sorry." The last thing he wanted to do was make her angry with him.

I'm already pressing my luck with Katrina.

Her aggravation seemed to dissipate in mere seconds as she stared into his gentle eyes.

It's so damned hard to stay angry at him.

Her graceful, pale hand reached up to caress the side of his face, and she appreciated the rough, masculine stubble forming on his cheek. She lightly patted him, and then playfully pinched his cheek with her fingertips.

"Twerp," she muttered. "Try to stay outta trouble, will ya?"

He reached up to caress her hand. "I'll try, just for you," he promised.

His warm touch sent a small tingling wave through her, as a lover's touch might. She snatched her hand back, as if lingering there might burn it.

"Good boy," she said. "Now get outta here. I've got real work to do."

He walked past her as she held the door open for him. However, as soon as he departed, she contemplated the fleeting sensations that he had just sparked in her.

Then she forced her thoughts to other matters, specifically how urgently Caleb had pleaded his concerns about the major and Dubravko. She shrugged and made a mental note to try and pay more attention to them.

"Yeah, in all my plentiful spare time."

*   *   *   *

Once the active session ended, Katrina and Alton met at length with Talise Penbroke for a private meeting in the conference room after the other attendees had departed. Alton hoped that Talise's expertise in contract law could be leveraged for mediation of some agenda topic disputes. Katrina suggested that an arbitrative role instigated by Talise might help appeal to the negative, extremist elements in the room. While dubious, at least Talise seemed sincere and promised to try.

By the time Katrina returned to the suite, it was late evening. She found Caleb lounging on the couch watching a movie on television. He sat up and grinned at her over the back of the couch as she entered, which quickly warmed her heart. For the first time in a few days, and despite his still-evident physical injuries, her mate appeared more relaxed and settled. It brought a wan smile to her lips as she crossed the distance between them to kiss him.

"You're late tonight," he casually observed. "How did everything go today?"

She shrugged. "Pretty much the same as the day before. I'm just glad that nobody has walked out. That must say something about our efforts, I suppose."

He took her by the hand and led her to the front of the couch, pulling her down to sit next to him. Turning her away from him slightly, he massaged her shoulders and neck with his strong fingers.

The sensations were both soothing and welcome and evoked small moans of pleasure from her. She concluded that it was the perfect physical greeting after such a long, trying day. Moreover, she resolved to get some real sleep that night for a few hours.

"You're precisely what I need," she complimented as his fingers continued their ministrations against her taut muscles.

He's definitely in a better mood.

He kissed her neck in response to her compliment and murmured, "I love you."

Best of all, he kept massaging. It was the first night since their arrival that things felt more like they were supposed to between them.

She only hoped that it would last.

*   *   *   *

Chapter 7
Hidden Places

*B*y midmorning the following day, misery seemed to prevail throughout the conference. Once again, Katrina was stuck in a room full of vampires who were either disgruntled with the agenda or frustrated that their peers bickered over minor details. She glanced sidelong at Alton, noticing the stately vampire's jaw was firmly set as yet another disagreement between two participants threatened to turn personal. It took everything she had to curtail the weary sigh building inside her.

Meanwhile, Caleb sat alone in the lobby, upset that his trip to Europe was neither memorable nor enjoyable, even as his fellow visiting humans seemed to be blissfully engaged in what he coined "tourist mode." His body still felt quite sore and achy, though the affects of Katrina's blood had done him justice, and he felt much better than the day before. His mood wasn't helped any by an email he had read in his college mailbox from the President, Dr. Patrick Beaumont, regarding the upcoming fiscal year's budget.

Dr. Beaumont suggested that by the first of July there was a real threat of employee furloughs and layoffs for the upcoming fall semester. The email mentioned that final budget information was forthcoming later that week. Caleb hoped it didn't come to layoffs. He was one of the newest faculty hired at the College and might find his position on the cutting block.

By midafternoon, Dori stopped by to inform Caleb that she was collecting additional information, which she hoped would be helpful to their investigations. However, she was still very hedgy about the nature of her sources. It wasn't long before he grew frustrated sitting in the lobby trying to distract his dark thoughts by thumbing through a biography on James Madison, waiting fruitlessly for something noteworthy to occur. He popped up off the couch and proceeded outside for a walk, hoping the scenic surroundings and fresh air would improve his disposition.

* * * *

Paige sat in the security office feeling bored while taking a shift at the video surveillance monitoring station. Upon spying the lobby camera view of Caleb going outside from his perch, she smirked.

That's right, kiddo. Get outside into the sunshine for a while. Being a spy isn't so glamorous, is it?

Part of her hoped that he would give up his unhealthy fixation with Baldar Dubravko. As she lamented her own situation, her favorite vampire physician walked in the door to the office with an inviting smile and bearing two large Styrofoam cups.

"Greetings, fellow servant of the people," Ethan grandly offered with a sparkle in his eyes.

He placed a sealed cup onto the desk before Paige while sipping from his own. The aroma from his coffee wafted her direction as she studied the sealed cup before her.

"What's this?" she asked, popping open the plastic lid. The smell of warm blood quickly assailed her sense of smell, making her mouth water slightly.

"Just thought I'd stop by and say hello," he said. "And I didn't want to come empty-handed."

She sipped at the warm blood, savoring the flavor. She hadn't fed regularly in recent days with all of the additional duties the major had foisted upon her.

"Oh, that's good," she complimented with a satisfied tone.

"Thanks for *not* bringing me coffee."

He inclined his head and idly chatted with her for a few minutes. In fact, she could have sworn that he was openly flirting with her. Not that she minded, of course. But while she appreciated the company of such a charming and attractive vampire, she momentarily considered her stuffy supervisor.

"You're sweet, but I'm not really supposed to have visitors dropping by," she noted.

"Me? I'm not a visitor," he countered. "I'm a peer, a fellow employee. This is just your run-of-the-mill water cooler chit-chat."

She appreciated his quick wit and raised an apprising eyebrow. His lean-muscled body was sculpted in a manner that any woman could appreciate. She absently imagined tracing her finger across and down his bare chest.

Ethan idly chatted for a few minutes about his day, albeit with the sound of a man who wasn't quite sure of how to broach a topic. Paige couldn't help thinking that he was working on an angle to ask her out.

Would I or wouldn't I say yes? she wondered.

As if on cue, and with the poor timing that only she could have predicted as of late, the major stalked through the office door. He quickly panned the room, only to adopt a stern expression as he noted the doctor's presence. She had seen that look before.

"So, I'd appreciate your consideration of a sturdier lock on the prescriptions cabinet in my examining room," Ethan spoke up as if finishing the topic. "Not that we've had any problems, mind you, but I've worked in hospitals where even some of the staff were tempted. And what with the increasing prices of prescription drugs today..."

"Sure, sure," Paige smoothly replied. "I'll look into that for you."

She admired Ethan's quick thinking.

The major suspiciously regarded them.

"Well, I'll be going then," Reynolds said. "Have a great day,"

he offered with a friendly tone to Major Pietari as he walked
past him to exit.

"Problems?" Pietari queried.

"I think I can handle it," she said.

At least, I'd sure as hell like to try, she slyly entertained as
the major continued into his office.

She studied her monitor as one of the surveillance windows
displayed the handsome Ethan Reynolds walking back to his
office. She couldn't help but smile.

*   *   *   *

Later that afternoon, Caleb's mood had improved slightly as he appreciated the beautiful forested mountain scenery
around him. He discovered a couple of small walking trails
leading into the nearby forest and took one on a whim. After
only ten minutes, his cell phone rang, and he noticed that the
number was from his college.

"Hello?" he asked.

"Caleb? Hi, this is Paul," the friendly voice offered.

Dr. Paul Wright was Dean of Social Sciences, namely, Caleb's division. He got along great with Paul and appreciated the
casual, first-name basis they were on since he had first started. Paul was a favored person around the College, and a great
dean. However, given the earlier email Caleb read that day, he
had a sinking feeling that the call wasn't strictly a social one.
A queasy feeling formed in the pit of his stomach.

"Hi, Paul. What's up?" he offered in a friendly tone despite
his misgivings.

"Uh, Caleb, I know you're in Europe and everything," Paul
began with a rueful tone. "I would've waited to see you in person, but I felt that I needed to let you know as soon as possible.
You may not have seen a message from President Beaumont
that went out two days ago –"

"Yeah," Caleb interrupted, "I just saw it this morning when
I was checking messages. Doesn't sound too good for budgets

this year, does it?"

"Well, uh, no, not really, Caleb," Paul hesitantly replied in an uncharacteristic manner. "Actually, that's why I'm calling. Listen, there's still a lot that could happen between now and fall, but..."

Caleb thought he was going to throw up. "Looking like lay-offs, isn't it?"

The pause that followed was nearly painful to him.

"Yeah, Caleb, I'm afraid it is," Paul conceded. "Each division had to select some potential staff for layoffs based upon seniority, you see, and well, I had to add your name for our department. I'm really sorry, Caleb. Listen, it's not for certain yet-"

"But likely, isn't it?" Caleb pressed.

"Yeah, it's looking that way," Paul said. "Believe me, it's nothing personal and certainly not a reflection on your performance. You're one of my best, Caleb; your enthusiasm's made quite an impact on the students, as well as your peers. It's just, well, it's just a damned shame. And, hell, I just thought you deserved to know where things stand."

Caleb's mind raced as he felt his future spiraling into uncertainty.

"Any idea when you'll know for sure?"

"Probably the next couple of days, I think. Listen, I probably shouldn't have called you about this."

"I won't tell anyone, Paul. Besides, it means a lot that you'd warn me. You've been really great, so no matter what happens I'll always appreciate all you've done for me."

Paul swallowed aloud.

"Dammit with this seniority crap. Believe me, there's a couple of burnouts around here that I'd much rather see retire instead of letting fresh talent go."

"Ah, the tenure conundrum rears its ugly head."

Paul chuckled. "You'd valiantly jest in the face of a hurricane, wouldn't you?"

Caleb's tight-lipped expression demonstrated otherwise.

He just hated the idea of Paul's being riddled with guilt over the situation. *It's not his fault, after all.*

"Someone once told me that even if you don't have control over what happens to you, at least you have control over how you choose to react to it," Caleb offered.

"You're wiser than your years," the dean quietly offered.

Caleb shrugged. "I dunno about that. But listen, will you do me a favor?"

"Sure, if I can," he replied.

"Call me the minute you know something for sure, okay?"

"You got it. It's the least I can do," Paul promised.

The two said goodbye, and Caleb fell into a daze as he contemplated how both the trip and his personal career seemed to be going to hell all at the same time. His mood quickly grew dour, and he wandered into the forest while considering a host of prospective options for his uncertain future.

As he walked through the serene forest appreciating nature's own form of silence, the surroundings complemented his reflective mind. However, it also seemed lonely and added to his sense of melancholy. The sun had nearly set, and all that remained was a reddish-orange spectrum on the horizon, which seemed analogous to the sun's setting on what was his burgeoning career in academia.

Though the light was fading, it was still ambient enough to see where he was walking. He wondered what alternate paths he might soon be compelled to walk in life, as well.

Will they be lit well enough for me to see them?

After a time, he stopped in the middle of a small clearing. A couple of large trees appeared to have fallen against some of their neighbors, creating the small open area. It was peaceful, and the fallen trees reminded him of how things seemed to be going in his own life lately.

I'm practically ignored by Kat given the conference issues, he bitterly determined. *Now, the career I've barely started might be cut short just days from now. Damn.*

He stood as still as a statue, shallowly breathing in an almost trancelike state and contemplated the situation he might face upon returning home from the Slovenian conference. He felt so powerless over his circumstances, having no influence over the fiscal conditions affecting his college or the final staffing decisions to be made. While his confidence in the leadership at the College was strong, he also realized that unsavory decisions sometimes couldn't be avoided, no matter the good intentions of the decision makers.

What will be, will be, he conceded with resignation. It wasn't the first time that he had faced undesirable prospects.

His mind snapped back to the present upon hearing a shuffling sound behind him, like some animal walking past a bush. Then a small, snapping sound followed, and his muscles tensed. He slowly turned to his left while gazing around the area with a frown. After turning nearly completely around, his eyes settled on Paige.

She wore a pair of faded blue jeans and short-sleeved Interpol rock concert t-shirt. Curiously, the shirt had a black and red image of a deer in a forest being watched by a camera. As she casually leaned against a tree trunk staring at him while snapping a thin length of tree branch into smaller pieces, he found the image on her t-shirt somewhat ironic for his circumstances. Of course, he was playing the part of the deer.

Her bright blue eyes stared back at him with a piercing intensity, which he found slightly unnerving.

"Trying to be subtle. Didn't want to scare you," she offered.

"You? Subtle?"

"Whatcha up to, tiger?" she asked, ignoring his sarcasm.

"Just taking a walk and thinking," he replied while folding his arms before him.

"Saw you take a walk on the video cameras earlier. But then you disappeared from around the complex, and nobody knew where you went. Kind of worried me," she said, noting his body language. "So, I had just enough time to change outta the stupid khakis and sport coat before sunset and figured I'd come looking for ya," she added.

"Thanks," he replied.

Of course, the fact that Paige is here and not Kat means my mate is blissfully unaware of the development.

Paige noted his dark mood and absently dropped the remaining pieces of branch to the ground.

"Shouldn't be out in the woods alone," she mildly chastised. "It's almost dark, and there are wolves around, you know."

He's seriously troubled over something.

"Yeah, well I haven't seen any. So, I'm feeling pretty safe right now."

The edges of her mouth upturned slightly as she adopted a fully-upright stance and playfully corrected him, "No wolves? I'm a bit of a wolf, remember? In fact, after I acquired a general idea of where you went, I tracked you here by your scent, Mister Rabbit."

He smirked at her comment, recalling a happier time just months ago when they had analogized her as a wolf and him as a rabbit.

"Ah, but don't forget, you're a friendly one, Miss Wolf," he fondly recollected. Then the fleeting moment faded as the recent, disappointing phone call replayed in his mind.

Paige's eyes flashed for a second before returning to their previous state, and she took two subtle steps in his direction.

Time to have some fun with him.

"Me? I'm not a friendly wolf, kiddo. I'm only friendly to you because I want to be," she clarified in a deliberately ominous voice. "We're predators, remember? I get really unfriendly when the mood strikes me."

He was unsettled by her suddenly edgy demeanor, but anticipated that she was just trying to distract him. Instead, her comment only increased his chagrin over his current situation.

"Tell me about it," he muttered while turning his back on her. "You vampires get all interested and friendly, and then suddenly you disappear or turn off like a damned light switch. And frankly, it just pisses me off."

"Hey, what gives?"

"Aw, crap. Just leave me alone, Paige," he fumed. He wasn't in the mood to play games.

She was completely taken aback by his retort and froze in her tracks as her mind raced to understand.

What the hell? Is it something I did?

She noted the tension in his body language and the fact that he had turned his back on her.

Okay then, rejection. Problems with the old lady maybe? But that's not all, I'd wager.

"Well, I'm here now. So why not talk to me?" she invited in a friendlier tone, all pretense of playing with him put aside for the moment.

Big sister's on duty now.

He shook his head and walked a few steps away to sit on the edge of one of the large, fallen tree trunks. While he kept his arms folded before him, his eyes softened somewhat as he looked at her.

"Never mind," he said. "You've got enough on your plate right now."

She shook her head.

Once again, tiger, you're trying to shoulder everything yourself.

Perching beside him, she placed a supportive arm across his shoulders. At first his muscles were tight, but then she felt him relax somewhat. She used her free hand to reach up and turn his face towards hers, insisting, "Hey, I'm your babysitter, your surrogate vampire. Talk to me, kiddo. Spill."

He stared back at her as darkness continued to fall around them. Then he shrugged.

"Well, first, Kat's been so distant with the conference distractions. Of course, that's when she's actually in the room. Most of the time, I never even see her. She's obsessing over Alton's latest project."

Paige remained silent as she lightly ran the tips of her fingernails across his shoulders.

It's a pretty big project, too, something not tried at this scale before. In the vampire world, this is "big time."

"And I got a phone call today," he continued. "It was from Dean Wright at the college. He said that the way the budget's looking, I may not have my faculty contract renewed in July."

Her eyes widened with surprise, and she began to realize how both of the things he mentioned were culminating to generate his bad mood.

He loves teaching.

"Okay, that's bad, I'll admit," she conceded while pulling him to her in a side-hug. "But it's not the end of the world. There are other teaching positions out there. Time to go job hunting. I mean, you nailed the position at your current college. You can do it again."

He incredulously stared back at her.

"You have no idea what you're even saying," he corrected with exasperation. "Do you know how lucky I was to land the job at the college in the first place? Think about it, Paige, isn't it a little strange that I'm a twenty-six-year-old straight out of graduate school, and yet I'm a full-time college professor? That just doesn't happen in the real world. Listen, it sucks to admit this, but I wasn't exactly their first choice on the hiring list."

Her eyebrow rose with surprise. "You weren't?"

He looked away. "No, I was at the bottom of their list of finalists. Of the four finalists, I was *fourth.*"

"So, what happened there, then?" she asked.

He paused. "Dean Wright was pretty candid with me after I was hired. He said their first choice got a better counter-offer from another college. The second guy didn't like the salary range, and the third candidate didn't pass the pre-hiring drug test. So, that only left me. It sounds like I was just a name to pad out the finalist's sheet. Although I think Paul told me the story right off so I'd buckle down from the start. Yeah, as if I needed any incentive to do that."

Okay, that's pretty surprising, Paige admitted. *Not that it changes my opinion about him, though.*

"Does Katrina know that?" she asked in a quiet voice.

"Are you kidding?" he chortled. "It's not something you go bragging about to your five-hundred-year-old, supermodel-looking, successful vampire-mate, now, is it?"

She winced at the pain evident in his voice and immediately regretted asking. Her mind searched for the right thing to say, but all she managed to do was increase her grip around his shoulders and hug him closer to her.

I wish I could fix this, but it's a little out of my league. It's not like I can just bleed dry the people who fire him, right?

Then she evilly smiled before discarding the idea altogether.

"Red's not going to think badly about you," she reassured him. "Hell, she loves you more than life itself, and I should know. What I'm trying to say is it doesn't matter in the end whether you're a professor or a window-washer. She loves you, the same as I do."

He peered into her bright blue eyes and noted her sincere look of sympathy. The edges of his mouth upturned slightly, and then his lips pressed together into a fine line again.

"But you see, it does matter," he insisted. "It matters to me. Being a professor was the one thing I could claim as my own special talent, my own niche in life. Soon, that may be gone too."

"Listen, if it's about the money..."

"And yeah, it's also about the money," he interrupted. "Geez, I'm already feeling inferior that she pays for these trips we take. Then I don't even pay more than the cost of groceries at the estate. Hell, if I lose my job, I'll be complete deadweight!"

She couldn't help smiling a little bit at his retort, which he found infuriating.

"Just what's so damned funny?" he demanded.

Her expression turned serious. "Listen, tiger, I don't know if you've given it any thought or not, but a five-hundred-year-old vampire has had a lot of time to build up a nest egg. And consider that Alton, 'Mister Capitalism' himself, was her mentor. Doesn't a little light bulb pop on in your head? I mean, look, I'm only about a century old, and I'm doing okay, if you know what I mean. Thanks to some financial tips from Katrina, of course."

He appreciated all of that, but it really didn't help to alter his feelings over the matter. In fact, it made him feel a little worse.

"Well, yeah, I see a light bulb coming on," he sarcastically replied. "And it indicates that what little means I had to make my own way is about to go away. So, now I'm supposed to just completely mooch off all the wealthy vampires in my life?"

Paige's eyes flared with anger, and she popped him on the back of his head with the flat of her hand in a manner that nearly knocked him off the tree trunk.

"Hey!" he barked. "Take it easy!"

But instead of apologizing, she stood up before him and glared back at him.

"You -- You're just so full of crap, Caleb!" she admonished. "Do you think that you're worth is in any way balanced by your ability to pay your own way? Let me tell you something, twerp, you're being an idiot!"

He started to jump up from the log, but she moved in a blur and pushed him back onto the trunk.

"Dammit, Paige!" he shouted back at her while barely catching his balance from falling backwards. The effort twisted his still-achy back somewhat, causing him to wince slightly.

"No! You listen to me now," Paige demanded. "Money is just a means to us, a necessary facet. It's all just material stuff. It makes life easier. But it's not what we're about, Caleb. We're mostly about the blood, and, trust me, you've got some good tastin' blood for a human."

Her mind easily recalled the smell and taste of his blood when she had helped heal his chest wound just prior to last Christmas. It had taken all her control not to drain him dry, actually. He tasted amazing to her.

His eyes suspiciously narrowed. "Just what the hell do you

mean by that?"

She adopted an almost cruel expression and paused for a moment to consider him.

Time for a way-overdue dose of reality, young one.

"That wonderful red stuff running through your veins right now means more to a vampire than a truckload of money," she pressed. "But it's more than that. With you, Katrina gets a mate. She gets your love, your body, your devotion, your companionship, and your blood. Don't judge us by conventional human values or goals. Money has no motivation for Katrina, or to me, for that matter. Hell, her savings practically compounds itself faster than you could ever spend it."

He blinked with surprise, his mind trying to process everything that she was telling him. His heart raced in his chest as he tried to make sense of it all. Meanwhile, she crossed her arms in front of her and silently stared at him as if watching time pass before her eyes.

I just don't want to be a mooch, he fumed.

"Okay, so maybe I didn't realize everything," he stammered. "I just felt –"

"...sorry for yourself," she interrupted him.

His mouth snapped shut, and he looked away.

Maybe a little bit, he conceded.

"I just want to be useful for *something,*" he absently whispered. "I want to contribute."

Her temper had abated somewhat, though she observed him with narrowed eyes before reaching out to grasp him firmly by the upper arm. He took notice of her hand before looking back into her eyes, which he gratefully noticed were no longer glowing.

"Your worth is determined by who you are as a mate, friend, and companion," she stipulated. "Not by your bank account, credit score, career, or job title. There may come a day when all that would be useless to your circumstances anyway."

He was taken aback by her comment and pressed, "What does that mean?"

"Play your cards right, and you may find yourself a little more than human someday," she alluded.

His eyes widened at the mention of a forbidden topic between him and Katrina, one of the seven all-important rules he had promised to uphold.

But it's not a forbidden topic between Paige and me, he realized.

"You mean, I may actually be turned," he ventured out loud.

Turned into a vampire.

Paige's mood abruptly shifted from intense to off-handed, and she merely shrugged.

"Who knows," she equivocated. "It's not something that's been discussed with me. But you never know, I suppose."

Not my place to offer, she silently berated herself. *He belongs to Katrina, not me.* The latter realization generated a momentary pang of both regret and longing in her.

A series of silent moments passed between them, and he realized just how dark the forest had become while they argued. If not for Paige's pale skin, he might lose sight of her in her dark clothes. Most of the nearby trees were merely dark images around them. It was a little unnerving, and he was suddenly grateful for her proximity.

"Listen, I didn't mean to piss you off," he offered with resignation. "I'm just an idiot sometimes, like you said."

She sighed. "Yeah, well, I didn't mean to belittle your circumstances, I suppose. Just grow up a little bit, will you, tiger?"

"Yeah," he acknowledged with a nod. "I get it."

She flirtatiously smiled and added, "But don't grow up too much, okay? I like a little occasional immaturity in my men. Keeps you playful."

He rolled his eyes and shook his head.

"I'm just sayin'," she added, sensing his mood improve by the moment.

"Whatever," he countered in his best Valley Boy impression.

She effortlessly watched him in the darkness with her vampire-enhanced vision and felt encouraged.

"Friends?" she softly asked.

The hint of a smile formed on his lips, and he nodded.

"Friends."

She slowly moved forwards and embraced him in a tender hug, perching her chin atop his shoulder. He wrapped his arms around her and appreciated both their closeness and the closure of their argument. Then she turned her face towards him and pressed her soft lips against the skin of his cheek in a gentle kiss.

"You mean a lot to me," she tenderly whispered. "Love you, kiddo."

He sincerely whispered, "Love you too, Paige."

A warm feeling passed through him, and he momentarily wished that a similar experience could be shared between him and Katrina again soon.

One problem at a time, he resigned.

"Don't say anything to Kat about this layoff stuff, okay?" he stipulated. "It's not completely a done deal yet."

"Sure," she conceded, though she wasn't left feeling very hopeful.

It really doesn't sound good for the poor kid.

After a couple of moments, she gently disengaged from their embrace. She playfully patted her hands against his body in a rapid flurry of slaps, demanding, "Okay, you moonlight-groper, back to the hotel already."

"Yeah, probably a good idea," he agreed and headed into the trees to their right.

Unfortunately, he was going in the wrong direction. Paige shook her head with disgust and darted forwards. She grasped him by the hand, pulling him after her as she stomped head-first into the forest in a completely different direction.

"Come on, Daniel Boone, let's get you back to civilization," she half-teased, half-admonished.

As they walked among the trees, a wolf howled in the distance.

"Hey, that's a wolf," he said with surprise.

"See? Told you," she muttered with satisfaction.

By the time they returned to the hotel, it was rather late in the evening. Paige agreed to sit with him while he ate dinner in the main dining room, during which time she noted something odd. The few human patrons in the room furtively glanced at Caleb, and some whispered to each other after doing so.

She carefully listened in on some comments from nearby people and discovered that one patron viewed Caleb and Dori's recent experiences with the local police negatively. Another comment suggested they had brought it on themselves. It took her practiced sense of control not to rush over to give the person an earful over that.

"Not real popular lately, are you, kiddo?" she asked before sipping from a glass of Coke, which she intended to exchange for a mug of warm blood sometime soon because her formerly ignored hunger was approaching an unpleasant level.

He looked up from his plate of chicken paprika, a local dish made with a creamy sauce containing spicy, red paprika served over noodles. "Not so much," he conceded with a gander at the room's patrons before returning to his pasta.

Admittedly, it bothered him, but he had much bigger problems on his hands to contend with.

A clerk from the main desk strode into the dining room and headed over to where they were seated. The lady extended a small white envelope to Caleb.

"Mr. Taylor, this was left for you at the main desk," the young woman pleasantly offered. "I was going to deliver it to your suite, but one of the other clerks said they saw you enter the dining room."

"Thanks," he replied as he turned the envelope over in his hand. It was labeled *Mr. Caleb Taylor* in an ornate script.

Paige curiously stared at the retreating desk clerk and then focused on the envelope. "Something from Red?"

He slipped open the seal and withdrew a white piece of paper with a single sentence: *The vault – 10 pm -- tonight.*

"Strange," he remarked and handed the message to Paige.

She peeked at her watch. "Hey, it's 10:10 already."

"Let's go then," he excitedly insisted while rising from the table.

"Whoa, tiger," she admonished, grasping his wrist with a sweep of her hand. "Let's ask ourselves why someone wants you where you know you can't go in the first place?"

As escape from her grasp seemed futile, he capitulated.

"Yeah, but what if they altered conditions so that I can?" he countered.

She released his wrist, pursing her lips. "Interesting theory. Let's go see."

They left enough cash to cover dinner and departed the nearly empty dining room in the direction of the main lobby. They proceeded to the main elevator, where they were the only people waiting for the car. The area was relatively devoid of traffic since the vampires were still in conference.

Inside the elevator, Paige pressed the button for the lower level where the vault was located. Much to her surprise, the LCD screen next to the small keypad immediately indicated the message: *Code accepted.*

The car descended, and Caleb looked at her with a surprised expression.

"I'm just as puzzled as you are," she said simply.

When the doors opened, they stepped into a large, dimly lit storage area that had all the trappings of being a large basement. Heavy-duty metal shelves were arrayed into rows and appeared stocked with boxes and crates of supplies and materials.

"Not very impressive," he dryly observed.

"It was just a basement storage area before the vault was installed, after all," she explained. "The vault's at the very back against the foundation wall."

They proceeded down a couple of aisles of shelves, continuing to the back of the concrete-walled basement. A shiny metal-looking vault stood at the very back of the bay area.

Using her keen senses, Paige detected no other presence besides them. She thought that everything seemed in place, except that the large shiny vault door was ajar.

The vault door looked like one belonging in a bank or financial institution. From the front, the dimensions of the vault were twelve feet wide and nearly ten feet tall, and it was composed of thick reinforced steel. An electronic control pad was at the left of the door on the wall facing about four feet high from the floor.

"Well, the vault door's certainly open," she noted.

With her leading the way, the two of them went to the door, which she easily pried open the rest of the way. She peered inside and noted that the interior lights were bright. The walls to the left and right were lined with locked safe deposit boxes of various sizes, except for a smaller section of wall immediately before them, which blocked her view into the main interior. They stepped inside and walked around the small section of wall, revealing a black, executive-sized briefcase on the floor at the opposite side of the vault.

"Well, there's something worth checking out," Paige noted and led the way into the vault.

They made their way across the twelve-foot span to the back of the vault where the briefcase was sitting. Paige reached down and popped open the latches, which weren't locked. Inside, there was nothing but a single folded piece of white paper.

She unfolded the page as Caleb peered at it while crouching next to her.

It read: *TOO BAD!*

Paige looked up with surprise just in time to see the vault door slamming shut behind them. The petite vampire sped across the distance to the door in a blur, but not fast enough to stop the door from closing into place. She slammed into the door with the force of her body, but the locking mechanism had already initiated itself.

"Open this door!" she yelled so loudly that Caleb winced. There was no response.

"Don't worry. The security person covering the surveillance monitors will see us on the camera," she assured him.

"Somehow I don't think so," he slowly replied as he pointed up to the surveillance camera that's indicator light was off.

She looked up at the camera with disdain. "Okay, that sucks."

"Can't we just yell until someone hears us?" he asked.

She grumbled, "It's practically soundproof. We're sealed in here until that door opens."

He threw up his hands in irritation, feeling like a rat caught in a trap.

Then the lights went out, leaving them standing in complete darkness.

He looked around with alarm, feeling as if he were floating in empty space. A wave of disorientation washed over him, and his heartbeat substantially increased.

"It's okay, Caleb," she offered in a soothing voice. "It's just you and me in here, so there's nothing to be afraid of."

She decided not to scare him further by telling him that vault had an airtight seal.

He stared in the direction of her voice and saw her blue eyes glowing at him from across the room.

"Paige," he carefully asked. "Are you angry right now?"

She rolled her eyes and snapped, "Pretty much."

"Good, better than being hungry," he absently observed.

Her bright glowing eyes widened as she stared back at him. "Actually, I am a little hungry, now that you mention it."

His eyes darted to hers. With his growing vampire knowledge and experience, he knew full well that being alone and trapped in a room with a hungry vampire wasn't an enviable prospect for a human. It had a tendency to shorten one's life span.

He snatched the cell phone from his belt and stared at the illuminated screen, only to have his hopes instantly doused.

"Dammit, no signal," he groused.

Having already anticipated that, she nevertheless looked at her own cell phone for confirmation and muttered, "Yeah, pretty much crap."

He felt a stab of anxiety and began to back up slowly to the nearest wall, stopping only when he felt the cool metal deposit box doors at his back.

She observed his action, capable of seeing relatively well in darkness, and moved to his side to place a supportive hand on his shoulder.

"Listen, no worries," she soothingly offered. "I'm here to protect you. Hell, I've saved your life on two occasions in the past year."

He contemplated how she had earned the amusing title of babysitter by her actions against a houseful of armed mercenaries that had attacked them while they were held up in Katrina's mansion. She had single-handedly killed all the attackers, except one that he had disabled with a crowbar.

Then he recalled that it was an injection of Paige's blood that had saved his life from a near-fatal knife wound to his chest soon after the mercenary attack when Chimalma had attacked him. All in all, she had proven to be a formidable friend and protector. However, he realized that a vampire's hunger might eventually trump their normal, rational decision-making capabilities.

"You may not have a choice if your hunger grows too strong," he ominously countered. "Kat said that younger vampires need blood more frequently. And even at nearly a century old, you've told me yourself that you're considered a teenager by vampire standards. And most teens have a hearty appetite."

She paused to consider his statement.

"We still have some time. Katrina and the others will probably find us before it comes to that."

"How much time?" he pressed.

"Three, maybe four hours," she calculated.

"Three or four hours?" he retorted. "You're supposed to be

able to go over a day without feeding!"

His heart rate raced as he calculated just how little time they might have before things turned ugly. He checked his watch and noticed that it was nearly 2 am and realized he just might end up being for breakfast.

"I've been kind of busy, if you haven't noticed," she pointed out.

He immediately tried to calm himself, appreciating that angering a hungry vampire was probably a bad idea, no matter how dedicated she might be to protecting him.

"Look," he gently apologized, "I'm sorry, I'm just a little unnerved, okay? My bad."

Paige's eyes flashed, and she snapped, "Just stop that, Caleb. I'm fine! You're starting to weird me out a little bit."

His mouth snapped shut, and he just stood silently against the wall of miniature doors.

"Well, so much for being Supergirl," she commented, recalling her analogy with Katrina back in Atlanta.

"What?"

"Aw, nothin'," she whispered dejectedly.

He smirked as he contemplated his DC Comics knowledge.

"If anything, you're more like Wonder Girl. She was a cute, short-haired blonde with blue eyes, just like you. As a matter of fact, she was a Teen Titan and a pretty cool one."

After only a moment, he felt Paige's warm breath against his face. Her soft lips lightly pressed against his cheek to place a quick, appreciative kiss.

"You're such a nerd, kiddo. But you're *my* nerd," she offered before sitting on the floor near his feet. "Hey, have a seat, and let's try to relax, all right?"

Rather, let's conserve the air. His agitated state would use up more oxygen.

Her tone was more like the optimistic vampire that he had grown to know and adore, and he slipped down the wall until he sat next to her.

The minutes seemed to last forever as they waited. Finally,

he leaned his head back against the wall and started dozing. His sleep patterns had been disrupted by all the erratic events since their arrival, so he made the best of an opportunity to rest.

As she contemplated matters, Paige reached over with one hand to gently guide his head to lean against her shoulder.

Not a good situation.

* * * *

The impasse over the latest topic within the conference room was enough to make Katrina scream. They had come so close to agreement upon the simple premise of performing a poll of vampires abroad on common points of vested interest. Yet, minutes later, an argument ensued over who would tally the results and how transparent reporting would be conducted in a timely fashion.

She wanted to strangle Dominic Ambrogio for his series of obstructionist objections since the conference began. Though Ambrogio attempted to be subtle by adopting the Socratic method of inquiry, it was becoming obvious to both her and Alton that the vampire had to be part of some organized conspiracy against the conference's success.

A knock sounded at the door, creating a sudden lull in the discussions. One of the guards outside entered and handed a small folded piece of paper to Alton before smartly departing the room.

Alton unfolded the note as all eyes in the room gravitated to him. After mere seconds, he passed the note to Katrina.

She read: *Paige and Caleb missing. Video surveillance disruptions hampering the search. – Dori*

Her eyes widened with immediate concern, and she rose from her chair. Alton grabbed her wrist to stop her, and she glared at him.

"I apologize, but a security matter has risen that requires immediate attention," Alton announced to the group. "There's no need for immediate concern by you or hotel guests, but I recommend that we adjourn at least until tomorrow morning. Additional information will be forthcoming. We're adjourned."

Katrina jerked her arm free from Alton's grasp and was the first one to barrel through the door on her way to the lobby. Alton closely followed at her heels with a tight-lipped expression.

Upon entering the security office, Dori looked up from the video surveillance workstations. Major Pietari stood beside her, and a security officer sat at the desk.

"Status report," Alton ordered before Katrina could say anything.

"We're having problems with the video surveillance system," the major crisply replied. "It's nothing serious, but we experienced a blackout period a few hours ago. We're rebuilding the video streams manually leading up to the outage."

"And what about the whereabouts of Caleb and Paige," Katrina demanded.

The major frowned. "Their whereabouts are currently unknown, but our security officers are trying to locate them now. However, we have no reason to believe anything untoward has occurred."

"So, your captain of security just disappears without notice, as well as a hotel guest, and you see nothing suspicious about that?" Katrina sarcastically challenged. She was beginning to dislike the major.

Pietari's jaw clenched, and he glared back at the red-haired vampire. "Ms. Rawlings, the captain was off-duty. It's not as if she needed to report her activities. And I'm to understand that she's some sort of surrogate to Mr. Taylor, so it's possible the two of them went out together or something. At this point, I have no evidence to suggest anything nefarious has taken place. Besides, I'm confident she's more than capable of handling herself."

Alton stared at the major, and then looked at Dori, whose expression was pensive.

"What do we know about their last known location?" he

asked.

The major started to speak up, but Dori interrupted him, "We just brought the last good video streams online. The lobby camera showed them heading towards the main elevator. Then the feeds all went offline."

"Institute a room-by-room search immediately," Alton ordered.

The major's eyes narrowed. "Mr. Rutherford, I'm afraid I must object. That seems quite an overreaction. I think that it's in everyone's best interests to consult the hotel manager first."

Alton's eyes flashed bright hazel, and his steely gaze locked onto the major's.

The office door abruptly opened to reveal a bleary-eyed, middle-aged man wearing casual slacks and a slightly wrinkled dress shirt. Katrina immediately recognized him from a photo on the information board in the lobby as Stanislav Vlaeva, the hotel manager. He had the look of someone who wasn't happy to be up at such a late hour.

"What's going on?" Vlaeva asked.

"Merely a video surveillance failure," the major offered. "I'm sorry you were disturbed over –"

"Yes, yes," Alton irritably interjected. "Captain Turner and Mr. Caleb Taylor have also gone missing, which seems to coincide with the time of the surveillance failure. I just instructed the major to begin a room-by-room search."

"I respectfully object," Pietari blurted.

Vlaeva briefly eyed Alton and then focused on Major Pietari. "Do it," he flatly ordered.

The major appeared visibly taken aback by the manager's sudden deference to Alton.

"As you wish," he curtly acknowledged. He turned and walked over to a small radio unit nearby to issue the order.

Katrina's impatience was nearly uncontrollable as her mind raced to consider multiple variables at once. Alton motioned to Dori with a nod of his head and tapped his hand in the small of Katrina's back to get her attention. He led the two women out into the main hallway.

"What happened?" he asked Dori upon ensuring that the hallway was relatively clear of bystanders.

"I went to find Caleb with some new information that I acquired," Dori explained. "He wasn't in his suite, which seemed strange at such a late hour."

"You entered our suite?" Katrina interjected.

Dori adopted a meek expression. "He didn't answer the phone, so I stopped by to knock at the door. Given everything that's happened, I was afraid that something might be wrong, and since Alton had a master key..."

Katrina wasn't entirely pleased with that revelation, but let it slide for the moment.

"And?" Alton gently prompted while tentatively glancing at Katrina.

"He wasn't there, so I went to consult with Paige," Dori continued. "I learned that she was off-duty, but nobody could reach her by cell phone or radio. That also concerned me, and that's when I found out from the officer on duty that there was also a system wide surveillance outage. It all seemed too coincidental."

"Good instincts," Katrina complimented, despite her misgivings about the master key.

"Thanks," Dori gracefully accepted before refocusing her attention on Alton. "Thus far, the guards are all searching inside the hotel, but primarily in the publically accessible areas."

"What about the grounds?" Alton asked.

Dori shrugged.

"I'll run a circuit outside," Katrina offered. "Maybe I can still catch a scent or other clue." She was happy to do anything besides sit and wait.

"Fine, but make sure that you're cell's online, or better yet, take a radio. It will be easier to monitor the situation," Alton said.

Katrina entered the security office to acquire a radio. She realized that Paige was more than capable of handling herself, but she worried over what the two of them may have run into.

*   *   *   *

Caleb was jarred slightly from the midst of a weird dream about wandering aimlessly in the dark. He illuminated his watch and lamented that nearly two and a half hours had already passed. Then he observed Paige's blue eyes shining like two orbs in the darkness. It seemed that they were brighter than before his brief nap.

"Paige?" he softly asked. "How are you doing?"

"Much hungrier, unfortunately," she said in a tight voice.

He swallowed, realizing that he was also feeling a little thirsty, although his thirst didn't involve attacking his nearest friend.

Then inspiration struck; an idea that seemed logical, albeit somewhat unorthodox.

"Hey," he ventured, "what if you just feed on me now, while you can still control your urges? Just a little, enough to keep your hunger under control."

She conceded the logic of his idea. "Nice, but what's rule number three, kiddo?"

He thought back to the rules that Katrina had made him swear to obey and recited from memory, "I must never willingly give or submit myself to another vampire."

"Exactly," she said with a note of finality.

Then her eyes narrowed, and she turned to stare back at Caleb with surprise.

"What?" he asked.

"You were right about feeding before the urge gets too strong. But you can't offer me your blood, according to Katrina's rules."

He remained silent, not really seeing how that helped matters.

"But if I take your blood instead of you giving it, then you're not at fault," she carefully explained. "You won't get punished, and I won't go into a feeding frenzy. It's a win-win solution for everybody."

"Wait a minute. Why does it even matter? It's just us. Who'll know the difference?" he challenged.

"Already thought about that, kiddo," she offered. "Listen, we're both gonna get interrogated by Katrina once this is over, and she's going to tell in a second that you're lying. You're her mate, Caleb. Don't ever lie to her...ever."

He shivered slightly at the tone of her voice.

"Rule number seven. Repeat it," she ordered in an uncustomary stern voice.

"Never lie in matters concerning any of the aforementioned rules," he said with exasperation. "Okay, so it would've been a mistake, wouldn't it?"

"Big mistake," she soberly agreed.

Particularly given how strict Red is about these things.

Silence reigned for what seemed like an eternity.

Finally, Paige quietly asked, "Listen. Turn away from me for a second, would you please?"

He frowned. *Strange request.*

Then he shrugged and scooted on the floor until he was turned away from her. In the span of a second, he felt Paige's soft arm slither underneath his arms from behind, placing him in an effective arm bar. Using only one arm, she immediately applied enough pressure to immobilize his arms behind him. Fortunately for him, while her efforts had surprised him, it had caused no unbearable pain.

"Hey!" he exclaimed. "What the hell's this all about?"

"I care about you too much to let you break the rules," she replied with concern. "I'm going to feed from you now."

"Fine, I'm not trying to fight you," he retorted, deliberately relaxing his body while in her grasp. "This was my idea, remember? So, start nibbling."

"Right, but you need to struggle a little bit here or you won't have an alibi. You *can't* offer your blood to me."

"This is stupid. Forget it," he refused.

She irritably growled. "Listen to me, tiger, and listen close-ly."

His body tensed, unsettled by her dark tone.

"I'm counting to three, and then you better try like hell to get away from me," she ordered. "Or I'm going to bite you in the neck, but *without* the nice numbing effect that you're used to. Remember how it felt when Katrina tore into your shoulder last year?"

A chill went down his spine as he recalled the time when Katrina had a post-traumatic experience in the form of a night-mare as she slept next to him. She had abruptly attacked him; brutally tearing into his shoulder. He had experienced pain and trauma unlike any other.

"Paige, don't do this," he pleaded.

"One," she counted in a flat tone.

"Please, don't," he begged.

"Two," she continued unabated.

His muscles tightened, and he came to an immediate deci-sion, despite his reservations.

"Three," she whispered harshly into his ear.

Her hot breath felt like the first belch of an erupting volca-no. But he struggled to remain calm, even while steeling him-self for the pain that was sure to follow.

"Fine. Do it. But I love you, and I refuse to resist when I have the ability to give you what you need," he boldly declared. "Your very own blood saved my life after Chimalma nearly killed me. The least I can do is offer mine to you. I give it freely and without reservations. To hell with the consequences."

She held his arms in a tight vise-like grip, knowing full well his shoulders probably ached. But then she abruptly re-leased him from the arm bar.

Damn him!

She struggled to dissipate her frustration and reclaim a sense of calm.

"Lean your body back against me," she finally relented in a subdued tone.

He scooted backwards until her outstretched legs were flanking him and leaned back against her warm body.

She positioned her back against the vault wall and wrapped her right arm around his chest from behind. Reaching up with her left hand, she soothingly ran her fingertips through his hair. She felt the tension in his muscles abate. Then she firmly grasped a handful of his hair in her fist and pulled his head to the left to expose the right side of his neck fully to her.

"Ow, ow, no hair pulling!" he complained as a stinging sensation shot through his scalp.

"Sorry, I'm really just trying to help with those 'compliance issues' when you have to recount this later," she teased.

However, she also took a perverse pleasure in doing it to him, partly from the frustration over his defiance and partly from an innate desire to be assertive with him. She pulled his hair in a steady fashion until his head was tilted exactly where she wanted him. In the darkness, she could hear the throbbing of his heartbeat and the blood rushing through the arteries in his neck.

"Nicely done, kiddo," she purred in a satisfied tone. "You're complying really well."

His head lay against her left shoulder as she craned her head around to reach his neck with her lips. Then she slowly, ever so lightly, kissed the exposed side of his soft neck once, twice, and a third time.

She relished that moment; the feeling of a prey's submission was thrilling. Then she stopped, silently berating herself for thinking of him as prey. He was so much more than that to her.

Despite his anxiety, he appreciated her attentions. The effect was somewhat soothing and satisfying, but then she jerked his hair again, and he winced.

"Hey, what gives?" he demanded.

She giggled. "Can't let you enjoy this too much, just for the record, you understand."

He scoffed out loud, thinking that it was she who was enjoying this a little too much. Then he felt her soft lips form around a spot on his neck, followed by her silky moist tongue pressing against his skin. She lightly flicked her tongue back and forth, and it tickled. He wriggled slightly in her arms from the sensation.

"Everything okay?" she asked. Despite her earlier aggravation, she wanted to make the experience special for him.

"Your tongue. It tickles," he whispered with the formation of a grin.

Kat never does this to me, he noted.

She smiled against the skin of his soft neck and murmured, "I know. This is just for you, tiger."

The entire experience took on a special significance for him. When Katrina and he shared this experience, it always felt like a communion. And though a feeding of necessity for Paige's benefit, the significance of the moment felt so much more.

He felt the telltale numbing sensation forming around the area where she intended to bite him. The numbness was soothing, and he was suddenly very grateful for it.

"Thank you," he appreciatively mumbled.

She playfully tugged at his hair again and whispered into his neck, "Oh, hush. Hold still."

He froze in place and felt two light pinpricks against his numbed skin, followed by a slight increase in pressure in his neck. The handful of his hair that she held in her left hand ensured that he remained still as her mouth sealed against his skin. Within seconds, he heard little suckling and slurping noises as his blood effortlessly passed into her mouth.

He further relaxed his body, and she released her grip on his hair, instead soothingly massaging his scalp. Time seemed to stand still for him, and he closed his eyes, listening to her feed on him. It was similar to his experiences with Katrina, but somehow different, almost as if Paige had a different technique for the process. Despite an act of necessity, it somehow felt as if he and Paige were growing closer to each other, sharing something equally intimate between them. The realization surprised him.

After a period of time, she ceased drinking, and he felt increased numbness in his neck. She was healing the puncture marks that she had made, as well as reducing the soreness that he might have otherwise felt in the wound area, precisely as Katrina always did for him.

The seal of her lips against his neck ceased, and she affectionately kissed him on the cheek.

"I'm grateful to you for providing your blood to me," she softly said. "You have no idea just how painful the hunger for blood can be when it becomes urgent."

And you have no idea how utterly amazing your blood tastes, she silently added.

He knew what it was to feel intense hunger, though the concept of a vampire's blood urge was something totally foreign to him. In truth, he had no basis for comparison. He only knew what Katrina had told him about it.

I'm happy that I could help Paige. She means the world to me.

As if sensing his thoughts, she used her hand to tilt his face towards hers and lightly kissed him on the lips. Despite his surprise, he gently returned her kiss in kind.

A momentary surge, like an electric shock, ran through her, and her eyes widened with surprise.

"You're a pretty good kisser, kiddo," she complimented. "I see why Red likes smooching on you so much."

He felt himself blush. "You're not too bad, yourself."

A pang of guilt followed as he realized just how much he had enjoyed it.

The petite vampire breathed in, suddenly sensing just how little air was remaining in the relatively small vault.

What if nobody finds us in time?

Perhaps it was that simple moment's realization of potential doom, or that her partaking in his blood created increased feelings for him. Either way, Paige resolved that there were things that she wanted to say to him just in case conditions worsened.

"You mean so much to me," she said. "I can't imagine life without you, in fact. I—I love you, Caleb," she whispered as her throat tightened from that earnest declaration.

The powerful level of emotion behind her admission frightened her. It was a unique feeling in her century of existence, and she was happy that the darkness precluded him from seeing the emotions reflected on her face.

"I love you too, Paige. You're so much more than just a friend after all we've been through together. I can never repay you for saving my life -- twice, no less."

She paused, uncertain that he appreciated the depth of her feelings, or the revelation that she had just shared. It was a dangerous admission on her part, and she resigned herself to the satisfaction of knowing that at least she had said it to him and fully embraced it within herself.

"In as much as I'm your surrogate vampire, I suppose you've become a sort of surrogate companion to me, kiddo."

She was almost shocked at laying her feelings out in the open as she did and at the sense of emotional vulnerability that accompanied it. Yet a part of her worried that if someone didn't find them soon, it might be her only chance to reveal such things to him.

He was extremely flattered and humbled by her declaration, though he found it somewhat odd that she would take such a moment to reveal those feelings. Their circumstances made it all seem strange, somewhat out of place.

"I've felt that about you for some time, too," he confessed. "I realized that when I came out to California to find you. But Katrina's my mate, and I'd never want to compromise that."

"I know that," she said. "And I would never want to put you in a circumstance where you'd have to compromise yourself. You and Kat are great together, and it makes me happy just to see you both so happy."

However, part of her was genuinely jealous of her red-haired friend and angry that fate could be so ironic where her heart was concerned.

"Except that I broke a serious rule in this vault," he darkly concluded, not looking forward to the time when he would have to confess it to Katrina.

"Hey, this was a special circumstance," she cautioned him. "You're not taking the fall for breaking any rules. I'll damn sure set Red straight about this."

"I wish you could find a worthy mate, someone who'd make you happy," he whispered, recalling how poorly her previous boyfriend, Gil, had worked out for her.

She scowled in the darkness.

"Don't worry about it. I'm okay for now," she declared, though perhaps more for her own benefit than his. "But if I were looking for a mate, I'd want him to be a lot like you," she whispered as her eyes watered slightly.

He grinned at the compliment, unable to see the strain reflected in her features.

"But, of course, somebody that's much more assertive and rugged than you. And someone who dances somewhat better than a Muppet," she teased, trying to break the solemnity of the moment. She fondly recalled the humorous comment that he had made about his dancing back in February, which suddenly seemed like a lifetime ago.

He started to chuckle, but felt as if it required some effort to take in a full breath. As he started to scoot away from her, she reached out with both arms and easily pulled his body back against hers. The temperature in the vault was very cool, and her body felt warm and soothing for him to lean against.

"Rest now. I'm sure it won't be long before someone checks the vault," she optimistically offered as she gently used her hand to press his head back against her shoulder so that he would be more comfortable.

The truth was that she was beginning to have doubts as to their chances of being discovered in time and wanted to make him as comfortable as possible without alarming him to the danger. A surge of sadness coursed through her system as she felt so powerless to rescue him from their circumstances. *If it's the last thing I do, somebody's going to pay for this,* she angrily vowed.

Caleb mulled over their trapped circumstances as he leaned his head back against Paige's shoulder. Then time passed, and he felt increasingly tired. He failed to take note of when he lost consciousness.

*   *   *   *

Chapter 8

New Guests

*N*early two hours had passed as Dori watched over the shoulder of the security officer at the video surveillance console. She deftly sidestepped Major Pietari's concerns over her continued presence by pointing out that she had extensive background working with video surveillance in a previous job. As the officer systematically reviewed each camera's views leading up to the mysterious blackout, she closely watched the monitors for anything noteworthy. Finally, the officer changed to the live camera feeds.

"That was our second pass, and still nothing other than seeing the captain and Mr. Taylor near the lobby elevator after leaving the dining room," the officer said.

Dori scanned the miniature screens before her and thought that something looked out of place. "Wait, can you pull up the shot of all screens just prior to the blackout?"

The screens reverted to a still-frame of all camera views, which Dori closely scrutinized. "Okay," she prompted, "now go back to a live view of all cameras."

The miniature boxes all reverted to live feeds, and she studied the multiple monitors before her. "There's one missing from that monitor," she prompted with a pointed finger to a grayed out box which had been populated earlier on the right-most screen. "What is that?" she asked.

The security officer cocked her head to one side and clicked on the small gray window. When the cursor hovered over the window, it popped up with the message: *Vault – View Disabled.*

"Activate it," Dori ordered in a suddenly authoritative voice.

The small screen was black instead of gray, but still showed nothing.

"It's the vault interior," the officer explained. "The camera must have become disabled during the malfunction."

Dori flashed the officer a dubious look. "Can we turn a light on in there?" she asked.

The officer pulled up another screen and activated a button for lighting. The view of the small window lit up to reveal two people sitting on the floor, leaning against the wall of deposit boxes.

Dori grabbed the radio and announced, "This is Dori. They're in the vault!"

* * * *

Paige was startled by the sudden whirring sound coming from the vault camera. She took note that the red operational light was illuminated, and by its glow they could see the camera point in their direction. Then the lights brightly snapped to life with glaring intensity.

She unwound herself from around Caleb and leapt to her feet, leaving him slumped against the vault wall. He tried to rouse himself and squinted against the bright ceiling lights, but he was having trouble moving in a coordinated fashion. He was also unable to catch his breath for reasons that he had trouble fathoming.

Paige turned her body slightly and stood in front of where he lay so she was in a position to defend him. Fortunately, a vampire's physiology could operate in a much lower oxygen environment than was possible for a human.

Moments later, the vault door lock mechanism made a loud series of clicking sounds, and the large steel door began to open.

Paige relaxed once Katrina, Alton, and the hotel manager appeared in the doorway with relief evident on their faces. Caleb craned his head around to see the incoming individuals and tried to move but found himself still feeling lethargic.

Katrina's eyes focused like lasers upon his struggling form. A feeling of concern surged above the relief she felt from finding him safe.

Paige surveyed Caleb and quickly knelt down beside him as Katrina moved towards them.

"Caleb," Katrina's soft voice issued, laced with urgency.

Paige pulled him into her arms as she knelt beside him in order to stabilize him better. Alton and the bank manager remained silent as they observed Katrina's and Paige's attentions to the young man.

Caleb's cloudy thoughts began to clear, and he struggled to fill his lungs with fresh air. At the same time, he felt a returning sense of control to his limbs. He stood with success, momentarily swooning as he established his footing.

Katrina's hand appeared out of nowhere to stabilize him.

What's wrong with Caleb? She gazed at Paige searchingly.

"Minor oxygen deprivation," she replied.

Katrina then realized how dangerous the pair's situation had become before the vault was opened. She sharply looked up at both Alton and the bank manager, who displayed similar expressions of concern.

Caleb pulled free of Katrina's grip, resulting in a surprised look on the redhead's face. His mind raced with a series of confused thoughts. However, he remembered some of the last topics that he and Paige had discussed before he lost consciousness, including his regret at having broken a cardinal rule by offering his blood to another vampire.

"We have to talk, Kat," he tersely stated. "I'll confess everything. These rules just are a death sentence waiting to happen."

He barreled unsteadily towards the open doorway, though it was crowded with figures by that time, including four other vampires: the major, two security guards, and a very concerned-looking Ethan Reynolds.

Katrina and Paige stood statue-still with perplexed expressions while watching him depart.

"What happened?" Alton insisted with a curious expression as most of the faces in the small vault looked first at Paige and then at the departing stormy figure of Caleb.

Katrina appeared bewildered as she watched Caleb whisk past her without saying a word. Her mind raced with why he would be so angry about the rules at a time like this.

A broken rule? she pondered as he stormed away.

"We received a cryptic note from the front desk about the vault. It was unlocked when we got here around ten-thirty or so, and then someone locked us in here," Paige irritably recounted to Alton.

"I never got a look at who it was, and they shut the door too fast for me to reach them. They had to be a vampire to move that fast. You can see the briefcase on the floor over there that drew us both in here in the first place. This was a trap, pure and simple, and I was an idiot not to see it from the start."

"What's wrong with Caleb?" Katrina demanded with a steely voice.

Paige heatedly retorted, "Wrong? I'll tell you *exactly* what's wrong. I had to feed, and I think it almost came close to costing me your friendship, that's what. Instead, you have a mate and a best friend riddled with guilt. So, thanks for all the helpful rules that we had to confront in here."

Katrina stared at her with a stony expression.

What gives? All I'm trying to do is figure out what had happened.

Paige pushed past the group to exit, and Katrina demanded, "Now just where are you going?"

"To try and stop my friend from making a mistake," she grumbled on her way out of the vault.

Ethan's soft brown eyes caught hers as she exited, and he started to say something. However, she paused only briefly to acknowledge him before proceeding after Caleb.

Alton and Vlaeva watched Paige depart then looked at Katrina, expressions of curiosity evident on their faces.

"Well, I don't very well know either, now do I?" she fumed as she turned to follow Paige to get to the bottom of what was going on. *Why the hell do I end up being the bad guy half the time?* she fumed as she stormed from the vault. All that she ever tried to do was keep Caleb safe, but she felt that everyone was always so critical of her.

"We better look into this carefully," Alton suggested while pointing to the briefcase. "However, I'd wager that an equally intriguing story just left the room."

The hotel manager studied Alton introspectively.

"Indeed."

*   *   *   *

Paige darted in a blur to reach the elevator doors before they closed, arriving a moment too late.

"This wasn't your fault, Paige," Caleb barked from the other side of the closed doors as the elevator car ascended to the floor of his suite.

Her eyes blazed bright blue in momentary frustration as she turned to head for the stairwell fire escape. Katrina just managed to catch up with her at the steel exit door and looked at her friend with a mix of concern and aggravation.

"Paige, what the hell's going on?" Katrina demanded. Her concern was changing quickly to irritation, and she wanted some answers.

"Oh, just follow me and find out," Paige insisted as she flung the door open and sprang up the stairwell.

Wasn't an alarm supposed to sound when I opened that door? she fleetingly pondered.

The two vampires exited the stairwell door on the floor where Katrina and Caleb's suite was located and were waiting beside the elevator by the time that the doors opened.

"Crap!" Caleb exclaimed as he was startled by the sudden appearance of both vampires. He frowned at his poor track record involving surprises and elevators.

"Paige, just let me do what I have to," he declared while barreling past both of them. Proceeding down the hall towards his room, he added, "Kat, I have a confession to make, and I'd rather do it in private."

Katrina raced ahead to snatch his arm, catching him in midstride. She spun him around, causing him to teeter slightly. Stabilizing his stance with her hand on his arm, she stared into his eyes with concern. He refused to meet her gaze, however, which bothered her even more.

"What happened?" she demanded in a calm voice.

"Nothing, except that I tried to help a friend," he explained. "But thanks to the rules, Paige decided that she had to practically rape –"

"Don't you dare use that word, Caleb Taylor," Paige interrupted him with narrowed eyes. "That's not what would've happened, and you know it."

Katrina's eyes widened with surprise as she frantically tried to decipher why he would try to use such a harsh word to describe what had happened. She also wondered which rules he was referencing.

"Let's take this inside," she quickly suggested as she maintained a hold on her lover's arm while gripping Paige's upper arm in her other hand. She didn't want to discuss the topic in an open hallway on a floor occupied by curious vampires with keen senses of hearing.

Time to get to the bottom of this.

She towered above both of them with a determined expression, and neither tried to resist her as she led them to her and Caleb's room. He already had his card key out, and since Katrina's hands were full, he unlocked the door.

Katrina pushed them both into the suite before her and slammed the door behind them. *If I have to get a little rough just to get some answers, then so be it.*

"You," she ordered with a pointed finger at Caleb, "sit quietly on the couch."

He silently perched on the edge of the couch with his arms defiantly folded before him.

"And you," Katrina stated, pointing her finger at Paige, "start talking."

Both vampires moved into the living room with Paige sitting on the chair across from Caleb while Katrina sat next to him on the couch. She calmly listened as Paige recounted what had happened in the vault, including all the details related to their rules dilemma and the final solution for Paige to feed successfully.

"You know, I'm the one dying of thirst now," Caleb impatiently interjected.

Katrina said nothing, but moved to the small refrigerator in the kitchenette area to retrieve a bottle of water for him. She felt a momentary pang of guilt at having neglected to consider how thirsty he probably was after being locked in the vault. She made a mental note to ask if he were hungry after they finished discussing what had happened.

"Please continue," she instructed Paige as she handed the bottled water to Caleb.

Paige proceeded from where she had left off, and Katrina's face was stern as she listened quietly to her friend. However, Paige deftly excluded details from the intimate discussion that she had shared with Caleb involving her feelings for him.

Katrina patiently listened as her friend recounted the events that both led up to, and followed, being locked in the vault. She casually observed Caleb in her peripheral vision as he drank the entire container of water. She couldn't help but notice that he appeared tense and agitated.

Once Paige finished, Katrina felt a host of emotions cascade upon her: anger towards whomever had trapped both her friend and mate, frustration over the seeming ineffectiveness of the security systems, and a pressing uneasiness over what had transpired between Paige and Caleb while isolated in the vault. In the end, she merely sighed with resignation.

"Who could have predicted that such a situation might occur? This is the first time that I know of where a human has been co-sponsored in some way between vampires," she insisted. "But you two should be lawyers given how handily you interpreted and generated loopholes to my rules for him."

Paige resented her tone and snapped, "Thanks, Ms. Sarcasm. Why don't you take another minute to try to understand our circumstances? The air was being used up pretty quickly by the time that I finished feeding. The situation looked pretty dire, though I wasn't about to tell him that."

Katrina was surprised by her friend's candid assessment of their plight within the vault.

"That bad?" she quietly asked.

"That bad," Paige confirmed. "You saw how debilitated he was when you entered the vault. Another hour and who knows if you would have found him alive."

Katrina sat stunned, while Caleb's face washed with shock.

"You never told me that," he quietly accused.

Paige paused. "What kind of guardian would I be if I inflamed the situation at times like that? Besides, you'd just get upset and use up the oxygen faster."

Katrina admired Paige's grasp of sound logic.

Hard to be upset with either of them, I suppose. Paige made the sensible decision. Would I have acted any differently?

Caleb's irritation dissipated, and he turned to grim thoughts as Paige's comments sank deeper into his mind. He glanced up at Katrina with a serious expression, only to find her intently staring at him. Her green eyes were penetrating but not angry, and he noticed that the corners of her mouth were upturned ever so slightly.

"I'm not angry with either of you, my love," she reassured him. Truth was, she was merely grateful that they were still alive.

He was somewhat surprised by that revelation. "But what

about the third rule?"

She shrugged. "I suppose that we'll need to start consider-ing that one in a situational context in the future, won't we?"

Despite knowing full well that both of them were trustwor-thy, it took a conscious effort on her part to be flexible about her control issues.

Maybe there's hope for me yet, she entertained.

Both Caleb and Paige considered her with upraised brows, and then exchanged curious glances with each other.

Katrina was amused by their reaction, but cautioned, "However, let's not get too crazy with the whole feeding thing, okay?"

They both nearly simultaneously replied, "Got it." Their eyes darted to each other over the coincidence.

"Okay then," Paige resolved, relieved that her best friend's concerns had been somewhat placated and that her own strong feelings for Caleb remained effectively unmentioned. "First, I'm still kind of thirsty, so I'm gonna go round up some more of the red stuff. Then I'm getting to work on finding the asshole that locked us in the vault."

Someone's going to become very dead very fast when I find them.

"Keep me posted," Katrina grimly instructed.

Her eyes darted to her mate, and the horrible thought of his near-death in the vault flashed in her mind. It had been a close call, and she intended to see that justice was handed out swiftly to those responsible.

"I'll check in with you later," Paige promised. Her eyes briefly fell upon Caleb. "Besides, kiddo here needs some rest."

She flashed him a smirk then rose to depart the room with a nod to Katrina.

"Paige?" Katrina prompted before she had reached the door to exit the suite.

"Yes?" she suspiciously asked while glancing over her shoulder.

"I'd rather that you not drink from him recreationally," Katrina informed her friend.

"Understood," she replied while gazing at Caleb in a penetrating fashion that slightly unnerved him. Then she winked and departed, closing the door to the suite behind her.

Katrina rose from the couch and went to lock the door to the suite, while Caleb wearily leaned back into the couch cushion. When she turned around, she maintained a neutral expression, but her eyes had a calculating look about them.

She joined him on the couch, warmly embracing him in her arms. Her arms protectively encircled him, and she felt his rapid heartbeat against her body. She sensed that something else was bothering him, something beyond the vault incident.

"I trust both of you, you know," she reassured him. The possessive nature of her personality railed against her declaration, but she bent it to her will.

He drew in the sweet scent of cherry blossoms emanating from her body and appreciated the soothing quality of it. "I'm glad. I'd never violate my fidelity to you, and I doubt that Paige would want that either."

"I appreciate that, my love," she contentedly replied. She trusted him implicitly and was merely happy to have him safely in her arms again.

He marveled at how understanding she was about the situation and hoped that she realized that his commitment to her was sincere. In his mind, there was no other prospective mate for him.

Her soft lips found his, and they tenderly kissed. Her fingers caressed the side of his face as their lips met again and again, until finally he had to pull away in order to catch his breath.

She realized that he must have felt exhausted. "Time for a shower and some oxygen-rich sleep, I think," she quipped.

He hauled himself upright with a tired groan and began stripping out of his shirt. She watched him walk towards the bedroom, appreciating his masculine form as the removal of his shirt revealed his lean chest and back muscles. She found him so attractive, and she tentatively bit her lower lip as carnal visions played across her thoughts.

"Well, maybe some sleep after I'm finished with you," she slyly muttered as she slipped her shoes off.

She purposefully slipped off the couch to follow him into the bedroom.

* * * *

Paige barely had time to finish a quick shower and pull on some sweatpants and a t-shirt before a knock sounded at her suite door. Still drying her hair with a towel, she flung open the door, expecting it to be the major or perhaps even the hotel manager.

Instead, Ethan Reynolds stood in the hallway holding a large Styrofoam cup with a lid on it. Her eyes flashed to the cup before looking up into his eyes, which reflected concern and maybe something else.

"Ethan?" she asked. Her eyes appreciated the way that his jeans perfectly fit his slim waist, as well as the snug fit of his black t-shirt against his muscled chest.

He started to say something, but stopped and instead extended the cup to her.

"Brought you a little something," he said with a supportive smile. "I was worried and wanted to check in on you."

She reached out to accept the warm cup and caught the faint scent of blood. Smiling, she gestured for him to come inside.

Realizing that she still held a damp towel over her hair, a wave of embarrassment washed over her. "Sorry, I'm a bit of a mess right now," she stammered as she closed the door behind them.

He entered and turned to look down at her. "Nah, you look great, actually," he assured her.

She casually tossed her towel on the nearby couch and popped open the lid to the cup. The scent of blood permeated the air, and she took a moment to drink from it. The warm liquid tasted amazing to her, though not nearly as much as Caleb's had earlier.

"I raced down to the basement when I heard they found you," Ethan gently offered. "I was pretty worried, but then I saw you both standing inside, and I felt so relieved."

Her blue eyes darted to his, and she glimpsed the sincerity reflected in them. Surprisingly, it deeply touched her that he felt that way. She frowned at the confused feelings she had, but registered a more familiar sensation run through her as she practically ogled him: desire.

"Sorry about earlier," she apologized, recalling how she had barely acknowledged him at the vault. "It wasn't that I —" she began.

She was interrupted by the sudden crush of his lips against hers.

He moved like a whirlwind, sweeping her into his strong arms and nearly lifting her from the floor. Her earlier feelings of desire peaked, transforming into a wave of sexual energy that cascaded throughout her body. The sensation was almost electric as their lips pressed together in a prolonged kiss that nearly took her breath away.

Still in his arms, she lifted her legs and wrapped them around his waist. His lips pressed to hers, drawing the breath from her lungs. He swung the two of them onto the couch, pressing her into the cushions with the strength that only another vampire could wield.

The heat streaming from both of them was palpable, and Paige's dormant sexuality sprang to life. Her body's reaction surprised her, but she relished every second. Only then did she fully realize the impact of the subtle tension that had been rising between them ever since the evening that Caleb had introduced them.

Much to her satisfaction, his body was everything that she had previously only playfully imagined. His body pressed against hers, and she felt firm fingertips against her soft skin.

Her lips locked onto his, and she felt her t-shirt being lifted upwards.

In a matter of moments, clothes were shed, and their bodies were joined. And finally, time stood still.

*   *   *   *

Early the next morning, Katrina slipped out of the suite while Caleb slept. She joined Alton to strategize for the upcoming resumption of the conference, or as she preferred to call it, the "organized debate and argumentation" sessions. While happy that Caleb was once again safe, she couldn't help wondering what was coming next.

Maybe I should've handcuffed him to the bed, she darkly reflected as the conference prepared to reconvene. *That might actually keep him out of trouble.*

Later that morning, Caleb made his way to the dining room for something to eat. He was keenly aware that a number of staff and guests stared at him as he passed. Embracing his newfound, notorious celebrity, he simply waved or politely wished them good morning.

He sat alone at a table in the corner, glowering into a cup of hot tea as he waited for his food to arrive. After massaging his sore eyelids with his fingertips at length, he stared wide-eyed across the table at Paige, already seated and intently studying him over a cup of coffee.

"Morning, tiger," she merrily offered.

He felt a rush of happiness at the sight of her. "Good morning, babysitter."

She adopted a playful grin as the waitress set a large plate of eggs, sausage, hash browns, and biscuits before him. He thanked her and hungrily appreciated the array of food as she departed.

"That's a honkin' plateful," Paige said in a mock-southern drawl.

He reached for a packet of grape jelly.

"Hey, I gotta make enough blood for two nowadays, you know," he countered.

Paige's smile faded a little as the memories of feeding on him in the vault washed over her. She recalled the rich taste of his blood and felt a momentary urge for more. Instead she sipped at her coffee, admittedly a poor substitute, and refocused her thoughts.

The revelations of mere hours ago washed over her. Despite her surprising, yet satisfying interlude with Ethan, she nevertheless felt a strong emotional draw to the young man before her.

After shoveling in a few forkfuls of food, he looked up to note her contemplative expression. He absently reached up with one hand to touch the place on his neck where she had bitten him, which immediately drew her attention.

"Sore?" she softly asked.

"Nope, never better," he replied with a shy smirk.

It was no worse than when Katrina drank from him, actually. Yet, there was something more to having shared his blood with her. He couldn't explain it, but he felt an increased closeness and an increased sense of affection between them.

Following a few bites of food, he looked up to find her staring at him again. "What?" he asked.

She was caught between conflicting feelings at that moment. As she stared at him, she saw an attractive, innocent man who she had sworn to protect, as well as someone who was a best friend. Granted, she enjoyed flirting with him and occasionally contemplating sex with him. But it was much more than that. She loved him, unlike anyone else she had ever known. And then with sharing his blood the previous night, those feelings were heightened. It had been more than feeding; it was intimate.

Even the sex that she had shared with Ethan, while surprisingly good, had been merely that: sex. Oh, she liked the handsome doctor, but then, they hardly knew one another. The sex was easy to understand and manage, unlike the complex spectrum of feelings that she felt for Caleb.

"Paige?" he asked with a perplexed expression.

She looks almost dazed.

She broke from her reverie. "Yeah, I heard you, kiddo," she answered. "Eat up."

He shook his head and continued to eat. Minutes later, Dori appeared and plopped down into a chair between them.

"There you two are," she energetically said. "I've been looking for you, Caleb. We have interesting things to talk about, you and I."

"Yeah?" he asked between forkfuls of egg and sausage.

Before Dori could respond, Ethan appeared at the tableside wearing the trappings of his trade in the form of a white lab coat over slacks and dress shirt. Completing the look was a stethoscope lazily draped around his neck.

"Good morning, everyone," he greeted in a friendly tone.

The three of them all looked up with smiles, though Paige's was more of a satisfied grin. His eyes caught the blonde vampire's only briefly before fully focusing on Caleb.

"How are you feeling this morning, young sir?" he asked in a practiced tone.

"Uh-oh, he's got that doctor's voice going on," Caleb teased. "Me? I'm fine today, Doc. All the oxygen's returned to my brain."

"Leaving only the usual minor damage," Dori quipped. "We hardly noticed the change."

"Ha, good one," Paige snapped and happily slapped open palms with the brunette.

Caleb adopted a bland expression and cast a withering look towards the women. "Oh, so very funny...not."

"Well, if you notice any blurred vision, disorientation, or headaches, come see me immediately, okay?" Ethan insisted. "Enjoy your day," he added and turned to walk away.

Paige's eyes followed him as he walked away, and then turned to notice that her two tablemates were watching her with curious expressions. "What?" she snapped.

Caleb and Dori innocently shook their heads.

"Oh, whatever," Paige blurted and rose from her seat. "I gotta run down some leads on last night. I'll let you know what I find out."

She quickly departed the dining room, leaving the two humans with perplexed expressions.

"What was that about?" Caleb asked.

"Not sure that I care to say right at the moment," Dori wistfully observed with a knowing tone.

Then she noted Caleb's curious expression and changed the subject. "Listen, I finally have some information related to our little storage building excursion."

"Like what?" He felt that the topic was old news given all of the recent excitement.

Dori explained that she had acquired old photographs of mines in the surrounding area from museum archives. One photo clearly showed the same area where they had been apprehended by the authorities. As recently as thirty years prior there had been an actual open entrance into a mine where the storage building presently stood.

Caleb was encouraged that they hadn't been barking up the wrong tree in their search of the site.

"Did you show everything to Alton?" he inquired.

"Yes," she glumly replied. "But he wasn't as interested as I expected him to be."

He silently pondered their situation. "So, with our being under virtual house arrest, how are we supposed to get back there?" he asked.

"We sneak out, of course."

"Lady, I like your style. What's the plan?"

"I'm working on that, but I should have something by tonight," she said.

"What can I do to help in the meantime?" he asked before lifting another forkful of food to his mouth.

She rose from her seat. "For now, just try to stay out of trouble. Think you can manage that?"

He rolled his eyes and offered her a sour expression as she

walked away. Then he happily returned to his breakfast.

*   *   *   *

By midafternoon, Paige was silently fuming during a protracted interview, or rather interrogation, from Major Pietari pertaining to her and Caleb's experiences leading up to and during their vault detainment. His insistence that she go over the details three times merely to be thorough sounded rational, though she somehow had the notion that he was enjoying himself.

However, she didn't give him the satisfaction, and instead patiently recounted the information upon request. In the end, it had seemed to her to be a waste of more than two hours of valuable time.

Finally, she was able to return to her duties, which meant engaging in her own investigation. Sitting before the video surveillance monitors, she poured over the stored video streams from the previous night just prior to her and Caleb's entering the elevator, as well as anything potentially useful that had been recorded after the systems came back online.

In addition to the vault camera's having been switched off, she noted that the basement cameras were unable to capture anything useful, either. Someone had been quite artful and clandestine in avoiding any other camera viewing angles.

An inside job, she resolved.

She reverted to a live video feed, quickly scanning the plethora of images before her, and zoomed in on a view from the shopping area near the main lobby. Caleb walked into one of the shops with Maddy Baker and Aiden Henderson in tow. She was pleased that he was interacting with other humans, instead of obsessing over Baldar Dubravko or any other vampires at the conference.

Upon further consideration, Paige considered it likely that their unplanned detainment had been part of a darker scheme. To her, the two most important questions were: which vampire took the initiative to act, and upon whose authority or sanction? The minutes passed as she reviewed the conference participants and any known affiliations for those who were representing absent parties. Despite her dedication to the investigation at hand, her mind wandered a couple of times. And on both occasions, the subject of such wandering was none other than the handsome and charming Dr. Ethan Reynolds. To her surprise, she found herself smiling like a school girl who was experiencing her first crush.

I need to get laid more often, she chastised herself, refocusing on the task at hand.

* * * *

Caleb spent the afternoon visiting with Maddy and Aiden and actually enjoyed himself for one of the few occasions since his arrival at the conference. For a brief period of time, he was able to stop dwelling on recent events, vampires, or mysterious upcoming plans with Dori. For a few hours, he was nothing more than a tourist enjoying the company of friends, or at least, burgeoning friends. He admired his newfound human companions and appreciated their diverse backgrounds and personalities.

He found Maddy to be happy-go-lucky, magnetic, and witty. In some ways, she reminded him of Paige, including their early twenty-something appearance. And yet, there seemed to be an underlying seriousness to her; focused and intent on where she was and what she was doing at any given moment.

Aiden was an electrician, a skilled tradesman in his own right, and a person with a sharp intellect coupled with a comradely demeanor. He was Caleb's age, though he carried himself in a confident, self-assured manner that one might expect from someone much older and experienced.

Caleb appreciated the social and emotional respite provided by the two of them. However, by late afternoon, the three had once again gone their separate ways. Maddy returned to her suite to shower and change before dinner. Aiden wanted to catch one of the late afternoon shuttle rides into Podjelje to purchase some gifts for family back home in Connecticut. Caleb had no immediate plans or obligations and decided to take a walk outside. On his way through the lobby, he ran into Dori, who was furiously scribbling on a notepad.

"What's up?" he asked. "Any progress?"

Her violet eyes caught his with an energetic zeal. "Working on it. We'll talk soon," she promised before whisking across the lobby in the direction of the elevator.

He shook his head with amusement as he proceeded towards the exit. He briefly wandered through the well-maintained flowerbeds and envied the skilled hands that had meticulously given to each bed. Though he had lived on an acreage as a child, he had moved to the city before learning much about tending gardens. Once in the city, his mother, as a single parent, rarely had the time to devote to gardening.

Caleb wandered in the direction of the nearby forest. Unlike the manicured gardens, the forest presented nature in its native, unbridled decorum. The unexpected cool breeze that swept across the mountains felt refreshing on that sunny late afternoon. The looming canopy of trees was quickly being overshadowed by the nearby mountain as the sun continued its westward track behind it. In a couple of hours, it would be dusk.

Unlike the main conference grounds, the forested area was devoid of people, aside from a single human guard who acknowledged Caleb in passing on his march back towards the conference center. Caleb offered a friendly greeting, but noticed that the man stared at him rather suspiciously.

Well, I am the resident troublemaker, after all, he conceded.

After no more than fifteen minutes of wandering, he heard the birds and other wildlife suddenly fall silent. Something triggered in his subconscious, and his eyes panned the area. Seeing nothing, he shrugged and continued his stroll.

A couple of minutes later, he looked up in the direction of a rustling sound in the bushes less than twenty feet to his right. His eyes immediately fell upon a pale-skinned woman with short, auburn hair wearing a security uniform worn by the conference site officers.

Instantly, he recognized the vampire that he had seen back in Atlanta in his backyard at the estate and at the Italian restaurant.

At first, she surveyed him with disdain. Then her expression transformed to a sneer, and she shook her head slightly.

"Of all the luck," she said.

Instead of fear, he registered surprise. "What are the odds?" he whispered.

He half-expected her to respond aggressively, but was dumbfounded when she merely winked at him. Then she turned and raced through the trees in the opposite direction, leading deeper into the woods towards the nearby incline of the mountain base. It was at that moment that he weighed the flight or fight reaction that any normal human would experience.

Yet, his decision was something that made him doubt his own sanity: he pursued her.

"Wait!" he yelled, plunging headfirst into the forest after her.

It took less than a minute of running for him to realize that she could easily outdistance him, leaving him lost in foreign surroundings with no sense of direction. A pang of doubt clouded his initial decision. Determined, he ran faster as he tromped across the uneven ground before him.

Soon, he came to the perimeter fence that surrounded the vast conference site property and which the vampire effortlessly seemed to slip through. He ran towards the location, wondering what magic trick had just been displayed.

As he drew closer, he quickly recognized the subtle manner in which the links had been cut to appear intact, while providing easy access through the barrier. Slipping between the cut links, he caught his shirt and scraped his hand, but made it to the other side.

The chase was on again, though he thought that she must have stopped to observe him because she wasn't much further ahead than before. Skirting a felled tree trunk, he leapt over a small depression in the ground, barely maintaining his footing as he propelled forward.

To his mutual surprise and satisfaction, he caught a glimpse of her through a break in the trees in the distance. *Well, she hasn't turned on her vampire super-speed yet, and she hasn't tried to kill me.*

"Hold up!" he yelled, but kept running, despite feeling a little winded.

He tried to maintain visual contact on her as she stopped to look back at him. Suddenly, his body lurched forward as he caught a tree root underfoot. His eyes darted downwards, and he flung his arms before him as a large rock sped towards him on his plunge to the ground. His left arm raked across the side of a rough-barked tree as he tried to grasp at anything nearby. At the last second he instinctually closed his eyes prior to impact, but felt something wrap around his torso, suspending him in midair.

His eyes snapped open to see the rock just inches from his face. His head swiveled up and to the right to see the auburn-haired vampire holding him with one arm.

She had an aggravated expression on her face and spat, "My God, you're clumsy. And insane!"

"Busted," he conceded with a hopeful expression.

She immediately dropped him to the ground beside the rock.

"Umph!"

"I don't believe this," she muttered with exasperation while perching her hands atop her hips.

He hefted himself up from the ground and sat up and back on his heels.

"Thanks," he appreciatively offered as he examined his left

arm.

She rolled her eyes and shook her head in disgust. "Give me one good reason why I don't drink you for dinner," she chided.

The gravity of his circumstances quickly washed over him, and he adopted a nervous smirk. "Um, perhaps because I'm charming in an annoying kind of way?"

She fought back a scowl with only partial success. "True," she agreed. "On the annoying part, that is."

The fear that had been growing inside him began to dissipate, but only slightly. His motivations for doing what he had were cursory at best, and he quickly acknowledged that he was facing a situation that could turn negative at any moment.

As if in time with his thoughts, the vampire demanded in a serious tone, "So, why are you following me? What's your game, human?"

"Actually, we both have the same questions, I think," he hedged. It was the best that he could come up with in a pinch.

She seemed taken aback at first, but resumed her serious, piercing focus on him. "And?" she demanded.

He swallowed hard, straining for something relevant to counter with. Then his memory played back to the conversation with the tall, dark vampire in Katrina's backyard before their trip.

"Take me to your leader?" he weakly ventured.

She winced at his lame reference. "Oh, I can't wait to see what Hazi says about this," she muttered.

She reached down to grab him by his uninjured arm and effortlessly pulled him up from the ground like a rag doll. He lurched upwards and struggled to gain his balance while in her grasp.

She spun him around and propelled him forwards in the direction that she had been running earlier. He nearly lost his footing, but managed to right himself.

The waning light around them gave the forest an edgy appearance, and he swallowed hard, wondering if he had made the right decision or not. However, at least the delay in walking with her allowed his racing thoughts more time to settle so that he could think more clearly.

"I don't even know your name," he muttered.

At first, she said nothing. Following a prolonged pause, she replied, "Mara."

"Mara. A beautiful name," he offered in a cheerful tone. "I'm Caleb."

"I know who you are," she sternly responded and pushed him from behind to encourage a brisker pace.

By the time twilight fell, there was barely enough light for him to see where he was walking. Fortunately, she allowed him to slow slightly, enabling him to maintain his footing. That was not to say he didn't stumble now and again, occasionally eliciting a disparaging response from Mara.

A short time later, they broke through the dense forest to enter a small clearing at the base of the mountain. A dark-skinned vampire casually leaned against a large, moss-covered boulder. He was the same vampire who had confronted him in Katrina's backyard just weeks prior.

Unfortunately, Caleb couldn't remember his rather complicated proper name, though he recalled Mara referring to him as "Hazi." However, something Katrina had once said about vampires and nicknames made him reject the idea of using such an informal address with the stranger.

"I've been pondering who might be accompanying you," the yellow-eyed vampire announced, sounding mildly intrigued.

Caleb walked towards him, but Mara grabbed his arm to halt him before he was six feet from the vampire.

"I ran into this one while approaching the perimeter," Mara explained. "Since he's probably the only person at the site who might recognize me, I thought it best to abort my plans."

One side of the man's mouth upturned with amusement.

"And you didn't kill him instead?" he asked.

She hesitated and grumbled.

"A soft spot for this one, perhaps?" he inquired.

Caleb started to turn to gauge her reaction, but she promptly popped him in the back of the head.

"I'm still contemplating dinner," she wryly remarked. "His blood smells inviting to me."

He took stock of his wounded hand and noticed that the blood was starting to dry where he had gouged it on the fence. His left arm ached slightly from the abrasions he had sustained earlier. He realized that it wasn't a good idea to chum the air with blood around a vampire.

"Well said," the man replied. Then he turned to address Caleb directly. "You remember me?"

"Yes, sir," Caleb politely replied. "Although I'm ashamed at the moment not to recall your name properly."

"So polite," he remarked. "I am Hakizimana."

Caleb attempted to brand the name into his mind while inclining his head in a gesture of respectful deference. Hakizimana seemed impressed by that, and the edges of his mouth upturned slightly.

Caleb viewed the growing darkness as an ominous blanket around him, and he had trouble clearly seeing the vampire's expression. He warily surveyed the area as if half-expecting a contingent of other vampires to appear out of nowhere.

"We are alone...for now," Hakizimana offered. "What can you tell me about the status of the conference, Caleb?" he asked with an authoritative tone.

Though Katrina had been kind enough to discuss the meetings in general terms, Caleb had very little specific information from the meetings. However, he understood that both she and Alton were suspicious of the motives of some of those in attendance, and the tone of the proceedings seemed less than fruitful. Despite his own growing reticence about the conference, he paused to consider what might be prudent to reveal.

"Well, it hasn't exactly been successful," he hinted.

That seemed to please the tall vampire, who smiled enough to display pearly white teeth for the first time.

"I thought as much," he replied. "Alton Rutherford is far

too presumptuous concerning his personal projects."

"Even though I'm anxious for it to be over, I somehow don't get the impression that failure is a good thing in this case," he reasoned.

"Oh?" prompted Hakizimana.

"Well," Caleb began, "Alton's agenda may not be the one you need to be concerned about."

Mara orbited around Caleb to gaze into his eyes, while Hakizimana moved closer towards him. He tried to remain calm, but nevertheless tensed from the rapt attention suddenly being paid to him.

"What do you mean by that?" Hakizimana asked.

Caleb swallowed, deciding, *In for a penny, down for a pound.* He shifted in his stance slightly so that both vampires were in front of him.

"There's a vampire named Baldar Dubravko, you see. And between him and another vampire named Dominic Ambrogio-"

"We already know of them," Mara interrupted.

Hakizimana held up his hand to silence her then nodded for Caleb to continue.

Caleb's eyes darted between the faces of the two vampires before him, but settled upon Hakizimana. He hoped the sincerity of his next statements would ring true to him.

"They seem to be doing everything possible to disrupt the conference and its attendees," he explained. "It's as if they're quite satisfied that things aren't going well."

"So?" Mara challenged.

"Well, I've been watching them," Caleb ventured. "And though I can't say for certain yet, it does seem as if they're up to something. I'm fairly certain that I almost suffocated to death in a vault just from demonstrating an overt interest in them."

Hakizimana's brows furrowed.

But Mara scoffed and urged, "You're just speculating in generalities, human. Hazi, we're wasting time. Let me drain this one, and I'll still have time to check things out for myself."

Caleb's pulse surged, and he nervously eyed the woman.

Perhaps he had been hasty thinking that she had taken a liking to him at all.

"Wait," Hakizimana ordered. His yellow eyes bore into Caleb's despite the darkness. "What is it that you think they're up to, exactly?"

Mara shook her head and settled her hands on her hips.

Caleb couldn't help thinking that this was his all-or-nothing gamble for either redemption or doom. He silently deliberated over everything that he had acquired from his own observations, coupled with anything Katrina or Paige had said to him. Then he replayed all the ponderings that he had contemplated during his numerous hours of boredom.

Finally, he shrugged and tried sounding as innocent as possible, "Well, if they're so adamant against the conference, maybe that doesn't just indicate disinterest in the proposal. What if the conference's failure removes an impediment to another competing interest? And if Alton's proposal is open and voluntary to anyone who wishes to join, what form of alternative or counter-agenda does that open the door for? Maybe nothing. Or maybe something that's oppressive and less voluntary in nature."

Mara blankly stared at Caleb, while Hakizimana thoughtfully tapped his chin with a fingertip. Seconds felt like hours as Caleb stood helplessly before the two vampires, wondering if his life were about to end.

I should've just run like hell for the conference center, he belatedly determined.

Eventually, Hakizimana sagely nodded his head.

"An interesting possibility. Granted, it's a great deal of speculation, but it's worth considering."

Caleb felt cautiously hopeful for the first time that evening. Then something else occurred to him.

"Um, if you don't mind me asking, why don't you infiltrate the conference and find out for yourself?"

Mara groaned. "What do you think I was trying to do when you saw me?"

"No," Caleb countered, "I mean, from the inside."

"And how do you propose we do that?" Hakizimana asked.

"Easy," he explained. "Just attend the conference."

Mara stared at the tall vampire next to her. The dark-featured man's eyes widened with some surprise.

"You have a gift for guile, for a human," he observed. "As if Alton's going to just invite me in, much less Katrina, who I'm sure won't be very pleased to see me."

Caleb admitted the logic of his statement. It was time for another gamble.

"Okay, point taken. But what if I could guarantee your safe admission to the conference?"

"And precisely what is your method of guarantee?" Mara demanded.

"Me," he offered. "I'll personally guarantee your safe consultation with Alton about this. My life for my word."

"We could take your life now," she flatly ventured.

Caleb contained a shiver at her cold tone and countered, "Yes, but it won't get you admission into the conference if you kill me now."

Hakizimana chuckled. "Well played, young man. Perhaps we'll consider your boon."

Caleb optimistically regarded the tall vampire.

"Any other bargaining chips up your sleeve?" Mara inquired.

He grinned. "Well, maybe..."

*   *   *   *

Paige strolled outside among the flowerbeds at the front of the conference center, appreciating the cool evening breeze. The shuttle bus pulled up before the hotel entrance with returning guests who had taken an earlier journey into town. She peered up at the partial moon in the sky and inhaled the fragrance of the nearby flowers. She also detected the telltale scent of a certain aftershave.

"Lovely night for a stroll," Ethan offered, appearing seemingly out of nowhere. Devoid of doctor's coat and stethoscope, he looked like a tourist in his casual slacks and collared shirt. She looked up at him. "Sure, if you like that whole romantic walk in the park sort of thing."

"You don't?" he asked with some surprise.

"I never said that," she demurred.

Her radio suddenly crackled to life with the voice of a tense security guard. "Captain Turner to the west exterior side of the conference center immediately! We've got visitors."

Paige and Ethan moved like a blur as they raced to the other side of the facility.

When they arrived on the scene, four vampire security guards were pointing submachine guns at Caleb and two other vampires whom Paige didn't recognize. She sensed his anxiety and immediately noticed that his left hand had been recently injured. Her concern for him was quickly superseded by building anger directed towards the two vampires flanking him whose appearance matched his descriptions of the two vampires who had confronted him in Katrina's backyard, as well as the woman at the Italian restaurant.

"Who are you, and what have you done to Caleb?" Paige demanded. She sensed Ethan's solid presence beside her.

"It's okay, Paige," Caleb reassured her. "It was an accident."

"We're here under a flag of truce. We merely need to speak with Alton," Hakizimana calmly explained.

"If that's true, then let the young man come over here," Paige negotiated.

Mara moved closer behind Caleb, gripping the top of his left shoulder in her hand and firmly squeezing.

"Um, I'm kind of guaranteeing their safety," Caleb tensely countered.

Paige growled, and Mara's grip immediately lessened, resulting in a sense of relief on Caleb's face.

"Get Alton out here now," Paige commanded into her radio,

knowing that if Alton came, so would Katrina.

Minutes later, Caleb watched as two figures virtually materialized out of the darkness to stand to the right of Paige. Alton maintained a neutral expression, while Katrina's was virtually livid, her emerald eyes brightly lit. Between her visage and her red hair shifting in the evening breeze, she looked liked a beautiful demon from hell ready to unleash both fury and brimstone on those around her, and Caleb shivered slightly.

Mara's eyes widened as she sensed the tension in his body, and she readjusted to a more aggressive stance.

"You rang, Hakizimana?" Alton quipped as he soberly studied the tall vampire.

The tall vampire inclined his head in greeting. "Alton Rutherford, I've come to request admittance to your conference."

Alton's eyebrows curiously rose. "I see. And what, may I ask, caused you to reconsider my offer of nearly a year ago? An offer you pointedly rejected twice, as I recall."

"Remarkably, this young man," the yellow-eyed vampire matter-of-factly replied.

"Really?" Alton incredulously challenged.

Katrina appeared astonished, but said nothing.

"Well, kiddo's just full of surprises," Paige whispered.

Alton dismissed the gun-wielding vampires around him with a wave of his hand. They looked at Paige for confirmation, and she curtly assented.

The four vampires shouldered their weapons and quietly slipped back into the night.

"And what, exactly, did Caleb say that piqued your interest?" Katrina demanded. She was quite unhappy to see Mara's hand on her mate's shoulder and even more displeased to see his wounded hand and arm. The scent of his blood played in the air between them with each passing breeze.

Hakizimana appeared circumspect for a moment. "He shared some compelling arguments concerning the *best interests* of those in attendance. And then, of course, there were other perks."

"Perks?" Alton pressed.

"Um, I may have mentioned that we could comp them for their suites," Caleb spoke up. "Perhaps one of the larger suites?" he tentatively added.

Paige groaned and tightly pinched the bridge of her nose between the fingers of one hand. Katrina rolled her eyes, and Ethan artfully stifled a laugh.

"I think we can arrange something," Alton diplomatically offered. "You're welcome to attend the conference, of course. You may be surprised to discover that I actually appreciate your participation."

"Thank you for your hospitality," Hakizimana offered with a slight inclination of his head.

"Are there just the two of you?" Paige guardedly inquired.

"Just Mara and I," Hakizimana replied. "However, I represent a number of other interested parties," he added.

"How many?" Katrina asked.

"Close to three dozen, including the two of us," the tall vampire replied.

Alton was immediately intrigued, and he shot a meaningful glance to Katrina.

"Excellent," he replied in a self-satisfied tone.

Katrina regarded him suspiciously, but quickly refocused her attention back on Caleb.

"And what of my mate?" she demanded with narrowed eyes.

"Naturally, I remand him back into your custody," Hakizimana offered, at which Mara released her grip on Caleb's shoulder.

Katrina crooked her finger at Caleb and wiggled it in a slow, beckoning fashion as she glared at him with a penetrating stare.

He swallowed hard, fleetingly wondering if he didn't feel more comfortable in Mara's grasp. Nevertheless, he moved away from the two vampires to within a few feet of Katrina.

"Perhaps we should arrange for your accommodations," Alton politely suggested to the two visitors with a gesture of his hand towards the conference center.

Hakizimana inclined his head in a gracious manner, and he and Mara followed Alton. Paige cast a curious, yet concerned, glance at Caleb before turning to fall in behind the trio. Ethan quickly surveyed Katrina's displeased features and looked at Caleb with concern.

"Let's have a look at those abrasions, Caleb," he reassuringly suggested and moved towards the young man.

Katrina held up her left hand, insisting, "I think that I've got this. Thank you for your concern, Doctor."

Ethan looked at Caleb, who shrugged.

"Thanks, Doc," he replied. "But don't wander too far," he sheepishly quipped. "I just might need you later by the look of things."

Katrina cast him a withering expression, though his comment elicited an amused smile from Ethan.

"I'm always a mere call away," he politely affirmed and turned to walk back towards the conference center.

"Very funny," Katrina remarked, somewhat relieved that her mate's sense of humor had returned. "Let me see your arm," she insisted, reaching out to him.

He stepped forward, extending his left arm to her.

She observed him in a stern manner that might chill a simmering volcano, but gently held his arm in her soft hands as she scrutinized his abrasions.

"Let's go back to the room, and I'll seal these," she suggested.

He nodded with resignation and fell into step beside her as they walked to the hotel. While there was no denying that he was happy to be back safely at the conference site, he was nonetheless concerned about Katrina's mood.

"I thought I was trying to help, but as with everything lately, all that I managed to do is make you angry," he lamented.

She looked at the man who had captured her heart, draping one arm around his waist as they walked.

"I realize that you mean well, my love," she conceded. "You're so young and full of adventure, but there are moments when you lack the wisdom to make sound decisions. It's a burden of youth, I'm afraid, and something that will develop with time."

She only hoped that she could keep him alive long enough for wisdom to set in.

He tried not to feel offended by her critical observations. "Alton seemed quite pleased with the results this evening," he tentatively ventured.

"But your methods are reckless, occasionally bordering on foolhardy," she snapped. "You're going to get yourself killed, Caleb."

He winced slightly over her biting admonition while simultaneously struggling to contain his irritation at being scolded almost like a child.

She caught herself before she continued her rant, and instead made a conscious effort to settle her temper as they walked.

Heaven help me, I sound like some horrible, angry bitch, she shamefully realized.

"Look," she patiently attempted, "this is hard for me. The stakes are escalating, along with the danger, and I don't want to lose you."

"I don't want to lose you either," he blurted, not fully realizing the intensity of his feelings, or their implied double meaning, until that moment. Given Katrina's lengthy obligations to committee sessions, it already felt as if he had been practically alone on the trip as it was.

She halted in midstride while encircling his waist with her arm and turned to stare into his gentle, pale-blue eyes. For as much as he was a capable young man by human standards, he appeared somewhat vulnerable to her.

"You're not going to lose me, my love," she calmly reassured him.

He offered a wan smile, and she bent down to kiss him warmly on the lips. Appreciative for her intimate attentions, he gratefully returned her kiss.

"Honestly, none of this is easy for me, either, and I'm trying my best to adapt to situations as events unfold. I want to prove to you that I can actually handle adversity. I know that you worry about me, and I'd like to promise you that I'll stay out of trouble, but I just can't make any guarantees," he earnestly offered.

She couldn't help but admire how determined and sincere he sounded. A previous, fanciful thought from earlier that morning gravitated to the forefront of her mind.

"Really? I think I can help with that," she resolutely remarked. "I'm half-tempted to handcuff you to the bed. Perhaps that will keep you out of trouble."

"What?" he countered with a wide-eyed expression.

"Just during the day, my love," she equivocated as she ushered their renewed walk back towards the hotel.

"Um, I think not!" he heatedly challenged while half-heartedly attempting to pull free from her grasp.

She slyly chuckled.

My sense of humor's still intact too, it seems.

* * * *

Chapter 9

Dark Places

*B*y the following morning, Caleb's demeanor had improved, and he was feeling more content. His arm had almost fully healed, thanks to liberal use of Katrina's saliva. Of course, the fact that she had not actually handcuffed him to the bed before she departed for the day's conference session was also encouraging.

He shaved and dressed with a hopeful feeling as he contemplated what plan Dori would have for their investigation of the mountain shack just outside of town. Then a pang of guilt followed as he recalled Katrina's concerns from the prior evening. She wouldn't be happy if she knew what he and Dori were planning.

He wondered if he shouldn't simply abandon further investigations both for his own welfare and for his mate's peace of mind.

A knock at his suite's door interrupted his thoughts, and he pulled a t-shirt over his head on the way to answer it.

Dori's really early today, he estimated.

As he opened his door, he was surprised to see Paige, once more relegated to her security outfit.

"Morning, Mister Trouble," she greeted.

She playfully dangled a pair of chrome handcuffs in her left hand at eye level before him.

"Katrina said to drop by," she slyly added.

"No way!" he challenged, immediately swinging the door

closed against her.

At the last second, her hand slapped the door and effortlessly pushed against his full weight to sweep it open again. She slipped into the room, laughing as she closed the door behind her.

"Whoa, tiger," she offered with a giggle. "Red said that I'd enjoy your reaction, and boy, you sure didn't disappoint," she added, sliding the pair of cuffs into her back pants pocket.

His heartbeat raced while slowly stepping backwards and watching her with a wide-eyed expression.

"I thought –"

"Yeah, I figured as much. Red told me about her little threat."

Her eyes narrowed in a predatory fashion.

"Don't worry, kiddo," she assured him in a sultry voice, "If I ever do handcuff you to a bed, I won't be leaving you alone."

"Oh really?"

"I'm just sayin'."

"Well, since you put it that way," he suggestively countered with a smirk and deliberately reached out to take her by the hand.

I can tease, too.

She felt a momentary charge tingle across her skin as he grasped her hand, and her eyes darted to his. She was surprised how pleasing the thought of sex with him was to her, but was equally unnerved by her silent admission. Her gaze took in how well his t-shirt fit his muscular chest and how his blue jeans hugged his lean waist. Then she caught herself and quickly rotated her hand to grab his wrist.

"Enough kidding around, you perv. Let's get you some breakfast. Nice healing job on your arm, by the way."

She pulled him towards the suite door, thankful that she had not succumbed to a fleeting desire that she would later regret.

"Sure," he agreed while eyeing her suspiciously.

Despite his sense of fidelity to Katrina, he couldn't help

feeling aroused by the fleeting idea of having sex with her. He considered her to be a powerfully attractive woman for whom he cared deeply. And his experience in the vault with her had only increased that sense of affection.

The two proceeded to the main dining room, platonically discussing a host of decidedly safer topics.

* * * *

Katrina sat at the head of the conference table to the right of Alton while appreciating the reactions from a number of vampires around the table as both Hakizimana and Mara secured their respective seats at the opposite end of the room. The yellow-eyed vampire had quite a reputation among his peers, almost like an ancient celebrity in his own right merely from his longevity. Certainly, he was the eldest vampire in the room, which was saying something with Alton being over eight hundred years old.

While not overly enthusiastic herself, Katrina particularly enjoyed the reactions of both Baldar Dubravko and Dominic Ambrogio over the newest participants. Both vampires seemed beside themselves and were lulled into silent contemplation versus their usual instigation of arguments among attendees.

Wonders never cease, she mused.

"At the risk of seeming obstructive," Hakizimana politely inquired, "Would it be possible to briefly enumerate the topics at hand?"

"Certainly," Alton neatly replied.

He proceeded not only to describe the active topics, but briefly recounted the other topics that had been argued into stalemates or had been tabled for later discussion.

Hakizimana briefly commented on the merits of some topics, while diplomatically conceding the difficulties of others. Most surprising to Katrina was how a number of the previously tabled topics garnered renewed life with the seemingly unbiased promptings of the ancient vampire.

Within an hour, a number of formerly reserved or silent attendees were openly discussing the merits of some of the previous agenda topics. It was perhaps the first time since the conference started that free-flowing dialogue was occurring.

"Point of order," Dubravko abruptly spoke up. "Shouldn't someone other than the chair recommend that previously tabled topics be revisited for discussion?"

One of Alton's brows imperiously arched, and he swept the faces in the room for someone to speak up.

Katrina sat up in her chair, meeting Dubravko's golden-fleck eyes directly.

"I motion that previously tabled topics be reopened for discussion at the discretion of any participants," she offered. "Who will second?"

Silence reigned for only a few seconds. Then no less than three vampires spoke up simultaneously in support. The final vote resulted in the vast majority of attendees favoring the motion. Dubravko, Ambrogio, and three others were among the only dissenters.

In and of itself, it was a momentous victory for the tone of the conference. Dubravko silently fumed across the table from Katrina, but she merely reflected quiet satisfaction.

Civil dialogue seamlessly resumed as if no interruption had occurred.

*   *   *   *

During breakfast, Paige absently watched Caleb eat while sipping from a Styrofoam cup of warm blood. She was determined not to let her appetite get the better of her in the future, obligations or not. Staring at the young man before her, she couldn't help thinking about his two-fold accomplishment from the previous evening.

First, he had been able to bring a powerful and elusive vampire to participate in the conference. And second, he had lived through the risky endeavor.

Glancing up from his plate of food, he noticed her staring at him.

"What?" he asked.

"You surprised me last night, kiddo," she conceded. "Quite a lot, actually."

"I'm full of surprises sometimes."

She giggled. "More like full of crap sometimes."

He cast her a dirty look as he speared a sausage link and bit off one end.

"Actually," she earnestly whispered, "I'm impressed and proud. I just wish that you wouldn't –"

"Take so many chances?"

"Yeah," she grimly agreed as tightness formed in her throat.

His clumsiness is glaring at times. I'd rather he not turn up dead anytime soon.

He was touched to see the depth of caring and concern reflected in her bright blue eyes.

"You and Katrina both," he quietly noted.

She sipped from her cup, trying to refocus her thoughts on something more constructive. In turn, he concentrated on finishing his pancakes. The remainder of their time together passed relatively quickly and quietly. Yet, there was a sense of contentment between the two of them in just sharing the table together.

Following breakfast, Paige disappeared to pursue a host of requirements placed upon her by the major, leaving Caleb to his own diversions. He strolled through the merchants' area at one end of the conference facility, absently perusing. Following a call to Dori's suite but getting no answer, he left voicemail about where she could find him.

He had grown somewhat bored, having seen the same shops on a number of occasions since being sequestered to conference property.

An hour into his wandering, Dori showed up next to him as he perused a rack of paperback books.

"Where's your cell phone?" she insisted, emphasizing her annoyance by prodding her fingertip against his shoulder blade.

He reached down to his hip and realized that he hadn't had time to pick it up when Paige had abruptly showed up at his suite.

"Oh, yeah. I must have left without it this morning."

"Yeah, well, you won't need it until later this afternoon anyway," she said. "Let's go outside and enjoy some sunshine."

They walked outdoors to the park bench on which they had sat together just days prior. Caleb noted the location was ideal to chat privately, allowing them easily to notice anyone who might approach. They sat quietly, appreciating the scenic surroundings for a short time before either spoke.

"I've figured out how we can sneak out," Dori finally offered.

"Yeah? How?"

"There's a linens truck that stops outside the loading zone at the rear of the building every day. The cameras are set up to observe the loading area, but the back of the truck obstructs the full view enough that we might be able to hop in unnoticed," she explained.

"What about guards?"

"Yes, there's always one on duty there, so we'll need a diversion," she agreed.

That seemed to be the sticking point, until something struck him.

"What if we could get someone else to help us?"

"You have somebody in mind who can keep it to themselves?" Dori asked.

"Maybe. How about Aiden?"

She observed him for a moment.

"Perhaps. But it's better if we don't tell him where we're going, just in case one of the vampires questions him."

He considered her qualification and realized that "one of the vampires" included Alton, Kat, and Paige. Excluding them wasn't something that he was proud of, but he also realized that they wouldn't support their venture, either. Still, he was convinced that what they were planning to do was imperative. *Besides, maybe we'll get lucky like I did last night.*

"I'll talk to Aiden," he resolved.

They agreed to visit again after he met with Aiden. It was another half-hour before he was able to acquire Aiden's cell phone number and arrange to meet him somewhere private. In the end, they agreed upon the Frisbee golf course. Fortunately, Frisbee was something Caleb was well acquainted with.

The two enjoyed a couple of rounds against each other before Caleb felt comfortable bringing up the subject at hand. Finally, after neatly tossing his disc into the goal, he subtly broached the topic.

"Great," Aiden chided. "Now you want me to get labeled a troublemaker, too. You're a real pill, Taylor."

Caleb shrugged. "Hey, I just thought you'd care enough about Talise to help us make sure there was nothing to our suspicions, that's all."

Aiden's green eyes narrowed, and he glared at Caleb. "Whaddaya mean by that?"

"Nothing, maybe," Caleb casually replied. "Only that sometimes I get it right, that's all. And I'm all for making sure that nothing threatens Katrina. Or Paige."

Aiden scowled. "I see what you're doing. You're trying to play on my fears. Well listen, try playing to my intelligence instead. Why don't you tell me where you think some threat might be coming from, and I'll determine if it seems reasonable or not."

Caleb admired the man's logic and moxie. However, he didn't feel comfortable spilling all the details, just as Dori had warned him.

"Dori uncovered some new information that leads us to believe that Baldar Dubravko has an agenda focused on the failure of this conference. That's another reason why the newest additions to the group, who, I might add, formerly weren't in-

Jaz Primo

terested in being here, found my argument compelling enough to attend."

Aiden tossed his Frisbee, missed the goal entirely, and cursed. Then he turned to stare silently at Caleb at length before nodding.

"Okay, but when you're done playing spy, I want to know the full details. So, what is it exactly you want me to do?"

Caleb was visibly pleased. "Agreed."

The afternoon was waning by the time Caleb was able to locate Dori. He had no sooner made it back to the main lobby when he noticed vampires milling around. A number of human companions were among the crowd. Frowning, he looked around for someone who he felt comfortable asking for details.

Seemingly out of nowhere Katrina appeared on the far side of the lobby, staring at him with an amused expression. He tentatively smiled back at her. She crooked her finger in the same telltale manner as the night before and wriggled it at him in a beckoning fashion.

She didn't seem upset or worried to him. Quite the contrary, she looked like a hunter who had just bagged its prize prey. Caleb swallowed, and his smile faded somewhat. Her emerald eyes were penetrating as he strode slowly across the lobby towards her. For that reason, he wasn't entirely sure that he wanted to know why she wore such an expression.

"Surprise, my love," she slyly offered and bent down slightly to kiss him on the lips.'

At least, something is destined to be a surprise, she silently affirmed.

"It sure is," he agreed. "The conference let out early today, I presume?"

"Given that it was the first positive meeting since we started, we thought it would be a good idea not to be greedy," she wryly explained. "Besides, it gives those attendees with partners an opportunity to spend quality time with them. Like us, for example. We won't reconvene until tomorrow morning."

"Oh," he replied.

It figures. Just when Dori and I finally have a plan of action, now I get to spend time with Katrina.

She took note of his distracted mannerism. "How does dinner sound?" she queried.

I wonder what's on his mind?

He took notice of the main dining room and saw a short line of people waiting to be seated.

"Sure, that sounds nice," he ventured and wrapped his arm around her waist to lead her in that direction.

But her body remained firmly planted in place, and his torso twisted with a lurch to look at her curiously.

She's like a statue when she does that, he marveled.

"Actually, why don't we briefly run by Alton's suite and pick up him and Dori? They can join us for dinner," she prompted.

It won't take long at all.

He suspiciously frowned. "Well, okay. That's a nice idea, actually."

He quickly wondered if his and Dori's plans would still be actionable after dinner or not. He doubted it with neither of their vampires preoccupied.

"Excellent. Let's go," she said, taking him by the hand to lead him to the nearby elevator.

Caleb knocked on Alton's suite door, glancing up at Katrina for what must have been the third time in two minutes to gauge her expression. For some reason, he couldn't help thinking that she was up to something.

Then again, between her and Alton, they're always up to something.

She contentedly looked down at him and soothingly rubbed his lower back.

Dori was the one who answered the door, and she looked none too pleased to be there. Her violet eyes were hard, as if she had just been arguing. She warily fixed Caleb in a manner that made him feel like turning to flee back down the hallway to the elevator. It was like a rabbit silently warning a fellow bunny, "Danger! Run!"

"Hi, Dori," Katrina warmly greeted her. "Caleb and I thought that you two might want to join us for dinner."

Dori absently reached over her opposite shoulder to scratch at her back. "Certainly," she politely replied. "We'll meet you downstairs."

"Dori," announced Alton's diplomatic voice from inside. "That sounds like Katrina and Caleb. Have them come in, why don't you?"

She said nothing and stepped aside to allow them to enter. Katrina pleasantly smiled at her as they passed.

Good girl, she noted.

Alton appeared to be tinkering with items from a large, black briefcase made of a composite material. Since the opened case lid was facing him, Caleb couldn't see what was inside. He observed Dori again, and she looked back at him with a miserable expression.

"Why don't you two have a seat, and I'll be right with you," Alton suggested.

Katrina's arm slipped around Caleb's waist, guiding him over to the couch, and he looked up at his mate with a curious expression.

She wistfully looked at him and murmured, "I love you."

"I love you, too," he sincerely replied.

"Caleb? Perhaps you would be so kind to remove your shirt for a moment?" Alton asked.

Caleb froze and then looked back over his shoulder at him. He noticed that the tall vampire was holding what looked like a large metal syringe, and it almost made him cringe.

"Just what the hell is *that* for?!"

Alton innocently shook his head. "It's really nothing."

"The hell it is. That's *something*."

Katrina reached over to help lift his t-shirt up, but he quickly slapped at her hands and pulled it back down.

"Just wait a damned minute! Somebody better tell me what the *hell* is going on here!"

"Shhh, nobody's doing anything to harm you, my love,"

Katrina soothingly offered as she patted him on the shoulder. "Just take your shirt off for a moment, and it'll all be over soon. It's a completely painless process."

"Oh no, not until somebody tells me what this is all about," Caleb insisted.

Another fleeting glimpse of Dori's visage indicated that he wasn't going to like the answer.

"We're merely inserting a small implant on your shoulder," Alton explained as if it were the most common thing in the world. "It rests just beneath the skin. You'll never even know it's there. Katrina will even numb the area for you."

"What *kind* of implant, Alton?" he pressed.

"It's a tiny tracking beacon," Katrina answered. "It's for your protection so that we can locate you in the event that you mysteriously disappear again."

He suddenly realized why Dori seemed so unhappy. Apparently, she had one installed, as well.

Well, that puts a big damned wrinkle in our plan.

"Great," he sarcastically retorted, "It's just like tagging a herd animal. Is that what we are now?"

Katrina's mouth became a thin line, and she frowned at him. "That's insulting, Caleb. Nobody's trying to demean you. We just want to keep you both safe, that's all."

"I think I'll pass," he flatly retorted as he stared into Katrina's eyes.

She briefly closed her eyes. When she reopened them, Caleb stared into the determined eyes of a resolute vampire.

"I'm afraid that's not an option, my love," she declared with a note of finality.

Enough games, Caleb. This is for your own good, after all.

"No," he repeated, though his resolve was shaken somewhat by her visage.

"Remove your shirt. Now," she commanded.

Her arm reached across him and firmly planted him against the cushion. She stared directly into his pale blue eyes and deliberately willed her eyes to flash at him brightly for a mere second.

He pulled away from her at that fierce sight. Then he realized that he wasn't going to win the dispute at that point. All he had left to maintain was his dignity.

"Fine," he relented and began stripping his shirt off.

It didn't give Katrina any pleasure to force her lover's hand in the matter. But more than anything, she couldn't endure another helpless feeling of wondering if he were okay, as well as where he might be. He was too important to her.

Caleb looked away from her and dejectedly sat with his shoulder slightly slumped forwards. He allowed his torso to be turned away from her, offering his back to them. Alton moved closer to him from behind the couch, and he felt Katrina's lips on his skin a little higher above his left shoulder blade.

She kissed him once, and his muscles tensed in response.

Despite the audience of Alton and Dori, Katrina deliberately kissed Caleb's shoulder twice more with her soft lips. Finally, she placed her tongue against his skin and waited for a time until it was properly numbed. Alton waited for her to pull away then deftly injected the tip of the needle. With a single push of the syringe, a tiny metal object was deposited just beneath his skin.

Before bleeding ensued, Katrina pressed her tongue against his skin, waiting for the entry point to seal.

A moment later, she lightly kissed the spot and said, "There. Done."

Now I'll have some peace of mind for a change.

He started to reach over his shoulder to touch the spot, but she lightly swatted his hand.

"Leave it alone for a short time so it can properly heal," she insisted. Then a brief memory of kissing his wounded arm as a child played through her mind, and she recalled having said the same thing to him as an eight-year-old boy. It was an odd recollection.

He slipped his shirt back on as Alton happily asked, "Well then, anyone hungry?"

The four of them proceeded to the main dining room for dinner, though Katrina and Alton did most of the talking over warm glasses of blood as Dori and Caleb traded dejected looks and mostly picked at their meals.

"I thought that we might take in a movie tonight," Alton merrily suggested. "There's a theater in Jereka that's open until midnight."

Dori forced a diplomatic expression. "I'm sure that's fine," she politely responded.

"I think it sounds delightful," Katrina replied in an upbeat tone.

Caleb was having none of it and merely frowned. He felt somewhat resentful towards both his mate and Alton. As Katrina's fingers lightly touched his hand, he immediately looked away.

Alton drove the four of them to Jereka in an SUV. Despite his aggravation, Caleb admired the vampire's keen driving skills on such a dark road. It seemed that the vehicle progressed at an unusually high rate of speed for the curving mountains road. He surveyed what little he could see through the side window of the back seat, pointedly ignoring Katrina beside him.

He's really angry about earlier, Katrina thought ruefully. *Still, it's for their own good.*

"I don't mean to seem impertinent, but I don't speak fluent Slovene," Caleb dryly observed. He had learned a few key phrases and courteously tried using them when possible, but he could barely hold a reasonable conversation with the locals in their native language.

"What?" Alton asked.

"The movie," Dori supplemented. "And neither do I, for the most part."

"It's in English," Alton supplied as he deftly maneuvered through a tight curve at a brisk speed.

Caleb gritted his teeth and wondered how the stately vampire had managed to arrange that little feat.

He probably purchased the theater or something, he speculated.

Once in Jereka, Caleb was impressed by how busy the small city was in the evening. People bustled about much like they would in any city in America. The theater was a quaint-looking structure reminiscent of an earlier period when theaters were a special and unique civic attraction.

Inside, people milled around as Caleb noticed that the movie posters were all labeled in Slovene. The universal smell of popcorn permeated the lobby, and his mouth watered. While Alton purchased the tickets, Katrina casually observed Caleb and Dori as they stood quietly waiting.

The film was a modern romantic comedy set in New York City entitled *Love, Unexpected*. A number of people were seated in the theater when they entered, most appearing to be college-aged. In an almost herding fashion, Alton led the way to their seats while Katrina brought up the rear, effectively ensuring that Caleb and Dori sat between them.

Caleb hastily mentioned, "I think I'll run to the restrooms before the movie starts."

"Me, too," Dori agreed.

Both were surprised when Katrina and Alton kept their seats. Once in the lobby, Caleb turned to his newfound friend.

"What do we do now?" he insisted. "Aiden already offered to help us."

"Oh, I am so furious at Alton," Dori fumed. Her eyes darted left and right in a flighty fashion that seemed out of character for the normally confident woman. "I don't know yet. Just give me some time to think about it. I'm not even sure if the implants poll us constantly or not."

"How do you even know about stuff like this?" he asked. There was so much that he still didn't know about Dori. She was a virtual mystery for all their time together.

Katrina appeared through the doors of their theater and swept the busy lobby to locate them.

"Kat's on us already," Caleb warned, turning his back on

his mate.

"Just act as normal as possible, and we'll meet up tomorrow after the conference starts up again," Dori urged. "I should have some answers by then."

She quickly walked over to the nearby women's restroom, darting through the door to enter.

"The men's is on the other side of the lobby," Katrina pleasantly offered from behind Caleb.

What are you two up to? she wondered.

"Oh, thanks," he said.

Katrina waited for them to return to the lobby and accompanied them back to their seats. Then she disappeared again while Dori and Caleb reseated themselves next to Alton. Caleb noticed he had already acquired Cokes for each of them.

A few minutes later, Katrina quietly reappeared in her seat next to Caleb, handing him a large bucket of fresh popcorn.

"Popcorn? Extra butter and salt, just as you like it," she encouragingly whispered as the previews began.

"Thanks," he accepted good-naturedly and munched on the tasty snack. Dori snatched a handful or two as well.

The movie was enjoyable, and by the end of the film each of them had openly laughed a number of times. The romantic aspects of the feature weren't lost on Caleb, and at one point he gently grasped Katrina's hand when it appeared on his thigh. Despite still feeling annoyed with earlier events, he couldn't deny that he loved her.

For Katrina's part, she endeavored to keep the evening light-hearted. For one fleeting night, she wanted to act like any normal couple out on a date and leave all the dramatic vampire-themed events of the present behind them. Granted, such things would return to the forefront of their lives in mere hours, but she desperately needed to show Caleb that she could still be what she enjoyed being most of all for him: his mate and companion.

It was very late by the time Alton drove them back to the conference site. Dori dozed in the front passenger seat, while

Caleb yawned nearly the entire time. He fought the drowsiness that threatened to overcome him, determined to see as much of his surroundings as the pervasive darkness would allow. The conference site had begun to feel like an oversized prison to him.

By the time Katrina and Caleb finally stood outside the door to their suite, he was no longer able to fight his fatigue. His red-headed mate observed him with amusement as he opened his mouth in a cavernous yawn, one that he thought would unhinge his jaw. He quickly squeezed past Katrina to enter the dark suite, making his way directly to the bedroom for much-welcome slumber.

Unfortunately, he ran directly into the back of the couch with a resounding "Umph."

"Careful. And try not to fall asleep before I can give you a goodnight kiss," she teased.

She shut the door and reached out for the light switch. It wasn't as if she needed the illumination, but she didn't want Caleb injuring himself on his trek to the bedroom.

As she flicked the light switch, every lamp or light fixture in the room snapped on. However, instead of the muted lighting that she expected, the room was filled with much more penetrating light.

"What the hell?" Caleb snapped as the lights in the bedroom and bathroom all popped on at once.

Katrina immediately felt intense pain, and her skin began to sizzle like bacon on a hot grill.

The next seconds passed like a lightning strike as Katrina's hand slammed into the light switch, though it failed to extinguish the lights. Her other hand reached for the suite's door handle, which fell away in her hand, leaving the door closed in place. She darted nearly blindly towards the bedroom but only saw more lights, so she sped into the coat closet beside her.

"Kat!" Caleb yelled with alarm as he had only caught a fleeting glimpse of his mate's scorched skin.

He immediately realized what was happening as he felt increased heat emanating from the nearest lamp. It was like the entire suite was a giant tanning booth. Grabbing one lamp, he jerked its cord from the nearby receptacle, rendering it harmless.

"Don't worry, Kat! Just hang on!" he shouted while racing to the various light switches in the room, though none of them extinguished the lights.

He wielded the lamp pedestal in his hand like a bludgeon and ran to each light fixture on the walls to smash the bulbs until they were dark and useless. He had to jump up in order to break the ceiling-mounted lights, but quickly progressed through the living room until all lights were broken. Then to save time, he raced to the bedroom and slammed the door shut, leaving him standing in complete darkness.

His momentary night blindness hampered his efforts to cross the room as he barked, "It's okay, Kat! The lights are out."

His efforts were met with his shin's painful, abrupt impact against the coffee table, which tripped him.

"Dammit!" he cursed while trying to maintain his balance.

He thought that he heard the nearby closet door open and felt a blur of movement nearby. The smell that followed nearly made him gag. It was like burned meat, and he shuddered upon realizing it was his mate's flesh.

"Oh God, Kat," he gasped.

"I'll be okay," her terse voice tried to reassure him.

Her anger was barely kept in check as she effortlessly moved through the darkness to part the curtains covering the windows. Although it was nighttime, the meager light filtering in through the coated glass from outside would allow her mate to see more easily.

"Jesus! Are you okay?" he insisted as his eyes began to adjust enough that he could make out her form near the windows.

He felt a blur of air rush past him again, and she disappeared from view. An acrid smell assailed his nose in her wake.

She opened the small refrigerator in the suite and withdrew two packets of blood she had stored there for convenience. She quickly assessed that her skin was only slightly damaged, and that fresh blood would speed the healing process.

"What can I do, Kat?" he asked. "You can have my blood right now," he immediately offered.

"No, my love," she countered while emptying the blood into a large ceramic coffee mug, which she placed in the nearby microwave.

He felt useless while watching her by the dim light emanating through the microwave's glass door, and his mind raced with a host of questions all at once. She moved to the nearby phone and punched a few digits even as her skin throbbed with pain from the burns that she had endured.

"Alton? Get to my room immediately. Something's happened," she ordered in a flat voice before pressing a button to end the call and get another dial tone.

She dialed again as Caleb carefully negotiated his way to her.

"Paige, grab your boss and get up to my room. There's been an event," she ordered and hung up the phone.

She turned to the microwave and retrieved the mug of blood. The thick substance felt soothing as it washed down her throat and into her stomach. She could almost feel the healing effects begin to accelerate as her body's cells began converting the blood to useful energy.

Vampires are nothing if not highly efficient biological machines.

Her eyes swept the room, falling upon the helpless, tortured expression on Caleb's face, and it almost broke her heart.

"It's okay, my love," she reassured him. "I'm going to be fine."

His tension abated somewhat, quickly changing to anger.

When I find out who did this...

A knock at the door interrupted his tumultuous thoughts.

"Katrina?" came Alton's voice from the hallway.

"Move!" Paige's voice ordered, followed by a clicking sound

in the door lock mechanism.

Somebody rattled the exterior handle, but the door remained shut. Abruptly, a loud thud preempted the crashing of the door as it slammed into the wall and swung closed again. Finally, the door pivoted open, casting a swath of light across the floor of the suite as Paige, Alton, and Major Pietari crowded through the doorway.

"Why are the lights off?" Paige queried as her gaze swept the room. Her vision settled on Katrina's face, and her breath caught in her throat. "And what the hell happened to you?!"

"UV-light bulbs happened to me. Caleb broke out the lights because the switches were disabled," she added, noting Dori's cautious appearance in the suite's doorway.

Paige noted the light emanating underneath the doorway to the bedroom and moved in that direction. Caleb's arm swept out, managing to encircle her petite waist.

"Same thing in there," he snapped. The last thing that he wanted was for more vampires that he cared about to get hurt.

Paige's eyes darted to the young man and back to the bedroom door. "This took some time," she absently noted while affectionately patting his arm.

"We've been away all evening," he interjected.

"Are you okay?" Alton asked, staring at the red-headed vampire.

"I'll be fine," Katrina replied.

She sipped from the mug of blood and stepped into the light of the hallway so the major could get a better look at her burns, which were already beginning to heal. The pain still throbbed through her body, but at a greatly reduced rate.

Caleb stared at his mate, recalling memories of when he was only eight. That was when he first met her on that fateful summer day after she had been severely burned by the sun. Her skin had appeared scaly and blackened. His earlier grudge against her for the implant in his shoulder suddenly seemed somewhat petty.

Her eyes met his, and she tenderly smiled back at him,

despite her obvious discomfort.

"The door handle was disengaged on the inside," Dori pointed out.

"She should've just kicked the door off its hinges in the first place," Paige admonished.

"I was caught off-guard and just wanted to block the painful radiation at the time," Katrina retorted.

"Somebody went to a lot of trouble to hurt her," Alton observed.

"I'll check the maintenance logs to see if anyone noted any contractors arriving on site," the major offered. "We took the surveillance system offline for a time tonight to diagnose and reinitialize the system, but I'll check the video logs to see if we can see a glimpse of the culprits." He looked at Paige. "Get this cleaned up and fixed, Turner."

He turned and barreled from the room like a man on a mission.

"Yeah, sure," she irritably replied. Somehow it didn't surprise her to get stuck with the cleanup detail.

A thought occurred to Caleb, and he moved to the nearby phone to dial one of the rooms in the hotel. Nobody paid him any attention as they continued to chat about what had happened. He heard someone pick up on the other end. It was Talise.

"I'm sorry for calling so late. But can I please speak with Aiden? It's important," he apologetically inquired.

"Who are you calling?" Paige asked.

A sleepy male voice on the phone asked, "Hello?"

"Aiden? It's Caleb. Listen, something important just happened, and we need your help," he insisted.

"We do?" Paige asked as the others watched with perplexed expressions.

"Just get dressed and get over to our room," he ordered and hung up the phone.

"What are you up to?" Alton asked in his crisp English accent.

"Somebody just pulled off a big electrical job here. Who better to help sort it all out than a master electrician?" Caleb asked with a sly expression.

By the time Aiden and Talise arrived at the suite, temporary lighting had been set up around the room. Additionally, the light bulbs had hastily been replaced in the bedroom and bathroom with ordinary ones. Paige and another security officer were discussing further investigative topics, while Alton and Katrina stood in a corner quietly conversing.

Caleb quickly briefed Aiden, and the sleepy-eyed young man used a multi-purpose tool to remove the panel from the light switch nearest the door. Dori and the vampires in the room quickly gathered around to watch.

Caleb noted with satisfaction that Katrina's skin only looked like it had sustained serious sunburns instead of the scarred tissue from earlier. Her skin was reddened and blistered-looking. She patted him on the shoulder with a reassuring expression.

"Wow, this is sophisticated," Aiden observed as he viewed the wiring before him. "Somebody really knew what they were doing here. See this? They installed a mini-breaker to act as the kill switch when the contact was activated."

"Hmmm," Alton murmured. "Rather elaborate for such a limited effect. Surely, they realized their trap wouldn't actually kill Katrina before she managed to escape the room."

"Yeah, but it's a hell of a message," Paige blurted.

And I need to find out from whom, she resolved.

Aiden politely passed through the group, making his way to another light switch, only to discover the same alteration to the wiring. The young man frowned and sharply looked at Caleb.

"Somebody had to crosswire all the suite's switches in series to all the other light fixtures, as well."

"Can any electrical contractor do that?" Dori asked.

Aiden shrugged. "Yeah, sure. But they'd need the electrical blueprints to know how everything was already wired. Normally, we'd balance everything so you didn't overload any one circuit in a suite like this, so you'd want to know how they tie into the main breaker panel. The phases all have to be balanced, you see."

Paige glanced meaningfully at the security guard standing next to her.

"I'll check the electrical room on this floor," the guard offered before departing.

"So, it wasn't necessarily an inside job," Talise ventured.

"Oh, there was an inside component to this, I'm sure," Paige said. Katrina nodded. "Somebody de-programmed the door to the suite, too."

"Yep, I've installed those types of locks on some of my previous construction jobs. They're pretty standard in places like hotels. Each door has a standalone lock, so it takes someone with access to the master key cards or somebody with one of the handheld programming units to make the changes," Aiden said.

"But it allowed me in the first time," Katrina countered.

"Aw, those locks are pretty dynamic, actually. You can program them to reset, or even deactivate, after the first swipe, if you want," Aiden explained.

Talise appeared impressed and moved to stand next to Aiden. "You're pretty handy," she observed in an approving tone.

He winked and kissed her on the cheek in response.

But Alton appeared less than amused exchanging knowing looks with both Katrina and Paige. "A rat in our midst, for certain," he said.

"I'll run down who has access to those components," Paige promised. She looked at Aiden. "Mind if I tap your expertise on this?"

He shrugged. "Sure. Not like I've got any other plans."

A couple of tired-looking maintenance men showed up outside the suite and politely knocked on the door jamb.

"Is this the suite with the faulty door?" one of the fellows asked in thick Slovene-accented English.

Everyone turned to stare at the men, who stood directly beside the ruined door as it barely hung from one hinge, seemingly aloof of its condition.

"You're kidding, right?" Paige incredulously asked.

"No offense, but you're gonna want to call somebody else, I think," Aiden sardonically whispered.

* * * *

As the process of repairing things in the suite was going to take time, and rather than bothering to transfer to another suite, Paige offered the use of her room to Caleb and Katrina. When Caleb woke the next morning, he rolled over to stare into the perky-featured face of Paige as she lay fully dressed on top of the covers, perching her head on one arm.

"Well, look who's sleeping in my bed," she playfully chimed with a sparkle in her bright blue eyes.

He sleepily peered back at her. "Chasing me out?" he asked.

"Are you kidding? I've been waiting forever to get you like this," she teased. "Wanna try my handcuffs on for size now?" she asked with a daring gleam in her eyes.

Following a roll of his eyes, he stifled a yawn while stretching his muscles. "Maybe later. But thanks for letting me crash here. Where's Kat?"

"Too bad," she mock-lamented with a pouty expression. "Your old lady left for the conference room a couple of hours ago. Alton was pretty anxious to inform the group of last night's events in order to gauge their reactions."

"Think it'll help?"

"Not so much," she soberly replied, rolling off the bed to stand. "Some vampires are good at feigning their reactions."

"Any leads yet on who altered our room's light fixtures?" he asked while sitting up.

"Not yet. As the major said, the security system was offline for a while, which was probably when they snuck in to do the job."

"Perfect timing, wasn't it?"

"Yeah, a little too perfect."

He yawned and plopped back down onto the bed.

She adopted a more upbeat expression, planted her hands on her hips and badgered, "Hey, time to get up, twerp. Whaddaya think I'm running here, a hotel?"

After showering and changing into the fresh clothes he had brought from his suite, Caleb went to the lobby to acquire a card key to his and Katrina's new suite. Much to his surprise, there was a similarly-sized room available at the opposite end of Paige's floor. He couldn't help but wonder if either of the two most important women in his life had a hand in that.

Probably both, he determined. Still, it made him feel happy to know that Paige wasn't far from him. *Well, that's when she's actually off-duty, which isn't very often lately.*

As he turned to head to the dining room for something to eat, he caught a glimpse of Paige in a freshly pressed security blazer and slacks standing near the elevator intently watching him with her arms crossed before her.

He held up the new room key for her to see. She adopted a mischievous smirk and winked at him.

He deliberately went out of his way to walk past her on his route to the dining room and teased, "How convenient. Making access easier to feed on me?"

"That," she conceded in a light tone, "and I like to keep troublemakers close by."

He stuck out his tongue at her over his shoulder, and she giggled.

Once seated in the dining room, he ordered brunch and waited for his food to arrive. While he was perusing a day-old copy of *The New York Times*, Dori appeared at his tableside and pulled up a chair next to his.

"Why is it that I'm always finding you down here?" she teased.

He looked over the top of his paper at the beguiling brunette, hoping that her positive demeanor portended good news.

"I happen to like eating."

"Your appetite is epic," she remarked with a smirk.

"Somebody got up on the right side of bed."

She shrugged and accepted fresh coffee offered by a passing waiter.

Watching the man depart, she informed him, "I have discovered something interesting about Alton's new toys."

His eyes darted to her with rapt attention and he laid his newspaper aside. "Such as?"

"The handheld tracking device is fairly large and operates as a proximity detection unit," she said. "It's still nestled in the briefcase as of this morning, which means they intend to use it only if we turn up missing."

"How does that help us?"

"It means that as long as we slip out stealthily enough, we'll have a short time to investigate before they notice," she explained. "Then they have to take the time to hone in on us, rather than receiving immediate GPS coordinates for our position. If we do our job right, we'll have all the information we need before they locate us. Then, if we're correct, they'll be happy that we uncovered useful information."

"Yeah, but they're still going to be majorly pissed at us," he said.

Especially Kat.

She shrugged. "An acceptable risk for proving our point, I should think."

"You don't know Kat," he groaned and did a double-take when he saw her openly grinning at him. "What?"

"Your choice in women," she wistfully contemplated with a shake of her head. "Both of them."

He started to inquire further, but she took a final sip of her coffee and rose to leave.

"Do something relaxing today," she instructed him. "Then you and Aiden meet up with me in the gardens at four o'clock. And be sure to bring a small flashlight with you."

He watched her go with a puzzled expression, but he was

quickly distracted by the arrival of his food.

Following his meal, Caleb spent the day fishing at the miniature lake at the rear of the conference property. He had been able to rent a rod and tackle at the courtesy shop skirting the small dock. The water was clear and the fish plentiful, but he released everything that he caught.

He savored a relaxing day appreciating the beautiful scenery around him and even ate lunch lakeside. In truth, it was the first day since his beating at the local police station that he actually felt "normal." Nearly all the soreness had abated in his muscles, thanks to Katrina's blood injections, and he had finally managed to avoid dwelling on the uncertain budget situation at his college.

It's not as if I have any control over what might happen, so I may as well try to live in the moment while things are enjoyable.

He reveled in his surroundings, frequently gazing across the lake's shoreline or up at the looming mountains blanketed in lush forest. Despite the recent dangerous events, it was an amazing place to visit, and he wished there weren't so much drama associated with his trip so that he could embrace it in earnest.

Maybe Kat and I can visit again someday. Only next time, alone.

The day quickly passed, and four o'clock came sooner than expected. He returned to his new suite to shower and change clothes, selecting a dark t-shirt and jeans. Though they hadn't coordinated their wardrobe, he found Dori similarly dressed as she stood beside Aiden. However, in lieu of t-shirt she wore a fashionable black cami and suede bolero jacket. She also carried a small leather satchel in one hand.

Caleb weighed the merits of his own ensemble and considered whether to return to his suite to change clothes.

I thought this was a spy mission, not a fashion show.

"The truck's already parked at the facility's freight entrance," she informed him, ignoring his self-deprecating expression.

The plan was simple and relied upon Aiden's skill with deception. Granted, there were a number of other unplanned variables, but it was the best opportunity available to them. It wasn't as if they could just blatantly commandeer a vehicle without being noticed and pursued.

"I just hope you two know what you're doing," Aiden offered. "But we had better do this quick. Captain Turner wants to meet with me in an hour. She had a few questions about the electrical fiasco from last night."

Caleb's eyes darted to his. "Don't even mention us while you're with her, Aiden. She picks up on things like a hawk. It's uncanny, really."

The young electrician held up his hands.

"Hey, no problem. I'm just planning to talk about electricity, nothing more."

They gave Aiden time to make his way to the freight area, and then took a circuitous route to a spot not far from the freight entrance. Caleb was pleasantly surprised when everything seemed to go according to plan. They watched as Aiden was able to distract the human guard, and only two other staff milled around the area.

As Dori predicted, a linens service truck was parked in the freight dock area. The driver and a hotel staff member placed two large loads of linens in the back of the truck and returned inside. Nobody noticed as Dori and Caleb slipped into the back of the truck. Even better, there were already large piles of sheets, towels, table cloths, and a host of other things to hide behind. After a final heave of linens onto the top of the piles, the truck departed the conference site property and made its way towards town.

Following a half-hour drive, the truck came to a final halt, and the engine shut off. After hearing the driver's side door open and close, Dori and Caleb waited for a minute to determine if the rear doors were to be opened or not. A flashlight snapped on, and Dori took note of the time.

She made the universal symbol for silence and crept to the rear doors. Carefully cracking open one door, she peered through the sliver. Following a quick motion of her hand, Caleb cautiously maneuvered his way to her.

The truck was parked at the rear of the cleaning service building in town. Dori slipped out and visually scanned the area before urging Caleb to follow. They stood in a wide alleyway serving as a rear shipping access for the two rows of buildings facing each other.

Making haste, they went down the alley to the main street and proceeded along lesser-traveled side streets towards their destination. The sun was on its downward trajectory to sunset, and Caleb anticipated that they only had a few hours before needing to worry about lurking vampires.

Within twenty minutes, they had made their way to the familiar field that led into the forest overlooked by the nearby mountain. Caleb admired Dori's keen sense of direction and wondered for the hundredth time about the woman's mysterious background.

When they finally arrived at the small storage building, Caleb noticed the lock had been replaced, and a heavy-duty metal bracket had been installed across the door and frame. But Dori seemed prepared and withdrew a small set of lock picks.

"You're a regular *Jane* Bond," he quipped.

She cast him a demure look and went to work on the lock with alarming efficiency.

He peered overhead at the sky, remarking, "It'll be sunset soon. We better do this quickly."

She cast him a wry look, asking, "So, now you're afraid that vampires are going to come swarming out here to get us?"

His voice was tight as he replied, "Aren't you?"

"Yeah, kind of," she admitted as the lock snapped open with a clink.

The door opened to reveal the same ramshackle interior they had seen on their previous visit. Dori reached into her leather satchel, retrieving a small electronic device about the size of a deck of playing cards. It was black and only sported a couple of buttons and multi-colored LED lights.

"What's that?"

"Hopefully, something that'll save us some time. I've been giving this shack a lot of thought since we were last here."

She pressed a button on the device and began waving it close to the benches and walls inside while closely watching the LED lights. When she waved it near the back wall where the tool-laden pegboard was mounted, the LEDs lit up like the Fourth of July. She continued waving the device in the manner of a magician performing a show until she had swept the entire back wall area.

"Find something?"

"Yep," she replied and moved the device to an area just to the right of where the pegboard ended about halfway between the floor and ceiling.

She pressed another button, holding it while a high-pitched tone emitted from the device. After what seemed like an eternity, Caleb anxiously peered outside the building, half-expecting someone to show up at any moment. He turned back to her as a mysterious clicking sound emanated from the wall.

The length of wall covered by the pegboard suddenly separated along its rightmost edge from the rest of the wall. Dori pressed on that section, which swung open to reveal a darkened cave-like corridor before them.

The scent of stale, moist air wafted out to greet them as Caleb muttered, "Well, I'll be damned."

"The photos were accurate, it seems," she noted with satisfaction. "This, my friend, is the entrance to the mine that was active until just a few decades ago."

She swapped the small handheld device for a flashlight from her satchel. He started forward with his own small flashlight, but she stopped him by pressing her palm against his chest.

"I think we'll overlook chivalry for now," she cautioned.

"This time, it's ladies first."

He shrugged and followed her into the darkness.

* * * *

Katrina sat in the conference room, appreciating the more positive tone of the meeting that day. Nearly the entire session had been productive at some level. She had to admit that the reappearance of the ancient Hakizimana had a positive effect on the other attendees. At least some things were finally falling into place, or so it seemed to her.

However, they were no closer to discovering who had installed the UV bulbs in the light fixtures of Katrina's suite. Everyone had reacted with surprise, shock, or concern upon Alton's announcement of the development. She was convinced, however, that someone in the room had some nefarious level of knowledge.

A knock at the door caused a pause in the discussions, and everyone looked up as one of the vampire security guards from outside carried a small note into the room.

"My apologies for the interruption, but an urgent message needs to be passed along," he announced and scouted the room for the recipient.

The guard strode over to Dominic Ambrogio, who accepted the message with a slight nod of his head. The dark-haired vampire quickly scanned the message as others curiously watched him.

"I'm afraid that I must withdraw early," he politely offered. "A matter of urgency requires my attention."

Katrina closely watched as the vampire rose and quickly departed the room behind the security guard. Her eyes darted to Alton, who watched with equal curiosity.

After the door closed, the discussion continued, and Katrina tried to refocus on the topic at hand.

* * * *

As Dori and Caleb proceeded into the silence of the cave-like corridor, he was struck by the oppressive feeling of the environment. The darkness pressed in from all sides, while the rock walls had an eerie subterranean aura. Large timbers appeared at intervals to reinforce the makeshift walls and ceiling. A quick sweep of light to the ceiling revealed metal light fixtures placed at intervals.

"Hey, there are lights in here," he observed. "Let's find a switch."

They backtracked to the entrance where a nondescript switch was set almost flush with the cave wall. A flick of the switch bathed the corridor in a dull yellow illumination. The true depth of the corridor became eerily evident as they gazed down its length.

"Come on," she urged and led the way forwards.

After a couple of hundred feet, they noticed a darker, unlit corridor branching off to the right. A flash of their lights confirmed that it was lengthy and curved to the left again further in the distance.

Dori flashed her light down at the floor.

"Lots of settled dirt with no footprints," she announced. "Let's follow the lights."

Caleb followed her lead down the corridor.

Another corridor branched off to their left and was lit like the current path. They stopped and curiously looked down its length.

"Which way now?" he asked.

She seemed indecisive and nervously chewed her bottom lip with a contemplative expression. "Left," she decided aloud.

After following the side corridor a hundred feet or so, they noticed a sturdy metal door set into the wall. It creaked as Dori opened it, and she had to shine her flashlight inside to see. It appeared to be a large storage room of some kind. Heavy wood workbenches lined the walls, and a metal storage cabinet stood in the corner. The tables were strewn with a variety of hand tools, including light fixture ballasts. Cardboard boxes of various-sized light bulbs were stacked in a corner.

Dori peered further down the corridor and saw it bend to the right. "Let's move on," she suggested.

Around the bend, the passageway led on for another hundred feet or so until finally ending with a heavy-set metal door like the one on the supply room. It was closed and securely locked by an industrial-looking deadbolt lock. They retraced their steps until reaching the original passageway and proceeded further up its length.

After more than an hour of investigation, they uncovered two additional locked metal doors and a series of unlit corridors.

Caleb reached out to grasp Dori's arm to halt her. She curiously looked at him, and he consulted his watch.

"This is turning out to be a dead end," he said. "Listen, it's almost sunset, and I don't want to be caught out when the vamps come out to play. Besides, somebody's going to miss us before long. At least we can say that we tried."

"It's a little disappointing," she admitted. "You're probably right, though. They'll be missing us soon, if they haven't already noticed us gone."

They turned and walked back through the oppressive passageway towards the entrance. After passing the first illuminated side corridor, they picked up their pace. They abruptly heard Slovene-accented voices coming from the direction of the entrance, and they stopped dead in their in their tracks.

Caleb heard a voice that he recognized, and a sour feeling formed in the pit of his stomach.

"Why did you idiots wait on me?" complained Dominic Ambrogio. "Get in there, you fools!"

"Shit," whispered Caleb. "Sunset already arrived."

Dori reached into her satchel, retrieving an automatic pistol.

Caleb's eyes widened, not expecting a firearm, and he stared at her.

"Who are you?"

"Never mind that. Start backing up as quickly and quietly as you can."

He quietly retreated back down the passageway with Dori covering them.

"I can smell them," Ambrogio seethed. "And I recognize one in particular."

A shiver went up Caleb's spine as he heard the pounding of multiple boots coming closer towards them. Within seconds, a man wearing a woodland camouflage uniform appeared around a slight bend, immediately raising and firing an assault rifle. Bullets ricocheted around them, causing Caleb to crouch involuntarily.

But Dori expertly raised her pistol, firing twice. The man groaned, falling to the floor clutching his chest.

"Run!" she yelled.

The sounds of firing and ricocheting bullets reverberated through the corridor as they fled headlong into the darkness. Dori managed to grab Caleb's arm to divert him down the illuminated side corridor to their left. The echoing sounds of gunfire were nearly deafening in close quarters.

"You!" Ambrogio shouted from the end of the short passageway.

Dori turned and fired twice as Caleb dove headfirst into the storage room they had investigated earlier. A roar that chilled Caleb's soul followed, along with Dori at his heels. He turned to see the vampire's pulsating blue eyes and look of rage as blood ran down his forehead.

Dori managed to push against the door, but the vampire's arm reached inside, preventing it from fully shutting.

Caleb grabbed a solid-looking metal pipe and swung it downwards with all the force that he could muster from all the years of playing baseball in college. The pipe impacted the vampire's arm with a bone-crushing thud, eliciting an anguished, painful scream.

The arm disappeared, and Caleb helped Dori shut the door.

Gunshots sounded, followed by the impact of rounds against the door. Fortunately, they failed to penetrate. Dori quickly slammed the door's deadbolt into place.

Both were breathing heavily while leaning against the door. Then a huge object slammed into the door, causing a reverberation that rumbled through Caleb's chest.

"Oh, he's mad now," Dori announced.

"Gee, you think?"

He looked back at the wooden benches and hurriedly pushed one against the door with Dori's assistance. His vision fell upon some empty cardboard light bulb packaging labeled *UV Fluorescent* along with high-value wattages.

Suddenly, he realized where the menacing light bulbs used in their suite must have come from. Dori caught his gaze and looked down at the tabletop.

"One mystery solved," she acknowledged. "Now if we can just live long enough to reveal it."

He didn't like the way she said that, but he found it hard not to concede the gravity of their situation.

*   *   *   *

Chapter 10

Choices

*P*aige sat at her desk in the security office listening to Aiden describe a series of advanced concepts in modern building electrical circuitry layout. Until that day, she had a functional understanding of basic AC and DC circuits, but lacked the advanced knowledge to fathom some of the intricacies of what had happened in Katrina and Caleb's suite.

"Am I going too fast?" he politely asked.

"Nope, got it."

The young electrician shook his head with wonder. "Well, you're the first person who's new to this type of information that grasped everything we've talked about in only a single conversation. I mean, it took me months of studying and hands-on apprenticeship to become comfortable with this."

She shrugged. "Survival mechanism for vampires," she offered. "You either learn quickly and adapt, or you're dead. Anyway, I've tinkered with basic electrical work before."

"Okay, then. Let's move on."

Following two additional hours of discussion, including a sidebar of questions for clarification, Paige felt more comfortable with the theory of operation for the advanced concepts. At least, it all made sense to her after he had explained it. Granted, it wasn't as if she were ready to become a trade electrician, but she would at least be able to conceptualize the things he had described.

"Thanks, Aiden," she offered. "I owe you one."

Then she turned to the female vampire manning the surveillance system.

"Hey, Satish. Get hold of Caleb and get him down here. I have a few questions to ask him."

"Right away, Captain," the vampire replied and reached for a nearby phone.

Aiden tried to ignore the exchange while gathering up the notes that he had written out for Paige. He neatly arranged them and handed them over to her. Then he gathered up his can of Sprite and headed for the door.

"Thanks for the drink," he remarked while reaching for the handle.

"He's not in his room," Satish remarked. She quickly scanned the video screens before her and spoke into her headset, "All eyes for Caleb Taylor. Report."

"No problem, Aiden," Paige absently remarked.

Then she looked up. "Hey, do you know where I can find Caleb?" Aiden paused but didn't turn around.

"Me? Nah, haven't seen him since this afternoon." He opened the door and stepped across the threshold.

She frowned, noting the discreet tension in the man's body. "Aiden," she prompted.

Satish looked up from her screens and turned to face Paige. "Captain, all units reporting in. Nobody has eyes on Taylor, and the screens aren't showing anything. He might be in another guests' room," she ventured.

Aiden turned to look at Paige with an innocent expression. "Yes, Captain?"

Paige's bright blue eyes bored into the young man's, and he swallowed hard. It was just a hunch, but she decided to play it.

"Where exactly did you last see Caleb?"

*　*　*　*

Katrina idly wondered what Dominic Ambrogio had been in a hurry to attend to, while also partly listening to some very good suggestions being offered by Hakizimana. In particular, he suggested a cooperative agreement for the use of Sunset Air services and other resources as an incentive for membership towards a worldwide consortium of vampires. She was really surprised by how many useful suggestions the ancient vampire had brought up.

And to think, he had been opposed to even being here leading up to the conference. Alton must be beside himself with glee now.

A knock sounded at the door, ushering in a hush across the room. This time, instead of the security guard, a very concerned-looking Paige Turner entered, directly walking to Alton and Katrina.

Katrina's optimistic features fell, and the pit of her stomach soured.

Paige handed a note to each of them, saying, "My apologies for the interruption. An urgent matter."

And how, she grimly thought.

Katrina's features turned to stone as she read the note: *Caleb and Dori both missing. Aiden helped to distract a guard so they could leave the property.*

"Bloody hell," Alton cursed under his breath in uncharacteristic fashion, trumping Katrina's own pending exclamation of surprise.

Instead, Katrina immediately rose, demanding, "Gather an escort."

Paige nodded, and Katrina followed her from the room in a rush.

"What's happened?" demanded Rianne.

Everyone else looked up with a mix of concern and curiosity.

Alton clenched his jaw. "I'm afraid we must adjourn for the day, everyone. An urgent personal matter has arisen requiring immediate attention by both the chair and the co-chair."

Baldar Dubravko chuckled, breaking the silence in the room. "Let me guess, Rutherford. Your humans are running amok again, aren't they?"

Alton ground his teeth and marked the vampire with contempt in a stare that would freeze open flames. "We will resume discussions tomorrow. My sincere apologies for any inconvenience."

With no further comment, he stalked from the room.

*   *   *   *

Katrina and Paige watched as Alton quickly removed the tracking unit from the black storage case in his suite. Within seconds, he had powered it on and was initializing the system for use.

"I just don't understand what they're trying to pull," Katrina angrily complained. It was upsetting that not even the threat of homing transmitters could keep the two troublemakers on site.

It's worse than raising teenagers.

"Any idea where they went?" Alton demanded as the system finished initializing.

Paige's expression spoke volumes of the worry that she felt. "Maybe. From what little the surveillance cameras show, they likely hopped into the back of a linens truck bound for town."

Alton paused, sharply looking up at Paige.

Katrina took immediate notice and demanded, "What? What are you thinking?"

"The mines," Alton muttered. "Dori tried to tell me there was something suspicious about those damned mines near the storage building where they were first apprehended. I told her that she was grasping at straws."

The tall vampire strode to a nearby closet, removing a leather briefcase. Inside was an array of small weapons. He tossed two combat knives to Katrina and withdrew a knife and automatic pistol for himself.

"Come on, let's go," Paige insisted. She fingered the hilt of a large combat knife tucked into her waistband and concealed beneath her blazer.

"No," Alton countered. "I need you to stay here and coordinate efforts. If I need more people, you'll need to dispatch them. I don't have confidence in the major's competency as of late."

Paige didn't like staying behind, but she immediately took note of Alton's suspicions concerning the major. A number of things didn't set well with her either, but she had thought it was just because she personally didn't like the guy.

"Fine," she reluctantly conceded. "There are four guards sitting in two SUVs waiting out front for you."

Alton and Katrina stormed from the suite in a blur of motion.

* * * *

Dori and Caleb stacked three more benches in front of the storage room door. The sound of a large object battering against the other side of the door reverberated through the room, jostling the benches with each impact.

Their expressions mirrored the fear and anxiety that each felt.

"That won't hold them forever," Dori warned.

The battering stopped, and moments later, all the lights went out. In the darkness, the only sound was their heavy breathing.

Then the battering began again on the door.

Caleb activated his flashlight, and his mind raced for any useful ideas. His light beam swept the perimeter of the room, and he noticed three small crates labeled as explosives.

Dori stared at where his light shone and began shaking her head.

"Don't even think about it, Taylor," she warned. "It'll kill us all."

He jolted as another massive impact hit the door. He continued sweeping the area with his flashlight and found the UV light bulbs. Nearby, he noticed electrical extension cords alongside light ballasts, and an idea formed.

"How many bullets do you have left?" he asked.

She paused to count. "Twelve, spread between two magazines."

Another crash landed against the door, and the hinges squeaked loose.

He steeled himself for what was coming. "If...When that door comes down, I'm gonna need you to shoot any humans that you can."

"There's also at least one really pissed off vampire out there."

He grabbed some side cutting pliers from the floor and began stripping back one end of electrical cable from one of the light ballasts.

"True. But I've got an idea."

*   *   *   *

The tracking device didn't register any beacon signals from the immediate vicinity around the conference site, but as Alton and Katrina's entourage raced towards town at breakneck speed, a faint blip registered. The sun was already hidden by the horizon, leaving only a fading glow that illuminated the countryside barely enough for a human to see without artificial light. The ambient UV radiation was more than tolerable for vampires, for which Katrina was particularly grateful.

The two SUVs raced through the center of Podjelje, heedless of the display they were making. Upon arrival at the small garage near the souvenir shop, Katrina pointed to the small dirt road leading into the forest towards the mountain.

"There," she urged, at which Alton gunned the vehicle down the road.

"I can go faster by foot," she argued while reaching for the door handle.

"No," he admonished. "We still have to conceal our existence to the general public. Things are bad enough, and containment's going to be questionable as it is."

She grit her teeth as countless seconds passed. Once the vehicles were heading through the trees, she leapt from the vehicle and ran well ahead of them.

Dodging trees in a blur of movement, she quickly arrived outside the small storage building where she spotted three vehicles: a police car, a small truck painted in forest camouflage, and one of the tinted-glass SUVs from the conference site that was parked right next to the building's entrance.

She approached the small building and immediately spied a secret entrance into a darkened cave-like interior. Hearing the sound of pounding inside, she entered as the two SUVs pulled up outside.

A man wearing a hunting outfit and carrying an assault rifle appeared in the entryway. Rather than speaking, he immediately raised his weapon to fire.

Katrina sidestepped the burst of gunfire and threw one of her combat knives, squarely catching the man in the chest. Additional rounds ricocheted harmlessly around the room as the man spun to the floor.

Alton appeared inside the doorway, quickly assessing the situation. He heard shouts of voices from inside and motioned to the vampire guards as he brandished his automatic pistol.

"Two inside, two outside. Eliminate anyone who's not ours," he ordered.

Two of the guards sped past him into the mine, and the other two took up positions outside. Katrina darted in behind the guards with Alton closely following.

Fresh gunfire quickly erupted.

*   *   *   *

As Paige paced the floor of the security office waiting for word from Katrina and Alton, some motion caught her attention beyond the front office window. She saw the major talking to Baldar Dubravko in the lobby. Pietari hastily surveyed the lobby and gestured towards the security office with one hand. Something that Alton had said earlier replayed in Paige's mind, and she reached into her desk drawer to withdraw a small digital recorder. Picking up a handful of reports from her desk, she moved like a blur to enter the major's office.

She tossed the paperwork onto his desk and activated the recorder, which she slid behind a line of books on a shelf suspended from the wall behind the desk.

The door to the main office opened and Pietari and Dubravko entered. Paige acknowledged them in passing on their way to the major's office.

"Papers on your desk to sign, Major."

"Fine, thanks," Pietari distractedly replied and closed the door behind them.

She returned to her desk and scowled.

For once, there'll actually be a fly on the wall. Or at least, in the bookcase.

*   *   *   *

Caleb relied on Dori's flashlight so that he could use both hands to work. He had already rewired one of the small ballasts to a long, heavy-duty extension cord. After inserting two of the fluorescent UV bulbs into the ballast, he picked up the connector plug at the other end of the cord. Using his own flashlight, he located an electrical outlet that had been spiked into the mine wall and anxiously looked up at Dori.

Another heavy impact strained against the door's hinges. The top bracket barely remained secured to the rafter.

"Let's hope they only turned out the lights and not the entire system," he suggested and plugged the cable in.

A warm glow emanated from the bulbs.

"Yes!" he exclaimed.

The echoes of gunfire erupted from beyond the door, but they sounded more distant than earlier. In addition, the pounding on the door abruptly ceased.

"Help me move the benches," Caleb urged as he slipped on a pair of old gloves lying nearby.

"You're insane!" Dori seethed.

"Hey, everyone says that the best defense is a good offense," he countered.

She shook her head and helped him push the benches aside.

The sounds of additional distant gunfire continued outside. Then the pounding on the other side of the door renewed, and it nearly came off its hinges.

Caleb signaled to Dori to open the door, and with one fluid motion, she disengaged the bolt and flung open the door.

Ambrogio appeared surprised as the door opened to reveal his grimacing face. Caleb turned the full force of the light ballast onto the vampire, and his exposed skin immediately sizzled.

The vampire screamed and fled down the corridor.

Dori gripped her pistol with the flashlight held alongside it and peered out into the corridor. The two of them moved together as Caleb also shone his light ahead of them. The sounds of gunfire ceased, and he thought that he heard the fleeting sounds of air rushing past the far end of the corridor.

Dori paused briefly then slowly proceeded forwards.

* * * *

Alton's two vampire guards had neatly dispatched the armed humans, leaving Katrina free to barrel ahead through the corridor. Fortunately, as a vampire, she had a perfect sense of direction and low-level vision in the mine and confidently proceeded in search of Dori and Caleb.

She heard a pained cry and stopped. A vampire swiftly moved ahead of her. She rushed forward at best speed and quickly overtook the staggering vampire.

It was Ambrogio, and he appeared to have been burned.

A wave of raw fury coursed through her as she assumed

that Ambrogio had something to do with Caleb and Dori's disappearance. He hissed with bared fangs and grasped her by the neck, but she slammed a combat knife into the vampire's chest.

Gripping his wrist with one hand, she slammed her opposite fist into his burned face with a jarring impact. As his head popped backwards, her hand deftly grasped the hilt of her knife that still protruded from his chest. With a single motion, she withdrew the blade and buried it into the vampire's eye with a squishy thud.

Ambrogio's body limply fell to the floor as Alton watched from a short distance away.

"UV light!" yelled one of Alton's vampire guards from back down the corridor.

"Shoot it out then," suggested another guard.

Katrina and Alton exchanged glances and made their way that direction until they saw a burst of UV light blaring from one of the side corridors. They stopped well short of the passageway, and Alton brandished his pistol.

Suddenly, amidst the odor of burnt flesh and gunpowder, Katrina smelled her mate's scent in the air.

"Stop! It's them!" she shouted.

Alton sniffed the air. "I believe you're right."

There was a silent pause, and Caleb's voice inquired, "Kat? Is that you?"

She nearly collapsed with relief, and the sick feeling in her stomach began to ebb slightly.

"Are you okay? Where's Dori?" she shouted.

"Here," Dori replied. "We're okay."

"Stand down. It's them," Alton alerted the guards.

"Well, they better turn off that damned UV light then!" one guard bellowed.

"Oh, yeah," Caleb faintly conceded in the distance. "Sorry about that..."

Katrina grinned despite herself and caught a glimpse of Alton as he shook his head.

Moments later, the lights came back on to reveal Katrina hugging Caleb in her arms while Alton warmly embraced Dori.

"I'm so glad you're okay, my love," Katrina muttered with relief. "But now I'm going to strangle you."

"My sentiments exactly," Alton agreed.

* * * *

While sitting on the couch back at the suite, Caleb required a couple of beers before he was able to come down from his adrenaline high. And given the manner that Dori drank her glass of wine, she must have felt the same.

Caleb silently admired the young French woman, marveling at how capably she had handled herself at the mines and with such amazing presence of mind.

Who is she, exactly?

Paige, Alton, and Katrina sat at the small dining table adjacent to the living room reviewing information gained from the cursory investigation performed immediately following the excitement. Reports were still coming in via cell phone, making the suite a sort of impromptu command post.

A knock sounded at the suite door, and Caleb rose to answer it, but Paige pointed her finger at him and shook her head. Instead, the blonde vampire moved to the door in a blur.

A waiter rolled a cart into the room and hastily departed. The smell of food made Caleb's mouth water, and he determined that he must be feeling better if his appetite had returned.

"Despite the spectacle they generated, Caleb and Dori's discovery of the UV light bulbs was rather timely," Alton conceded.

"Tell me again how our boy made a UV flamethrower," Paige urged.

"Maybe later," Katrina countered dryly.

"He's a regular MacGyver," Paige proudly quipped.

"Who?" Dori asked.

"It was this pretty cool TV show from the 80s about a resourceful guy who could use bits of nothing to make tools and gadgets," Caleb began, but then paused with a perplexed expression. "Or was it the 90s? I only remember it in reruns, actually."

Paige groaned and pressed one of her palms to the side of her face. "Just never mind."

Alton cast them a strained expression, but continued as if uninterrupted. "The explosives are another matter altogether," he said. "Those were high-yield, military-grade explosives, not for mining. And it appeared that less than half of the original contents were still intact in their crates."

"Aren't you glad I didn't let you use them," Dori prodded Caleb with a knowing look.

He blushed and caught a glimpse of Katrina's wide-eyed look of shock from across the room.

She shook her head.

"Let's eat," Caleb remarked to change the subject while moving to peruse the food cart.

He smoothly commandeered a plate adorned with a cheeseburger and fries and moved over to the unoccupied end of the dining room table. Dori moved from her seat and began picking at the vegetable tray on the cart.

"What concerns me is that, despite the compelling evidence in our favor, Ambrogio's death will probably create a suspicious stir among the attendees," Katrina pointed out. She was convinced that the vampire was merely part of a larger scheme, though she lacked further evidence for corroboration.

"Probably true," Alton ruefully agreed.

"Additionally, there's the leadership angle to consider," Katrina added.

Caleb rose from his chair and returned to the cart, searching for condiments. Finding none, he walked towards the suite door.

"Hey, where do you think you're going?" Paige demanded.

Everyone looked up to stare at him.

"Ketchup," he innocently replied.

"Forget it," Paige dismissed. "You're grounded for the time being."

"Hello? Fries need ketchup," he insisted.

"We often use mayonnaise in France," Dori interjected.

Caleb's look of horror was his silent reply.

"For Pete's sake," Paige retorted, slapping a palm to her forehead. "Just cool your jets, Ned McNeedy. I'll get your ketchup."

"Ned McNeedy? Is that some character from a Philip Marlowe mystery?" he teased.

"Don't dis Marlowe."

"I'm just sayin'."

The short vampire narrowed her blue eyes.

"Watch it. And don't be stealin' my catch phrases, either," she admonished before disappearing through the suite's door.

He watched the door close and fondly reflected on his surrogate vampire. She had practically squeezed the breath from his lungs in a bear hug upon their return to the hotel that evening.

"I worried about you, kiddo," she had whispered in his ear.

A warm, satisfied feeling flowed through him at the memory.

"Ned McNeedy," he muttered. "What a hoot."

When he turned back to everyone, Katrina and Alton were intently staring at him.

"What?" he asked with an innocent expression.

"As I was saying," Katrina continued with an exasperated tone, "Ambrogio was a follower, not a leader. I doubt that he was the only one involved in things that have transpired. Recall that it was Baldar Dubravko who Caleb first saw at the dirt road leading back to the mines, not Ambrogio."

Caleb looked up from his burger, recalling that night and how hard it had been to get anyone but Dori to believe him. He scrutinized the mysterious brunette, watching her nibble on vegetables and cheese while sipping her wine. She noticed his attention and smiled at him from the reading chair across the room.

"I wonder if there's a relationship between the London sect that you uncovered in the train tunnels and this group," Dori pondered.

Caleb wondered precisely how much she knew about their March exploits in London.

I've got to find out the real backstory on this lady.

"We should know more once my agents finish pouring over the site," Alton replied. "We're fortunate not to have to deal with the local authorities on this yet."

Katrina was happy for that small blessing. At least the mines were far enough from town that nobody seemed to have overheard the gunshots.

Granted, the battle took place almost exclusively within the mines.

In what must have been record time, Paige reappeared through the suite door holding a bottle of ketchup. Caleb grinned while gratefully accepting it and created a veritable pool of it near his fries.

"Makes me thirsty," Paige mumbled, staring at the red substance on his plate.

"Pour you a glass of ketchup?" he quipped, holding up the bottle.

She promptly, albeit lightly, smacked him on the back of the head.

"Check ya later, funny boy," she retorted. "There's something I need to look into."

*   *   *   *

Paige returned to the security office and motioned to Satish at the surveillance station. She wandered over to her desk, discreetly noting that the major's office was empty.

"The major say anything about signing those reports?" Paige asked.

"Didn't say anything to me, Captain."

Paige wandered into the major's office, picked up the reports from the out basket on his desk, and quickly extracted the digital recorder from the bookcase. It was still on, and she fingered the power button to Off. Slipping it into her pocket, she walked back out to her desk.

She downloaded the audio file to her computer and password protected it in a nondescript folder on her system. Then she slipped the recorder back into her pocket and used a headset to listen to the audio file. Within moments, she heard the major's door shut, followed by his and Dubravko's nearly whispered voices.

"...thought you said you could handle Turner?" demanded Dubravko.

"...staged the vault, just as you insisted. The video surveillance snafu was damned difficult to manage, and then Taylor brought Turner down there with him. It was a stupid idea in the end; they both survived, which only made them grow more suspicious," Pietari chastised. "You should've let me do things more directly."

Paige gritted her teeth. Hatred surged through her system, and her fists clenched across the desktop.

"You'll do as you're told," ordered Dubravko.

"What next then?"

There was a long pause.

"Let me worry about that," Dubravko said. "I'm still waiting to hear back from Ambrogio. I should have a better idea by then."

The two exchanged benign information about the conference, and both vampires departed the office. Then silence.

Paige closed the audio application and locked her workstation. Anger roiled through her as she replayed the audio recording in her mind.

I'm going to kill Pietari, she vowed.

Paige once again focused on how she and Caleb had very nearly asphyxiated inside the vault, and the major's recorded statements replayed in her thoughts.

You bastard. Trying to kill me's one thing. But almost murdering Caleb? There's hell to pay for that.

"Captain?" Satish inquired as she studied Paige with concern. "Are you okay? The major's requesting your location on the radio."

Paige's bright blue eyes flashed, and she deliberately struggled to regain her composure.

"Sorry, got some bad news in email," she neatly replied. "Where'd you say the major is?"

Minutes later, Paige met the major, who was speaking with one of the uniformed vampire security guards at the loading dock area at the rear of the facility. He was studying a surveillance camera mounted on a corner of the building.

The blonde vampire suspiciously followed the major's gaze.

"What's going on out here, Major?" she asked.

Both vampires scrutinized her with perplexed expressions.

"You ask that as if there's something wrong with our being here, Captain," Pietari retorted. "Actually, I'm considering how that human of yours managed to elude our surveillance system so handily today."

She speculated that, given all that had happened, it was probably a good thing, despite the danger in which Caleb and Dori had placed themselves. So much had been brought to light thanks to their successful efforts.

Of course, it's easy to be cavalier when they're safely back under our protection.

Then her anger threatened to rise again as she focused upon the traitor before her. She barely managed to keep her fury in check.

"Captain?" the major asked with a quizzical expression.

Paige blinked. "Sorry, just wondering about that myself. I'm sure we'll make a better effort to track him and Dori from now on."

"I was considering house arrest, myself," the vampire offered.

The other guard warily watched both the major and Paige. "You don't have a mate, do you, Major?" she asked.

He regarded her coldly. "As you so succinctly put it not long ago, that's none of your damned business."

"Fair enough," she flatly temporized, at which the guard uncomfortably looked away from them both as if studying somewhere in another area of the complex.

Paige glanced at her watch.

"I think it's about time for Satish to be relieved at the surveillance desk," she suggested. "Tegins, would you mind relieving her until I return?"

The guard gave the major a questioning look.

Pietari shrugged. "Fine. Go ahead."

"Yes, sir," the guard replied and turned to depart, visibly pleased to be leaving.

"As I was saying, Captain, we need to eliminate the blind spots back here, for one," he noted. "I expect you'll get on that as soon as possible."

"Really? What other blind spots?" she inquired.

The major surveyed the exterior length of the building towards a tall, wooden fence surrounding some of the facility's massive air conditioning units. He pointed to them.

"There are large blind spots around those units, for example."

She considered the placement of the cameras on that side of the building, and the corners of her lips upturned slightly.

"Yes, you might be right," she said and began walking that direction. "Still, there's something I need to talk to you about."

Pietari walked beside her. "Really? Such as?"

Her mind settled upon an immediate course of action, though she didn't think that Alton or Katrina would later approve.

Too damned bad.

"I'm considering a change in my life, Major," she offered as they got closer to the fenced area.

"That so?"

"Yep," she confirmed, stopping next to the fence and gazing around at the nearest camera. "Oh, and you're right about the cameras, by the way."

"Indeed. About that *life change*, Captain?" he impatiently pressed while following her gaze to the camera she was staring at.

"Oh, yeah, that," she said while gazing up at the camera with a devilish grin. "Thinking about taking a job as head of security."

"Mm-hm," he absently murmured. "Where?"

"Here." Her blue eyes burned brightly with hatred. Her hand slid beneath her security blazer, grasping the hilt of her knife.

"Huh?" he asked, turning to stare at her with surprise.

She brought the blade up, slamming it down at an angle into the lower left quadrant of his chest, penetrating all the way through his heart and into his lung.

Pietari gasped and jerked towards her.

"Trying to kill me is one thing, but going after Caleb really pisses me off!"

She moved in a blur to grasp his head in her hands and twisted it around with all her speed while bearing her full weight until the major's neck snapped with a sound like a breaking tree branch.

She brought her leg up and viciously kicked his body against the brick wall of the building, where it bounced off and onto the ground with a heavy thud.

"Rot in hell, you bastard," she seethed through clenched teeth. Then she calmly reached under her jacket for her cell phone.

"Alton? Boy, do I have the scoop on something good," she stated in an evil, satisfied tone as her eyes pulsed in the darkness.

As she slipped her cell phone back into her blazer, she spied Ethan Reynolds standing at the corner of the building staring at her in surprise. He warily studied her.

Oh crap, she thought. *Friend or foe?*

"This isn't what you think," she reassured him.

"I think you just killed your supervisor."

A quirky expression formed on her face. "Well, you got me there, I suppose."

A flash of uncertainty flashed in his eyes as he calmly observed her.

"Wait, I can explain everything in good order."

Ethan shook his head. "Lady, I sure as hell hope so."

Well, there goes date night, Paige thought.

* * * *

Alton, Katrina, Dori, and Caleb all stood outside around the prone, dead body of Major Pietari. Ethan stood with his arms folded before him, remarkably calm and quietly observing everything. No less than three security guards and a sergeant crowded around the periphery of the group, confused as to what had happened.

"What happened here?" Katrina demanded.

Paige calmly pulled out her digital recorder. "Everything's on here," she explained.

"What's this all about, Captain? Should we mobilize the entire security staff?" one guard demanded. "Do we have an intruder on site?"

"Nope. This is one of the bad guys, believe it or not. Wrap him in plastic and get him outta sight."

The sergeant stared at Paige as if she were insane. "You're kidding me."

"Do it, Sergeant," she coldly demanded, her eyes suddenly blazing.

"Yes, ma'am," the guard replied and ordered another guard to help him remove the body. The two other guards looked at each other and then back at Paige.

"You two, keep your eyes open for anything suspicious," she ordered.

The two guards looked at each other before turning to walk back to the south on patrol. Ethan patiently watched, and both Katrina and Alton turned to consider him.

"What were you doing out here, if I may ask?" Katrina suspiciously asked Ethan.

"Me? I usually take a stroll during the evening, so I went by the security office to ask Paige if she wanted to join me. They said she was outside..."

"It's okay. He's okay," Paige interrupted.

I hope so, anyway.

Katrina appeared dubious, but Caleb confidently spoke up, "Really, he's one of the good guys."

Ethan smiled at Caleb appreciatively as Katrina weighed her mate's comments and shrugged, but nevertheless she moved to stand closer to him.

"Play it," Alton insisted, staring at the recorder in Paige's hand.

Everyone expectantly watched Paige as she shrugged and hit *Play*.

By the time the conversation between Pietari and Dubravko had finished, Katrina's jaw was firmly clenched. Dori appeared surprised, and Caleb stood quietly, entranced by Paige's angry blue eyes. It sent a shiver through him, which caught both Paige's and Katrina's attention.

Paige's expression softened following his reaction, and Katrina wrapped one arm around his waist, pulling him closer to her.

"Well, isn't this just a night filled with revelations?" Alton postulated.

"What do we do now?" Paige asked while tentatively surveying the immediate area.

Alton's eyes glistened with intrigue. "Do nothing. Leave the rest to me."

*   *   *   *

Later, Caleb and Katrina were finally alone together in their suite for what felt like the first time in an eternity. He closed his eyes and relished his shower, rinsing the shampoo from his hair and appreciating the feeling of hot water cascading down his tired body. Then he heard the shower curtain moving.

"Kat?" he called as the water ran over his head.

He felt soft hands massage his shoulders.

"Who else, my love?" her gentle voice asked.

It had been too long since he had heard her voice sound so soft or relaxed.

"Paige, maybe?" he mischievously teased.

She loudly slapped his bare buttock with the flat of her palm, making him jerk slightly with surprise from the impact and sting.

"Wrong answer."

He chuckled and finished rinsing the last of the shampoo from his hair. Turning around and opening his eyes, he gazed upon the woman he considered to be the most beautiful in the world.

Katrina's long red hair fell around her shoulders. Her pale skin was like porcelain, and her green eyes bore into him with an almost magical intensity. His eyes panned the length of her nude body, which he found simply irresistible.

She stepped forward, passionately kissing him on the lips. His body instantly reacted, and he pulled her against him. Then time stood still.

Lying in bed together following their shower, she laid her head against his muscular chest, appreciating the steady rhythm of his heartbeat. She lightly ran her fingernails across and down his arm, and he practically purred with appreciation.

"Roll over and I'll do your back," she offered.

He rolled onto his stomach and immediately appreciated the sensation of her fingernails lightly scraping across his skin.

"Ohh, thanks," he moaned.

She allowed the silence to grow between them. After a few

minutes, she brought up a topic that had been on her mind all evening.

"You have to promise me that you'll stop trying to go off on any more risky adventures, my love."

His body tensed, and his ire rose slightly. "Only if you promise to start taking me more seriously when I bring something to your attention."

He thought that if any of the vampires in his life had given more credibility to his suspicions early on, maybe a lot of what had happened could have been avoided.

She mulled over his reaction and finally conceded that she may have dismissed his concerns a bit too hastily due to her focus on the actual conference.

"I should give you more credit, I suppose," she temporized. "You're just so young and inexperienced. Sometimes it's just easier for me to think –"

"That I'm a child?"

She frowned and stopped scratching his back. It hadn't been that long ago since Paige had made a similar accusation over her treatment of him.

Is that it? Does some subconscious part of me still perceive him as that fragile, vulnerable eight-year-old whom I met two decades ago?

The idea unsettled her, though she doubted that there was any truth in the notion. She resolved that, if anything, it was her desire for control that was at play. Ultimately, she recognized that the heart of the matter was focused upon wanting to keep him safe from harm.

She slyly smiled and purred, "You're certainly no child, Caleb. You're a grown man in every sense of the word, I'm happy to say, and I have very *mature* feelings towards you."

He wriggled his back slightly, and she continued running her nails across his skin.

He moaned with pleasure. "You trust me, don't you?"

"Of course I do," she replied. "Perhaps a compromise: if I promise not to discount your observations, you'll promise me not to go off adventuring without conferring with me first."

He contemplated that for a moment. *So, as long as she's aware of my actions, I'm free to act as I see fit? That seems fair enough.*

"Done," he replied.

She was content that something very important had been agreed upon.

"What about tomorrow morning, Kat? What's Alton planning to do?"

She stared across the dark room while considering all the angles.

"I'm not entirely certain," she conceded. "But I know he means well, and I trust his instincts."

"And, um, what about the plan for me tomorrow?" he asked, unsure if he were technically still in trouble for that day's events in the mine.

She adopted a shrewd expression while glaring down at her young mate.

"As for *you*, I expect you to stay around the hotel, of course," she insisted. As if to accentuate her point, she pressed the tips of her fingernails against his skin in lieu of claws.

While not enough to break the skin, it generated an unpleasant sensation. His body tensed, and he swallowed hard.

"Got it," he quickly agreed.

She happily continued scratching his back.

The next morning, Katrina rose early to confer with Alton on the day's plan prior to the start of the session. A discreet inquiry assured her that Dubravko was still at the hotel, and she took the additional step of asking Paige to keep an eye on her mate.

Caleb slept later than he had planned, waking well after nine o'clock. The previous day's adventures had taken a toll, and he appreciated the additional rest. For some reason, he felt much more hopeful, though perhaps that was partially attributed to the neutralization of two previous vampire-related threats on his life.

Additionally, he hoped that the tense rift between him and Katrina had been somewhat mended, and he fondly recalled her previous evening's attentions.

After shaving and pulling on some jeans and a concert t-shirt from The National, Caleb made his way to the lobby. He had no sooner stepped off the elevator than he noted a few straggling vampires making their way in the direction of the conference room. A rush of air washed past him, and Paige appeared at his side.

"Whoa!"

She smoothly fell into stride beside him on his way to the dining room.

"I promised Red I'd keep track of you today."

He made a sour expression. "Let me guess, you're the –"

"That's right. Babysitter's on duty."

"Aw, man."

The mere term suggested that she would probably be stuck to him like glue. And with her being a vampire and its being daytime, he was likely on "house restriction" for the day.

"I wanted to go fishing again," he lamented.

"Well, I'll send a human guard, or two, to keep an eye on you then. Meanwhile, let's get my boy something to eat."

Once seated at their table, his pale blue eyes settled upon her.

"How is your staff doing with the news this morning?"

She thoughtfully contemplated him. *You mean, how's everyone taking the news that I murdered their boss last night?*

"I briefed everyone this morning and explained that additional information will be forthcoming later today. Most of them are curious, but generally supportive. I've managed to build considerable respect with the majority of the guards. That's something Pietari never garnered during his brief tenure."

Thank goodness, or I'd have serious loyalty problems right now.

He listened with a serious expression. Then his visage softened, and he wanly smiled at her.

"What's that expression all about?" she asked with a chuckle. It looked endearing to her.

"I'm really proud of you," he whispered. "You're kind of amazing, really."

Paige was an anomaly to him in so many ways. *Part fun-loving, part lethal, but always a true friend, even when she's annoying the hell out of me.* He not only adored her, he loved her.

She stared into his eyes, appreciating the gentleness reflected in them. His expression was full of adoration, akin to how someone might gaze upon their hero.

Oh, I could so get used to that.

"Thanks, kiddo," she said, returning his smile.

"So, what happens next?"

Her smile faded. "That's really the million-dollar question, isn't it?"

* * * *

The vampires assembled in the conference room sported a host of demeanors, including curiosity, wariness, and various levels of concern. Alton and Katrina sat at the head of the table, patiently waiting for the murmuring to subside before beginning.

Katrina spied Dubravko across the table, and she took interest that he appeared surprisingly calm under the circumstances. That suggested that he was either completely oblivious as to what might be coming, an unlikely prospect, or that he had another angle of his own ready to spring on everyone. The second notion bothered her more than she cared to reveal.

Once the din of voices had abated, Alton addressed the group.

"Many of you have had an opportunity to hear varying degrees of information related to multiple events that unfolded late yesterday afternoon and early evening. I can accurately confirm the deaths of two vampires: Dominic Ambrogio and Major Kivo Pietari."

A murmuring reignited among the attendees, except for Dubravko, who listened with a stoic expression.

"The deaths were over separate events, but related," Alton continued.

A series of questions issued forth from multiple members at once, each demanding details. Alton held up his hand for silence and informed the group of what had transpired that led to both deaths. The recollections took some time, though the gathering was polite enough to allow him to complete his presentation.

The subsequent questions were mostly for clarification of previously stated details. However, when the queries turned to one of context, Alton moved to the next phase of his presentation.

"I'm afraid there's some rather uncomfortable information accompanying these events," he began. "That is, beyond the participants already cited. I'm afraid we're looking at a conspiracy to disrupt these proceedings."

Dubravko's expression turned stony, and he leveled a hard stare at Alton. The corners of Katrina's lips upturned slightly.

"I have some evidence that I'd like to share with you that I believe will explain everything," Alton said while removing the small digital recorder from his blazer pocket.

Everyone waited expectantly.

*   *   *   *

After Caleb finished eating breakfast, he and Paige walked into the lobby. A vampire security officer with lieutenant's bars on his shoulder approached her.

"Captain," he politely began, "the sergeant and I would like to discuss some important staffing concerns with you in the maj -- that is, in the main office. There are two of our human guards who have been acting suspiciously following last night's events. We'd rather address things earlier rather than later, if you catch my meaning."

Paige studied Caleb. "Sure, makes sense," she replied.

"Why don't I just hang around here until you get back?" Caleb suggested.

She turned to him and firmly ordered, "Fine, but you had better sit here in the lobby waiting for me. I'll be back soon, so don't get any ideas about leaving, or..."

"I know, I know," he interrupted with a roll of his eyes. "Retribution, angst, and a host of painful punishments."

She grinned. "Yeah, something like that."

The lieutenant pointed up to a nearby lobby camera and noted in a mock-ominous tone, "We're watching you, human."

This guy sounds like a lame Bela Lugosi, Caleb mused.

He plopped down on a nearby couch and watched them walk towards the security office.

"Good one. I like that," Paige told the lieutenant.

A few minutes later, Maddy happened by and noticed Caleb give a slight wave in her direction.

"Hey, Trouble," she quipped.

He rolled his eyes. "Whatever."

"Rianne told me a little bit about what's been going on," she offered, plopping onto the couch next to him. "It looks as if a lot of us owe you and Dorianne an apology. I would've never imagined all that's happened the past few days. It's kind of shocking to learn that some nefarious people have been operating in our midst all this time."

Caleb knew all too well how things, and people, often weren't what they claimed to be. He realized how street-smart he was becoming since meeting Katrina.

Actually, my entire personality's been undergoing a bit of an overhaul, he realized. He felt much more self-confident and self-reliant since becoming involved with her. But then, he was a much happier person, as well.

"Earth to Caleb," Maddy teased.

"Sorry," he broke from his reverie. "I was just thinking

about what you said, that's all."

"Sure, I get it. Face it, your life's a lot more exciting than I gave you credit for when I first met you."

Boy, that's an understatement. A lot more than I prefer, actually.

"You're one lucky guy, Taylor," she said. "Having two beautiful women in your life like you do, and both vampires. Frankly, I'm a little envious."

"Only one of them is my mate, however," he stipulated.

One of her eyebrows dubiously arched, and she chuckled. "Boy, are you in for a surprise someday," she knowingly whispered.

He frowned, but light-heartedly countered, "Well, just keep your hands off either of them. I don't need any competition."

She rose to continue on her original errand and smirked. "From what I see, Taylor, they're way outta my league. But then, I love Rianne too much to stray."

"Good thing for me then," he credited.

She proceeded towards the lobby exit, and he watched the happy-go-lucky blonde walk away while pondering her observations with a puzzled expression.

"Better not let Katrina catch you girl-watching," Aiden chortled.

Aiden's sudden appearance startled him, and he swiveled to stare at him.

"Hey, there's no competition there," he awkwardly countered.

"Yeah, that one's batting for the other team," the young electrician observed.

Caleb acknowledged the truth in his comment. "Okay, there's that, too."

Absently, he noticed two hotel employees hauling luggage through the lobby towards the main desk. It appeared that someone was checking out, and he wondered who it might be. Turning to gaze towards the glass doors of the lobby, he noticed a few staff members arranging an awning over a black limousine with dark tinted windows.

Maybe a vampire departing, he thought.

The two staff members at the counter took the luggage outside to the rear of the limousine.

"Wonder what's going on there?" Aiden asked. "I didn't know folks were already leaving. Is the conference ending early or something?"

Caleb was curious about that, as well.

*　*　*　*

Before Alton pressed *Play* on the digital recorder, there was an outburst.

"What kind of theatrics are you trying to pull, Rutherford?" Dubravko demanded.

"I'm just offering everyone a chance to listen to the truth," Alton calmly explained.

"I've heard enough of this ridiculousness," Dubravko complained. "This conference has been a complete waste of time, and I intend to report that to the parties that I'm representing here. First, I see an inability to reach a viable structure for continued dialogue. Next, the inability to solidify a standardized base of common principles. And finally, you're trying to use conspiracy theories to manipulate group dynamics. Preposterous!"

Dubravko's gold-flecked eyes glared at Alton and then at Katrina as he rose from his chair.

"You're fools if you stay for anymore of this," he warned the rest of the participants. Then he grabbed the folder and notes before him and angrily stormed from the room.

The assembled group traded curious or concerned glances with each other, and a few vampires acted as if they were preparing to rise from their chairs.

"Please," Alton diplomatically offered. "Please listen to the evidence, and then you can judge for yourselves. Nobody, least of all me, is trying to force anything upon you."

The few who had started to rise sat back in their chairs. Others erupted into individual hushed conversations, while Katrina just stared into Alton's eyes. *That was both odd and unexpected.*

* * * *

As Aiden and Caleb talked about all that had happened the previous day and evening, Caleb noticed Dubravko storm into the lobby, headed straight for the main desk. The surly vampire removed a cell phone from his pocket and appeared to be texting with someone. Then he abruptly put away his cell phone and locked eyes with Caleb. The imposing vampire sneered at him and proceeded to the main desk.

"Is my car ready?" he demanded.

"Yes, sir," the woman at the counter assured him. "Your driver arrived not long ago, and we're loading your luggage now. Thank you for staying with us, Mr. Dubravko, and have a pleasant journey home."

"Thanks," the vampire replied. "I'm looking forward to it."

He proceeded through the main doors to the dim area of the awning-shrouded limousine and slipped inside.

"That was weird," Caleb noted.

His mind screamed that something seemed very odd about the display, but he couldn't quite place what.

"Hey!" Paige exclaimed from nearby. "Was that Dubravko?"

Caleb acknowledged her, but was still distracted by his thoughts.

"Yeah, the guy just stormed out of here like a bullet," Aiden supplied.

"What the hell is Alton thinking?" Paige hated the idea that the vampire would get away after being neatly implicated in recent events.

Then something occurred to Caleb like a light bulb snapping on. It was Dubravko; something was definitely missing.

"The briefcase," he muttered.

"What?" Aiden asked.

Then another image flashed from Caleb's memory, and a look of horror formed on his face.

"Oh crap!" he exclaimed. "We gotta see Alton. Now!"

Paige wanted to press him for information, but he had already leapt up from the couch and was racing towards the conference room.

* * * *

Following Dubravko's hasty departure, the room seemed to erupt in a litany of simultaneous comments or arguments over the events of the prior twenty-four hours. Seemingly, everyone had an opinion, some better-informed than others.

"Please, if we could all quiet down so that I can play the recording for you," Alton urged.

The door to the conference room opened to reveal a harried-looking guard. "Uh, sorry Mr. Rutherford, but this young man —"

"Alton! You've gotta listen to me!" Caleb yelled from the hallway. "The briefcase!"

Katrina's eyes widened, and she rose from her chair with concern. "Caleb?"

"Let him in," Alton ordered as he rose from his seat.

The room burst into hushed whisperings as all eyes intently focused on the young man.

Caleb quickly squeezed past the guard then momentarily froze as he took in the roomful of vampire eyes all focused on him. He gathered his wits and concentrated on Alton.

"The briefcase," he blurted.

Alton stepped closer to him, abandoning further attempts to calm the mutterings of his fellow vampires, resigned to the fact that order had been lost.

"What briefcase?" Alton asked.

As Katrina watched her mate with a frown, Caleb scanned the room and circumnavigated the conference table until arriving at two empty seats, one of which Dubravko had been seated in.

He slowly pulled the chairs away and looked underneath the table as the nearest vampires stopped chatting and turned to observe him.

Paige appeared in the doorway and announced, "Dubravko's leaving."

"What?" Alton demanded. "It's broad daylight. He's not going anywhere."

"Hello? They pitched the awning over the car," she clarified.

"Bloody hell," Alton cursed under his breath.

As Caleb peered underneath the table, he saw Dubravko's black leather briefcase and looked up, pointing to it.

Katrina and Alton had followed him around the table to watch.

"That can't be good," Caleb urgently noted.

Katrina and Alton saw that red LED numbers on the briefcase's lock code display were counting down rapidly. Alton immediately grabbed the briefcase and turned to hand it to the vampire guard who had entered the room to announce Caleb.

"Get this outside and far away from the building! Now!" he ordered.

The vampire carefully took the briefcase in hand and hastily exited the room with it.

Katrina insisted, "We've got to clear the outdoor vicinity of any humans."

Paige turned to speed from the room in a blur.

"Everyone needs to account for their human companions immediately," Katrina barked at the other vampires milling around the room.

The room erupted with vampires disappearing from around the table. Caleb watched the disarray while his mind grasped an important concept.

It's daylight; these vampires can't leave the hotel!

He slipped from the room as Katrina and Alton urgently

spoke with Hakizimana. When he arrived in the lobby, the vampire guard holding the briefcase was heatedly arguing with a human guard who was refusing to accept the briefcase.

Dorianne stood near the lobby entrance with a puzzled look on her face as she watched the arguing guards. Caleb rushed over to the two and caught Dori's attention. He mouthed the word "bomb," and her eyes widened with realization. One glance at the numerals on the briefcase indicated that they didn't have much time left.

He grabbed at the briefcase, and the vampire guard glared at him.

"Get back," the guard ordered.

"You sure as hell can't!" Caleb objected. "And this guy's petrified."

He instantly relinquished the case to the young man.

"Door!" Caleb shouted as he rushed for the first set of glass doors.

Dori's expression immediately turned to one of understanding. She launched herself at the glass doors as Caleb raced to them. She held the door open as he passed and then sped outside in close pursuit.

"Just throw it as far away as quickly as you can and get the hell out of there!" Dori shouted.

Katrina entered the lobby just as Caleb and Dori were exiting.

"Caleb!" she screamed as she raced to the lobby's exit.

She rushed past the first set of double doors, immediately feeling the intense burning affect of UV radiation from the sunlight beyond. Alton's hand wrapped around her arm and jerked her back inside, where they nearly tumbled to the floor.

"*No!*" she screamed with anguish as her head rotated towards the coated glass windows to see her mate rushing outside across the large expanse of grassy field before the conference center.

All of the people in the lobby, both vampires and humans, ran to the UV-protected glass windows and strained to watch

Caleb. Alton and Katrina rushed forward to command a front spot at the glass, and Alton placed a supportive arm around Katrina's shoulders as the two vampires collectively held their breath.

"For God's sake, just throw it and run," Katrina urgently whispered.

"Everyone get away from the damned windows!" Paige harshly ordered, though her eyes were filled with horror as she tried not to think about Caleb.

Then she stood in a veritable daze, transfixed to the view beyond.

* * * *

Caleb felt sheer terror rise in him as he immediately realized the death sentence that he faced if he didn't hastily ditch the briefcase. With a determination born of both desperation and fear, he ran across the expanse of manicured turf that constituted the frontage of the hotel grounds towards the looming cliff facing into which the road leading to the conference center had been cut.

"Throw it, Caleb!" Dori yelled from somewhere behind him. "There's not enough time!"

His mind raced with where to throw the briefcase to minimize the possible damage to innocent lives and the hotel itself, which he knew was covered in panes of glass along its façade. Then he spied the looming cliff that fell to the road below, and he spotted the dark limousine in the distance as it made the gently graded turn towards the road.

Given the short time that had passed, he just knew that the limousine occupant had to be Dubravko. The car had been delayed by the rolling length of street that wound its way around before tying into the road below.

He willed his legs to run as fast as possible towards the cliff's edge. He swallowed to loosen the growing tightness in his throat and kept to his course. Reaching the edge of the sharp drop-off, he saw the black limousine making its steady way directly below where he stood.

Thankfully, the only vehicle in view was the oncoming black limousine. His eyes darted to the briefcase as its three LED digits transmuted into two.

In a panic, he used all of his upper body strength to throw the weighty attaché down to the road below. It plummeted through the air in a spinning arc and flatly landed onto the pavement with a bounce at the side of the roadway.

He started to run, but turned back to see the limousine sail past it. As the tail of the vehicle passed the briefcase, a huge explosion erupted. The shockwave was enormous, and the blast threw Caleb onto the ground.

Dori was standing halfway across the grassy field when the explosion erupted, and the concussion from the blast knocked her to the ground. A plume of red fire and black smoke mushroomed upwards into the sky above the cliff line as the onlookers inside of the hotel all simultaneously gasped. The glass vibrated all along the front side of the hotel. Some panes cracked, but thankfully remained intact.

"Caleb!" was all that Katrina could helplessly shout as the palms of her hands pressed against the glass. Alton placed a supportive hand against her back, though his face was a mask of concern as he stared at Dori's prone form.

Paige was still wide-eyed with shock as she struggled to discern the state of Caleb's body as it she saw it lying still on the ground. A grim possibility clouded her thoughts.

Please, please, please...not that.

*   *   *   *

Caleb felt strong hands grasping his body and rolling him onto his back as high-pitched ringing sounded in his head. He was groggy, and his eyelids felt so heavy that he had trouble opening them.

"Caleb? Caleb, can you hear me?" Dori pleaded from somewhere that sounded far away.

He pried his eyes open and saw Dori's face come into focus, as well as three men wearing hotel security jackets. The sky beyond alternated between sunshine and dark puffs of smoke.

"Can you sit up?" one of the men asked.

"Y-Yeah," he stammered as they helped him sit.

His head felt woozy, and his balance escaped him slightly as he almost swooned. Firm hands gripped his shoulders, and Dori squatted down on her knees before him. She reached out and lifted his eyelids as she gazed into his eyes.

He ran one hand across his face and felt something sticky. When he finally focused on his hand, he saw fresh blood.

"Is my nose bleeding?" he asked.

"He might have a concussion," Dori surmised. "Get the cart over here."

A golf cart appeared nearby, and they helped him onto the passenger seat. Dori moved around to the driver's seat while one security guard stepped onto the passenger side and held onto the roof to keep Caleb from falling out. The cart slowly pulled away towards the main entrance of the hotel.

"What happened?" Caleb asked.

Dori looked at him sidelong. "The limousine flipped over lengthwise and exploded. I saw one person lying on the street. Well, most of him anyway. Then I saw another body on the ground, but it was smoldering in the sunlight. It had to be Dubravko."

He tried to nod with understanding, but a sudden pain shot through his head and neck.

"Ow," he muttered while reaching for the back of his head.

"Just sit still," she suggested as she pulled alongside the main hotel entrance. "I think you need some attention."

He chuckled despite his fatigue and muttered, "Oh, I think I'm about to get that, all right."

Katrina's going to be pissed.

He was half-carried through the main doors leading into the lobby by Dori on one side and a male security guard on the other. The room was a shouting match of voices and activity, and Caleb winced from the painful effect on his ears.

He was no sooner through the doors when he smelled the scent of cherry blossoms.

"Caleb," Katrina whispered in his ear while gently cradling him in her arms. "Are you okay, my love?"

He managed a lopsided grin. "I am now."

Her soft lips pressed to his, kissing him.

Alton and Dori watched with concern as Alton protectively encircled her with his arms, pulling her body close to his. Paige hovered over both Katrina and Caleb, trying to gauge the young man's condition.

Caleb's hearing began to buzz loudly, and the voices in the room sounded distant in his ears. The crowded lobby of vampires and humans seemed to spin around him, and he started losing his balance.

Fortunately, Katrina already had hold of him and neatly swept him into her arms. A moment later, darkness enveloped him, and he lost consciousness.

Ethan instantly appeared at her side.

"Let's get him into the examining room," he urged, leading the way towards his office.

It took less than a minute for the vampire physician to diagnose the young man on the examining table before him. Alton, Paige, and Dori all entered the room.

"I think he may have a mild concussion at the very least," Reynolds determined with concern.

"What do we do?" Katrina demanded.

"He needs an MRI as soon as possible to check for traumatic brain injury," Ethan explained.

"Is there a hospital nearby?" Alton asked Paige.

"There's one in Jereka," Paige supplied. "I'll arrange a vehicle."

"Time's of the essence, everyone," Reynolds soberly insisted.

Alton immediately suggested, "Helicopter would be preferable."

Paige nodded. "I'm on it."

Katrina stared down upon her mate with both concern and a growing sense of fear.

* * * *

When Caleb awoke, he vaguely realized that he was lying in a hospital bed. His eyelids fluttered slightly as his vision focused on the dimly lit room around him. Heavy curtains covered the windows, but he could still see soft light emanating into the room from above them.

Is it sunrise or sunset?

A sense of time displacement washed over him, and he wondered how long he had been unconscious.

"Finally awake, are we?" a middle-aged nurse asked from across the room. Her accent was thickly Slovene, but pleasant.

"Where am I?" he asked as the woman came into view beside him.

"Jereka General Hospital," she replied while holding his left wrist to measure his pulse.

"How long have I been here?" he asked.

"Almost four hours," she replied. "It's nearly evening now."

He relaxed somewhat, confident in knowing he hadn't been in a lengthy coma or anything. The events leading up to the explosion replayed in his mind, though he only recalled bits and pieces after that. His head still ached, and he was having trouble thinking clearly.

"I'll let the doctor know you're awake," she offered before turning to depart. "He'll want to speak with you."

"Um," he prompted to get her attention. "Is anyone else waiting for me?"

"I'll check the waiting area for you," she offered.

"Thanks."

Lying in the bed contemplating all that had happened, he almost didn't notice the doctor slip into the room. He was a tall gentleman with slightly graying brown hair and a bushy mustache. He displayed a polite demeanor as he observed Caleb. "Mr. Taylor, how are you feeling?" the man asked. His accent wasn't Slovenian, but Scandinavian. "I'm Doctor Stian Flagstad, Chief of Neurology here at the hospital."

"Hi, Doc," Caleb politely offered. "What...How bad am I?"

Flagstad smiled. "You're a very lucky man, Mr. Taylor."

"Caleb," he prompted the doctor.

"Certainly, Caleb," Flagstad continued. "We performed an MRI, and everything appears normal. However, I'd like to perform some additional tests and examine you further before making a final diagnosis."

Caleb's eyes swept the room as he fully digested what the doctor had told him. It was as if his mind were struggling to keep up with what was being said. He stared at the curtained window, and when he looked back at the doctor, he saw Katrina standing at the back of the room.

She looked beautiful to him with her red hair falling around her shoulders. However, she wore a concerned expression, and her arms were tightly folded before her.

His eyes widened with recognition, and he whispered, "Kat?"

The doctor frowned and turned to look over his shoulder with surprise. "Oh, I'm sorry, I didn't realize you stepped in. I'm Doctor –"

"Flagstad," Katrina finished as she stepped forward to shake the doctor's hand. "I'm Katrina Rawlings. You were saying about Caleb?"

Flagstad seemed a little unnerved. "Ms. Rawlings, are you family?"

She moved to the side of the bed, reaching down to run her fingers through Caleb's hair.

"We're common-law partners. I also have a power of attorney to authorize any medical or billing forms that require attention."

As she observed her mate in support, Caleb looked up at

her and squeezed her hand.

"I'm glad you're here," he said.

The doctor paused for a moment, as if assessing the couple before him, before continuing. "We need to run some additional tests, and I'll be happy to brief you further."

"Thank you, Doctor," Katrina responded.

"I'll let the two of you visit briefly," he offered and left.

One of Katrina's eyebrows arched as she focused upon her mate.

"You're going to be the death of me someday. You know that, don't you?"

"I'm sorry." Worrying her was the last thing that he wanted to do. His head suddenly ached terribly, and he pressed his fingertips to his eyes. "My head's pounding."

"I'll see what they can do about that," she promised.

He laid his head back against the pillow and closed his eyes. The next few hours were eased by some medication given to him by the nurse, though it made him dopey, and he phased in and out of consciousness.

He thought that it must have been the middle of the night when he stirred, only to see both Katrina and Paige sitting in guest chairs next to his bed. He quickly fell asleep again.

When he awoke sometime later, it was to the voices of Dr. Flagstad, Katrina, and Ethan. He only vaguely followed what was being said, though the topic involved his diagnosis. He abruptly fell back asleep.

The next morning, Caleb felt much more rested. His head hurt less, and he had undergone a series of additional examinations and tests. By mid-morning, Dr. Flagstad briefed Katrina and Ethan on his condition, which involved a concussion, though with no expected long-term neurological or traumatic injury. He received brief instructions on what symptoms to expect, as well as advice to visit both his primary care physician and a preferred neurologist when he returned to Atlanta.

By late afternoon, he was anxious to be released. Alton ensured that a limousine with protective window screening was dispatched to pick him, Katrina, and Ethan up at the hospital. It was briefly tricky as the two vampires rushed from the shaded entrance of the building into the back of the vehicles. Each only suffered minor effects that appeared much like a bad sunburn, partly aided by shielding themselves with jackets over their heads as they rushed into the car. Fortunately, few people were nearby to see the strange display. On the drive back to the conference center, Ethan reminded Caleb to take one of his prescribed pain medications. Caleb dozed in and out of sleep as Katrina nestled his head against her shoulder with her arm draped around him. He recalled the beautiful sunset as the vehicle pulled before the hotel entrance, but was only partially aware during the wheelchair ride to his suite.

* * * *

Katrina gently laid Caleb onto the bed in their suite and pulled his shoes and socks off for him. Drawing the bed's comforter over him, she made sure that his head was only slightly elevated on the pillow. Then she lightly kissed him on the lips.

"Kat?" he asked, stirring slightly.

"I'm here, my love," she assured him while perched on the edge of the bed.

"I love you," he urgently whispered. "I love you so much, and I need you to know that."

She lightly ran her fingertips across his forehead. "Oh, my brave angel. I love you dearly, too."

She loved him so much that she didn't have the heart to tell him how his nearly lethal heroic actions had almost devastated her.

If he had died...

She shook her head and tried not to contemplate that further.

Following a knock at the door to their suite, she moved like a blur to answer it. Alton and Dori stood outside, and she ushered them into the room.

"Paige just mentioned that you had returned," Alton began as Katrina closed the door behind them.

Dori quickly relayed the latest details garnered following the explosion, including the secretive forensic confirmation of Dubravko and his aide's demise. She indicated that the local authorities were fully cooperating with Interpol on the investigation, though Alton had intervened, using key contacts in order to handle Dubravko's vampire remains to mask them from general discovery.

"Well, that's something at least," Katrina darkly said. "Thanks for your help, Dori."

The young French woman smiled in return. "My pleasure."

"But we still don't know who Dubravko was specifically representing at the conference," Alton pointed out as the three moved towards the bedroom where Caleb was resting. "And we have no idea if the attempt with those explosives was specifically sanctioned by the lobbying parties or not."

Katrina's expression hardened, and she muttered in a quiet, lethal-sounding voice, "Well, we're going to discover the answers to both of those questions. And there's going to be hell to pay if I don't like what I learn."

Alton silently sat for a moment as he gathered his thoughts. "It may take some time, but believe it or not, I agree with you fully."

Dori remained silent, moving to sit in a chair not far from the bed.

"Count me in," Caleb mumbled to everyone's surprise. "But before all that, does anybody have any aspirin?"

*   *   *   *

Chapter 11

New Beginnings

Caleb sat up in bed and gratefully accepted the anti-inflammatory medication for his headache. As he lay back down, his pale blue eyes swept the room until resting upon Dori. So much had transpired so quickly in recent days that he had never been able to get to the bottom of one key question.

"Who are you, exactly?" he asked.

"Me? I'm just a simple French girl," she demurred with a shrug.

Caleb scoffed as Alton suppressed a smirk.

Then her smile faded, and her visage turned serious. "I'm a Special Agent in Charge for Interpol, Caleb."

Even in his slightly impaired state, he was both surprised and impressed. "Interpol?"

Dori nodded. "I've been with the agency for almost ten years now."

Katrina frowned. "I suspected something of that nature. But precisely how did you meet Alton?"

Being on Interpol's radar doesn't bode well for our kind.

The woman fondly gazed into Alton's hazel eyes.

"Alton and I met one night while I was on a surveillance mission," she recalled with a distant expression. "Unfortunately, I didn't realize my target knew about our presence. My partner was killed before I realized what was happening, and Alton saved my life just as a knife blade flashed in my peripheral vision."

"I've a soft spot for lovely ladies," Alton interjected with his charming English accent.

Somehow that didn't surprise Katrina. She knew long ago that Alton's *modus operandi* often involved old-school chivalry.

"We dated for some time afterwards," Dori continued. "Though I must admit that it took me quite a while before I became suspicious of our frequent evening-only rendezvous. Eventually, he revealed his secret to me, and once I got over the shock of it, I found that I wasn't bothered. In fact, there's something quite romantically gothic about the whole premise."

"So," Katrina assessed, "you're the special contact he used to acquire information about Chimalma when we were tracking her last year."

Dori looked at Alton, who shrugged.

"Indeed," he confirmed. "And a valuable resource she was, as well."

Katrina's eyebrows rose with curiosity, but her thoughts were interrupted by yet more knocking at the suite's door. She answered it, and Paige strode into the room with a wide-eyed expression.

Alton and Dori stepped into the living room as she entered.

"What's wrong?" Alton asked the petite vampire.

"I've never heard of anything quite like this," Paige ventured with near-excitement in her voice. "Most of the vampires are mingling in the main dining room among their human companions. There's a lot of talk about Caleb and how he risked his life like he did. Some want to confer a monetary offering, while others are talking about oaths of fellowship or something like it."

"Really?" Katrina asked with surprise.

In all her centuries as a vampire, she had never heard of such a thing before. But then, in her lifetime, events on the scale of the conference had never been tried, either.

"That boy continues to surprise me," Alton murmured almost to himself.

He walked to the bedroom to peek in on Caleb.

"How are you feeling, son?"

Caleb peered down the length of the bed past his feet to get a better view of Alton in the doorway. "Better, thanks. Just tired, mainly."

"Well, get some rest," Alton offered. "You have a number of well-wishers downstairs, in addition to the ones in this suite, and we all need for you to feel better soon."

"Thanks," he replied.

I have more new friends. Human and vampire friends.

"Oh, and Caleb," Alton said. "Brutally honest, what you did today was impressive. I'm very proud of you, young man."

"Brutal honesty?" he asked.

It was a term that Caleb and Alton used to indicate that their statements to one another were entirely forthright, without reservations or patronization. It meant a great deal to him to know exactly where he stood in Alton's eyes, particularly given how Katrina looked up to him as her former mentor.

"Brutal honesty," Alton confirmed.

"And what might the repercussions be for killing a vampire today?" It was only after saying it that such a fact solidified in his mind, and he felt almost numb.

Oh my God, this can't be happening. I killed a vampire today and his human aide. I've never killed anyone before.

He anticipated that a human killing a vampire was likely an unpopular act, no matter the justifications or circumstances. But the starkest realization in his mind was that, despite the death of both a human and a vampire at his hands, he didn't feel the remorse over the deaths that he would have expected.

Alton warmly responded, "Among those here at the conference, you're most assuredly 'in the clear' in a phenomenal way. I've also spoken with the Slovene authorities, and they consider your actions as a 'heroic act in their own country's war against terrorism,' or some such thing."

"Among those here," Caleb repeated as Alton's comments slowly replayed in his mind. It occurred to him that those present might be sympathetic to his actions, but perhaps those allied with Dubravko wouldn't feel so forgiving.

As if divining the young man's thoughts, Alton continued, "The vampires that Dubravko represented won't take kindly to their emissary's death, but even they would be hard-pressed to decry your actions openly without garnering negative attention from the vampire community. Dubravko attempted to murder a host of his peers, after all. However, that doesn't mean that you might not be a target of opportunity for them moving forward."

Caleb sighed with resignation.

Great, I'm a target again, he groused. Although it wasn't as if he would dream of taking back what he did. To him, anything was worth saving those that he cared about so dearly.

"But you've acquired many more allies than you had even a day or so ago, as well," Alton reassured him. "Mark my words Caleb; you have a number of powerful supporters behind you now, aside from those in this suite, of course."

The two female vampires stood in the living room listening to Alton's and Caleb's conversation. Katrina slowly nodded her head in determined agreement, while Paige glanced in Alton's direction with a steely-eyed resolve.

Caleb earnestly smiled. "Thanks, Alton. Thanks so much."

Alton's expression turned serious. "No, thank you, dear boy. Many owe you a significant debt of gratitude today. And vampires don't easily forget their debts."

The tall, dark-haired vampire turned and proceeded across the living room towards the door to the suite, wrapping his arm around Dori's waist as he passed her. They silently departed, pulling the door to the suite closed behind them.

"Someday, I want to know what that 'brutal honesty' term is all about," Katrina whispered, almost to herself.

"I bet it's probably some sort of guy thing," Paige said.

"Hm," Katrina said absently.

She had known Alton for centuries and doubted her friend's off-handed assessment. Alton was typically very precise and deliberate in his vocabulary. However, to her, that was a minor mystery that could easily wait. For the time being, she had Caleb's well-being and security to consider, as well as a host of other concerns related to the remaining conference agenda.

* * * *

Following a few hours of sleep, Caleb woke to discover a nighttime view through the bedroom window. The suite's curtains were pulled open, and he noticed that a moon had partially risen. He imagined the night was rife with wandering vampires outside the walls of the hotel.

Stretching his legs while lying in bed, he immediately felt a number of sore muscles ache from his efforts. Appreciative that his headache of a few hours ago had temporarily subsided, he once again felt more like himself.

A flickering light on the nightstand commanded his attention, and he noted that it came from the display on his cell phone. Reaching over, he flipped open the face and dialed voicemail. The message was from Paul Wright and was short and sweet.

"Caleb, it's Paul. I'm sorry, but I have bad news from the state regents and our president pertaining to next year's budget. As we feared, the cuts were deep, and things don't appear good at all. We've arrived at our worst-case scenario. Please call me when you get back."

So there it was: he was about to become jobless. His dream career of a lifetime was over, or at least, suspended. He wearily placed the cell phone back onto the nightstand.

Pivoting up from the mattress, he had barely pushed his legs over the edge of the bed and sat up, when he felt a sudden wooziness roll over him. He grabbed the side of the bed with both hands to steady himself and slowly proceeded to stand up.

His bare feet had no sooner touched the floor when he started to feel slightly dizzy, and two small hands wrapped around his upper arms from behind to steady him in place.

"Easy there, hero," Paige's voice warned. "What are you doing up?"

He smiled, grateful that his friend and guardian was watching out for him. "Where's Kat?"

"You know, I still can't believe she lets you call her that. She hates nicknames."

"Hey, you call her 'Red' and get away with it. Maybe I'm just a special case, or something."

She giggled, wrapped her arms around his muscular chest, and pulled him against her petite frame. A tingle ran through her body as a rush of desire threatened to surface.

He felt the appealing warmth from her body penetrate his shirt.

Then he felt her lips at his left ear as she whispered, "You are very special, kiddo. In fact, after today, I'd say that you're a human phenom of sorts to some folks. And, yes, you and I are both exceptions to her nickname rule. In truth, we probably get away with a lot more than she'd allow from anyone else. Actually, I'm sure of it."

She held the wonderful young man in her arms, silently cherishing the moment. Certainly, the dashing and engaging Dr. Ethan Reynolds had captured her attention, but Caleb had captured her heart. Of course, he was already taken, and by her best friend, no less.

Some women have all the luck.

Still, it wasn't as if she intended to challenge Katrina for Caleb's affections. She frequently saw the love reflected in her friend's eyes and refused to do anything to harm such a special thing. But there was sadness within her from not having anybody like that for herself, at least, not yet.

"I should just be grateful for what I have," she mumbled under her breath.

Although quiet, he registered her comment and blinked with surprise.

Paige froze and swallowed hard, suddenly sorry for her audible slip. She realized how vulnerable she felt at that moment and dreaded saying anything further. But her heart outpaced her mind.

"I wish you'd do something to make me hate you," she whispered in a tight voice.

"What?" he whispered as he pulled away from her, staring incredulously into her blue eyes.

Her pained expression spoke volumes.

"Sometimes it's so difficult for me, wrestling with such strong feelings, unlike anything I've felt before. Then knowing that it doesn't matter because you couldn't possibly ever love me in the same way that you do Katrina." She struggled as her brows knitted from the effort of holding back tears.

His heartbeat raced, and it tortured him that he couldn't return the same level of affection to her that he felt for Katrina. In any case, even if he could, he realized that it would never be fair to either of them to pursue them both. A choice had to be made, and he had made it long before meeting her.

And I have no regrets.

"But I do love you," he retorted as he turned to face her. "I'll love you forever. It's just a different sort of love. And I need you so very badly in my life," he insisted, tightly hugging her to him. He took note of her taut muscles, though they relaxed slightly after a moment.

Paige felt her eyes moisten as she silently nodded. She didn't trust her voice to respond as her small arms encircled his waist.

Moments passed before she lightly kissed him on the cheek and whispered, "Well, I didn't get a chance to thank you for saving my life today. So, thanks."

She allowed the silence to grow between them for a time.

"And as for that old lady of yours, she's out at the site of your exciting briefcase finale," she said, forcing a degree of levity into her voice.

He pressed a kiss against her cheek, which surprised her. She was awash with so many conflicted emotions that she felt like a circus juggler at that moment.

"You're welcome. I can't bear the thought of losing either Kat or you, much less both of you."

She silently considered him at length, deliberately stalling to appreciate the closeness they were sharing.

I love this little guy so very much, she mused, smirking from the irony that he was actually a couple of inches taller than she was.

"Are we okay?" he asked.

She parted from their embrace, pulling away from him slightly while her piercing gaze transfixed him. Then her visage softened, and she nodded affirmatively.

"We will be...someday."

He stared back at her affectionately.

"We better be. I won't settle for less," he challenged as a hopeful wave of relief washed over him. Somehow, he felt as if he'd just dodged some kind of catastrophic emotional bullet.

"So, how about a little evening stroll?" he prompted.

"Okay, tiger," she agreed. "But no more heroism for today. If you start feeling weak or overly tired, you tell me. Got it?"

"Got it," he calmly replied as he turned to lead the way to the suite's front door.

However, his mind was still flustered by Paige's emotional revelations.

*   *   *   *

The night was far more beautiful than it had appeared from the hotel room. The air was cool and dry, and the sky was awash with a spectrum of stars. The moon cast a romantic glow on the area, and occasional park lamps further enhanced the romantic ambiance.

Caleb breathed in deeply, appreciating the scent and coolness of the fresh mountain air. He walked across the expanse of ground that he had spanned earlier in the day, but for some reason, that same distance seemed much further in the darkness.

As he walked, he realized that Paige had fallen behind him a short distance away. He paused to glance over his shoulder at her, and she smirked back at him.

"Go get her, kiddo," she teased. "Or rather, be ready for her to come get you when she sees you standing there. I'm close if you need me, but do me a favor and stay away from the edge."

He quirked his lips at her odd comments and kept walking towards the edge of the small cliff from which he had flung the briefcase. As he approached the edge, he saw a glow of industrial spotlights encircling a huge crater in the roadway.

The fencing alongside the road had been blown down for a short distance on either side of the crater, and the small cliff on which he stood seemed to have been whittled away significantly. Down below, some heavy tractors and a backhoe filled the crater with dirt and gravel.

He noticed that the black limousine was flipped over and had been moved to the side of the roadway. It was basically a twisted metal frame, burned and battered almost beyond recognition. There were also scorch marks on the undamaged part of the roadway where a fire must have been. Approximately two dozen workmen attended to various activities at the site, as well as a half-dozen or more authorities.

Surveying the scene below him, he spotted Alton talking to Katrina as they watched over the activities at the site. Dori was nestled beneath Alton's left arm protectively draped around her shoulders. He was momentarily reminded of how Katrina often wrapped her arm around his own shoulders. It was a comforting scene, and he was pleased that the two seemed so happy together.

A handful of other vampires and some human companions watched from just outside the roped-off construction area. Caleb felt somewhat anxious as Katrina abruptly stopped talking to Alton and looked up to stare directly at him. He waved down at her, and she briefly returned his wave before adopting a concerned expression.

She doesn't like me standing here.

She moved in a blur from next to Alton and sprang halfway up the rocky façade of the cliff with a single leap. Then she appeared to half-claw, half-step the remainder of the way to the top where he was standing.

He was astonished that she was able to accomplish such a feat, and he staggered back a step or two.

"My God, Kat," he nearly gasped.

To humans, vampires in action could be breathtaking, if not terrifying.

Nature's perfect predators.

"You shouldn't be up and around tonight, my love," she stated with concern, drawing herself to her full height in an imposing stance. "And I can do much better than that. You just haven't seen me in action very often."

She was a vision of beauty in the moonlight, her pale skin illuminated against the night. Her emerald eyes glowed ever so slightly, but he wasn't sure if it were strong emotion or hunger.

Despite the way her red hair was pulled back in a tight ponytail, it seemed to glisten brightly in the moonlight. She was a vision of feral loveliness, and he momentarily wondered if biblical angels also looked that way to humans. To him, she was certainly an angel, the angel who had saved him from the hands of a cruel, abusive father.

"A beautiful angel," he whispered as his pulse increased from the desire that flowed through his mind and body. "My vampire. My love."

The corners of her lips upturned slightly, and then her eyes darted behind Caleb to see Paige standing close by. She nodded to the petite vampire before returning her full attention to Caleb.

My Caleb. But why are you here when you should be back at the room resting? A concussion is nothing to be trifled with.

"I need to be near you," he replied to the question evident on her face.

She moved across the distance between them like lightning, coming to an abrupt halt to stand before him, and gazed down into his eyes. Her arm wrapped around his waist as she bent to kiss him passionately on the lips. Much to her satisfaction, he returned the kiss in kind.

"I need you too," she whispered after parting from the kiss. "But you should be in bed resting, not standing next to the edge of a cliff."

He chuckled as his arms reached out to encircle her, and he hugged her to him. He felt her arms envelop him in return, and he smiled. It was exactly what he needed.

"How'd you sense I was up here?" he asked.

It was her turn to chuckle. "You're my mate. I'm keenly attuned to the scent and taste of your body and your blood. I recognize the rhythm of your heartbeat and the music of your pulse. I could pick you out of a crowd of people in seconds if I were blindfolded. And besides, if I can find you in a dark London subway tunnel, how much easier must it be in the open evening air?"

It was a heady experience that flowed through him as he considered her almost poetic response to his question.

How can I be so blessed to have her in my life?

"I love being your mate," he murmured as he rested his head against her shoulder.

"As do I," she endearingly replied, holding his body close to hers.

Katrina loosened her grip and rotated her body around to stand beside him. She wrapped her left arm firmly around his waist and slowly led him back to the edge of the cliff. She stepped behind him and wrapped both arms around his waist, her body remaining like a pillar grounded to the Earth beneath her as he was tethered by her arms.

"Let's give you a more secure vantage point. You can see that it's still a mess down there," she offered.

Caleb looked down over the edge, feeling very safe and secure in Katrina's arms. The anxiety of earlier had completely dissipated, and he could appreciate all that was taking place down below more thoroughly. He noticed a few of the vampires, including an uncustomarily grinning Alton, momentarily looked up at him. A couple of the vampires gave small waves to him, and he waved back.

Then he felt Katrina pull him away from the edge as she hugged him closely to her. He wanted to melt into her as he felt the warmth from her body penetrate into his own against the evening's cool breeze.

"Kat, there's something you need to know," he tentatively began.

She was immediately concerned by his tone, but lightly kissed the back of his neck. "Yes?"

"I sort of lost...What I mean is, Georgia's experiencing some steep budget cuts with the bad economy. And, well, I just found out that I'm being laid off from the college. I lost my job, Kat."

She mulled over his revelation for a moment and hugged him to her.

He loves teaching. It's so unfair.

"But don't worry, I'm going job hunting just as soon as we get home," he reassured her. He meant to prove to her that he was no slouch. However, he also realized that the major obstacle was more the country's "jobless economic recovery" than his determination to find work.

Katrina proudly regarded the man in her arms, touched that he was so concerned with her impression of him. As if he had to impress her after all that he had sacrificed for her.

He simply has no idea.

"Caleb, there's no shame in your circumstances. You were laid off, just like so many other people. The culprit is a faulty economy, not you. You speak of job loss as if I'm going to think less of you," she mildly chastised. "And yet, you nearly died today for me, for Paige, for strangers, for all of us."

He frowned. "But that was an easy decision, actually. You couldn't flee the building during daytime. I just can't live without you, not now, not ever. You're my everything, Kat."

Her arms tightened around him, but she relaxed her grip again to prevent hurting him. The thought of losing him to an explosion had been nearly too great to bear, and she didn't think that she could endure something like that again.

"I thought you were dead when that explosion went off," she said as her eyes moistened. "And I can't bear to see you take risks like that again. I need you in my life, and I need you to be alive to do that."

He let that sink in before saying anything.

"So, it seems that we're at an impasse, Kat. We need each other too much to see the other risk their life. Sounds like we need to risk our lives together, then."

Katrina fondly considered him as she held him in her arms. "An admirable philosophical argument, my love."

He tilted his head upwards to kiss her appreciatively as her lips met his. Then perspiration formed on his forehead, despite the cool evening breeze, and he suddenly felt very tired.

"Are you ready to go back to the room now?" she gently asked, having detected the change in his body.

"Are you really interested in my answer?" he playfully countered, though his legs were feeling more tired with each passing moment.

She adopted a sly expression. "I'm always interested in your answer, my love. However, I'm also taking you back to the room now."

"Well, I suppose I could use a shower and maybe something to eat."

"What a fortunate coincidence then."

Releasing him from her embrace, she affectionately held his hand as they walked side by side back towards the hotel. As they reached Paige, she fell into step alongside them.

"See? I told you *she'd* come get *you*," she teased Caleb.

*   *   *   *

The conference only continued for two additional days following Caleb's return to the hotel. The reconvening of attendees began with Alton's playing the complete digital recording of the conversation between Major Pietari and Dubravko. It wasn't as if Dubravko's failed attempt at murdering the attendees didn't convey the heart of the matter, but the digital recording added supplementary context to the events leading up to that. A number of attendees made statements, some quite elegant, concerning the important occasion that fate had placed before them.

In the end, it was agreed by the vast majority that an abbreviated list of fundamental premises for collaboration would be established to distribute worldwide to vampires for consideration. Additionally, a future conference would be scheduled for further discussion of those items by interested parties.

Alton was quite pleased.

Towards the end of the day, Caleb was invited into the conference room. Upon entering, Katrina beckoned him to the front of the table to stand between hers and Alton's chairs.

The assembled vampires issued a toast to him, using champagne glasses containing warm blood, no less.

Alton held up a thick manila envelope, informing him, "Caleb, this august group has raised a small token of our esteem and appreciation for your courageous and life-saving actions on our behalf. Each has pledged their support of your actions and bears no ill will for the inadvertent death of Baldar Dubravko. In fact, a roomful of allies would like to greet you and thank you in turn."

Caleb realized that any reference to the death of the limousine's driver was notably absent.

He likely didn't warrant recognition as Dubravko's aide. Was that because he was merely human?

He made his way around the table with Katrina closely behind him, politely nodding and shaking hands with each vampire in turn. In particular, he was pleasantly surprised that Talise and Rianne gently embraced him rather than merely shaking hands. Certainly, new alliances had been formed.

"We were glad to make new friends on this trip," Talise whispered in his ear, while smiling over his shoulder at Katrina.

"You'll both have to come visit Maddy and me, Caleb," Rianne warmly invited.

Katrina nodded.

When they arrived at Hakizimana, the ancient vampire looked upon him with an appraising expression as they shook hands.

"You've surprised me, Caleb. It's been some time since that's happened, and that's a good thing."

The hazel-eyed, auburn-haired Mara stood beside Hakizimana, inspecting the young man as she reached out to shake his hand.

"I suppose you're okay in my book," she reluctantly offered. "Maybe," she added as the edges of her mouth upturned ever so slightly.

Caleb's eyes darted to Hakizimana to see the vampire smiling at him in evident amusement as he continued around the table to greet the remaining vampires.

When he returned to the head of the table, Alton gestured to Caleb.

"We all genuinely thank you, young man," he said with a nod, gently dismissing him.

Katrina lightly ran her fingernails down the back of his neck and smiled at him before retaking her seat next to Alton at the front of the conference table.

Caleb turned to depart, but Hakizimana rose, asking, "I wonder if the Chairman might indulge the newest member of our gathering? I have a question for Caleb."

Caleb stopped and turned to look at both Alton and Katrina. Each nodded their approval, and he returned to stand between them at the front of the room.

"How can I be of assistance, Hakizimana?" Caleb politely asked, inwardly pleased that he had recalled how to pronounce the vampire's name properly.

"You've gone to great personal length to risk your life. In the end, the actions you have taken have certainly furthered the success of this conference. May I ask why all of this meant so much to you?" the dark-skinned vampire innocently inquired.

Caleb's face blanked as he grasped for a diplomatic answer, and instead, tapped into the emotions he had been feeling.

"I'd truly like to say something insightful or prescient, or something inspirational and noteworthy, but I'm afraid that all I can offer is this: I did it for those whom I care deeply about."

He looked at Alton, and then his eyes settled on the woman whom he loved so dearly.

"And if I may say, at first, this conference seemed such a novelty to me. But given all that's happened, it's obvious that novelty has given way to necessity. All of you must try to come up with a viable plan for the future because I'm quite sure that humanity isn't going to have a plan when the day comes that vampires are revealed to the world. I sincerely hope that you can succeed because, for me, it comes down to this: some of my favorite people are vampires, and I don't want to see them threatened."

Katrina warmly smiled at him.

I simply adore you, my love.

He winked back at his mate and looked up to scan the room of silent faces before him. Among others, Hakizimana appeared notably pleased.

"From the mouth of a young man who's a quarter of a century old," he observed. "Look at us, beings of history and longevity, many of us ten-fold older than he is, or more. Ask yourselves, how can we dare expect less from ourselves given what this beneficent human has already done for us?"

There were sobering looks and nods of silent approval as the tall vampire gracefully returned to his seat. Alton adopted a pleased expression, much like the cat that ate the proverbial canary, and looked up at Caleb with overt approval.

"Thank you, Caleb," he genuinely offered. "Both for your service and your welcome sincerity."

Caleb bowed slightly to the stately vampire and reached down to take the manila envelope on the table before him, but Alton gently placed his own hand over it.

"Don't worry, I'll take care of this for you, dear boy," he whispered.

Caleb observed him with a wry grin and quietly departed the room. He had no idea how much might be in the envelope, but was grateful for the gesture.

Any amount would be welcome. I'm unemployed now, after all.

*   *   *   *

After the conference ended for the day, Alton and Katrina met Dori and Caleb in the main dining room for dinner and were joined by Paige and Ethan, who arrived together. Caleb noted that the large manila envelope was on the table to Alton's left.

Following some cursory visiting and the arrival of wine for the group, Alton turned to Caleb, pointedly placing his hand atop the envelope.

"I hope you'll excuse my presumption earlier, Caleb," he diplomatically offered. "But Katrina and I feel that it's best to look after this for you. I have some wonderful investment plans for you that will grow and develop this little nest egg of yours into something formidable."

Despite feeling somewhat ashamed for discussing the matter before everyone, he was also dying of curiosity.

"Um, what kind of nest egg are we talking about, exactly?"

Alton withdrew a piece of paper from his pocket with a figure written on it and slid it across the table between them.

Caleb's eyes widened to the size of saucers. He had never envisioned that kind of figure in his earlier estimations. It easily reflected ten years worth of gross salary as a college professor...at one of the premiere ivy-league universities.

"Well, uh, that's pretty impressive," he stammered in

agreement and glanced up at Katrina, who was smiling.

"I'm confident that you'll like where this goes," Alton assured him. "And of course I'll send quarterly statements so you're kept apprised."

"Oh, sure."

This must be a dream, right?

"Now, a toast to us and the ones we love," Alton neatly interjected.

Everyone raised their glasses, and Caleb surveyed those at the table. Alton and Dori stared into each other's eyes while Ethan smiled at Paige.

Paige appeared surprised, but winked at Ethan, and then her blue eyes quickly darted over to catch Caleb's. She smiled at him as his eyebrows rose.

Caleb's gaze continued on its way around the table to settle upon Katrina, whose stare bored into his, appearing both sultry and sincere at the same time. A warm, satisfied glow spread across his face.

My vampire, my love, he thought while sipping his wine.

*   *   *   *

The final day at the conference was spent handling last-minute motions among the attendees and assigning post-conference activities and responsibilities. Naturally, Alton and Katrina were assigned a number of them, which she immediately lamented.

More time being distracted from Caleb.

Still, a number of the attendees did offer to assist in smaller ways, which held the promise of continued collaboration for the success of the endeavor.

After word spread about Caleb's comments at the prior day's committee, he found himself a bit of a rock star around the facility. Apparently, his off-the-cuff comments had gone over well, which he found encouraging.

He was busy the next day packing and saying goodbye to his

newest acquaintances, including a number of vampire guards. He spent extended time with Maddy and Aiden, clearly two of his favorite new human acquaintances. He promised the New England electrician that he would call to arrange a camping and fishing trip together. In Aiden, he found a kindred male spirit who also happened to have a vampire partner.

He did manage some additional fishing at the site's miniature lake. Though it was both therapeutic and relaxing, thoughts of his return to Atlanta pervaded the forefront of his mind on more than one occasion. He almost dreaded his return home, if only for his new career status in life.

Still, his current circumstances were better than he would have expected a few days ago, although one glimpse of the security guard perched not far away from where he fished confirmed that he was still notorious, despite his newfound popularity among vampires. The fact that the guard was both unassuming and congenial suggested a positive reputation, at least.

Towards the end of the day, Caleb found Paige and Ethan sitting in the small coffee shop near the shopping area. The two were smiling and chatting just like two old friends.

It made him happy that his surrogate vampire had found someone to spend time with. He wandered over to the pair, who looked up together at his approach.

"Hey, if it isn't the vampire world's newest diplomat," Paige teased with a sparkle in her bright, blue eyes.

"Hi, Caleb," Ethan happily offered. "How do you feel today?"

"Much better, thanks. Just a little dizzy now and again."

"That's to be expected," Ethan replied. "But we'll need to keep an eye on you for a time, just the same."

"I guess that's for the rest of today, then," Caleb suggested. "We're leaving for home tomorrow, after all."

Ethan's eyes darted to Paige, and he grew solemn. "Yeah, I suppose that's true."

Caleb adopted a curious expression and nonchalantly

asked, "So, Ethan, where's home, again?"

"Hamburg, for now," he wistfully replied. "Big city, interesting people," he added with a shrug.

Paige's expression turned somber as she listened.

Such a nice guy. The truth was that she liked the handsome doctor more than she cared to admit, which was unusual given how briefly she had known him.

Face it, good chemistry makes a difference. Of course, really great sex doesn't hurt, either, she thought.

Caleb observed his surrogate's reaction and ventured, "Ethan, I don't have a regular family physician back home and was wondering something."

"Yes?"

"Have you ever considered moving back stateside?"

Paige's eyebrows rose as her blue eyes met the brown-eyed doctor's.

He smiled back at her and then looked at Caleb.

"On occasion," he said. "I haven't been back in the States for years, actually."

"I'll be relocating to Atlanta after this, as a matter of fact," Paige interjected. "It'll be nice living closer to Red and tiger, here."

"Is that so?" Ethan replied with intrigue.

He glanced down at his cup of coffee with a probing expression. He patiently took a sip of the dark liquid and observed both Paige and Caleb over his cup.

After a few moments, he ventured with a smirk, "I suppose it wouldn't be good to abandon my new patient to a cold, cruel world of anonymous physicians, now would it?"

"That can't be ethical," Paige solemnly agreed.

Interesting, very interesting, she mulled.

"It's hardly in the spirit of the Hippocratic Oath," Caleb suggested.

The vampire physician studied Paige at length, as if weighing his options.

She regarded him with a thoughtful, yet hopeful, expression.

Finally, he smiled and nodded.

"Why not? Atlanta it is, then."

Paige cast an appreciative, nearly elated, expression at Caleb. Her attention quickly returned to Ethan, staring into his eyes like someone who had just won the lottery.

She grinned. *Oh, I can't wait to see where this goes. And I just love playing doctor!*

* * * * *